The Secret Bureau
(Vol. 1)

Charles Félix Henri Rabou

The Secret Bureau
(Vol. 1)

translated, annotated and introduced by
Nina Cooper

A Black Coat Press Book

ISBN 978-1-61227-510-9. First Printing. July 2016. Published
by Black Coat Press, an imprint of Hollywood Comics.com,
LLC, P.O. Box 17270, Encino, CA 91416. All rights reserved.
Except for review purposes, no part of this book may be
reproduced or transmitted in any form or by any means,
electronic or mechanical, including photocopying, recording,
or by any information storage and retrieval system, without
permission in writing from the publisher. The stories and
characters depicted in this novel are entirely fictional. Printed
in the United States of America.

TABLE OF CONTENTS

Introduction

Le Cabinet Noir, here translated as *The Secret Bureau*, was first published in a truncated edition in Belgium by A. Lebègue in 1849, before being reissued in France in a complete, five-volume edition in 1856 by L. de Potter. The story was then continued in three subsequent volumes, also published by L. de Potter: *Les Frères de la Mort* [The Brothers of Death] (5 volumes, 1857), *La Fille Sanglante* [The Bloodied Girl] (4 volumes, 1857), and *Le Marquis de Vulpiano* (6 volumes, 1858).

Apparently, a portion of the story was serialized in 1865 in the daily newspaper *Le Globe*, but it has otherwise never been reprinted since. To complicate matters, Rabou—or his publisher—affixed the wrong titles of *Frères de la Mort* and *La Fille Sanglante* on earlier volumes, making it extremely difficult to research the work and identify its various segments. We are indebted to Professor Henri Rossi who took the time to pull out the original editions at the Bibliothèque Nationale and compile a detailed and coherent table of contents for each of the four novels.

Contemporary critics and specialists of 19th century French literature frequently cite Charles Rabou (1803-1871) as the friend to whom Honoré de Balzac entrusted the completion of his unfinished novels, *Scènes de la vie politique* (*Le Député d'Arcis*) (1854), *Le Conte de Sallenauve* (1854), *La Famille Beauvisage* (1855), *Les Petits bourgeois,* and *Scènes de la vie parisienne* (1856). Rabou, however, was an author in his own right. He wrote ten novels from 1831 through 1860, an historical essay (1860), and contributed four novellas to *Contes bruns* (1832), a collection of stories published with Honoré de Balzac and Philarète Chasles. He completed a law degree in

Dijon, but never practiced law, working first as a journalist writing political and literary articles for *Le Quotidien, Le Messager des Chambres, Le Journal de Paris, La Charte de 1830*. He was one of the founders of *La Revue de Paris*, where he was editor from 1830-1833.

There is very little contemporary critical work on Rabou; the most complete and knowledgeable resume of his work is that of Éric Dussert in *La Clef d'argent, Littérature de l'imagination*.[1] Since Dussert's article is one of the few complete examinations of Rabou's work, pertinent passages are translated here.

"Second rank authors who have modestly enriched literature and remain, for the most part, held in respect by the shadow cast by the Great Men, are called minor. For them, there is no pardon. They are forgiven nothing; they fall, ashamed of their weakest pages, into profound forgetfulness, waiting for a reader more curious than others, less inclined to follow fashion, to go astray. In the case of Charles Rabou, he had to wait until 1951 and the publication of P. G. Castex concerning the French fantastic short stories from Charles Nodier to Guy de Maupassant to repair eighty years of neglect. But Rabou is not an ignored genius. His prose is unequal; his novels are not easy to get into. Not at all obstacles to the practiced eye, one says. Castex has revealed some nuggets, the best known of which is *Le Ministère Public*, first published in *Contes bruns*, which brought together in 1832 Rabou, Philarète Chasles, and Balzac, who was for some time thought to be the author. Fortunately, Charles Asselineau has, in his *Bibliographie romantique*, re-established Rabou's ownership.

"If one judges by the titles of his own novels, *L'Allée des veuves* (1845), *Le Cabinet noir* (1849), *La Fille sanglante* (1857), Charles Rabou fits perfectly in the company of romantic representatives of fantastic literature: Pétrus Borel (aka Le

---

[1] http://clefargent.free.fr/. Charles Rabou, *Le Mannequin, Le Codex Atlanticus: fantastique fin-de-siècle & bizarreries contemporaines*, no. 4, 1st. trim 1998, 24-34.

Lyncanthrope), Philarète Chasles, Xavier Formeret, Jules Janin. Their stories in several collections resemble those such as *Le Salmigondis*, *Le Conteur*, even *Le Sachet*. As for the fantastic macabre dance of *Le Mannequin*, it remains an excellent example of what these "frénétiques" know how to do: droll, morbid, and playful, a treat."

The "frénétique" literature Dussert mentions here is defined as literature written in the 19th century which gave free range to all the passions, in all their strength, without any kind of control. It carried to hysteria, passions such as the exaltation of the individual, a taste for horror, the fantastic, and the macabre. To play on the reader's nerves, it evoked the supernatural, brought forth cadavers from such sinister locations such as ruined chateaux or abbeys and cemeteries.

P. G. Castex defines "frénésie romantique" as "literature characterized by the need to free the human spirit from the limits imposed on it by reason, morality, and social order."[2]

Rabou's short story, *Le Mannequin*, which Dussert mentions as a prime example of "frénésie romantique" is also an excellent example of Castex' definition, as well as a helpful introduction to Rabou.

In *Le Mannequin*, published in Vols. 21/22, *Revue de Paris*, June 1830, a French painter, returning from a visit to Germany, stops for a short time in a Bavarian village, where he paints several portraits and is asked to paint a fresco for the village church. He agrees and has in mind something like Michelangelo's *Last Judgment*. But the painter says to himself: "It seems to me, in that motif, the burlesque could be happily married to the terrible." (p. 22) He finds he needs a model and asks the local gravedigger to find him a skeleton.

As he is arranging the skeleton's pose, his model gets up, greets him and goes out the door into the village. There, he is joined by other skeletons, coming from all directions. They form a dance group, singing, "Merrily, Merrily, the departed."

---

[2] P. G. Castex, *Frénésie romantique*, Cahiers du Sud, no. spécial de 1949, *Les Petits romantiques*.

Soon, a few skeletons break off from the group to go find those they left behind who had sworn to be faithful to them. The first is a young woman who goes to find her fiancé, the second a doctor who has left his unpublished scientific works to a colleague to have published for him, the third a man whose wife was disconsolate at his death. Each of these, and all the others who search for those they left behind, are cruelly disappointed and return to the group of singers. The mayor of the village was giving a ball. All the skeletons went to participate, empting the ballroom of all the living. The mayor's dead son played host, grotesquely greeting those he had known during his lifetime. But, as the music was about to start, the village clock struck 4:00 a.m. and the dead had to return to their graves. The villagers accuse the painter of having caused the revolt of the dead and give him three days to leave, accompanied by the gendarmes.

A 1979 edition of *Contes Bruns*[3] annexes reviews from the 1830s of the stories of Balzac, Chasles and Rabou contained in that volume. The following is an example of the tone of the reviews:

Tome XXXV: "I would willingly be more severe toward the third author, M. Charles Rabou, despite all the *Revue de Paris* owes to his able direction. M. Charles Rabou almost made me at odds with the whole human race. I defy the most intrepid optimist not to have an excess of misanthropy after having read *Les Regrets*, a dramatic series of distressing truths." (pp. 284-285)

This critic is less severe with Rabou's *Tobias Guarnerius*, saying he prefers that story in which "we see the artist pour his mother's soul into a violin. The fantastic in that story is excellent in that it does not exclude the moral, and if

---

[3] *Contes Bruns... par une tête à l'envers*, Éditions des autres, 1979, 46 rue de Richelieu, 76001 Paris. Annexes: *Revue de Paris*, Tome XXXIV, *Revue de Paris*, Tome XXXV; *La Caricature*, 16 Febr. 1832; *Le Figaro*, 9 Febr. 1832; *L'Artiste*, Quatrième série, Tome III.

one does not like the fantastic, it can still be taken as an ingenious parody of certain short stories from that Germany, where, as M. Ch. Rabou says, 'there is philosophy in the air.'"

The same critic finds *Sarah la Danseuse* truly philosophical. The sinful Sarah is condemned to dance throughout eternity without an orchestra to count the measure. He also finds *Le Ministère Public* the best story in the volume, but regrets that it is too short.

All the comments in the critical essays from the period affixed to the *Contes Bruns, 1979 éditions des autres,* prepare the careful reader for the fantasy, irony, and even the misanthropy of Rabou's novels. Although the examples here are of the "littérature frénétique" of the 19th century, the contemporary fan of television and movies will find the fantasy and subjects familiar. Lise Queffélec[4] explains:

"The 19th century is still with us; we haven't left it. The public infatuation and the critical anathemas which greet televised feuilletonesque series recall, even in detail, what was happening a hundred and fifty years ago. How could we not be struck by the glaring continuity which, from the end of the XVIII century, right up until our days, a form of the imaginary in fiction is offered to the wide public for its pleasure and diversion, while on the margins, in different degrees of deconstruction and elaboration of the imaginary, it tries to find new languages. To write the history of the serial novel of the XIX century is to write the pre-history of this time 'of the masses' expression and of the cultural communication in which we still live today."

Recent series of movies such as that of the adventures of *Indiana Jones* and the television series *The Walking Dead* are only two examples of dozens that could be cited to confirm the fact that the 19th century is still with us.

---

[4] Lise Queffélec-Dumay, *Naissance du roman populaire modern à l'époque romantique: le roman-feuilleton de La Presse de 1836 à 1848.*

11

If the contemporary reader is familiar with the present-day "littérature frénétique," he will also be familiar with the plot of *Le Cabinet Noir*. The technology has evolved, but the function of the Secret Bureau is the same in any country, the overreach of a government into the personal lives of its citizens, keeping it informed of the activities and intentions of its citizens, its friends and its enemies. Rabou has Louis XVI's minister, Maurepas, answer in the affirmative, in reply to the King's question as to whether "that abomination" still exists. Maurepas says that no government could exist without it, "for who would consent to govern?" Napoleon used it effectively, and all major nations today deny its existence, exploit it extensively, or maintain that it is used only for national defense, not against its own citizens.

Le Cabinet Noir is the first of a series of four novels; it was followed by *Les Frères de la mort, La Fille sanglante,* and *Le Marquis de Vulpiano*. The difficulty of getting into some of Rabou's novels that Dussert notes is clearly illustrated in *Le Cabinet Noir*. Rabou begins the book with a first Prologue, then an *Avant-Propos*, then a second multi-layered Prologue, with numbered sections, providing an introduction to, and background for, the rest of the novel. Rabou changes locations, adds new characters, jumps to another aspect of his story, with little or no transition. By the end of the second Prologue, the reader finds that this was deliberate. Rabou halts his narrative there to speak directly to the reader, a technique he will continue to use. Sometimes, he asks the reader to be patient, telling him that all will be explained later; at other times, he assures the reader that the next characters will be even more interesting than the ones he's just left; and he occasionally cautions the reader about making premature judgments. The reader learns that Rabou is playing with him, sometimes taunting, almost insulting him. He tells the reader about the last scene he sketched just before the end of the second Prologue:

"The time hasn't come to tell you the last word of that intrigue and a whole world of events and facts no less extraordinary remain for us to go through before the denouement.

"Right now, however, we can admit to the reader that the unidentified masked woman, with whom Lupiano [sic][5] had been seen around Paris, wasn't at all the same woman he had introduced to the police as his daughter. We will even go so far as to let it be known that the young woman he had substituted to deceive the law was none other than Georgiana, the 'Bloodied Girl' who had played the role of Madame Lelouard in Bordeaux and then had been abducted by King Radama.

"Given these few words between the author and the reader, just a few words of preface and explanation:

"In the vast and arduous development of what might be called an imbroglio, when curiosity and mystery must be one of the principal elements of interest, would the author be showing himself too demanding of those who want to follow the deduction to ask patience, which will always be given, for everything? Could he also be asked to pay attention to how the plot of the many incidents is developed, and finally asked to keep in mind some of the facts already recounted which will often be echoed or completed in a distant part of the story?

"For more clarity, the author, like preachers, has divided his material. Following the present prologue will come six divisions which, in advance, can be classified and labeled..."

The first of the six parts Rabou promises is a rather long story about the Hulet family which, for generations, has been the secret head of the government's spy network, the Secret Bureau, which intercepts and opens all private mail, as well as intercepting and decoding all foreign and domestic correspondence. The job passes inexorably from father to son; no first son fit for the job is allowed to decline the position. Those unfit are killed, imprisoned, or never allowed to succeed at

---

[5] Rabou will eventually change this name into that of "Vulpiano," but we have retained the original spelling in this book.

any other profession or in any aspect of their life, and no one can resign.

The plot begins with the Revolution of 1789, the Reign of Terror, the Convention to decide the fate of Louis XVI, the supremacy and then fall of Danton and Robespierre, and afterward the chaos and violence throughout France. It traces the ambitious Henri Hulet as he tries to avoid the fatal destiny marked out for him. He has been told only that he cannot avoid his fate, but has not been told the details, nor the true position his father has occupied his entire working life. Rabou leaves Henri Hulet at the beginning of Part II, promising to complete his story later. He then introduces a new plot, centered on the resourceful Maltese Gregorio Matiphous, while also bringing back some of the characters from Part I.

Among the bizarre characters introduced in the next two sections are: a man risen from his grave to write his memoirs, an Osage Indian cadaver that can leave its place as a medical exhibit, a young woman who wears a wax mask, a hangman and his family who are talented musicians, the daughter a pupil of Christian Bach, a surgeon who perfects a method to allow a hanged man to continue to breathe, a hermaphrodite, who is enormously wealthy, an accomplished swordsman and an excellent shot, a beautiful actress and her young lover, a prison based on the honor system, etc.

But, as Rabou tells the reader, he must be patient to find out how the plots are intertwined.

Nina Cooper

HISTORICAL EVIDENCE

Our readers know that the name *Cabinet Noir* has to be understood as a complex web where, in the name of the State, the violation of private correspondence is sometimes practiced. Sometimes also, with a dose of euphemism, the seat of that Inquisition is called *The King's Bureau.* With what secrecy, in every place and in every country, that mysterious Institution surrounds itself, abundant historical documents establish the long duration of its existence. We thought a rapid discourse on this subject would form an interesting prologue.

From the most ancient antiquity, and well before the invention of the post office, royal curiosity was occupied with looking into secret correspondence. After the assassination of Parménion,[6] Alexander the Great, believing he had discovered in the army he led to conquer the world, some symptoms of discouragement and sedition, found no other way to measure the intensity of this bad will than to secretly appropriate the soldiers' thoughts. He let them know that he was on the point of sending a courier to Macedonia, and that, in that way, they could have news passed to their families. All the letters he had caused to be written in this way were opened and read, and each one manifesting disapproval of his ambition and vast designs, was certain to obtain the conqueror's more or less explicit disapprobation.

In Rome, even during the Republic, secret correspondence underwent some audacious investigations. Almost all the citizens coming from distant provinces arrived carrying letters.

---

[6] (360-336). Macedonian general under King Philip II of Macedonia as well as under Alexander the Great. He helped conquer the Persian Empire with Alexandre the Great, but become too rich and powerful; both he and his son, Philotas, were executed by Alexander.

What we call today *taking advantage of an opportunity,* was then the usual means of epistolary communication. Those letters were not carried to their address; the one carrying them wasn't responsible for that. They were instead delivered en masse to employees called *portitores,* who were like customs officers or toll collectors. Each citizen went to them to find out if some missive had arrived for him; but prior to that, the eye of the State had gone over the letter, and, if some correspondence had been encountered where the Magistrate could hope to find revelations affecting the public order, it wasn't an error if he opened it. The comic and satiric poets were full of satiric verses regarding this method of government.

Now we come to France. It is strange that Louis XI, to whom we owe the institution of the *poste*, did not have the idea of looking into personal letters before anyone else. It seems that the practice was well part of his royal temperament and in the suspicious mentality of his government. But Louis XIV is generally regarded as the first who submitted private correspondence to constant and regular surveillance. On this subject, one can read in the *Mémoires* of Saint-Simon:

Louis XIV took great care to be well informed about what happened everywhere, in public places, in private houses, in the business world, in family secrets, and in liaisons. There were an infinite number of spies and reporters. There were all types: some who were ignorant of the fact that their information was going as far as the King; others who knew it; others who wrote to him directly and sent their letters by ways he had set up for them, and these letters were seen only by the King and always before anything else.

The establishment of the dangerous sections of the secret police was due to his curiosity. From that time, they have continued growing. In addition to the serious reports that came to him in this way, he diverted himself in learning about all the Parisian affairs and follies. Chancellor Pontchartrain[7] who had

---

[7] Louis Phélypeaux (1643-1727), Marquis de Phélypeaux (1667), Comte de Maurepas (1687), Comte de Pontchartrain

Paris and the Court in his Department, ingratiated himself a great deal to the King by that unworthy means, and it often helped him, as the King himself admitted, against the brutal attacks of those from whom, without that help, he would have succumbed.

But the most cruel of all the ways in which the King received intelligence was by *opening letters;* that's what gave so much authority to Pajot and to Roullier[8] who had charge of censorship that could never be added to or taken away for reasons so long unknown, and who so enormously enriched themselves at the expense of the public and the King himself. The promptness and thoroughness of that execution wasn't understood. The King saw extracts of all the letters where there were articles that the heads of the post, then the minister who oversaw them, judged should go so far as him, and entire letters, when they were worth the trouble because of their contents or by the consideration of those in charge. From there, the principal people at the Post, masters and employees, were in a position to do everything they pleased; and to whomever they pleased; and as few things are lost without some benefit, they didn't need to forge or follow some intrigue. A disparaging word about the King or about the Government, a joke, in a word, an article from a specious letter taken out of context with no foundation, with no perquisition at all, and this method was always in their hands. So, true and false, is it unbeliev-

---

(1699), known as the Chancellor de Pontchartrain, was a French politician. After serving as head of the Parliament of Brittany, he held office as Controller-General of Finances and as Navy Secretary and, from 1690, Secretary of State of the Maison du Roi. Lake Pontchartrain in Louisiana was named after him

[8] The Pajot and Rouiller family bought the Hôtel de Villeroy (built in 1370, rebuilt in 1640, and sold in 1671) for their postal service. The building, one entry on the Rue des Déchargeurs, Ist Arrondissement, was then known as the Hôtel de la Poste.

able how many people of every sort were more or less lost because of it. The secret was impenetrable, and nothing cost the King less.

Saint-Simon was far from having said everything about his subject, of which he had only a vague knowledge. Then let us also quote from the Memoirs of Madame du Hansset, the maid of Madame de Pompadour, where some more precise or more relevant details are to be found:

There was (that lady said) *two persons, the lieutenant of the Police and the Intendent of the Post, who played a great part in the confidence of Madame de Pompadour; but the latter had become less necessary because the King had had the secret of the Post, that is to say the extraction from the letters they opened, which M. d'Argenson* [9] *didn't have, despite all his favor. I heard it said that M. de Choiseul* [10] *abused it, recounting to his friends the amusing stories, the amorous intrigues, which the letters they unsealed contained, which, according to what I have heard, were very simple. Six or seven of the Post employees put aside the letters they were forbidden to open and, making an imprint of the seal with a ball of mercury, they then put the letter over a goblet of hot water, making the wax melt without damaging anything. They then opened the envelope, took out the letter and then closed it again with the seal. That's how I heard the thing told. The Intendent of the Post carried the letters thus extracted to the*

---

[9] René-Louis de Voyer de Paulmy, Marquis d'Argenson (1694-1757), statesman, councillor of state and friend of Voltaire; he had the reputation of being a conscientious man, but ill adapted to court intrigue.

[10] Étienne-François, comte de Stainville, duc de Choiseul (1719-1785), military officer, diplomat and statesman. Between 1758 and 1761, and 1766 and 1770, he was Foreign Minister of France and had a strong influence on global strategy throughout the period. He is closely associated with France's defeat in the Seven Years War and subsequent efforts to rebuild French prestige.

King on Sunday. He was seen to enter and pass for this formidable work before the King like the Ministers. Doctor Quesnay [11] *became furious several times in my presence about that infamous ministry, as he called it, to the point that froth came to his mouth. "I wouldn't dine any more willingly with the Intendent of the Posts than with the hangman," he said.*

In a letter addressed to Maréchal de Richelieu, Madame de Tencin, in some way, pointed out the abuse of that abuse in remarking that it often became, in the hands of the Ministers, a way to deceive Royalty:

The secret of the Post (that famous female intriguer said) *is in the hands of three persons: Maurepas,* [12] *Amelot et Ory.* [13] *Dufort* [14] *acts only after their advice. As Intendent of the Post, he had every means of directing them, so that the King saw only what they wished, and he could never learn the truth. He needed his own man who had no relationship with his Minis-*

---

[11] Note in the text: "The King's doctor and Head of the Economists Sect." François Quesnay (1694-1774) was indeed a French economist of the Physiocratic school. He is known for publishing the *Tableau économique* (Economic Table) in 1758, which provided the foundations of the ideas of the Physiocrats. This was perhaps the first work attempting to describe the workings of the economy in an analytical way, and as such can be viewed as one of the first important contributions to economic thought.

[12] Note in the text: "Minister under Louis XVI." Jean-Frédéric Phélypeaux, comte de Maurepas (1701-1781), son of louis Phélypeaux, seee Note 6.

[13] Note in the text: Ministers under Louis XV." Jean-Jacques Amelot de Chaillou 1689-1749), Intendant of the finances (1726), Secretary of State for Foreign Affairs (1737–44) and Surintendant des Postes (1737). Philibert Orry, Comte de Vignory (1689-1747), Controller-General of the Finances and Director general of the Bâtiments du Roi until 1745.

[14] Jean-Nicolas Dufort, Comte de Cheverny (1731 -1802), friend of King Louis XV.

ters, *who would always be interested in not letting him see anything but what could not harm them.* I don't know just to what point this way of intruding into others' secret can be approved. *Put into use under Louis XIV, it was perfected under this reign; but at least, since it's used, it must become useful to the King and not used by the Ministers to deceive him better.*

It seems that, by the principles proclaimed in the Revolution of 1789, that practice of absolute governments should have disappeared from the political morality of our country. It was even solemnly denounced before the opening of the Estates General. On this subject, the Etampes[15] records read:

The Deputies claim that there exists a Cabinet Noir *[Secret Bureau] to open all letters, to take excerpts from them, and even to destroy them at will. That odious Inquisition, a violation of the public faith, creates abuse of all kinds by the knowledge that it gives of family affairs; the suppression of this Bureau will be demanded.*

There is reason to believe that, at least momentarily, that this request was granted, since, a little later, we see a member of the Constitutional Assembly ask the Tribune that the official surveillance of correspondence be re-established; but, this time, on behalf of democratic ideas, to look for counter-revolutionary plots. It was on that occasion that Mirabeau pronounced this remarkable discourse, a fragment of which follows:

Is it right for a people who have just become free to borrow the maxims and the procedures of tyranny? Can it be right to wound morality after having been such a long time the victim of those who violated it? Let these vulgar politicians who put before justice, what in their narrow schemes they call the public good, let these politicians tell us, at least, what interest can color that violation of national decency. What will we learn from the shameful inquiry into letters? Vile, dirty, intrigues; scandalous tales of contemptible frivolities. Is it

---

[15] Town located about 30 miles southwest from Paris, home of many historical archives.

believed that plots circulate by ordinary postal carriers? Is it even believed that new politics of some great importance pass by that means? What great ambassador, what man charged with a delicate negotiation, doesn't correspond directly and doesn't know how to escape the espionage of the post? It is therefore useless to violate the secrets of the family, the business dealings of the absent, the trust of friendship, the confidence between men. Such a guilty procedure wouldn't even have an excuse, and it would be said of us in Europe, "In France, under the pretext of public security, they deprive citizens of every proprietary right over letters, which are productions of the heart and the treasure of confidence."

This last asylum of liberty has been violated without punishment even by those whom the nation has elected to assure all its rights. By this fact, they have decided that the most secret communications of the soul, the most hazardous conjectures of the mind, the emotions of an anger often with a bad foundation, errors often corrected the moment afterward, could be transformed into depositions against third parties; that the citizen, the friend, the father would thus become the judges, ones of the others without knowing it; that they could perish one day, one by the other, because the National Assembly has decided that it will use as a basis of its arguments, ambiguous and surprised communications that it was not able to procure except by a crime.

Mirabeau was right, and one thing to note, in fact, is that no conspiracy of any importance was never discovered by means of that so-called *Cabinet Noir*. So, following the speech that we have just reported, the Assembly rendered a degree proclaiming that: *Public morality must always be the basis of true politics,* and, as a result, rejected the police method that had been proposed.

But, despite that magnificent declaration of the Convention government, it didn't hesitate to put itself, somewhat later, in the same position as the *Ancien Régime,* violating the secrecy of letters, an energetic method of political surveillance. [16] Only, the government under the Terror used more naïveté and frankness than had the absolute monarchy. Letters, once unsealed, if nothing compromising was found inside, were sent on to their address, after having been stamped with the inscription "Revolution of May 31st"[17] as an excuse. What the somewhat Spartan government of 1793 did, it goes without saying, was imitated by the widening morality of the Directorate

Some apologists of the Empire and the Restoration wanted to deny that these governments had the same curiosity; but even though the idiosyncrasies of the two periods wouldn't be enough to weaken the value of those denials, documents are there to establish the fact that never, at any time, was the secret of letters less respected. The Emperor, in his *Memoirs from Sainte-Hélène,* made the following explicit admission on this subject:

Very few post letters (he wrote) *were read. Those that were returned to private individuals, opened or resealed, had not been read, most of the time; they had never been finished. The method was used a great deal more to prevent dangerous correspondence than to discover it. The letters really read, kept no trace; precautions were the most complete.*

Since Louis XIV there has existed a political police bureau to investigate relations with foreigners. Since this sovereign, *the same families have remained in charge of it.* The individuals and their functions were not known; it was a veritable lifetime employment. Their education was achieved at great cost in diverse capitals of Europe. They had their own particular morality, and lent themselves with repugnance to

---

[16] Note in the text: "See: Eusèbe Salverte, *Dictionnaire de la Conversation*: article: *Violation du secret des lettres*." Anne Joseph Eusèbe Baccibbuère de Salverte (1771-1839), poet, politician, singer, compromised in the Royalist uprising of 13 vendémiaire, Year 4, was condemned to death, but later pardoned.

[17] Note in the text: "The Fall of the Girondins."

examining letters of the interior. However, it was they who exercised it. As soon as someone was added to the list of that important surveillance, his arms, his signet ring, were also engraved by the Bureau, so well that his letters remained intact after having been read with no suspicious signs. Those circumstances, the serious inconveniences that they could bring about, the serious results they could produce, made up the principal importance of the Director-General of the Post, and demanded in his person, a great deal of prudence, of wisdom, of soundness of judgment.

In addition, the Emperor was not personally partisan to that degree. As for the political enlightenment that it could procure, he didn't think that this enlightenment could balance the expense that it occasioned, which was six hundred francs a year. As to the surveillance of the letters of citizens, he believed that it caused more bad than good:

Rarely (he continued) *as for personal opinions, the conspiracies processed in that way, they could become more deadly than useful to the prince, above all, with our character, such that, one I had treated badly when I rose, would write, during the day, that I am a tyrant; he would cover me with praises in the evening, and perhaps he would be ready to give his life for me the next day. The secrets of letters could then cause the prince to lose his best friends, making him take on an air of distrust; so much more so in that enemies capable of being dangerous are always rather clever in not exposing themselves to that danger; it is the same that I have never been able to intercept a letter from any of my Ministers.*

Even so, the Restoration didn't cherish in the *Cabinet Noir* the debris of the *Ancien Régime,* its suspicious character, which is that of every weak and instable government, that leads inevitably to censorship of letters. As police, the *Cabinet Noir* did little service, and it wasn't by this procedure that attempts against the State were foreseen or foiled. But spying on correspondence largely profited that harassment surveillance of opinions in which it looked for its security, and never, at any other period had the organization of this so-called "public service" received greater development.

Jealous guardian of rights and liberties, the Press did, under the Restoration, what it had not been able to do under the Empire and the government prior to 1789. Strongly denounced by newspapers, the existence of the *Cabinet Noir* was no less energetically denounced by the authorities! The question was finally carried to the Tribune. There, close up, the government defended itself badly; to sum up, a legislative document was given favoring public opinion and suspicions.

In the meeting of the Chamber of Deputies on May 3rd, 1828, under Minister Martignac,[18] who finally broke with the misguided ways of the retrograde politics, to report on a petition on the matter of the *Cabinet Noir*, which had just been abolished, and gave the following details:

This Bureau was the laboratory of a committee of twenty-two members. They took advantage of darkness to meet at an agreed upon time in an odious hideout, and never left without the greatest precautions to hide from public view. Thirty thousand francs each month were taken from the funds of a Ministry to support these vile employees. In the night of last January 31, this committee was dissolved. The furniture, the instruments, the tools and utensils, all the paraphernalia disappeared under the cover of night. A Ministerial revolution was enough in France to abolish the Cabinet Noir, *that has not, so far as we know, been re-established since.*

After the Revolution of 1848, the *Revue Retrospective* was in a position to publish several official documents of great interest. An article published in the *Comptes Rendus* about the secret funds of the Minister of Foreign Affairs proves, at the same time, that the *Cabinet Noir* existed and that it no longer exists: "Pensions for *former employees* of the Cabinet Noir: Sixty thousand francs."

---

[18] Jean-Baptiste Sylvère Gaye, Vicomte de Martignac (1778-1832), minister under Charles X from 4 January 1828 to 8 August 1829.

AVANT-PROPOS

I

Hoffmann, the famous author of the *Contes Fantastiques*,[19] died leaving a son. This young man possessed a great deal of his father's imaginative turn of mind. That was one more reason for the widow Madame Hoffmann to try to direct him toward a more positive career. She had kept a too poignant memory of the agitations with which the arts and literature had filled her husband's life to wish a similar destiny for her well-beloved son.

In 1833 the young Frantz Hoffmann was studying medicine in Paris. One evening, seated with some friends at a table in a little brasserie in the Rue de la Harpe, in a melancholy mood, he was drinking his share of a bowl of wine punch. He was thinking of his glorious father who, under the influence of the fiery blue-flamed liquid, had been lifted to great heights, to the infinite world of the imagination. There was lively talk among the dreamers. The budding Hippocrates[20] were telling each other funny stories about the medical dissecting theatre, just as painters, when they get together, recount stories about painters' studios.

Suddenly, Frantz burst out, interrupting an on-going story, pointing toward a person who had just entered:

"Oh, Gentlemen! Look over there!"

That person, in fact, was quite extraordinary. He was tall, had a receding hairline, and looked deeply troubled and

---

[19] Collection of horror and fantasy stories by German author E. T. A. Hoffmann, made into an opera by Jacques Offenbach in 1881.

[20] Hippocrates (c.460-c.370 BC) Greek physician during the Age of Pericles, considered the father of medicine.

melancholic. He was so pale and so desperately thin it was almost possible to see right through him. You would have thought him a subject especially prepared for an osteology study.

"He's a man who has the malady the veterinarians call '*le gras fondu*,' an inflammation of a horse's lower bowels," an intern at the Hôtel Dieu, the famous Paris hospital, said casually. Doctors, especially the young, have a habit of not being astonished at anything and of easily explaining everything.

The newcomer, however, had taken a table next to that of the students, and he wasn't long in exhibiting a new and curious eccentricity. As if expecting another guest, he had two cups of coffee placed in front of him. While savoring one of them with the appearance of the greatest appreciation, with a gesture of his hand he seemed to push away and keep at a distance an invisible table mate who had tried to drink out of his cup. Then, seeming to be exasperated by the perseverance of the invisible person, raising his voice he began speaking,

"But, sir, let my coffee alone; you have your own."

And with his finger he pointed to the other still full cup from which he hadn't drunk.

"You see, my friend, that he's a maniac. He has the looks and appearance of one," said the other students, to whom Frantz Hoffmann had pointed out this little scene. The young German didn't want to contradict them, but, in his opinion, he was far from believing that a simple mental derangement could explain everything about that man. It seemed to the naïve student that it made him shiver just to look at him.

He would have sworn the gas lights had grown noticeably dimmer since he entered the room.

Nevertheless, the hilarious stories continued to follow one after the other. Then there was one recounted by a fellow named Blanquillet, better known among his friends under the name of "Constant Cutter" because of his fanatic passion for surgical operations and dissections.

"As for me," that jolly fellow went on, "I must tell you a

story about a very bizarre and stupid thing that tormented me for more than six months. Are all of you familiar with the big cadaver in the anatomy display room at the Medical School? You know that big American Osage Indian skeleton in the clinic, whose superb muscular development was worth the honor of his preparation? One day, during my first year, passing near this big set of dry bones, I said to Bourdin: 'What a pity not to have had that fellow there to dissect!' While I was talking, I don't know what went through my head, but didn't I just then have an idea that that devilish savage was looking at me, that he didn't seem happy and seemed to be threatening me? The next day I went back just to visit him. Besides, it was too stupid to let such an imagination take hold, but that wasn't all. It seemed to me that, more and more, this "gentleman" was looking at me in the wrong way. Finally, in short, I didn't dare any longer walk near that big gallows-bird. To avoid him, on my word of honor, I was doing exactly the same thing as when you pass by the shop of a boot maker to whom you owe money and whose shop you no longer go into."

The skinny and pale character had not stopped paying careful attention during this tale. Leaning over toward Blanquillet, he said to him:

"You were certainly not wrong, sir, to have been afraid of that Osage Indian He's a very wicked man, you see! And if I told you the adventure that I myself had with him...!"

The officious interlocutor was prevented from saying anything more. The bowl of wine punch was dry, and just at that moment the boy from the billiard room came to notify the students that a billiard competition was about to begin. All the listeners immediately took flight and only Frantz Hoffmann remained to listen to the story announced.

Not seeming to notice the places around him that had just become vacant, the pale and skinny man continued:

"Sir, I am now such as you see me. Before the cholera epidemic I enjoyed the most robust and the most flourishing health."

"I understand," Frantz Hoffmann replied. "After an

attack of that terrible malady..."

"Not at all," the story-teller interrupted. "The epidemic, I can say, went by me without touching me. Precisely the day that the maximum mortality rate was published in the Bulletin, I recall having had lunch with some friends, philosophers like me. It was perhaps the gayest and the best that I have attended in my life."

Frantz Hoffmann regarded that new type of epicurean with admiration and, to himself, he noted that the poor man had severely declined since that pleasant meal.

"I must tell you," the narrator continued, "that I have a naturally thoughtful and melancholy disposition. After that luncheon, at which, I must admit, I had drunk a very reasonable amount, I found myself by chance in the vicinity of the Boulevard des Invalides. I began to walk along its long, silent and solitary streets, experiencing a certain charm in walking along there, thinking.

"There I had an encounter with someone who, at the time of such cruel mortality in which one then lived, had nothing extraordinary or unexpected in it. A victim of the plague passed by sadly in his last lodging, as the good La Fontaine says. And never, in fact, was there ever seen a sadder funeral cortege: not a relative, not a friend, walked behind that forgotten and solitary casket. Not even the dog, the convoy of the poor, accompanied it.

"I found myself very moved by this spectacle, and as if that obscure and unknown dead man had meant something to me, there I was, following that hearse in order to mask somewhat the hideous abandon.

"Arrived at the field of rest, I wanted to go through with my sad duty right to the end and see the mortal remains that I had escorted returned to the earth. My friend in extremis once in possession of his last home, I was going away with that interior satisfaction that a good deed never fails to produce, when a sad voice called to me.

"'Ah! Bourgeois, don't forget your gravedigger. If this was done through your generosity,' said one of those doleful workers.

"Finding that mendacity grafted onto the dead man:

"'Eh! I don't know that man,' I replied. 'Ask the family. I'm not related to him.'

"But I was dealing with a tenacious and jovial beggar, who answered me:

"'You can certainly see, Bourgeois, that he is the last of his family, reduced to going alone if you had not been there to go a few steps with him, this poor forsaken fellow.'

"In fact, I thought, these people have a hard job. Retracing my steps, I stopped at the edge of the grave, and looked about on me for my purse in order to take out a piece of change. And, in taking out my purse, I pulled out a little gold inlaid tortoise shell notebook caught in the mesh of the strings. In the jerk that I gave to tear it loose, I dropped the notebook, which opened in its fall and scattered on the ground the visiting cards which it held.

"Officiously, and in a hurry like a man who expects a tip, the gravedigger stooped down to pick up the money holder, into which his calloused hands put the visiting cards. Disastrously, a joker by nature, he had the bizarre idea to keep one. Then, brushing aside the bed of sand under which the funeral coffin was beginning to disappear, he slid this visiting card into a fissure of the poorly constructed pine box.

"That was assuredly an unexpected and extraordinary bit of courtesy done in some way to Eternity.

"Seeing where my visiting card was going: 'What are you doing there?' I shouted sharply.

"'Well, Bourgeois, I'm letting that man know the name of his benefactor, his street and its number.'

"'Your joke is as stupid as it is indecent. All right, get that card out and give it back to me.'

"The gravedigger did his best to do as I asked, but the card, caught too tightly, couldn't be retrieved. Another cortege coming in with a grave to be dug, the miserable man took his pick and shovel and left me with my problem.

"As I left the field of rest, the Sun was going down and it

brought that bitter wind which never stopped tormenting the Parisian atmosphere all the duration of the cholera epidemic. Already ill-disposed in mind and body, a sharp cold penetrated me, and drawing my overcoat over my chest, I hastened to regain my lodging.

"After having a big fire lit, I ordered my man servant to prepare me some strong tea, into which I poured some rum. I drank several cups without stopping in order to get my circulation going again.

"At the end of a quarter of an hour, a gentle sweating penetrated me and told me the success of my dosage. Commanding my domestic then to keep my door closed to anyone who might arrive, I took a place in a comfortable chair at the corner of the fireplace. I told him not to light the lamps so that nothing might disturb the somewhat feverish sense of wellbeing into which I felt myself descending.

"The room in which I was then seated was decorated in somber and severe taste. Its black oak furniture, its Cordouan wallpaper, its Japanese vases, some Bernard Palissy,[21] and some wall hangings and fabric with Venetian designs made it somewhat resemble those XVI century interiors the Flemish painters were so fond of.

"In the absence of any other light, lit by the reddish reflections from the living room, all the objects surrounding me took on a fantastic aspect, little by little. And while around me real life slowly became prey to a progressive sleepiness, my head was filling with strange visions. I seemed to see sculptures on my furniture; the faces painted on my porcelains made hideous grimaces at me and the characters on the wall hangings appeared about to get down from their canvas so as to approach me.

"Suddenly, awoken by a sixth sense, I thought I heard knocking at my door, followed by an interval of silence, then a

---

[21] Bernard Palissy (c.1510-c. 590), French Huguenot potter, famous for having struggled for sixteen years to imitate Chinese porcelain.

second more distinct knock, which no longer left me in doubt.

"No one could have come in. My domestic would have entered without knocking and my door was expressively closed to all visitors. The same noise was renewed a third time.

"'Come in!' I shouted in a loud voice with a marked tone of impatience. Then the door opened and there entered, in fact, a character whose looks and shape were such as to cause more than a little astonishment. He was tall, dressed in black, with a sad face and a worn and emaciated appearance, like that of a man just recovered from a serious sickness.

"'Who are you? How did you get in here?' I asked him, marked by a curtness under which I took no pains to hide a certain excitement.

"'I am, sir,' that man replied, 'the person that you were good enough to accompany right up to his last resting place. I had the honor of receiving your calling card. I am paying you a return courtesy call.'"

II

"Ah! Well!' said Frantz Hoffmann, interrupting, "You were undoubtedly dreaming."

"A dream!" responded the story-teller. "Would to Heaven it had been! But I was, unfortunately, only too wide awake. I must not even hide from you the fact that hearing my guest state who he was, I felt something like a little shiver run through my hair. Nevertheless, I tried to look unaffected and, rising, in order to push a chair toward him, continued:

"Please sit down," I said resolutely to this deceased man.

"He acknowledged my offer with a deep nod of his head and took a seat in the chair I offered him.

"For a moment we looked at each other in silence, which made me notice something else. From the eyes, nose and mouth of that strange visitor there escaped a pale phosphorescent light whose inert clarity was without heat. In the shadows it somewhat resembled the light produced by a glow worm.

"This seemed to me more and more serious. To go immediately to the source of my doubt, I quickly approached the questionable character and clapped him on the shoulder in a friendly fashion.

"'It was good of you, old fellow,' I said to him, 'to be thus in a hurry to visit.

"But my hand, sir, met nothing but emptiness and made its way unobstructed across a form like a cloud that couldn't be touched. Seeing this attempt, the dead man began to smile, and said in a rather joking tone:

"'You wanted to see,' he said to me, 'if I was really there. You acted like St. Thomas in reverse. You must begin to believe. You touched nothing.'"

"'I admit,' I answered, 'that our encounter seems to me quite extraordinary. How to explain it...'"

"'Is there communication between the living and the dead?' my guest interrupted. 'The return of people from the dead is not something that dates from yesterday. So what do you find so new and unusual in an apparition from beyond?'

"'There must be for you,' I answered quickly, 'some great interest in this visit. The dead, so far as I know, don't trouble themselves for simple social politeness. Have you come to reveal a crime to me? Did your wife poison you, blaming it on the cholera? They say that sometimes happens.

"'There you have human prejudices!' answered the phantom, shrugging. 'Can't we make the least little escape without Hamlet's father, the statue of the Commander, or Banquo's ghost? Thank God! my dear host, we aren't so ceremonial. Your charitable act brought forth my gratitude. Your calling card established between you and me what I will call a galvano-magnetico-tumulaire current. Just consider me the most ordinary of visitors. If you don't mind, let's talk.'

"'Let's talk,' I replied, delighted with the friendly tone. As for me, finding the occasion good for informing myself of a number of things, I already had a series of serious and important questions on my lips. But my interlocutor didn't leave me the choice of subjects. Raising his voice, and with that special tone which seems to be calling attention rather than beginning a conversation, he asked me:

"'Sir, what do you think of that famous Secret Bureau which was so much talked about during the Restoration?'"

"'What!' I answered, 'that secret den where the Government daily violated personal correspondence? No one has a complaint of that odious inquisition more than I. On this subject I have gathered much information. When the time is right, I will make certain revelations.

"'My dear sir, there's no book to be written on that subject,' the dead man then said to me in a peculiar tone.

"'And why wouldn't I write it?' I asked.

"'For a very simple reason. It's already been done.'

"'And by whom?'

"'By your guest, if you please. During my lifetime, which will explain to you the solitude of my funeral, I was one of the employees of the secret bureau, and it seems on the subject we're talking about, I know more than you do.'

"'But where did your book appear? In what format? In what year?'

"'My book hasn't yet appeared. I had laid it out, organized my notes, and there was nothing left for me to do but write it when death struck me.'

"'Then it's an aborted book,' I noted.

"'No, I can dictate it.'

"'But how can you find someone for that task?'

"'Helpful and compassionate as you are, am I wrong then to count on you?'

"'What! On me? That's a service that I don't at all agree to render you.'

"'But that wouldn't at all interfere with your affairs. I'll come only at night.'

"'And what about sleep then!' I replied, and without adding what I was thinking, that such a daily prolonged contact with such a visitor had nothing very healthy or attractive in it.

"'Well, my dear fellow,' the man from the tomb impertinently said. 'You will have eternity in which to sleep. And, besides, you go from dancing to gambling all the time, and pass sleepless nights, which are, certainly, a great deal worse employed.

"I answered in the same tone: 'If I spend them that way, it's apparent it pleases me to do so. Besides, I have never been anyone's secretary, and it's not with you, my dear fellow, that I intend to start.'

"'Perhaps!' answered the phantom in a somber and cadaverous voice.

"'And who will force me to?' I asked, not letting myself be intimidated.

"'There are ways,' said the posthumous man, with a frightening smile.

"'Threats!' I shouted, beginning to lose patience. "'Please leave my house immediately!'

"And I rose impetuously.

"'I'm comfortable here and I'm staying here,' answered the audacious person. 'I understand perfectly your little game. You just want to get rid of me in order to steal my idea.'

"Faced with that base and ignoble accusation, I had no other choice. Rushing to the bell cord to call my servant, I rang it excitedly. An instant later my domestic appeared, bringing a lamp. When I looked at the place where the phantom had formerly been sitting, I no longer saw anyone. He had disappeared."

"That was very understandable," Frantz Hoffman started to say, still following his idea of his interlocutor's having had a nightmare.

"What! Very understandable! You'll see," continued the storyteller in a tone that meant even stranger revelations must be expected. Then, continuing his story:

"The rest of my night," he continued, "passed somewhat peacefully, and the next day, when I awoke I had no trouble persuading myself that I had been the plaything of a dream. Nevertheless, throughout the day, I felt anxious and tired,

34

physically and mentally. It was only toward the evening that I was able to throw off that bad mood. The Opera and Mademoiselle Taglioni[22] having contributed a great deal to calm me, leaving the play, I spent another half-hour at Tortoni's[23] where I found some women I knew courageously risking some iced drinks despite the cholera. Considering all of that, it might very well have been 12:45 a.m. when I returned home.

"Past midnight, my servant was never obligated to wait up for me. He needed only to leave a lighted lamp in the vestibule. Then I turned the key in the outside door, and with that lamp in my hand I went through a rather long series of rooms to reach the study which I had the honor to describe to you. A fire was always lit for me there, because I usually spent an hour reading or taking notes before going to bed.

"When I opened the door of that room, judge, sir, my astonishment! I saw a person sitting on both sides of the fireplace. One of them, wearing a big red cloak, acting perfectly at home, was busy poking up the fire. Without rising or greeting me.

"'You're coming home very late,' said one of the intruders in a commanding and arrogant voice. At those words, the one poking up the fire, turned his face toward me, and then, would you believe it, whom did I recognize? Exactly that man who always looked askance at that fellow, your friend, that American Osage Indian in the Exhibit Room of the Clinic in 1827. In short, that big red and white harlequin that I had looked at twenty times on his pedestal and with whom, I really must tell you, I wasn't on excellent terms with myself either. Excitement had at first made me speechless, but as soon as I could speak:

"'You again!' I said angrily to the one who had spoken to

---

[22] Marie Taglioni (1804-1884), ballet dancer who perfected toe dancing.
[23] Popular 19th century restaurant located on the Boulevard des Italiens.

me.

"'*Again*?' my guest of the evening before said ironically. 'That's a word of reproach.'

"'What do you want here? Why is that man here?'

"'Will you take down my dictation, or will you again have your servant show me the door?'

"'No, I won't write and I ask you to leave.'

"'Be careful,' that miserable man then said to me. 'I have my gendarme here and you must not fool with me.'

"As I didn't want to deal with that uncouth man any longer, I ran over to my bell cords, but it was impossible to use them. They had taken care to cut the cords. Then I rushed toward the window, intending to call for help. At that movement, running to place himself in front of the rods which opened the French windows, the horrible phantom shouted to me in an insulting way:

"'One last time, will you write?'

"With the most unshakeable firmness, I protested that nothing would make me change my resolution."

"'We'll see about that,' said my abominable adversary, and pronounced this simple word: "'WASHINGASHA!'

"At this word, which you will probably recognize as Indian, jumping like a tiger, in two bounds the Osage was on me. With his iron muscles, he grasped and squeezed me as we rolled onto the rug together. Suddenly, at the height of that struggle, I felt myself torn apart by a sharp pain from my head to my feet. Then under that indescribable sensation, it seemed to me that life was flowing out of me, and I fainted.

"I must tell you, sir that, during his lifetime in his own country, that Washingasha was a circus strong man. As a consequence he was skilled in all sorts of magic and evil practices. That man was, most of all, deplorably practiced in the horrible practice of scalping. There was something that enraged him. He couldn't get over not having been able to enjoy Parisian life, since he was dead almost from the time he arrived at the hospital. Now, do I have to explain to you why he never stopped giving our friend Blanquillet, and me those evil looks? He'd been planning an escape from a long time. He felt sure that he could avoid being pursued and recaptured if he could find someone to take his place as an exhibit. It was I, sir, who was that victim. Can you then understand the frightening preliminaries? When I came to myself, I was no longer a man. I had been unexpectedly lowered in the ranks of existence. The two monsters had transformed me into the big skeleton in the Faculty of Medicine showcase. From that moment, my social position was to be a piece of anatomy."

Here the pale, thin, man sadly covered his face with his hands. The convincing tone of his speech drawing him little by little into the world of the fantastic, Frantz Hoffmann seemed to take a rather intense interest in the sad event of that metamorphosis.

"In such an abnormal situation," the speaker continued, "how can I tell you of my suffering and humiliation? In the hours when the exhibit room was open to the public, I had to submit to the stares of the lazy and the insolent of the students and the dirty-minded jokes of the student midwives. Later, when the doors were shut, locked up with all that horrible human garbage conserved there for the use of science, I was terrified by the silence and emptiness of those vast sonorous rooms. In the window frames, I could hear the muffled labor of the insects of destruction resuming the labor of Death, trying to return to him the petty thefts from his tombs.

"When the night hours came, it was another kind of torture. As midnight was sounding on the faculty clock, my terrible persecutor taunted me like Christ on his cross, asking me to descend from my pedestal and with a thousand other insults. He always came back to the object of our debate: 'Will you write?' 'Will you write?'

"Since it didn't seem to me possible that such a huge reversal of nature could go on indefinitely, I stiffened my resistance. From atop my pillory, I was able to defy my tormentor. But beware of the Devil!"

"'By the way,' he said to me one day, 'what do you think my friend the Osage has done with everything he filched from you so completely?'

"I disdained answering that insinuation, in which I saw nothing but a detestable mockery. But the monster continued:

"'Examined up close,' he said, 'that skin doesn't exactly fit him like a glove. But with these Red Skins that's no problem, and dressed up in what he borrowed, sleeping in your bed, spending your money, taking your place near your mistresses, do you know what that fellow does? On my word, what a life!'

"'What you're saying, is not possible,' I shouted, terrified by the new horizon of misfortune appearing to me.

"'Not possible! And why not?' the phantom continued. 'That's said every day in conversations: "I wouldn't like to be in your skin." 'He didn't find it distasteful. He really wanted to be in yours. He had a good time there and took full advantage of it.'

"'God in Heaven!' I then cried out in the last agony of despair. "'Have you allowed this to be the payment for my charity?'

"'Well, what I don't approve of,' the most hellish personage I have ever met continued with hypocritical concern, 'is that this escaped savage doesn't act with a little more restraint. To get drunk every evening, cheat at cards, sign IOU's, cheat merchants, and in addition to all that, refuse to fight a duel. You'll have to admit that's to abuse a personality a little too much. As for me, I was saying to him the other day: 'My boy, be careful. All this could well end in a jail cell.' To this he answered: 'What does that matter to me? That's the problem of the other one. I'll quickly bolt and give him back his cast offs, once the police decide to torment me.'

"Up to that point I had endured everything and defied everything, but with that view of my dishonor, I became broken, destroyed. He saw that I was weakening.

"'Cone, now,' my persecutor said to me, 'is it such a difficult thing to write, from the dictation of an honest man, whose mind and memory are full of them, a series of varied and extraordinary adventures?'

"'Use me, sir, but put an end immediately to this hellish enchantment so that at least I can re-establish my name!'

"By means of several passes by his hands, I plunged almost immediately into a magnetic slumber. The next day when I woke up I had been restored, but I was in my bed suffering horribly, so much so that the doctors, stubbornly in those days seeing nothing else, treated me as if I were suffering from a severe attack of cholera."

III

Finally you decided to write," said Frantz Hoffmann. "That was surely the best thing to do."

"It seems so to you, sir," replied the story-teller. "Nevertheless, that cowardly complaisance was for me only the beginning of an unendurable obsession. As soon as that maniac had finished dictating his story to me, he began again with variations, so that it would never be finished. In this sense my misfortune was aggravated. Unlike the Moon that each night rises more and more three quarters of an hour later, he moved forward the hour of his arrival. So, much before beginning our work, from the dinner hour to the theater, in the evenings when I could be invited out (the Osage's excesses having compromised me less than I had feared), I had to smell and see that horrible larvae at my side, and he even (you were able to see that a little while ago) comes right up to my cup, despite the care that I always take to give him his share, as if he still possessed a physical apparatus with which to be in touch with the exterior world, as if he wasn't a ghost and a spirit."

"But, I say," Frantz Hoffmann said judiciously, "you're expressing yourself very well there, it seems to me, about that dangerous man, in a very vivid manner and in a hardly measured way. Therefore he isn't near you at this moment?"

"No, sir," the pale and thin man answered. "He left me to go play pool. He has a frenetic passion for billiards, seemingly having been during his lifetime a man of not very steady habits who kept very low company."

"And you don't know any way to force him to part company with you?"

"Oh! Pardon, sir. There would be one way, and he has broached it to me rather clearly. His book written and re-written, he would consent to deliver me of his presence if I would get it published for him."

"Well! What prevents you from doing that?"

"But he doesn't want me to pay to have it printed, saying with reason, perhaps, that books self-published by authors don't sell easily. I saw, one after the other, all the publishers. What people, sir! They all clamor for something new and extraordinary. But when I took them that book, which certainly is rather extraordinary and rather new, they seem to say that I wasn't in my right mind and showed me the door with more or less courtesy."

Sharing the poor possessed man's sorrows, the sympathetic young man said: "Listen, I may be able to help you. I'm the son of a man who wasn't without some reputation among booksellers. You know *The Tales of Hoffmann*?"

"Do I know *The Tales of Hoffmann*! And you would be the son of that great man!" shouted the speaker with excitement, while a gleam of life appeared in his expression and for a moment colored the faded bones of his cheeks.

"Yes," the student answered. "Hoffmann was my father, and perhaps offered under the patronage of that illustrious name, your manuscript might be less badly received."

"Who could doubt it, young man. It will be at your place tomorrow...Your address, please."

At this request, Frantz took from his pocket a small embroidered velvet case, a present from his fiancée at the time he left for Paris, and taking out a little card he presented it to the poor secretary that he intended to help.

But that was to very thoughtlessly revive a painful memory.

"A card! A card to me!" shouted the maniac as if he had been threatened with a burning iron. "Ah! I see very well that you are a wicked joker like the others!"

Then, without wanting to hear any explanation, he tragically left the café.

The next day the young German was peacefully smoking his pipe in his furnished room, discussing with some of his friends of the night before the question of whether he was dealing with a weird personality or just with a deranged person. Suddenly there appeared in the gathering a young female student, a tall blonde named Clara.

"Here is something the concierge gave me for you," she said to the young Hoffmann, whom, as a fellow countryman she had come to visit. At the same time she put into the young man's hands a roll of papers with black seals and in addition a letter of large dimensions, with a thin border of the same color. That unusual missive was set up in the following way:

Sir,

My secretary is an imbecile and his frightened way of leaving you yesterday at your rendezvous at the Rue de la Harpe might well be such as to compromise the good and useful intentions that you had testified in regard to my manuscript. To leave you without even getting your address! Could anyone be more ridiculous and clumsier! Fortunately, I was able to repair his stupidity. I go about anywhere I like, and at the Medical Faculty, you can understand that, as a dead man, I have particularly free access. Therefore, I was able to remember your name that I had heard pronounced by your comrades. I went through the student registrations and found your address: Lemoine Hotel, Rue des Maçons, Sorbonne. I can only hope this letter will reach you punctually.

I can only thank you, sir, for your kind thoughts and beg you to be willing to continue them. The book that I have the honor to send to you is a work filled with unusual memories and is extremely conscientious, as you can see, because the manuscript that I confided to your care is the tenth version written at my dictation by the man named Charbonneau, whom I employ as a secretary. I will leave the rest entirely up

*to you for your corrections of the proofs. And at the same time
I hereby make a commitment to break off any kind of
relationship with the hereby named Carbonneau on the same
day the book is available for sale. I require, however, sin qua
non, that the bookseller pay for all the necessary publicity.
Those gentlemen, in that regard, need to be carefully watched.*

*Please accept, sir, the assurance of my great
consideration and do not take it unkindly, if, even with you, I
continue to keep my anonymity, and limit myself to signing:*

An ex-employee of the Secret Bureau

Written in the same handwriting as the letter, the
manuscript had, first of all, the merit of being magnificently
readable. In addition, it was embellished with rather curious
pen and ink drawings. At the head of the 1st notebook and
placed like an epitaph, was the following title:

THE LIFE AND ADVENTURES
OF FRANÇOIS-MAXIMILIEN DE KORMER,
MARQUIS DE LUPIANO;
TOGETHER WITH THE SECRET, PHYSICAL,
MORAL, AND ANECDOTAL HISTORY
OF THE
CABINET NOIR
FROM ITS EARLIEST TIMES RIGHT UP TO OUR DAY

Above the title was placed this epigraph, borrowed from
Titan, Jean-Paul Richter's most famous novel: *After which it is
well not to unseal letters dealing with matters of State, except
after resealing them.* (Titan, Volume II. Cycle LXXIV).[24]

Young Hoffmann's friends were very amused about that
entire letter. But he didn't put much store in all their jokes.
Clearing off a clean place on his work table, encumbered with

---

[24] This passage starting from "Written in the same handwriting..." was deleted from the De Potter 1856-57 edition.

notebooks and medical books, he seemed ready to consider seriously the nocturnal literary activities of the departed.

Somewhat scandalized by the candid young man's attitude, Blanquillet then said,

"Are you going to begin reading that silliness instead of coming with us to the Hôtel Dieu? Dupuytren[25] is supposed to perform two superb operations today."

"On my word!" Frantz answered. "I'm curious to find out what that man has been able to write. If he's insane, as you say, it seems to me that from the scientific point of view a book which has come from his pen must certainly have some interest."

"Decidedly," one of the young man's friends remarked, slapping him on the shoulder at the same time. "Like father, like son. My boy," he added, "you really are your father's son and to think they want to make a doctor out of you!"

"Well, look here. This looks rather nice," said the young girl student, who, as curious as an upstairs maid, had opened the manuscript and gone through it.

"Don't touch that, Clara," one of Frantz's friends exclaimed, laughing. "That will bring you bad luck. A dead man wrote it."

"Then that must be someone like Mr. Paul de Kock.[26] Would you like for us to read these papers together, Monsieur Frantz?"

"Gladly, dear lady," answered the young student, who nevertheless accepted with some embarrassment.

---

[25] Baron Guillaume Dupuytren (1777-1835), French anatomist. As an army surgeon, he treated Napoleon's hemorrhoids. In 1811, he was the head surgeon at the Paris Hôtel Dieu Hospital. His most important publication is *Treatise on the Artificial Anus*.

[26] Paul de Kock (1793-1871), novelist; he was the son of Jan Conrad de Kock, a Dutch banker guillotined during the French Revolution. He was popular throughout Europe, but less so in France, and here is insulted by Clara.

"All right, gentlemen, let's go," Blanquillet shouted. "Me, first of all. I want to get a good seat."

Once the students had left for their butchery, blonde Clara went to sit near the window so as to have daylight for a piece of embroidery she was going to work on. During this time, Frantz Hoffmann had gone to sit down at his table, and picked up the manuscript. It began thus:

PROLOGUE

I. The Invisible Ones

During the year 1819, a crime, accompanied by very extraordinary circumstances, was committed in Paris. A magistrate, enjoying esteem and general consideration was found one morning murdered in his bed. The weapon the murderer used was a dagger. The hand of a clever artist, whose imagination seemed to take pleasure in the horrible, must have made the design and fashioned the weapon. The handle was formed by a long, half naked, partially draped skeletal figure. On the blade, a horrible joke, in wavy letters could be read: *La lame donne le manche.*[27]

An ebony tag on a little bronze steel chain was hung on the instrument of the murder, still planted in the heart of the victim. On the black background, standing out in red letters was this single word: LIAR. At the same time a red stamp bearing the number 4 in the middle of a shield had been stuck on the dead man's forehead. It was as if it was the first number which seemed to announce a horrible series of murders.

That setting of circumstances had at first seemed very striking to the police. Working together with the family of the magistrate, whose private life the murderer was accusing in this way, the most absolute secrecy was kept concerning the circumstances of the unfortunate man's death. Another concern, that of forestalling the fear of the public, who might have believed they were menaced by a band of invisible hired assassins, brought about mysterious instructions. In addition, no indiscretion must be committed by the newspapers, then

---

[27] The blade brings death.

censured, and the *Gazette des Tribunaux*[28] didn't exist.

Several weeks passed, during which all the police investigations had been fruitless and there was a new crime and a new victim, a woman, highly renowned for religious devotion and virtue and who, recently widowed, had shown inconsolable sorrow at the loss of her husband. It had never occurred to anyone to suspect her sincerity. She was found dead in her bedroom, struck down while kneeling on her prayer stool. The same wound to the heart, the same dagger left in the wound, the same ebony wood tag on the murder weapon carrying the double accusation: ADULTERESS AND POISONER. Last of all, on the dead woman's forehead, the same red stamp and in the middle of the shield the number two.

The reasons that had advised secrecy about the first crime determined, a fortiori, the most complete discretion about the second. But a great complication was encountered in this affair. Alerted by the accusation cast on the memory of the victim, the police pushed their investigations in several directions. While it remained without any clue as to the audacious murderer who numbered his crimes, it acquired posthumous certainty that the woman society held to be the model of wives, had, in fact, stirred by an adulterous passion, been led to get rid of her husband by means of poison.

It's not necessary to say what doubling of zeal that discovery gave the police inquiries. To the exploration of their duty and their conscience, they had already added their ego. Was this not in fact for them an unwonted defiance, the existence of a kind of secret tribunal having its police and its executioners and allowing itself to know and to punish crimes which remained unpunished and ignored in public prosecution?

One evening, scarcely a month after this new drama, at a rather early hour, in the middle of a street and some feet from one of the great centers of Parisian traffic, an old man was

---

[28] Journal of jurisprudence and judicial debates.

struck dead. It was as if the murderers had wanted to gain public recognition from authority, which had until then been missing from their crimes. It was more than a reputation for honesty, it was a dazzling philanthropic renown that the murderers had given themselves in the task of stamping out in blood. Number three, as the red stamp on the victim's forehead named him, would have been, according to the tag appended to the dagger, an INCORRIGIBLE USURER. That accusation was in fact justified by the accounts revealed in his estate. However, the publicity that hidden justice seemed to want at any price for its executions failed it again this time. No newspaper was authorized to speak of the event, and as for some oral details which could have been put into circulation by the small number of persons present when the cadaver was taken away, they were dismissed and treated as ridiculous fables by the official newspaper, the *Moniteur*.[29] It's known that the government, the proprietors of a newspaper, make it an instrument of lying as often as an instrument of truth.

At the end of the same year, a last adventure which was stranger than all the unusual events which have just been reported to the reader closed this series of obscure attacks.

To the west of the Hell barrier, the entrée to a vast subterranean ossuary called the catacombs have galleries which extend under several Paris neighborhoods. On December 24th the wife of the guardian of this funereal warehouse had invited some friends to celebrate Christmas Eve with her. The meal was very lively, noting that in general the professions that live on death aren't usually given to melancholy. Wine and happy conversations were making the rounds when, in the somber empire of which he was the watchdog, the catacomb's custodian thought he could make out some subterranean noises resembling loud voices. Superstitious terror immediately spread among the guests.

---

[29] Propaganda tool of the French Government created on November 24, 1789, by Charles Panckouke. It ceased publication on June 30, 1901.

Since the guardian's dwelling was the only entrance into the mortuary galleries, the guardian thought that he was certain no one had been able to enter without his consent or to remain there unknown to him after having been let in. A former military man and scrupulously exact in fulfilling his duties, in spite of his wife's entreaties wanted to investigate the strange noises that he had heard. Since no one having dinner with him had the courage to accompany him, armed with two pistols and a lantern, he resolutely went down into the subterranean passages to explore what was happening.

Sometime later, his prudent dinner companions heard the sound of two detonations. That was all. Many hours passed without that kind of Aeneas who had descended into Hell reappearing. Night was falling; the police were then called. After arming themselves with torches, a large squad of officers began to search through the passages trying to find the cause of the noises that were said to have been heard and to confirm the fate of the man who had begun that exploration before them.

The result of these searches was horrifying. After a quarter of an hour, they stumbled on the cadaver of the unfortunate custodian. His two discharged pistols were at his side near his still burning lantern, placed on his stomach like a guiding light. There again appeared, with the eternal dagger, the red stamp which this time marked the number four with the label PRESUMPTUOUS CURIOSITY brazenly giving that as the reason for the murder. It was supposed that the unfortunate guardian had the misfortune to disturb and surprise some terrible mysteries.

As for the trace of the invisible murderers, it remained, as always, elusive. Everything in the profaned asylum of the dead remained silent and in its habitual order. Despite the minutest searches, the way through which the bloody men had entered the passages could not be found. Vainly, for several weeks there were daily and nightly rounds to aid the law's natural passion to penetrate the dark secret, but an inextricable obscurity continued to protect it. In addition, it, more than anything that had preceded it, was carefully kept from the public. Never had the powerlessness of the police against the dark scoundrels they were supposed to find been more scandalously demonstrated.

II. More Mysteries

About the time these black attacks were taking place, an event of a very different nature had caused some sensation in the Faubourg St. Germain. The Marquise de Camembert, one of the most elegant women of the Parisian aristocracy, had suddenly announced the intention of withdrawing from the world and entering the Ladies of the Sacred Heart of Turin as a nun. That resolution had appeared strange in every way. It was difficult to explain why a twenty-five year-old woman, endowed with gifts of the mind, face, and fortune and recently widowed by a seventy year-old man, had not found another way to use her youth and liberty.

However, a supposition had occurred to some clever people. They recalled that in the salons where she had had great success in conversations and in beauty, Madame de Camembert was at least as feared as she was welcomed and sought after. Having a reputation for loving intrigue, she was found to have such personal knowledge about the intimate life and secrets of a number of people, that there remained truly great doubt as to how this enlightenment was gathered. Such complete and so unusual scandalous gossip had even been about to give her the opportunity and the foundation for a great fortune. Admitted to an audience with Louis XVIII, who had a particular taste for gossip and slander, she had amused him in that meeting with so many racy revelations about Parisian society that he had immediately developed a sort of passion for her. It would also have taken very little for that grandson of Henri IV to have put her in possession of the role of favorite. Considering his obesity and his age, that was not exactly the sinecure that his infirmities would have indicated. However, supported by the congregation and by the Marsan

Pavilion,[30] another influence had prevailed. In the opinion of the onlookers, the Marquise' project of retirement had to be attributed to the miscalculation that royal kindliness nipped in the bud.

However that may be, when seeing the beautiful penitent distribute liberalities to her servants and to her friends, and get rid of or set aside all her fortune, absolutely as if she were at death's door, inflexibility and persistence couldn't be doubted. As to her entry into monastic life, she seemed to want it to be particularly rigorous and austere. In leaving for her pious exile, she informed all those who might have claimed some place in her life that she would receive no correspondence or visit. Her personality would be so completely absorbed in her monastic name that henceforth she must be considered as having never existed.

Before leaving France, Madame de Camembert finalized her ties to France by selling, among her properties, a magnificent town house she occupied on the Rue Notre-Dame-des-Champs, in the Luxembourg quarter. It had formerly belonged to a famous Controller General, Abbé Terray.[31]

The man who was to acquire that splendid dwelling was a very remarkable personage. In the future of this story, he is to play a considerable role, allowing us to give some explanations concerning him. Calling himself the Marquis de Lupiano, he fell to Paris from the skies one fine day without anyone being able to find out anything about his background, his country, his family, or, as some people went so far as to say, of his sex. It must be admitted that he was to reach the ultimate possible limits to eccentricity and incognito. The fact

---

[30] The section of the Louvre that ties together the Palais du Louvre and the Palais des Tuileries—here, meaning the occupants.

[31] Joseph Marie Terray (1715-1778), Controller-General of Finances during the reign of Louis XV and agent of fiscal reform.

is, apart from the mystery with which he appeared to want to surround himself, that man, was quite bizarre in his outward appearance. With a forest of gray hair, a sparse and thin beard, his face, with unusual paleness and delicacy, showed that deep, multiple crossing of wrinkles which is the particular trait of the old age of women. At the same time, because of the thin, high-pitched timber of his voice he managed to suggest the strangest interpretations. But on the other hand, the regard of this old man had something quite penetrating. His movements, despite his apparently weak constitution, were very commanding and strong. In short, at the time of a still famous duel with pistols, a fortunate winner in that encounter, he had demonstrated such prodigious courage and cool-headedness that stupid conjectures, confronted with such powerful moral attributes, could, after that, no longer be risked.

For a while, in order to reconcile everything, they claimed to see in this living problem a continuation of the famous androgyny that, under successive names of Chevalier and of Chevalière of Éon,[32] attracted so much attention at the end of the last century. But, examined more closely, that version wasn't for a moment sustainable. Born in 1728, the Chevalier d'Éon would have been, in 1820, more than ninety-two years old. Obviously, the Marquis de Lupiano hadn't reached that advanced age. In addition, settling everything, was the fact that, ten years earlier, May 21, 1810, the Chevalier d'Éon had died in London in the arms of Father Élisée,[33] Louis XVIII's principal surgeon, who did the autopsy.

---

[32] Charles-Geneviève-Louis-Auguste-André-Timothée d'Éon de Beaumont (1728-1810), French diplomat, spy, soldier, who lived his last thirty-three years as a woman, claiming to be anatomically female. Doctors, after his death, verified that he was anatomically male.

[33] Père Elisée, real name Marie-Vincent Talochon (1753-1817) was a famous master-surgeon of the time.

It must be admitted that at the period this story began it would have been rather difficult to see him walk about the streets of Paris. In the meantime, let us sweep aside the cloudy atmosphere in which the bizarre Marquis seemed to take pleasure. Let us note another peculiarity in his existence which, at least, was not problematic. Established in a rented house with a magnificent retinue, leading a truly princely existence, even before he had acquired the Hôtel Camembert at the cost of half a million pounds, he justified that prodigious expense by the very useful possession of enormous funds deposited in London, Paris and Vienna banks. In addition, he made an honorable as well as an intelligent use of that opulence. As often as he wasted considerable sums on the strangest fantasies, he also spent a great deal of money encouraging literature and the arts, of which he was an excellent judge. And numerous charitable acts were attributed to him, although, on the other hand, he was reproached for imperious, haughty behavior and for losing his temper. In a word, he showed all the signs of a profound estimation of himself, combined with a not less profound contempt for the rest of humanity. Appealing to general curiosity in so many ways, the Marquis asked for even more by attaching his name to a peculiarity which, in the time we're talking about, was very popular in Paris, without anyone ever having known the name for it.

All the contemporaries of that time can recall having heard the famous girl with the death's head talked about. According to public gossip, she was a rich heiress who could put her hand on an immense fortune at the disposal of the man courageous enough to look at her without trembling when she had taken off her mask in front of him. Now that unusual marriageable girl, whose existence, as we will see, was less fabulous than many had thought, was simply the Marquis de Lupiano's daughter. Accompanying her father into public places and into salons, she never showed herself without a wax mask on her face. But the cruel caprice of nature of which she was the victim, seems only to have reached the charms of her face. She had a tall, slim and admirably proportioned figure, beautiful, thick blonde hair, a perfect neck, and white hands of admirable shape. However, when she began to speak, there was a surprising exterior revelation of her infirmity. Even with care, there was mixed something sepulchral and cavernous

Taking seriously the offer of her hand that strange fiancée was supposed to make to the first suitor, several naïve suitors presented themselves at the Marquis' townhouse, and depending on the mood of the Marquis they were either pleasantly hoodwinked or harshly dismissed. Nevertheless, M. de Lupiano didn't claim to deny the hideous deformity of his daughter. On the contrary he was the first to confirm the belief by the explanation that he himself gave for it. According to that explanation, the Marquise, his pregnant wife, helping him with some archeological excavations, was suddenly startled by the sight of a human skull which had rolled under the picks of the workers. And because of the shock the sight caused the mother, the unborn child contracted the terrible resemblance that disfigured her. But, that sad creature whom wicked fate had disinherited from all beauty, was certainly not reduced to spinsterhood, the only choice that ridiculous gossip had spread about this matrimonial auction. With the superb dowry that she could dangle before the eyes of the suitors and the intellectual superiority which showed in her conversation, she was still an easily marriageable girl which more than one great name of the upper aristocracy would willingly arrange.

III. The Bloodied Girl[34]

The Marquis de Lupiano and his daughter had already lived in Paris for more than a year when one afternoon during the month of January 1820, we saw him walking through that dark lateral passage which, entered from the Rue Saint-Marc,

---

[34] This title will reappear and eventually be reused by Rabou (or his publisher) as the title of the third volume in the series.

had no other exit but the Panoramas Grand Gallery. He was at that moment accompanied by a man remarkable for his confident bearing and for his strong, resolute air. That man's name as well as swarthy complexion indicated a southern origin, but that was the only information which to that point could be obtained about him. Count Montalvi was one of those foreigners of doubtful background who led a most elegant lifestyle in Paris without anyone really knowing anything about either the source of the fortune that he dispensed, the names of the decorations that he wore, or the country from which he came.

To tell the truth, with his frail nature and his puny appearance, clinging to the arm of his imposing companion, to whom he was speaking animatedly, the Marquis de Lupiano formed a rather grotesque contrast. However, with the deferential and approving attitude with which the Count was listening to him, it could be suspected that he recognized great moral superiority in the spindly man speaking to him. A great nephew, an officer of the Italian police, is not more obsequiously attentive to every word of a little old uncle, from whom he expects to inherit.

At that time, the boutique of a toilette articles merchant named Madame Constantin was situated in the isolated passageway where the conversation of the two strollers was taking place. The usual various functions of that type of commerce is well known. Having kept girls as most of her clientele, whether she bought from them or sold to them, the retail merchant is always somewhat obliged to enter into the business of these Madeleine's[35] whom she frequently helps with her advice. The toilette article merchant, in general, has known a little about love and knows how to sympathize with it. She would therefore already know about those small kindnesses from the goodness of her heart and her inclination,

---

[35] Biblical character sometimes portrayed as a prostitute, witness of Christ's crucifixion, and first at his tomb of his resurrection.

when she doesn't already know, most of all, by her self-interest.

"On my word, a beautiful creature," the Marquis suddenly said, seeing, in fact, a remarkably beautiful woman who had crossed his path leaving Madame Constantin's shop.

"Something slightly risky in the plan," the Count remarked.

"Exactly what we need," Lupiano answered, "since, decidedly, we can't count on the help of our beautiful friend."

"By the way," Montalvi continued, "Providence is great, and, who knows? Just at the moment when we were least thinking about it, she's sending us the guiding Angel we were lacking." Saying this, he dropped the Marquis' arm and was about to hurry after the charming apparition, who was already almost out of sight.

"Oh! No! No!" said the Marquis, holding back his impetuous friend. "You're not going to act like a student or a law clerk and dog the heels of a woman. That merchant," he added, pointing to Madame Constantin's shop, "will certainly tell us everything we want to know."

And a minute afterward, followed by Montalvi, he entered the merchant's shop. Upon entering, appearing to be a serious buyer, the Marquis said:

"Madame, we would like to see some lace."

"English? Malines? Alençon?" the merchant asked, as much to show off the variety of her assortment as to know what they wanted.

"Whatever you choose, provided it's beautiful, however," Lupiano answered.

"Monsieur, here's a magnificent article, and what's more a very good buy," said the saleswoman, beginning to unroll several yards of Brussels lace wrapped around a cardboard holder.

Nothing is impossible to find in the shop of a toilette article vender. And everything can be found there by chance, from the dress worn by a young girl for her first communion even to dueling pistols. It wasn't astonishing, therefore, to see the Marquis brusquely interrupt the Brussels lace sale to enquire the price of a savage's bow and arrows that he had suddenly noticed in a corner.

"That, sir, that's Indian," the sales woman answered in a capable low voice, which meant that between the question and the answer the object that had so unexpectedly attracted the buyer's attention, had at least just doubled in price.

"No," answered Lupiano, who had traveled a great deal and was a connoisseur. "That's Hottentot and it's from the Cape of Good Hope. But it's not a question of where it comes from. I'm asking you what you want for it."

The merchant named an exorbitant price, which the Marquis, without bargaining, paid in gold. At the same time he asked that his purchase be held. He would have one of his servants come for it. A reason for his curiosity thus established, he asked:

"A very remarkable woman was in here a while ago. Do you know her?"

"A very remarkable woman?" the resale woman repeated, without seeming to know what was asked. That is inevitably the beginning of those kinds of conversations.

"Yes, a tall, pretty young woman who just left your shop, apparently one of your clients."

"Ah! Yes," said Madame Constantin, finding her memory again. "A brunette wearing green cashmere. The gentleman is certainly right. In my opinion, she's one of the most attractive women in Paris. And it can really be said that she's not where she should be, the poor child!"

"What do you call 'not where she should be?'" Montalvi asked.

"That is to say a woman who has no good luck. The gentleman knows there are some like that."

"But," the Marquis continued, "what does that 'no good fortune' consist of? It's already something to be beautiful and in Paris. A pretty woman is never unhappy except when she really wants to be."

"Damn, if the gentleman believes that losing a rich

protector, when it's not your fault and seeing your furniture seized is something to be glad about!"

"One protector lost, another found," Montalvi remarked.

"Hum! For Georgiana, that's already not so easy," answered the sales woman. "There are words that kill, you know!"

"What words that kill? You like to speak in word games, my dear Madame Constantin."

"Yes, sir, that's how men are, and very often it takes only a bad nickname to spoil you in their mind."

"Ah, well," said the Marquis, "to be labeled in that way by bad nicknames, that young girl Georgiana is therefore, consequently, a loose woman?"

"As to that, sir, you are very mistaken! Georgiana is a nice girl, gentle as a lamb, liking only to stay at home, incapable of deception and of arguing with anyone. But it's just her fate, that's all."

"That is to lose all her protectors?"

"Yes, sir, to see them all taken away, one after the other, but not in the way you would think, and not a long story of their leaving her. The way that came about was seeing death do away with them, and always by terrible deaths. So, for example, she would have one of them today killed in a duel; tomorrow, another one, while riding with her in the Bois du Boulogne, take a fall from a horse and not get up; the next week it's an English lord who, without rhyme or reason, committed suicide in her boudoir and caused her to lose a Persian rug worth at least fifty louis. There was also one in politics whose end came about through a conspiracy."

"The Devil! But that is in fact being born under an unlucky star," Montalvi remarked.

"And so, following all these disasters, what is the unfortunate name that she's been given?" the Marquis asked.

"Some young men began to call her," the resale shop keeper answered mysteriously, 'the bloodied girl.' You know, sir, after that famous novel where there's the nun? The name stuck and I'm not exaggerating. I today know some very sensible men, magistrates, peers of France, bankers, people with education and ability, who, fearing for their life, wouldn't even greet Georgiana in the street."

"Ah! So you say, 'the bloodied girl,'" said the Marquis, looking at Montalvi.

"Oh, certainly," said Montalvi in his turn, appearing to hit on an idea. Then speaking to the shop owner:

"Well! Tell us a little more," he added gaily. "Where does that murderous beauty live? Because we really wouldn't want to meet her in the street."

Madame Constantin appeared to take the question as a joke and, instead of answering it, asked the Marquis sweetly:

"So, Monsieur doesn't want to buy my Brussels lace?"

"On the contrary! On the contrary!" Lupiano said quickly. "It's you my dear lady, who hasn't yet told me the price."

The Marquis then having once more paid a very expensive price without bargaining, the resale shop owner said:

"Pardon, gentlemen, I have forgotten a very pressing appointment," moving at the same time to the door at the back of her shop. "Ernestine," she shouted to her shop assistant, "here is a shawl that must be taken immediately to Mademoiselle Georgiana, still at 31, Rue Roquépine. She isn't moving until the day after tomorrow."

Having innocently and ingeniously been given the fact he wanted to know, the Marquis, moving toward the door with Montalvi, said:

"Honored to have met you, Madame."

"You don't want me to have these articles sent to you?"

"No, that's not necessary. As I told you, someone will come to pick them up."

And the two friends left the shop.

Two days later a servant appeared at Madame Constantin's shop, coming to pick up the Marquis' purchases. The merchant was very charming toward that servant, and did her best to make him chat, but she couldn't have had worse luck. The only thing he knew how to say in French was 'Bonjour, Madame.' What's more, speaking Portuguese, he couldn't communicate with the shop owner except by means of a piece of paper he was carrying on which someone had written: 'Give to the bearer the bow and arrows and the lace bought by Monsieur Hernandez.'"

The servant, on leaving, left the paper in Madame Constantin's hands. She didn't waste any time examining it with extreme attention, and noted that it was the back side of a letter's envelope. On the front was written: *Monsieur de Hernandes, Wholesale Merchant, Cambridge Hôtel, Rue de Rivoli, Paris* and the stamp indicated that the letter came from Brazil.

As soon as the two strangers had left, the officious merchant had hurried to let Mademoiselle Georgiana know by means of a note the curiosity and the questions of which she had been the object. But the curious thing was that during the two days which had just passed, the carefree beauty had given no signs of her existence. And instead of coming to get news, which would have been quite natural, she had left Madame Constantin, whom she knew to be a very inquisitive person, in the most complete ignorance of the result of the excellent information given about her. Finally, not able to wait any longer, the resale merchant decided to go to the Rue Roquépine, to the lodging where we have seen her, with such perfect propriety, give the indirect location. But there, a first disappointment. The evening before that visit, Mademoiselle Georgiana, all her creditors paid, her chamber maid, a female confident she was much attached to, suddenly dismissed, had let it be known that she was leaving for Italy. The concierge, charged with paying Madame Constantin the balance of a small bill, was left without any information about when his beautiful renter could be expected to return. In addition, he had been given the job of selling her furniture.

Seeing enlightenment thus escape her, exasperated, the toilette articles merchant immediately decided on a bold step. Presenting herself resolutely at the Cambridge Hotel, she asked to speak to Monsieur de Hernandez, not being at a loss, when she reached him, to find whatever pretext for her bold visit.

Introduced without any great difficulty, a new and more serious setback awaited Madame Constantin. Monsieur de Hernandez was a gigantic Brazilian with a swarthy complexion, an exuberant frizzy head of hair, in which there was not the least resemblance to the two strangers who had used his name. It's not necessary to add that the bow, the arrows, and the Brussels lace were totally without meaning to him. Finally, bored by the persistence of his visitor's many questions, the merchant remembered that at the time this scene took place, people coming from Brazil were honored with very special attention by the police. He therefore suggested to the virtuous lady that he was inclined to consider her as having some mission to him for those vigilant eyes. He brusquely broke off that encounter with the questioner in a manner infinitely less polite. To her great despair, Madame Constantin had to stop the course of her investigations at that spot.

IV. The Lelouard Couple

At a time very near that in which the very unexpected departure of Mademoiselle Georgiana had taken place, there was gossip in the city of Bordeaux that the charms of a Parisian lady accompanied by her husband had registered at the Grand Hôtel de Guyenne. To cause that much sensation, it must be supposed that that woman, who, besides, had passed the time of her first youth, possessed very miraculous graces, because it's known that Bordeaux women also pride themselves on their beauty. And Bordeaux men, with that totally southern vanity, which has made the political fortune of many of them, would gladly persuade strangers that it is usual to meet women in their city who resemble Venus de Milo and Diane the Huntress.

In addition, what contributed even more to throw the attractions of the beautiful Parisian woman into even greater relief was the contrast with a husband already over the hill, who had no redeeming exterior advantages, and the cruel disparity of age between them, which was the first thing noticed.

That lack of harmony had even at first thrown a troop of very ardent admirers under the feet of the lovely stranger to whom the husband's disagreeable casual manner had offered little encouragement. But it must be quickly added that in less than a week that great competition and that compact, hassling crowd had considerably thinned.

Made very jealous, it seems, by the knowledge of his ugliness and his advanced age, to whom these two aggravating circumstances didn't seem to take anything away from his arm's muscular ability, the husband had begun by killing one of Penelope's[36] suitors in a duel. One evening, another adorer had been found stabbed at a cross street, without any proof, that's true, of the direct or indirect participation of the fierce Othello. But also without any other explanation of that tragic adventure but the indiscreet ardor, approaches and sighs which the victim had allowed himself.

It's understandable that those two murders had been sufficient to put an imposing chastity belt around the beautiful stranger. In addition, once the husband had been gotten around, there remained the difficulty of being heard by the lady, who seemed indifferent and disdainful rather than eager to receive adoration. They had to be content with admiring her at a distance, outside the balustrade. The cult of which she was still the object was a sort of embodiment of the popular saying, *Look, but don't touch.*

And, although they had arrived in a post carriage and were occupying the principal apartment of the most elegant hotel in the city, these glorious spouses hadn't brought any servant. That left even less chance of satisfying the curiosity

---

[36] Allusion to Penelope, Ulysses' wife, who was besieged by avaricious suitors until Ulysses' unexpected return from the Trojan War.

of which they were the object. They were rarely seen at the theater or out for walks. Almost all their distraction seemed to be, for the woman, to change outfits several times a day, and, for the man, to follow the activities of the port, either walking up and down the quay, or watching from his balcony the departure and arrival of ships.

As for how the husband and wife lived when by themselves, as much as could be found out, it was unusual. This husband, such a fierce guardian of his honor, never addressed a kind or tender word to his wife. And he treated her with an unequivocal coldness, if not with a certain disdain. On her side, that proud and so little encouraging beauty seemed hardly to except her gracious spouse from the glacial indifference with which she certainly seemed to honor all the masculine sex. In addition, having a great deal of money and having a considerable line of credit deposited with bankers in the city, never eating at the common hotel dining table, never receiving anyone, and avoiding with marked care any tie and all contacts, the more this unusual couple excited curiosity, the less they seemed disposed to satisfy it. The only precise thing that had been found out about these impenetrable strangers, was that they came from Paris and were named the Lelouards, a revelation found from their passport, which, besides, they had without any difficulty left with the hotel manager the very day of their arrival.

Little by little, discouraged by that meager amount of information, public attention was beginning to withdraw from those two irritating objects, which offered no solid ground for the most perseverant investigations, when a rival event suddenly occurred. This was a relief from the tiring inquisition which to that moment had been preying on them. One day, at the Stock Exchange, gossip spread that an official agent of the King of Madagascar, Radama-Manijaka,[37] had disembarked

---

[37] Radama I "the Great" (1793-1828) was the first Malagasy sovereign to be recognized as King of Madagascar (1810-1828) by a European state. He came to power at the age of 17

that morning with a large cargo of native products.

In any case, that news was interesting. First of all, beautiful material for speculation in a cargo to sell, the possible increase or decrease of certain foodstuffs, profits to foresee, a good commercial opportunity to take advantage of; in a word, a business deal was presenting itself. Coming next after this event was what publicists would call a political horizon. For people who knew about overseas trade, King Radama-Manijaka was considered to be a person of some importance, and the arrival of an agent accredited by him shouldn't be considered a fact of no importance.

Since 1665, with varying success, France had never ceased trying to set up trading agreements in the African island of Madagascar. And there, like almost everywhere else, she had encountered the bitter competition of England. Now, King Radama, at first just the chief of the Hovas tribe, had finally dominated the entire island. And after the conquest, as a civilizing monarch, wanting to bring the arts and enlightenment from Europe, he had seemed to want to direct his vague attempts at outside relations toward England. But

---

following the death of his father, King Andrianampoinimerina. Under Radama's rule and at his invitation, the first Europeans entered his central highland Kingdom of Imerina and its capital at Antananarivo. Radama encouraged these London Missionary Society envoys to establish schools to teach tradecraft and literacy to nobles and potential military and civil service recruits; they also introduced Christianity and taught literacy using the translated Bible. A wide range of political and social reforms were enacted under his rule, including an end to the international slave trade, which had historically been a key source of wealth and armaments for the Merina monarchy. Through aggressive military campaigns he successfully united two-thirds of the island under his rule. Abuse of alcohol weakened his health and he died prematurely at age 32. He was succeeded by his highest-ranking wife, Ranavalona I, his second cousin

now if he was sending a diplomatic agent, there had been a change in the direction of his political intentions. And our trade relations, until that point suffering and precarious, were therefore going to take new flight and offer new and unblocked exportations. It's easy to understand, that circulating in the Stock Exchange, a place where, without seeming to do so, great ardent imaginations fermented, these conjectures immediately produced a very great sensation. It really didn't take much to make a very great personage out of the newly disembarked.

Soon, more information surfaced and it all went back to the encouraging facts which were first seen. Intending, probably, to give his mission all the splendor and all the impact possible, the King of the Hovas' envoy arrived with a suite and a magnificent retinue. He brought with him his *vadibé*, or legitimate wife, a Malagache beauty of the deepest brown, and very closely related to King Radama, since she was the Queen's first cousin, then and still today, Ranavalo-Manijaka.

As for the plenipotentiary, at his arrival he had had a tailor called to dress him like a Frenchman. From the very deep copper tone of his complexion to the magnificent tattoo noticed on his stomach, everything made him appear to be originally from America. However his servants claimed that he was a European who came from who knows where to the coast of Madagascar. There, through his administrative and military talents, as well as by his distinguished manner in the frequent orgies to which the civilized king showed himself only too inclined, he rapidly gained favor with Radama. The King, after having made him his favorite, then one of his ministers, had finally made him his relative and now his envoy.

Several days passed, during which the Malagache diplomat made himself as generous of his presence as the couple who had thrown public curiosity off the track had been stingy of theirs. Then another twist came and began to circulate new gossip, in which the new and old objects of general attention were unexpectedly united and mingled.

To believe these strange rumors, as if to find a man in Bordeaux that he judged worthy of spending time with, the terrible Monsieur Lelouard needed an envoy of King Radama to show up there as soon as the dark Excellence was settled in the hotel where the unsociable Parisian lodged. The latter had shown an unmistakable intention to become human. Soon, living next door to each other, they had begun to develop certain habits, one of which was to eat together, and it was almost as if the two households, black and white, soon formed only one.

There was one more even more remarkable detail. King Radama's envoy, probably tired of the attractions of a colored regime, couldn't, without excited emotions, see the contrast of the resplendent beauty of Madame Lelouard. The husband, usually so little patient, didn't seem to take umbrage at the lively expression given to that admiration. And although the Envoy was less and less measured from day to day, he continued to find a patient, longsuffering husband, demonstrating no behavior to temper that admiration.

On her side, apparently encouraged by that sort of conjugal carte blanche, Madame Lelouard was far from showing herself disobliging toward the impetuous manifestations of the sighing African. Her sweet charm, according to the gossip mongers, had finally taken on a character so obvious that Queen Ranavalo's cousin had noticed it. Bursting to boiling point at that, the jealous Malagache would have exploded furiously and it would have taken very little, they added, for the *tanguin*, a strong poison very honored in Madagascar, where it is used in judicial proceedings, to play a role in that rivalry. In any case, in a situation so strained, such a denouement would become inevitable and here's how it all ended:

One beautiful night, the charming Madame Lelouard climbed furtively into the poste chaise by which she had arrived. Only, following a rather strong distraction, instead of having Monsieur Lelouard conjugally by her side, it seems that for a traveling companion the beautiful fugitive had taken the Envoy of the King of the Hovas.

At this bolt of lightning, reviving, but a little late, his marital vigilance, the unfortunate spouse had hurried after the traces of the infidels, who, according to all the information that could be collected, appeared to have taken the road to Paris. As for the illustrious and unfortunate cousin of Queen Ranavalo, a new Ariadne,[38] she had to temporarily continue to reside in the city of Bordeaux. Her ignorance of the language and the customs of the country where she had been abandoned scarcely left her anything to do but despair, except to later take a magnificent revenge, if she ever managed to put her hands on her flighty and perfidious spouse.

V. The Mysterious Crate

About two weeks after the arrival of King Radama's envoy in Bordeaux, January 13, 1820, a memorable date, since that was the day the unfortunate Duke de Berry was assassinated, there took place in Paris an adventure as little known as it was extraordinary and which caused the police of the period rather great anxiety.

That the event didn't get more publicity at that time is rather unusual, because, first of all, it looked very much like it was tied to the Louvel crime.[39] Probably, the little excitement was overshadowed by the great. It occurred in the middle of the preoccupation caused by the assassination which put in question the future of a dynasty. This explains why the perplexing state of affairs that we are going to take up with our readers slid by almost unnoticed. Just at the time the unfortunate Prince was felled by his assassin, Fate willed it

---

[38] Allusion to Ariadne, daughter of King Minos of Crete. Abandoned by Theseus on the Island of Noxos after having helped him slay the Minotaur.

[39] Louis Pierre Louvel (1783-1820), assassin of Charles Ferdinand d'Artois, Duc de Berry, last of the Bourbons. His wife produced a son seven months after his death on the scaffold.

that by a sad contrast this fatal event took place the night of *dimanche gras*.[40] Needless to say, there were many balls taking place in Paris.

The notary B***, among others, was giving a great ball that evening. The invitations expressly said that guests were to wear costumes. Among the guests was a young man named Maisonneuve, who was a particular friend of the B*** household. A son himself of a provincial notary, and destined for the judiciary by his father, that boy had been sent to Paris to pursue advanced studies in jurisprudence. As an old friend of the family, M. B*** had agreed to watch over him.

Not very intelligent, with a happy, ruddy and ordinary face, herculean shoulders, a steel disposition, and the greatest confidence of a fool that it's possible to have, the future magistrate had all the characteristics needed to fail to control a chamber of notaries. And it was particularly at the Prado at the Grande Chaumière[41] and other respectable places (where to use his expression, he had the greatest success with women) that he usually attended the classes of these advanced studies which, one day would let France have another Aguesseau.[42]

The 1820 carnival was the first Maisonneuve had spent in Paris. It must therefore have been an exciting time for the student and his day the 13th of February, in particular, must have been only one long and ardent sacrifice to the holy religion of the *dimanche gras* carnival.

As soon as he jumped out of bed that morning, dressed like a savage, his wicker club in his hand, wearing an Indian headdress and something resembling a leopard's skin thrown over a flesh-colored undershirt which emphasized his athletic and muscular build, he went to pick up a young shepherdess in

---

[40] Trinity Sunday, celebrated world-wide as a carnival season.

[41] Two 19th century bars and restaurants popular with students.

[42] A bit of irony. Aguesseau (1668-1751) was Chancellor three times and, according to Voltaire, the most learned lawyer in French history.

the Latin Quarter. She should in no way be confused with the chaste and pastoral patroness of the city of Paris. Under the pretext of waking them, he had, three quarters of the way, bashed in the door of two friends, a Harlequin and a Turk. They then received his visit and that of his tail wagging companion. The sextet, then completed by the addition of a Pierrot and a Poissarde, after an ample and early lunch, they grouped themselves picturesquely in a cheap, rented carriage for which they all contributed.

After the day spent in driving up and down the boulevards, our young men dined at the *Cadran Bleu*, and when night fell, after they had picked up some torches, they began a drive around all the somewhat notorious places where the carnival was taking place. About 11 p.m., Maisonneuve left his friends to attend the ball of the notary who lived in the Faubourg St. Germain. The partying band had gone into the Salon de Mars, Rue du Bac, and then, last of all, they had stopped at a first- floor Wauxhall, situated on the Quai Voltaire, in the abandoned church of a former religious community, where, by a bizarre combining of words, the name Bal des Théatins[43] had been given to this wicked place.

However, the festivity that Maisonneuve had not yet honored with his presence seemed to be doing rather well without him. It had already reached the highest pitch of animation, when the notary's attention was suddenly attracted by the noise of a heated discussion, or to put it better, by the noise of a brawl taking place in his antechamber. Hurrying to find out the cause of this scandal, M. B*** found that it was produced by a would-be interloper carrying a crate of rather considerable volume and weight on hooks. With this grotesque equipment, that he called his costume, this unusual guest, not withstand the energetic opposition of the domestic staff, was trying to enter the ballroom to present his greetings to the lady of the house.

---

[43] The Order of the Théatins was a Catholic religious order founded in 1525 by St. Gaétan de Thiène.

To judge by the masque the rowdy man was wearing, M. B*** thought it must be some carnival joke, and without finding it in very good taste, he confronted it with better grace than his servants had. After some talk, the mystery was finally explained and Maisonneuve was found under the burlesque equipment which was the object of all the debate. At first, the very natural way in which he had played his drunken porter role had made him unrecognizable.

At that time, those hideous and sloppy disguises which since have become so popular, were not in fashion. The notary therefore only partly understood the ill-fitting costume of his guest, and this time, largely relying on the right to censure delegated to him by the young man's father, reprimanded him sharply about the bad choice and the inconvenience of his costume. However, following rather long explanations, it was decided that despite his sleeveless forest laborer's costume, at least ten years before its time, the adventurous boy, at his risk and at his peril, could enter the drawing rooms. But as for the hooks and the crate, M. B***was unrelenting. They had to be left in the antechamber with the skins and coats in spite of Maisonneuve's insistence and protestations. He cried out in despair that they made him spoil his entry.

Nevertheless, the student's equipment had caused some talk in the ballroom. In general, some interesting surprise was expected and awaited from inside that gigantic box he had taken the trouble to transport and which the notary's puritanism had forbidden entrance. The bearer was therefore pressed with questions on all sides. But he acted mysterious, letting it be understood that a drama, a whole history, was contained, as in the Trojan horse, in the flanks of his case. He finally answered some women, whose curiosity had particularly persecuted him, saying, that this mystery wasn't one of those that could properly be spoken in the ears of angels.

Just then supper was announced. The ladies went into the dining room where, according to the customs at great gatherings, only they were seated at the table. The men stayed together awaiting their turn. The moment seemed right to get the student to confide that secret, since having nothing else to do made them even more curious.

Maisonneuve finally seemed ready to give in. However, before beginning his story, he took care to see M. B*** wasn't near enough to hear. The details he was going to be forced to reveal were probably not such as would edify that serious man responsible for his ward's good behavior and habits.

Once he was sure the notary, entirely absorbed in overseeing the cold buffet, couldn't come in to be outraged at the narration, Maisonneuve, no longer had any reason to refuse to give in to the general eagerness. Placed in a large circle of his listeners, he began something like this:

VI. Maisonneuve's Story

"Wanting to know the ins and outs, the moral and philosophical makeup of the Parisian carnival, about two hours ago, with a group of friends, male and female, I went into a dancing and smoking dive, commonly called *Le Bal des Théatins*. It goes without saying that I didn't find any of those venerable ecclesiastics there, but I did find a crowd of Pierrots and Polichinelles, that in the circumstances, I dare say replaced them very advantageously.

"My friends and I had very suitably dined. However, the ladies, as usual in our Latin Quarter, made it known that they wouldn't say no to having something to drink. We ended our evening with a bowl of warm wine. I drank so much that I found myself slightly excited and tipsy.

"In that mental state I decided to show off some exercises like Hercules. Without bragging, I can say that in these tours de force I'm not absolutely awkward. As a consequence, I offered to bet that I could lift a bench in the establishment on my arms. The said bench would be ornamented and garnished with a whole family of honest country folk with various faces, who had come in to watch the dancing.

"The friend to whom I offered that wager seemed to shrug it off, which caused me to forget, to a certain point, the rules of modesty, by bragging about several feats of strength not less extraordinary which I had done in my own province. To that my friend answered rather roughly that I was drunk and that I should go sleep it off.

"The thing was going to turn out badly because that insult was made in the presence of a number of listeners, who, up until then, had shown some interest in my story. But suddenly my anger was fortunately diverted. Across from me I saw a charming black Domino, whose eyes under her mask were sending signals, while a little hand, white as alabaster, was making an absolutely beguiling sign, in which a double meaning could easily be detected.

"In one way, it seemed to say: 'Come to me, my dear.' In another way, showing a terrible disdain for the menagerie that I was sitting at table with, it signaled an imperative command to hide the attraction which was beginning between the delightful Domino and myself.

"Understanding immediately what was happening, I stood up with a clever pretext and maneuvering with as much luck as ability, I had soon joined my unknown woman, some steps in front of me in the crowd where I didn't lose sight of her.

"Naturally I was expecting a witty and animated conversation, as is usual when you're masked. Not at all. In the arm I had passed through my own, I felt a trembling something like fear in the breast of that divine odalisque. Then, as I asked her if she was going to be sick, she said:

"'How does it happen, sir,' she said to me, (Pardon me if I cite her words literally,) 'that for a man gifted as you are with all exterior advantages, which indicate a good education and elegance, you appear to be satisfied with the ignoble company from which I have snatched you?'

"'Well, little mother, my friends are very good fellows, and if it's to give me a lesson in morality that you wanted to speak to me…'

"'Morality, I neither like it nor practice it, but vice, disorder, even orgy,' and she said this word with the accent of a tigress, 'I want them adorned with a veneer of sophistication and good company. You're handsome,' continued that siren, whose words I reproduce with regret. 'You have a noble bearing and manners. You have really all that's necessary to resemble the delightful roués of the Regency. And I find you here, embracing common little shop girls, throwing your pearls before swine, when life, already so short for more refined pleasures, asks only to be born under your feet.'

"That demon woman's words, like bubbling champagne, went to my head. However, I was still master of myself enough to turn her words against her.

"'Ah, as for that, beautiful mask,' I said to her, 'what are you yourself doing in these places, where by your charming talk and casual behavior, you seem to me to be terribly out of place also.

"'I? I came here to see just how low certain appetites could make a soul of mud, sink. I am outraged, amazed at the base rivalry which I have just seen, and now I want to take my revenge.'

"'And that vengeance, beautiful darling?'

"'There aren't two ways. That of women, the good one.'

"'But an accomplice is necessary. Have you thought about that?'

"'Why did I pick you out? Why did I signal you to come to me? Why are you squeezing my arm convulsively right now?'

"And you will note, gentlemen, that it was she who was squeezing mine, in the most frenzied way.

"'Impossible,' I said, 'that you aren't beautiful, a passionate person like you!

"'Yes, I'm considered passable. Let's leave. I'm suffocating in here.'

"We left and when we got to the sidewalk of the church, I wanted to call a kind of berlingot. The kind which we had been jogging about in all day, my friends and I.

"'That's not needed,' my charming one said to me. 'Two steps from here, at the corner of the Rue des Saints-Pères, I have my carriage and my servants.'

"More than that, mcney, I then thought. Servants and a carriage!

"In two jumps we were at the place indicated: a superb outfit, a coachman with a three-cornered hat and a big fur-trimmed coat, a Negro servant to open the door.

"Once we were inside: 'Where does Madame wish to go?'

"'To the town house,' and we rolled off."

To suppose that that good fortune came from Maisonneuve's memory and not from his imagination, some of our readers perhaps would already have remarked that it couldn't have befallen a more light-headed and indiscreet man. It must be believed also that such was the impression of one of the listeners, who had just instants before entered the drawing room.

This disgruntled listener said in a very loud voice: "It's inconceivable that anyone could have such conceit as to tell such stupid stories!"

Then, following that outburst, as he started toward the door seeming angry, Maisonneuve said: "Well! What's wrong with that gentleman?" And he watched the interrupter until he was out of the drawing room. Otherwise he attached no importance to that incident. And immediately taking up his story again:

"We drove for some time," he continued, "and the whole time as the driver wished. I paid very little attention to what was going on outside, busy as I was wanting to lift the mask off my adored one and doing other little impertinent things, which, I must say, to tell the truth, she resisted.

"Suddenly the vehicle stopped and both the doors opened noisily at the same time, which usually doesn't happen.

"'What a terribly awkward moment,' the Domino exclaimed, jumping out the left door.

"Me, I didn't jump out the door on the right. I looked

around and with astonishment you can imagine, I found myself in a place dark as an oven. They had taken the precaution of extinguishing even the carriage lanterns. I smelled the odor of manure and a chicken yard, which made me suppose we were inside a farmyard or some other stinking country site. Then, as an additional charm, I heard a guard dog being detached from his chain. They introduced him to me under the gracious name of Loud Boy and I could easily imagine the size and height of this frisky personage by the loud barks he gave in the silence of the middle of the night to celebrate the first moment of his liberty.

"During this time the door was still held open.

"'The gentleman is not going to get out?' the Negro asked me respectfully.

"'No! Saprelotte! I'm not getting out. What does all this mean and where have I been taken?'

"'The gentleman can't sleep in this carriage, however.'

"I tell you nothing could make me get out. I'm here in a rough place, but I'll withstand a siege if necessary.

"The damned Black then shouted: 'Lift!', and immediately, as if by magic, the vehicle broke into two pieces and left me under the open sky. At the same moment, I felt myself grabbed under the armpits from behind. From the front, a slipknot went around my legs and despite the vigorous efforts to get loose I made with my arms, I was quickly taken into a low room where they locked me up. With the most extreme politeness they asked me to please wait a moment. A novelist wouldn't have had any trouble describing that room. It had only the four walls as furniture and was lit only by a candle burning in a broken glass on the ground in a corner.

"If I had actually been overcome by drink as my impertinent friend had claimed, my word, there would certainly have been enough there to sober me up. And I must say that at first my reflexes weren't exactly up to par. Cursing women's duplicity and my foolish belief in good fortune, I could foresee the most sinister denouement. Begun happily, the carnival had turned disastrous for me. But at the word carnival, a more consoling thought came to mind. In Paris, I told myself finally, they play a lot of pranks. This is the holiday season. My adventure started at a dance. Could it just simply be that I was the object of a joke? ...I wasn't mistaken. A moment later, I heard a sst, sst, then I saw a paper pushed under the door. I picked it up. It contained, hurriedly written in pencil...

Here, Maisonneuve, as if a piece of proof, took from his pocket a paper folded over four times. He read the following:

Dear Sir

I am in despair over what has happened to us. This is a miserable joke they wanted to play on you, and far from being able to oppose it, I'm going to be obliged to take part in it. Otherwise, I'll have to let it be known that I came back with an unknown person. You aren't the person whom they believed they were waiting for. I even beg you, for my safety, not to take off your mask for any reason and to lower your voice as much as possible. If it's important for you to see me again, in order to avoid any suspicion, do exactly everything asked of you. It will be more ridiculous than difficult. Don't worry about the strange place where you are. For more secrecy, I've brought you by way of the servants' quarters beside the stables. In a little while it will be very different because these detestable jokers are going to make you go down into the cellar. For the rest, here is my name and the address of the house where you are now. One more thing, give in and don't be afraid. Tomorrow, as early as you wish, come to my house. I will await you with impatience, if only to offer you more ample explanations, all my excuses, and all my regrets.

That reading finished, Maisonneuve folded the paper and with an efficient air added:

"There followed a magnificent Spanish name and the address of a street in the Faubourg St. Honoré. I ask not to explain any further about that name and address."

Picking up his story again, he continued:

"I managed to read that consoling epistle by the light of the candle. The preparations for the joke, apparently finished, I saw two masked and bizarrely clothed individuals enter to start the comedy. They were wearing a black head covering like those that the executioners of the Porte-Saint-Martin and those of the Ambigu.[44]

"One of those grim individuals held a white handkerchief folded so as to serve as a blindfold, the other a sort of slipknot, probably to frighten me, just in case I showed signs of wanting to resist. It was always with the greatest kindness and consideration that these two species of jailers asked me to please go with them.

"While as a preamble I submitted to the formality of being blindfolded on top of my mask, the charming master said to me in a low voice, 'It's me. Don't worry.' At the same time he found a way to squeeze my hand tenderly. Next, we walked about twenty feet outside my prison. Then they told me to be careful and that we were going down. That really was what the cave's stairway required. Probably to make me believe that we really were going down into the bowels of the earth, we first went down a certain number of steps, which I wouldn't have failed to count if I had thought I was involved in a serious adventure. Then they made me go on solid ground, then go down again, then go up again, so many time that I began to tire of that exercise. But we finally arrived at the ground floor and they removed my blindfold. Everything seemed to indicate that I was at the place in the joke where the meeting would take place. I must admit that the gloomy place I had been brought to astonished me a little.

"Imagine a long, gallery poorly lit by a reddish, sepulchral light. The direction from which I entered was closed off by an immense red wall-hanging descending from the arch to the ground. On the right and the left the walls were

___

[44] The Theatre de l'Ambigu-Comique was founded in 1769, burned 1827, and rebuilt on the Boulevard Saint-Martin in 1828.

hung with printed fabric which represented long rows of human death heads and bones in frightful relief. At the other end, limited only by the deep shadows, this terrible place seemed to be infinity. But toward the end where the light seemed to fade away, the eyes stopped at a sort of throne on top of a platform. On each side of the platform there was a row of seats. I counted twelve of them. Only ten of them, in addition to the throne, were occupied by what seemed to be phantoms wearing red masks, red gloves, and red capes with hoods. That frightening color was also that of all the furniture and decidedly seemed to be the favorite color of the establishment.

"My two conductors, who didn't let me out of their sight, after having led me close to the platform, addressed the presiding officer with a silent salute, then took a place several steps back from my side. Beginning then in a cavernous voice:

"'Sir,' the high functionary began, 'I like to believe that, following my orders, you have been treated with the greatest respect. Nevertheless, I owe you, first of all, excuses relating to the kind of violence used to bring you here.'

"'How's that, President?' I answered. 'To be kidnapped by a pretty woman, is, on the contrary, very flattering and very gallant.'

"'Nothing pleases me more,' replied my serious questioner, 'than your casual behavior in a situation where many others would perhaps be concerned about apparent danger. Your gaiety proves that we are dealing with a man of courage and that we couldn't have chosen better for the important mandate we want to entrust you with. However, we're dealing with serious interests here, and perhaps you, like me, will find it proper to treat them seriously.'

"That sort of reprimand reminded me of the beautiful Spanish girl's instructions. She had strongly recommended that I play my role of dupe naturally. At the same time I remembered to soften my voice.

"'I am in your hands, sir. Speak,' I answered. 'What do you want of me?'

"'As you can see by the secrecy with which we surround ourselves,' he answered me, 'we are a secret society, and what's more, a political association. That means that under a government that is an enemy to all liberty, we come together in the midst of the greatest perils. We have been tracked by the police for a long time. At the present time, we are sold and delivered over by a traitor. Just this very night, on his information, our meeting place, where they believe they are sure to surprise us, must be surrounded by an armed force. We are meeting here for the last time.'

"'My word, that's a shame!' I couldn't help answering, deviating a little from the spirit of my role. 'The location is spacious, convenient, well aired, and above all, decorated with taste.'

"'We won't be lacking space,' replied the presiding officer, with added solemnity. 'Innumerable limbs of our society extend throughout the entire universe, which remains an asylum for us. But today, momentarily forced to disperse, we leave preoccupied with a serious concern, that is, to know the fate of our archives. No one among those presently here can take charge of overseeing their transfer. In a moment each member at this reunion will be on the way to a different point widely separated on the globe.'

"I interrupted and hastened then to say: 'I understand. It's a question, as they say, of giving you a hand to help you remove these documents?'

"'As you say, and believe that our gratitude...'

"'Gratitude! But I would be flattered. On the other hand, gentlemen, the gendarmes and the King's Prosecutor General!'

"'It's precisely the danger that makes it a service. If it were only a matter of taking charge of an ordinary burden, the first public porter in the street could render us this good service, and we wouldn't need the elite man we have singled out.'

"Enchanted for the preference, but I would take the honor of pointing out to you...'

"'President,' one of those seated then shouted loudly,

standing up. 'That man is hesitating and we're losing precious time with him. I ask that we look elsewhere, after having, however, disposed of this coward, who has come here only to discover our secret.'

"'Calm down,' the presiding officer replied. 'Between caution which takes danger into account and cowardice which declines it, there is some difference, however. I will have so much more confidence in the resolution of our agent in that he will have reflected on and calculated the extent of the danger.'

"'That's justly said,' I exclaimed. 'The other gentleman would wish that I had made my decision even before I had heard explained to me exactly what action the honorable society expects of me.'

"'Do you see that object?' the presiding officer asked me, pointing out in a corner a crate of huge dimensions on which the word Fragile was written more than was necessary in big readable letters. All the sealed documents of our society are in there.'

"'It was stamped that it was to be moved with caution so much that I would have bet it was made of Sèvres porcelain.'

"'That carton,' the man in red continued, 'you must carry on your shoulders, which are, Thank God, broad and strong. Carrying this, taking advantage of the darkness, you must go, apparently without any encumbrance to Rue Notre-Dame-des-Victoires to the office of the Express which leaves at 4:00 a.m. for Bordeaux. Using the first name of the sender that comes to mind, you will tell them to send it to the address written on the outside of the carton. That done, you will have accomplished your mission, In a few days, the society, without hoping to recompense you for so important a service, will, nevertheless, have a testimony of its high satisfaction sent to you'

"'But President, may I take it upon myself to point out that to carry this huge crate on my bare shoulders...!'

"'Everything has been taken care of,' the dignitary, seeming impatient, answered me. He really was playing his role with perfect naturalness. 'There are hooks, a complete porter's costume, including the medals, in case you are stopped by some patrol or policeman making his rounds. You can make no objection, if it isn't that at the moment of execution, you lack courage.'

"He really was charming, this dear President, with his no objection to make. That means there was a rubbish heap of them to answer him, if only you wanted to knock a hole in his nice proposition. For example, he could be told that there had to be supposed something a great deal more dangerous in his transferring documents than he wanted it to be believed, since in fact nobody in his friendly society had any enthusiasm to take charge of it. Again, in taking the commission for what it was, that is to say, for a joke, let the gentlemen, the mystifiers, know that their joke wasn't very cleverly planned. Nothing had less verisimilitude than their confidence given to an employee, the first man picked up in the street. But my role was not to argue. I knew the key to the enigma. The joke consisted in having me walk about Paris with this ridiculous crate on my back for some more or less long time. Assuredly, when I considered that the payment for doing that was the good graces of the charming Spanish girl, who really attracted me, I don't think it could be proved that I made a bad bargain.

"Pretending, then, to be truly wounded by the doubt the president's last words seemed to cast on my courage, in an instant, with the help of my two guides, I had put on the employee's costume. Next, there was a second edition of the blindfold formality which earned me a new and stronger hand squeeze, a strong recommendation, given in a low voice, to be accurate and punctual in carrying out my mandate. That done, two of the associates went ahead of us, carrying the crate and we were remounting the staircase. Back in the manure courtyard, they put me in a vehicle, but it was no longer the magnificent carriage. Without seeming to do anything, my hand slyly touched canvas, a tarpaulin. That told me I was in a cart. My exit was going to be that of a criminal.

"My traveling companion was the red and black gentleman who had introduced me. We rolled along some time with slow and measured steps like loaded transport vehicles.

Finally my conductor told me to step down. Doing the same, he helped me put on the shoulder straps for the hooks, on which he loaded the crate. Then jumping into the cart, which I then heard drive away, picking up a fast pace, he shouted to me, 'Good Luck!' and authorized me to remove my blindfold.

"The handkerchief lowered, I tried to orient myself, and the first thing that came to my sight was, if you please, the dome of the Invalides. The satanic jokers, when I was supposed to be taken near the Stock Exchange, had had me taken and abandoned at the edge of the Seine, near the Esplanade of the Invalides, between the Pont de la Concorde and the Pont d'Iena."

A general laugh having for a moment interrupted the orator, he was probably going to explain the chain of ideas or the circumstances which had led him to carry the famous crate to the notary's house instead of to the freight office as the unknown man had urgently instructed him.

But before Maisonneuve had time to start clarification, the ladies had finished supper and they were already crowding back into the drawing rooms. The moment having come to follow them, the student wasn't a man to let anyone get ahead of him.

Giving the slip then to his listeners and to his conclusion, he rushed into the dining room to take one of the first seats that had been vacated. It's easy to understand that the fatigue of his narration as well as that of carrying the crate, had made him work up what he called a ferocious appetite.

VII. The Contents of the Crate

The lady of the house had come several times to encourage the invited guests to hurry and finish their refreshments. The ball couldn't start again because of a lack of dancers. The table had been emptied little by little. Only some more unremitting gastronomes had continued to see what they could salvage from what was left of the banquet. Among the number of these last minute workers, was Maisonneuve, although he had been one of the first to begin. The brilliance of ideas originating from sensations, that infinity Napoleon felt he had in his head and in his star, Maisonneuve demonstrated that he seemed to have in his stomach.

For the second time, a charlotte russe, that he never tired of praising for its freshness and cream taste, was part of his hurried eating, when suddenly the notary with a severe and worried expression appeared, tapped him on the shoulder and said:

"Maisonneuve, come, I need to talk to you."

In the middle of gastronomic pleasure, the corners of his mouth decorated with cream, Maisonneuve answered that intimidation with all the appearance of no great haste. But in a movement that could leave no doubt of his extreme concern, the notary, taking the spoon, which Maisonneuve was still holding, out of his guest's hand, placed it firmly on the table. This time in a commanding and totally definitive voice:

"I'm telling you to follow me. I need to talk to you."

Seeing that it was decidedly a matter of something serious, Maisonneuve, while standing, still had the presence of mind to empty a glass of champagne, which he didn't want to abandon without anywhere to go, he said. Then he finally followed M. B*** into his office, the only room that had escaped the invasive disorder of the party. There he found a stranger, who answered his greeting with a serious and mysterious air.

Opening the question without an introduction, M. B*** said to the student:

"That bizarre story that you recounted in the drawing room a while ago which is making the rounds from mouth to mouth, what are we to think of it?"

"It's true. I'm not capable or inventing anything."

"I know that," replied the notary, stressing the reply in a not very complimentary way. "But I'm asking you if you believe without any doubt that you were the object of a simple prank?"

"But of course it was a joke, and a joke, to tell the truth, rather stupidly put together. If I was the butt of it, it was because it was convenient for me."

"Well! Me! I'll tell you that, on the contrary, in my opinion and in that of the gentleman present here, with your bird brain and the detestable company you keep, you've gotten mixed in a very serious and very important business and nothing proves to me that I mustn't fear the consequences on my own account."

"So, then," Maisonneuve said, shrugging his shoulders in the most perfect incredulity.

"Do you know what's happened, Mr. Funny Fellow?" the notary with even more seriousness and truthfulness retorted. "The Duke de Berry has just been assassinated."

"Bah!" the student retorted. "Who told you that story?"

"The gentleman you see here brought the news of this terrible event. And he has every reason to believe that his information is only too exact, since a while ago, when he was leaving a house where he had spent the evening, shortly thereafter, he met My Lord, the Duke d'Angoulême and My Lord, the Count d'Artois rushing to the place of the crime, the Opera."

"But did they say that the Duke died immediately?" Maisonneuve asked, beginning to be more serious in his replies.

"Right now," the notary replied, "they only mention a very serious wound. But that circumstance which is for the good servants of the Monarchy a consolation and a hope is perhaps for you, in particular, a misfortune and, in addition, a danger."

"Ah! Bah! You're making me seem like an idiot," Maisonneuve exclaimed, exasperated. "What can my story have in common with the unfortunate event you're telling me about?"

Dominating the conversation somewhat sententiously, the stranger said:

"Here, sir, is where there is a very distressing connection between the facts we've put forward. You certainly admit that the political crime that has just been committed can very likely be attributed to secret societies, which for any somewhat thinking man can no longer be in doubt today."

"I admit that, if you like," Maisonneuve replied, "but so what?"

"Well! This evening, whatever you may think, it is evident to us that you were drawn into the bosom of a serious secret society that must have been brought together foreseeing the catastrophe it prepared."

"All that is just conjecture; those aren't facts," the student answered disdainfully.

"Conjectures, if that pleases you," replied the stranger somewhat drily, "but to continue to reason, I will add that the unfortunate Prince not having immediately died, the society, following a partially failed coup, had to think of some measures of preservation. Now you will admit, sir, this transfer of its documents, for which you have been so unusually requisitioned, entered completely into this sequence of ideas."

"One more time," Maisonneuve replied, "I am morally and physically sure to have lent a hand only to a practical joke. Now, if you want to comment on that as long as you like…"

"But, you miserable, stubborn man," exclaimed the notary, taking the arm of the disbelieving man, and squeezing it in a kind of nervous clench, "your adventure is so little a joke that the description of the place where you were taken is completely in agreement with what can be known of the mysteries of certain societies. Thus, in the practice of L'Écossime, a more than suspicious offshoot of the Free Masons,[45] the lodge of the Supreme Council, or Thirty-third

---

[45] Rabou is incorrect. Free Masonry is said to have originated in Scotland, perhaps as early as 1598, and was therefore one of the foundations of Free Masonry in England and in France. Originally a secret philosophical and philanthropic organization, it became politically active and was sometimes credited with helping organize the French Revolution in 1789.

and last Degree of the order, is exactly hung with purple and funereal emblems, just like the supposed cavern to which you were led."

"After all," said Maisonneuve, not knowing how to answer this last argument, "is it that carton remaining in the antechamber that's bothering you? Well! Open it and look at its contents."

"Yes, of course it will be opened," M. B***, excitedly answered. "I don't want to aggravate suspicions of complicity even further, which its presence in my house could only too naturally be assumed. It will be opened in the presence of the authorities. What everyone did will be examined. The Police Commissioner has just been called. He'll be here in a moment. I warn you, you'll have to explain yourself to him."

"Good! Good!" said the student, rubbing his hands together. "We're going to have a good laugh and the venerable magistrate will have his share too. It's really too amusing, in Paris, at carnival season."

"Tell me," the stranger said to M. B***, "that suspicious object, it's hardly possible to inventory it in the antechamber. Don't you think it's appropriate to bring it here?"

"I'll be very careful about doing that," exclaimed the notary in comic fright. "I'm leaving that packet where that nincompoop brought it. The Police Commissioner will advise what to do."

At that moment a servant opened the door to the study where this serious deliberation was taking place. Thinking he was going to see a Magistrate whom he had called, M. B*** walked quickly to meet him. He was ready to show him all the regard and all the consideration that never fails to be shown to the police when there is no apprehension of finding oneself in some trouble.

But the servant wasn't announcing the Commissioner of Police. The stupefaction of the notary can be imagined when the man who entered began to tell him in a frightened voice:

"Ah, well, sir, it's decided that our house is considered a branch of the bureaucracy. There are four more crates and four more delivery men arriving!"

Hearing this, M. B*** and the stranger looked at each other as if to consult each other as to what to conclude about this new and curious incident. Decidedly the carnival seemed to have more a part of it than politics. This mutual exchange gave the notary no lucid explanation. He went over to Maisonneuve, who seemed very amused by the situation, and asked him haughtily the meaning of all that.

"Probably, the diverse secret societies in Paris have chosen you as their notary," the student answered, "and as a consequent of the assassination of the Prince, they have sent you their archives to guard."

That rejoinder, above all considering the level of Maisonneuve's usual wit, really wasn't too bad. It managed to outrage the notary, and, followed by the other actors of the scene, he left, furious, to put order in that kind of conspiracy that the Paris crate makers and packing companies seemed to be directing toward the house.

Just as M. B*** arrived at the antechamber, the fellows he proposed to roughly reprimand, had, despite what they had been told, already unloaded their burdens beside the one Maisonneuve brought. Four sisters of almost identical dimensions gave the room the deceptive look of a warehouse or a freight holding room and created a riot of crates and delivery men.

Energetically questioned as to the source and the destination of that enormous amount of goods, the delivery men, forming a chorus of gobbledygook, answered that a distinguished gentleman had come to wake them up where they lodged. He had paid generously in advance, considering the unusual hour in which he requested their services. He had then taken them near the Jardin des Plantes in a rented conveyance, and told them to take the four cartons as rapidly as possible to the address plainly written on the outside, that of M. B***, Notary, Rue de l'Université, Faubourg Saint-Germain, to which they were sent from Bordeaux by M. Britannicus.

If, before this burlesque incident, Maisonneuve had taken the trouble to read the address on the crate he had carried, and above all if he had been more intelligent, he would have been immediately struck by an unusual circumstance. He would have known that he himself had been charged to send the crate to M. Britannicus in Bordeaux, whereas now it was M. Britannicus of Bordeaux who had sent the crates to M. B***, a Paris notary.

But in the middle of the Notary's indignation, the delivery men's explanations in an Auvergnat accent, and the cross-fire of thirty questions from the guests, that the noise had finally brought out of the drawing rooms, everyone demanded answers at the same time. How could even the most observant keep his head?

Finally coming over to the opinion of Maisonneuve, who maintained that the delivery of the four additional crates was an undeniable continuation of his own adventure, M. B***, to cut short the ridiculous situation in which he saw himself placed, commanded the porters to pick up what they had brought and to quit the premises immediately.

While not obeying at first, with a certain mocking and laughing air, one could suppose the Auvergnat delivery men better informed than they claimed. Finally, making their retreat rather slowly, they had been gone more than a half-hour when the Magistrate arrived. Informed of the way in which the suspicious crate had been confided to Maisonneuve, he didn't at all agree with the student, considering the way Maisonneuve continued to contribute his adventure to a joke.

The cave and the fact of the red men immediately reminded the civil servant of that daring series of crimes that we previously reported. In his function as a police officer in the judicial system, he had participated in some of those investigations and he knew all the details. The invasion of the house by the delivery men seemed to him very significant and worthy of attention. He strongly reproached M. B*** for not having carefully kept these people until his arrival, not doubting that he would have been able to get precious information out of them.

Nevertheless, the fifth crate remained to be inventoried.

Taken into M. B***'s office, the magistrate, without expressing his thoughts aloud, walked around the crate a long time, and in sense smelled it, seeming to detect some suspicious odor. But, having already asked for tools to open it to satisfy his curiosity and that of those present, he was attacked by scruples. If proof of a crime sealed under those mysterious planks existed, would he be competent to prove it?

Shouldn't he limit himself to locking up the crate and leaving it to the King's Prosecutor?

Fortunately, that difficulty could be put off for the moment. M. B*** remembered that there were several magistrates among his guests. There were two among them who had indisputable qualifications to open the crate. Going immediately to requisition the first that came to hand, a young magistrate dressed up in the costume of a Roman Senator which he had chosen for the occasion, M. B*** pulled him almost forcefully from a hot game of cards and commanded him to perform his functions.

During all that delay, the grim news of the Prince's assassination had little by little entered the ballroom, where it had interrupted the dancing, but none of the guests had left. The magistrate's arrival had created excitement. Everyone wanted to know the key to the enigma to be found in the notary's office. By most, the most frightening revelations and mysteries were suspected and waited for.

Finally everything was known and we are ashamed to admit that Maisonneuve had bought off a great triumph. In that crate, the object of so many guesses, comments, and analyses, there was actually something ridiculous, five or six paving stones carefully wrapped in hay, old rags, and shredded paper.

VIII. Reports of the Major and Minor Police

Rather early the next day, the Director of the Royal

Police received three reports related to the bizarre and inexplicable adventure that was finally crowned by such a pitiful denouement. The first of the reports was that of the Police Commissioner. There was a suggestion that the nonsensical crate had been substituted for the real, serious and important crate, against which it had been placed. Since the magistrate related no new fact which the reader doesn't already know, it's not necessary to reproduce his report.

The second report came from a lower level policeman whom the Police Commissioner had accompanied when he went to the home of M. B***. The law of progression makes zeal grow and enlarge in relation to the humbleness of the functions. A man, employed in espionage at 900 francs a year, had believed he could, by force of his imagination in the absence of real, more positive information, shed light in the middle of this shadowy business. As a consequence, following a habit rather familiar to those like him, he gave as proof what were only suppositions.

Paris
14 February 1820
3:00 a.m.
To: The Director General
14 February 1820
(Note at the bottom of the page here: 'We don't think we should conserve the orthography of this report which made it almost illegible.)

France, lamenting and mourning from the fatal blow that has struck the grandson of Saint Louis and the august dynasty, requires that all good Frenchmen and the zealous servants of the King and his august family make an effort to discover the authors of the infamous attack that saddens every heart. That is why I must not hide the certainty that I can supply, de visu, relative to several very suspicious wooden coffers transported during the night of the 13/14 February 1820 to the home of M. B.***, Notary of the Paris, Seine District, living in the Faubourg Saint-Germain. It has been proved that secret *societies committed the assassination. Unable to raise the Faubourgs St. Marceau and St-Antoine to revolt as they thought they could, they were afraid and had their archives removed and transported to the home of M. B***, Notary. Not finding them safe, they had them picked up by men disguised as delivery men and put paving stones in the crates. It seems that the grate contained the given names, surnames, and all the home addresses of the affiliates of the terrible Red Society, whose goal is the assassination of every sovereign and crowned head. They like only the color red, which is the color of blood. It is moreover proved that the said Society's permanent headquarters is the underground situated beneath the Champs-Elysées. They were waiting there until the assassin, very surely one of their members named Louvel, had struck, as the Director General has probably learned.*

As to which, if my information is found exact and confirmed, as I flatter myself to believe it is, I will ask for a promotion. I have a right to ask for such for my services, because several of my brigade, younger than I am, have received theirs.

And I have signed:

Isidore Uraili

The third report addressed to the Police Commissioner is a work infinitely superior, by the content as well as by the style, to the stupid and ignoble denunciation that you have just read. It comes from the elegant and practiced pen of one of those white glove observers who profit by their entry into drawing rooms to keep the police informed of all that goes on there. Independent of a certain amount of more precise information about the mysterious intrigue the development we have followed, this report seems to us to present a rather true and curious reflection of the mores of the period. As a consequence, we are reproducing them *in extenso* despite the rather chatty long windedness and slander.

Dated from Paris, the morning of 14 February, it contains the following:

To the Director General:

I am reporting to you only a summary of the results of my presence in two or three gatherings during the terrible evening yesterday. There was a dance at the home of the banker I*** following the usual customs of that household, acrimonious talk in all groups against the order of things in the present government. A young man, whom I am told is one of the editors of the Constitutionnel,[46] *where he is in charge of the arts articles, stood out by an unremitting verve of impertinence and sarcasm. I believe that young man is very dangerous and he is certainly to be watched. I was told his name, which I unfortunately didn't have the presence of mind to take down.*

My primary effort was to transmit to the administration only absolutely perfect, pertinent, and exact information. But I can say at the moment that he is a man above average height, wearing glasses, and, in addition is remarkable for a low voice and by a very pronounced provincial accent.

Leaving that club, I went to spend a quarter of an hour in the Faubourg Saint-Germain in the house of the Duchess de N***. There, it goes without saying, was no dancing. The regular devotees of the house sacrificed to the divinity of the day by means of some of those smutty stories for which the aristocracy has such pronounced taste. That has always seemed very unusual to me. The old Commander de S***, whose Rabelaisian memory and wit everybody knows, was there with his immense repertory; Madame de M***, with her tea and cakes; and something unusual, the two daughters of

---

[46] French political and literary newspaper, founded in Paris during the Hundred Days by Joseph Fouché. Originally established in October 1815 as *L'Independent*, it took its current name during the Second Restoration. A voice for Liberals, Bonapartists, and critics of the church, it was suppressed five times, reappearing each time under a new name. Beginning in 1880, it saw a real decline and ceased publication in 1914.

the house, although saintly educated at the Sacré Coeur, they merrily took part in that risqué conversation. They laughed like the others at the smutty places exactly as if it had been decent and proper that they had understood.

The small amount of politics gleaned in this location took place in a window enclosure between M. V. de C***, belonging to the Doctrinaire Party, and Amphitryon,[47] *M. the Duke of N***, whose constantly immaculate white state you know. Our Prime Minister, M. the Comte de Cazes, was, I don't need to tell you, very roughly treated by those of the Marsan Pavilion who simply reproached him for being a Jacobin and for losing the Monarchy.*

M. V. de C*** defended the Minister with a great deal of verve. But it has to be admitted that tonight's horrible event gave, after the fact, much weight to a remark by M. the Duke de N***. "What!" he shouted. "Do you want a throne and a society to be conserved when a man of the ancient nobility dared to write in a pamphlet entitled The Organizer *that the death of the King's brother and that of the Duc de Berry would be less regrettable than that of the last of the industrialists? Someone to fill the position of the King's brother or nephew can always be found, whereas it takes study and aptitude to make an industrialist." To that M. V. de C*** answered that the author and the ones who printed the brochure had been arrested. "Yes, but they were acquitted by the jury." I didn't wait for the end of that as a catilinarian* [48] *kind of instinct drew me toward the costume ball hosted by M. B***, the*

---

[47] Amphitryon was a Greek general from ancient Thebes who was first mentioned by Hesiod, whence his name became a synonym for the word "host." Zeus had assumed his likeness to seduce his wife, Alcmena, and given a grand banquet. The real Amphitryon showed up and claimed to be the host, but the guests and servants figured the real host was the one who gave the feast.

[48] Named after Roman senator Catiline, who conspired against the government in 63 BC but was exposed y Cicero.

notary.

Very probably, sir, you have been presented with some report relating to a very bizarre incident that singled out that confused and difficult situation as a carnival trick about which the legal authorities were, at the end, definitely mystified. Nevertheless, given information which only I have and which I have the honor to transmit to you here, you will find that a great deal more serious character must be recognized in an affair I do not hesitate to call to you most pressing and our most serious attention.

The magistrate's search coming to an end, and while the crowd of the notary's guests before they separated started making comments you can guess, I hurried to leave. I wanted to put down in writing the results of my diverse observations during the evening that had just ended. When passing in front of a carriage parked near the house, I distinctly heard a woman's voice saying with animation to the coachman:

"Yes! M. Maisonneuve! Ask the concierge to let him know there is a lady downstairs asking for him and ask him to come downstairs immediately."

On hearing Maisonneuve's name, which was the name of the student to which a beautiful unknown woman had entrusted the famous crate, my attention was immediately aroused. Then, recognizing at the same moment that the woman asking for the young man was masked and dressed like a domino, my first impression was to call for her arrest. Through her, the key to the stupid joke or that of the wicked intrigue which had hovered over the house of the notary M. B*** for some hours could be revealed.

Sometimes, if it's a question of a simple prank, to force a person that the student's story indicated was very highly placed in society to let them be surprised in such a false position, wouldn't that be dealing with the situation with a very heavy hand? A less harsh, but equally sure, method coming to mind, I walked toward the mysterious woman. In a perfectly simple and natural way, "You want to speak to M. Maisonneuve," I quickly said to her. "I believe he's still upstairs and if you'll allow me to be your ambassador, I'll go let him know he's wanted here."

If the beautiful masked woman showed reluctance, I would call immediately for help and force her to get out of the carriage, whatever might happen. But she made no objection to confiding to me the mission I was offering. On the contrary, she showered me with excuses and thanks. I met the young man right on the stairway and told him what good luck he had just had. The hare-brained fellow gave me a thousand thanks and ran down. Me, I dashed to my carriage and was immediately on the trail, since, after a very short chat, the hero of all that adventure had gotten in beside the lady and the carriage started off.

We traveled the Rue du Bac and the Pont Royal like a convoy and it seemed to me that in a very brief delay, I would possess the address of the beautiful Domino. Where could our lovers be going? At that hour, and following the terrible news already spreading, all the bars and public balls had closed their doors. On the other hand, it was not probable that a lady, however little respect she might have for herself, would go spend the night in the lodging of a young man that I had been told was a student in the Latin Quarter, a quarter, besides which we were just leaving. Everything then made me think that they were going to the lady's home. But, reaching the area near the Palais Royal, the carriage suddenly stopped and turned around. It finally stopped on the Rue d'Argenteuil in front of a shabby-looking house. There the coachman was paid and sent away, the evident conclusion being that they were going to spend the night at that place.

I myself, having sent away my carriage, began to consider that lodging. Its appearance gave me a great deal to think about. A memory suddenly came back to me which explained why the mysterious couple had decided to take shelter in that house.

Without being absolutely a bad place, the house in front of which I was posted was of highly suspicious morality. Occupied for the most part by artists freed from the inconvenient surveillance of a porter, on the third floor, as well as I could remember, it had a certain lady, widow of a colonel, as a renter. In the sad economic state to which she was reduced, Madame de Saint-Brice had rented and furnished a rather large space. She had reserved for her own use only a miniscule portion. The rest of the apartment was comprised of several bedrooms, which fortunately did not connect to each other. They formed a sort of asylum where, at any hour, day or night, for a fair price, lovers, if they came with a recommendation, or only with a certain appearance, however little elegant it might be, were sure of finding shelter.

A light wasn't long in illuminating two windows on the hospitality floor, where there had been no clarity at all before. I no longer had any doubt about my memory. Consequently, I no longer hesitated. Finding out without too much trouble how to open the exterior door, I climbed the staircase. I decided to knock at the door of the helpful widow, using all possible discretion, however, so as not to frighten the turtledoves in their nest.

Following some negotiations through the door, Madame de Saint-Brice decided to let me in. I began by putting money in her hand and asked her very solemnly for a private interview. Once seated in the matron's bedroom, I explained to her that a lady had just entered with a young man and I had many reasons to believe that miserable woman was my wife. I added that my intention wasn't to create a scandal in a respectable house, but just to verify the worst case that I had suspected.

I asked that I be allowed to occupy the bedroom adjoining the one the adulterous couple was now in. The extraordinary acuity of my ears would give me, through the partition all the information that I would need. There was great indignation by the virtuous hostess at my so clearly formulated request. Her house wasn't at all what I seemed to believe. The lady who might be in her house at the moment was one of her friends, a perfectly free person whom neither a husband nor a lover would have the right to spy on. So, an

95

absolute refusal to furnish me the means of spying on anything.

I then changed tactics. Laying bare my role of the unfortunate husband, I mysteriously confided to my incorruptible widow that her two protégés were suspected of being part of the great political crime which had just been committed. But instead of following that lead, the duplicitous and subtle woman took advantage of the sad news I had just told her to throw herself into the most immoderate sorrow. It was necessary to be done with it, however, and my ultimatum was posed like this: If I continued to be refused the official and devoted assistance that I had a right to expect, beginning the next day, the person not cooperating could expect that her beneficent industry would be revealed to the Prefect of Police. Just to what point her furnished clandestine hotel was compatible with the rigor of the regulations would be examined.

Phrased in that way, Madame de Saint-Brice could no longer have the shadow of a hesitation. She immediately took me to, and with a little noise, got me settled in a bedroom perfectly situated to become an observatory. When I was alone, making some small holes in the partition with a small drill I always carry with me, I considerably increased my chances of getting good information. After that, I had only to listen and watch as until then, I must hasten to say, things between the young man and the Domino, who hadn't taken off her mask, couldn't have been more proper. Our people, seated one on either side of the fireplace, were chatting quietly about their business. To explain why he had carried the crate to the notary's house instead of, following his instructions, to the baggage room, the young Maisonneuve was in the middle of answering that, a dupe of a prank, he didn't feel obliged to follow the intentions of the creators point by point to the baggage room, lugging about a burden which never stopped being rather inconvenient to carry.

'I thought,' he continued, 'it would be rather funny to arrive thus equipped at M. B***'s house. And as a matter of fact, my idea was successful, because it revolutionized everything at the worthy notary's.

'But after all,' the Domino continued, 'I insisted that you fulfill blindly the order you were given.'

'Agreed, but persuaded that there was nothing serious, and besides, having a lot of time between the departure for Bordeaux, I saw nothing troublesome about allowing myself that little stop.'

'That's what comes of trying to be witty and trying to interpret things.' the lady then said. 'On the contrary, it's a matter of the most delicate secret.'

'But then, why did you make me think it was a carnival joke?'

'First of all, because I had taken an interest in you, because I feared some resistance on your part that could have put you in some danger, and because I could be more certain of your docility by talking to you about an insignificant joke to which you would agree because you were attracted to me.

'So I really did have the archives of a political society on my shoulders?' Maisonneuve asked.

'Eh! No. You were carrying expensive contraband objects. Lace valued at some hundred thousand francs was almost seized and confiscated by your imprudence.'

'Lace! Come now, to weigh that much....'

'To throw off suspicion it had been wrapped up with paving stones, like those found in the crates that arrived after yours at the notary's house in order to spread the confusion that repaired everything cleverly.'

'Well then, come now, little mother,' the student then objected, 'in drawing me that way into an ambush, did you think you were playing a very friendly and distinguished role?'

'What I did, I was forced to do. My husband, head of a contraband group, to avoid the most bizarre and diverse traps, had the idea of going to pick up a dupe in one of the public balls. You yourself, in posing as Hercules, were his choice. It was he who, by his threats, because he makes me the unhappiest woman in the world, forced me to approach you and get around you. It was he who, disguised as a Negro, opened the carriage door and then climbed up behind the landau.

'Ah! Well!' Maisonneuve remarked, 'to have such horses and a carriage at its disposal, your contraband group is rolling in silver and gold?'

'For his share of that dangerous industry, my husband draws eighty thousand a year. He is also very highly placed in society, where he enjoys all sorts of esteem and consideration. Last year he was almost named a member of the Chamber of Deputies. With his prodigious ability, I don't doubt that he will soon become Minister of Finance. No one understands customs and public credit like he does.'

'That doesn't prevent him from being a very disagreeable spouse,' the young man replied.

'Yes, he often mistreats me, because as much as possible, I resist being an accomplice to his criminal practices, or because I try to persuade him to cash in what he has made and renounce his dangerous profession.'

'Then I understand that idea of revenge you told me about at the ball.'

'Ah! Let's talk about more serious things,' the Domino said, avoiding the question. 'If I risked everything to see you again, it was to warn you of the dangers surrounding you and not to hear your silly talk.'

'Bah!' replied Maisonneuve like a true student. 'When it shows up you can see it coming. Now we are alone, safe. You detest your husband. I'm fortunate not to displease you. Let's enjoy life!'

And while saying this, he tried to pull off the lovely Domino's mask.

'In any case,' retorted the lady, defending herself, (and you will agree, Director General, that that is a rather nice way of putting it), 'I will not let you see my face, since, being out in society every day, I might encounter you. Then, believe me, sir, don't lose any time to escape from the vengeance of these terrible associations. While you were very imprudently telling our business in M. B***'s drawing room, you were pointed out to them by a person whose departure you probably noticed. They swore to take revenge on you, and if you knew the power of those people!'

'Come now, this group of contrabandists, men of the world, must not really be so mean.'

'Eh!, sir, you can't imagine what they are capable of; it's actually your life that's in question.'

'So much more reason to indulge in voluptuousness now.'

And the student showed himself moving forward to that end.

Defending herself, but without anger:

'In fact,' continued the beautiful, unknown woman, 'this house is perhaps the best place of refuge for you. So, I'm going to leave you here, and in a few hours I'll have made all the necessary arrangements for your safety sent to you. But the first step, the most indispensable, will be to leave Paris, without quibbling, don't you see?'

'It's possible that I'll leave Paris tomorrow, if you order me to do so. You, my absolutely beautiful one, won't leave me right now.'

'Mon Dieu!' answered the Domino. 'How unreasonable you are. You know I'm not free. I'll already have a lot of trouble explaining my absence to my husband, and you want to keep me here indefinitely?'

'No, not indefinitely, but, what the devil, be a little nice if you want me to let you go.'

'You're talking when you're comfortable. A while ago you were sitting at a table, but I'll have to tell you, I'm dying of hunger. The trouble of that crate to be picked up, and then the care of providing for your safety, hasn't left me any leisure to eat anything since this morning.'

'Good! Let's eat,' Maisonneuve exclaimed. 'Myself, thanks to that imbecile M. B***, I haven't had anything but a bite. Only, here's the question: Would our worthy hostess have anything to serve us?'

'That's more than probable,' answered the lady.

'All right, I'm going...' the student said, standing up.

'No, let me do it,' the lady answered. 'I know where the old witch hides the good things. She would offer you some left-overs.'

'Ah! You wicked thing!' said Maisonneuve, 'you know so well all the people in this saintly house and act like a tigress towards me!'

Unable to answer that victorious remark, the charming Domino let a kiss touch the end of her mask and left laughing. The helpful provider came back an instant later carrying the results of her search. She said: 'I found only some ham, some Bordeaux and this opened bottle of Madera.'

'Fine, the Madera. Opened or not, that's not such a bad find,' Maisonneuve answered.

And the table settings put rapidly on the table, they began their banquet. The student, counting on the seduction of the headiest wine, didn't want to touch the Bordeaux, but his tablemate insisted on drinking nothing else, and she mixed a great deal of water with it. Maisonneuve, on the contrary, indulged exclusively in the Madera. At the end of a quarter of an hour, his exaltation had reached the highest level. In that mental state, becoming bold even to the point of impertinence, the student wanted to see the lovely Domino's face at any cost. Catching her off guard, with a sudden movement, he managed to tear off her mask. But then, Director, judge his terror when the so-called beauty, whose face he had just uncovered, was none other than that famous daughter with the death's head. She has been talked about in Paris for several months and you have probably met her in drawing rooms with that unusual father, the old Marquis de Lupiano.

Taking advantage of Maisonneuve's surprise and terror, the horrible girl exclaimed:

'You are despicable! But I will pay you back!' Rushing out at the same time, she double locked the door. She did the same to my door almost immediately afterward. I had clumsily let the presence of someone be known by leaving the key on

the outside. That double precaution taken, the clever creature calmly left the apartment and after a few seconds she was safely outside the house.

Thus caged, the student began to create a terrible row. But his insistence to be let out was of short duration. The matron, either through an agreement with the woman who had just left or because the noise hadn't awakened her, without making a movement, let Maisonneuve's first energy die down. Soon he began to yawn, stretch out his arms, and appeared to be fighting against a pressing need to sleep. Then he threw himself on a bed placed in a corner. It wasn't long before he was letting out harmonious snores.

Seeing him fall asleep so quickly, my first idea was that he had been given some narcotic, but that could also be explained by the heady wine he had overindulged in.

On my side, I was very restrained. My helplessness was no less disagreeable to me. But to create a scandal to obtain my deliverance would perhaps be to attract the student's attention and let him know that I was on his trail. After a deadly quarter hour waiting, that ridiculous situation was crowned by a sad denouement.

I at first heard groans and inarticulate words following the sleeper's happy snoring. Then I saw him twist and roll about on his bed, and finally, he showed all the symptoms of being seriously sick. Suddenly, struck with a horrible idea, I thought I should no longer be quiet. I finally attracted the attention of my hostess, who freed me.

Going immediately into the young man's bedroom, I found him pale, haggard, and already starting to vomit. I then ordered the matron, who, by the expression of real terror on her face, seemed to be acquitted of complicity, to have the sick man drink some warm water. Getting the address of the nearest doctor, I ran to wake him and take him back with me. When we arrived, the poison seemed to have made its way into the entrails, which it terribly upset.

After writing a prescription, the doctor tasted the suspicious wine that had a small quantity left in the bottle. He *found it had a disagreeable taste. The mass of the ingredients with which he had been drugged, had probably settled to the bottom where they were stronger.*

My attentions to the sick man now no longer necessary, I had a more pressing worry: to alert the police and, sir, more especially to report to you. However, before leaving the scene, I wanted the opinion of the doctor. I asked him what he thought about that case. He answered me that in such a situation one is never very sure. First of all, the liquids had to be analyzed. But here, unfortunately, there was the greatest appearance, and in his opinion, until there was more ample information, the unfortunate young man appeared to have been poisoned.

IX. Where Several Things Are Explained.

Evidently, from the reports coming to the Police Commissioner from various directions, everything seemed to indicate a new and more frightening resurgence of those invisible criminals. For a considerable time the search of them had been the despair of the magistrates. But there suddenly seemed to be some hope of finally picking up their traces. These men mysteriously assembled in a subterranean place, which, according to the description given by Maisonneuve, must be the Catacombs. These came naturally to mind because of the murder of the unfortunate guard.

What's more, wasn't their predilection for the color red a definite clue? This had already been noted in the type of frightful ceremonial with which these invisible murderers slaughtered their victims and was again found on this occasion. By a new step from that, it seemed that the personality of one of their hired assassins and probably the head of their association had been identified.

That woman with the death's head, who, after having played such a large role in the affair of the Crates, had become mixed up in a poisoning. Wasn't she notorious as the daughter of the Marquis de Lupiano? The strangeness and the oddities that surround that man's life, don't they marvelously support suspicions that a last and more transparent revelation point to him?

Let us add to those different indications that vague presumption which seemed to attach all those shadows and bloody past to Lupiano's sword. It's understandable that the next day after the ball given by M. B***, the notary, the police descended on Lupiano's town house.

The Marquis received the magistrates with the air of a great lord, but tempered however with perfect courtesy. He listened without any apparent embarrassment or emotion to the long exposé of charges that they heaped on him and gave perfectly freely all the explanations asked of him. Then he summed up the accusation:

"So," he said, "all the suspicions of the police originate, and the circumstance in particular which gives me the honor of this visit, is the sad infirmity of my daughter? Recognizable by a description which admits of no equivocation, she would undoubtedly have marked her presence in the mysterious occurrence which is now the concern of the magistrates?"

On their affirmative response:

"Well!, gentlemen," the Marquis continued, "I myself, before you order it, asked for my daughter to be examined. For you, the first in Paris, she will take off her mask. Yesterday she would have perhaps have made some difficulty in agreeing to your request, but today the mystery is over. Henceforth her face will be uncovered everywhere she shows herself."

That said, Luciano rang for a servant, and ordered him to let his daughter know he was waiting for her. Shortly thereafter an elegant young woman dressed in an elegant morning *negligé* appeared. The Marquis having assisted her to lift a thick veil of black lace which covered her features, the onlookers made a gesture of disgust and fright on finding themselves face to face with a hideous likeness of a skeleton. But at the same moment, the Marquis moved behind the accused and pressed a small spring hidden in her hair. There was then something totally different. In the place of a wax mask, which, on being detached, broke into pieces on the floor, there appeared the ravishing face of a woman. And she even, God forgive her, seemed to be laughing in the face of the magistrates.

Seeing all the scaffolding of the accusation fall apart, the police didn't seem beaten. And claiming they had the right to be curious, which, to a certain point, appeared justified, they demanded a reason and the goal of this hideous disguise which was carried on such a long time.

"If I had to," replied Lupiano, "I think I could avoid answering, because I don't know that having taken a fantasy to create horror, a woman must answer to the police. However, to explain what our action has of the bizarre, I think a few words will suffice. My daughter is married. Her husband has had to be separated from her a long time. As he has a naturally jealous and suspicious nature, he wouldn't allow her to stay in Paris, where the air is reputed to be bad for conjugal honor, except on the condition that she live here in complete sequestration.

"With a view of getting her out of this rigorous regime, while nevertheless leaving her in the conditions desired by her lord and master, I was the one, gentlemen, who had the idea of that funereal masquerade. I was very sure that no serious suitor would come up against the terrifying caprice of my imagination. The absent husband arrived precisely last night. Henceforth, protected by his presence, my daughter has received permission to resume the use of her charms. I am happy, gentlemen, to have been able to offer you the first sight of her fortunate and pleasant transformation."

The police, as is well known, when they think they have their hand on a prey, don't knowingly let it be snatched away. The visitors didn't lack arguments against the Marquis' explanations, claiming they would accept them only by a compulsory inventory by force.

At this, Lupiano began to show some emotion, but only that of impatience. And speaking in a tone which appeared to want to cut short any discussion:

"If your intention and your need," he continued, "is to find at any price the guilty persons, I don't see, in fact, gentlemen, why you don't go look for them somewhere other than in my house. I must, however, warn you that here where you stubbornly look for the traces of a crime, you are greatly exposed to gather nothing but a burlesque result. One of my friends, present at ball of the notary, M. B*** saw the beginning of the ridiculous story which stirred up the police. He had the curiosity to keep up with what followed. According to the news he transmitted to you a little before your arrival, the young Maisonneuve is right now in very good health. And that should seem to you no doubt, as to me, to exclude any idea of poisoning. About two hours ago he received a note saying almost this:

Sir, you are so stupid that you don't deserve a crime. You claim to have been poisoned. Just to teach you to carry out errands better in the future, good and worthy young man, learn that you have been purged.

"I am," the Marquis continued, "entirely at your disposition and ready, as is my daughter, to be your prisoner. But perhaps you would find it wise to verify the truth of my information."

Lupiano's confident and peremptory tone couldn't keep from making an impression on his guests. They already felt very embarrassed to continue, when a letter sent in all haste from the Chancellery arrived to confirm the oral explanations of the Marquis and to notify them, considering the high rank of the personage, not to go forward with the questioning begun except with extreme propriety.

Coming around in their turn to Maisonneuve's opinion, the magistrates believed as he did in a carnival joke organized at a high level. They explained to themselves that the story, then so popular about the death's head and the fantastic society of red men, long known by some people, had been put together and found to play a role in that vast hoax.

Well. It has to be recognized that the police, once again, followed the wrong trail. If, persevering in their first investigation, they had interrogated the Marquis more strongly without discovering a connection between the mysterious crate and the Louvel Crime, which, in reality, never existed, they would have found the key to a mysterious intrigue. They were unaware of the entire plot that only we knew. The time has not come to say the last word about that intrigue. A whole world of events and facts not less extraordinary, remain for us to go through before the denouement.

Right now, however, we can admit to the reader that the unknown masked woman that Lupiano usually showed around Paris, was not at all the same woman that he had presented to the magistrates as his daughter. We can even go so far as to let the reader know that, in order to deceive the police, the person who was switched was none other than Georgiana, the Bloodied Girl. It was she who had played the role of Madame Lelouard in Bordeaux and had afterward been whisked away by the envoy of King Radama. Given these first clarifications between the writer and the reader, here are a few short words of preface and explanation.

In the vast and arduous development of what could be called an immense imbroglio, in which strangeness and mystery must be one of the principal elements of interest, will it be too much to ask patience from those who would really like to follow the line of deduction? The explanations for everything will always finally be given. Could they also be asked to pay attention to the creation of multiple incidents of the plot that must be disentangled and call to memory some facts already related at a much earlier point that often will be echoed or finally resolved?

For more clarity, the author, in the style of preachers, has divided his material. Following the present Prologue, there will be six parts which may be thus classified and labeled in advance:

Part I. THE HULETS

Part II. GREGORIO MATIPHOUS. THE SLEEPERS'

CLUB[49]

---

[49] Included in this volume.

PART I: THE HULETS

I. A Man's Vocation

In 1774, the Advent sermon was preached by a man named Hulet. The choice of this preacher had seemed strange, a man completely unknown, belonging to no order whose reputation would have procured him the honor of speaking before Their Royal Majesties. He was a simple little vicar from one of the parishes in Paris, Saint-Landri, situated on the Ile de la Cité.

His good fortune, however, had nothing about it that can't be explained. One day, by chance, the Princess of Lamballe [50] had heard Vespers at Saint-Landri. And following Vespers she had heard a sermon by Abbé Hulet. The talent the young preacher showed on that occasion had so much more struck the Princess, as she hadn't expected to meet him in such a place. On her return to Versailles, she had spoken of him to the Queen in terms of this highest admiration.

On the word of a person who had her complete confidence for everything, Marie Antoinette was curious to see this so out of place Bourdaloue.[51] Some days later the

---

[50] Princess Maria Teresa of Savoy-Carignan (Marie Thérèse) (1749-1792) was a member of a cadet branch of the House of Savoy. She was married at the age of 17 to Louis Alexandre de Bourbon-Penthièvre, Prince de Lamballe, the heir to the greatest fortune in France. After her marriage, which lasted a year, she went to court and became the confidante of Queen Marie Antoinette. She was killed in the massacres of September 1792 during the French Revolution.

[51] Louis Bourdaloue (1632-1704), Jesuit priest, rhetorician and philosopher.

prodigious distinction mentioned was bestowed on him. However, what at another period the Jesuits had easily obtained for the least subject of their order, with the help of the steward of her house, the Queen had some trouble making it possible for her protégé.

Old de Maurepas,[52] the one who, when he was younger, had written a dirty, inelegant poem about Madame de Pompadour that he paid for with a prolonged disgrace during all of Louis XV's reign, found himself, at the beginning of the following reign, the all-powerful minister. Without his approval Louis XVI wouldn't be permitted to ask for anything. And when it was a question of the Advent preacher, even in the presence of the enthusiastic sponsors supporting his advancement, the oracle was consulted.

"Hum!" M. de Maurepas then said: "To have the honor of preaching in Court, I don't actually say that he has to be from the nobility…"

"That's how it seems to me," Madame de Lamballe, quickly interrupted. "Massillon[53] was the son of a notary."

"Yes, but at least his family was from the acceptable bourgeoisie, whereas Abbé Hulet's father…"

"So! What about Abbé Hulet's father?" Marie Antoinette asked impatiently.

"I can't tell the King the obstacle I see to the Queen's wish; it's a state secret."

And in the ear of the one whom he could very well have called his royal student, M. de Maurepas said some words in a low voice.

"What! That villainy is still here?" exclaimed the King in a strong tone of righteousness.

"Yes, undoubtedly," replied the old Minister, "and it has to continue or, otherwise, who would take charge of governing?"

"However," the Queen said," I don't find anything as

---

[52] See Note 12.
[53] Jean-Baptiste Massillon (1663-1742), Catholic bishop.

impolite and discourteous as a Secret of State. It seems to authorize, before women, no matter what their rank, whispering and the most disobliging things in the world said to one side."

With his usual weakness for his beautiful companion, the King, said, "I can certainly tell my wife…"

And that time, without consulting the old Minister, who didn't seem to very much approve that indiscretion, he spoke confidentially into Marie-Antoinette's ear the secret of Abbé Hulet's unworthiness.

The content, whatever it was, seemed to make an impression on the Queen. She seemed disposed to sacrifice the poor vicar, saying with seeming regret,

"But then, whom will we choose?"

The only one left out of the State Secret, and hurt by the general desertion prejudicial to her protégé, Madame de Lamballe became petulant and to the question posed by the Queen, she answered:

"But Your Majesties, have the young Abbé de Périgord. He is, that one, I think from a rather good family."

Monsieur de Talleyrand, he who was later Priest of Autun and one of the eminent diplomats of modern times, was then twenty years-old. He had just finished his ecclesiastic studies and had come to attention by some not very edifying adventures. He was the one Madame de Lamballe had just mentioned and it is, in fact, regrettable that the ironic advice she offered hadn't then been followed. To that life so filled with such strange fluctuations, it lacks what that of Cardinal de Retz[54] did not lack, the bizarre circumstance of having preached an Advent sermon.

"In such a case, however, birth is not everything," replied the King, who hadn't noticed that the Princess had spoken mockingly.

"It is so little, that it is nothing," replied Madame de Lamballe with animation. "My opinion, in so far as a woman

---

[54] Jean-François Paul de Gondi, Cardinal de Retz (1613-1679).

can know about these things, is that for the priest, there is no family affiliation. All his family antecedents are absorbed in his quality as Minister of the Most-High. And it will always seem strange to me that when God finds a man with good enough ties for His Service, which an earthly sovereign, even if he is the King of France, thinks he must look into the fact of his birth."[55]

And de Maurepas, who laughed about everything (his politics and his character have been so summed up), greeted the Princess' sally gaily, but Louis XVI, who had a great deal of what was later called liberalism was strongly struck by the dart of truth that had just been thrown at him. And after the exchange of several more words, the strong and beautiful argument of Mademoiselle de Lamballe won the decision.

Abbé Hulet, despite what his father might have been, took his place, therefore, in the Pulpit where Bossuet, Fléchier, Bourdaloue and Massillon [56] had stood. And although he hadn't risen completely to the height of these illustrious priests who had preceded him, his sermon on the first Sunday of Advent was greeted with distinct favor. At the same time, gossip circulated around the court that he also had become greatly recommended by the ladies of the court. It was said that his entry into the priesthood had been the result of an unhappy love affair. He was almost seen as another Abbé de Rancé.[57] That story was both true and false. In fact, here's the way things really happened.

---

[55] Note in the text: "*Je commençais mes sermons de l'Advent dans Saint-Jean-en-grève, le jour de la Toussaint.*" *Mémoires du Cardinal de Retz*, Part II.

[56] Renowned theologians and rhetoricians: Jacques-Bénigne Bossuet (1627-1704), Louis Bourdaloue (q.v.); Jean-Baptiste Massillon (q.v.) and Valentin-Esprit Flechier (1632-1710).

[57] Armand-Jean le Bouthillier de Rancé (1626-1700), Canon of Notre Dame de Paris and Abbot de la Trappe, who, inheriting great wealth, led a profligate life, but turned later to an austere religious life, reforming the Trappists.

Despite the moving religious fervor of his speech, Father Hulet was nothing more than a magnetic personality. His religious vocation, like that of the celebrated reformer with whom they wished to compare him, was motivated by a great deal of ambition and an ardent desire for a temporal fortune. Love, if you wish, had been the starting point, but it had not been the sacrifice that gained him so much sweet sympathy. There are a thousand ways to love without tenderness of heart. One can love with his senses, with his reason, with his ego, with his self-interest, with his boredom, and even through habit. At nineteen years-old, and even before it was a question of his entering the priesthood, in his own way, and in so far as he was able, he had become attached to the daughter of a gentleman named Boisbrunet.

Son of a somewhat well-off petty bourgeois, who had some obscure job as a clerk in the Foreign Affairs Department, Hulet was not in a position to aspire to the hand of that rich heiress whose fortune and superior birth seemed to make unapproachable. However, as a result of an important service that the senior Hulet had had the opportunity to render to the Marquis de Boisbrunet, who was grateful, a great friendship between the two families was created. From their childhood, the two young people saw each other daily and as soon as they were old enough to feel emotionally involved, love, which cares nothing for distinctions and social distances, began to creep into their relationship. Their mutual attachment didn't long stay a secret from the Marquis, but, contrary to immemorial custom, he approved of the sentiment.

Following a friendship of fifteen years, happy to have an opportunity to repay the good services of the senior Hulet, M. de Boisbrunet had himself come to propose a *mésalliance* and had spoken of a marriage between their children. But following the same reversal of all the established rules, the humble man protested strongly against that suggestion. His said that his son was not of a social station by birth to be able to accept the honor offered him. And although the Marquis pointed out to him that it wasn't up to a man of the common people to hold such scruples if the gentleman found the alliance a good one, the senior Hulet had held firm in his refusal. And that was done in terms of an unusual self-denial which apparently was not feigned.

Not able to reason with such a stubborn resistance, M. de Boisbrunet had finally put the negotiation in the hands of the one he was thinking of making his son-in-law. The young man had thought that success wouldn't be difficult nor long in coming. It seemed to him that his father, after having given his extreme delicacy as much time as was reasonable, must give way to the instances of friendship and consideration of his son's happiness.

However he had made many miscalculations in his expectations. Not only did the young Hulet not obtain the consent that he hoped from the author of his days, but he saw himself very strongly reprimanded for having dared to carry his pretentions to such a high level. And he finally came up against a persevering and inflexible determination which he had to see that he would not overcome.

Carried then beyond the limits which filial respect should always maintain, the young man dared to insinuate that only an egotistical puritanism or an unfortunate desire to make himself stand out could explain a decision that would upset the whole economy of his future. He added that he thought he didn't need to be concerned with such a bizarre caprice and such cruel tyranny.

The person he had just spoken of with so little respect, answered him:

"My son, you are nineteen years-old. Next year I must confide a family secret to you. After that you yourself will have realized that this marriage that you are talking about is impossible. As for the present, I am not permitted to explain myself any further. But understand this: it is a duty of honor and delicacy for you not to think any further about this union."

There is no need to say what terrible curiosity that half-confidence raised and with what innumerable questions it was met. Actually, all the unhappy young man could learn was that, for a long time, those of his family and race had to reckon with a cruel duty, in which there should be seen something of the fatality of the ancients.

"That fatality that weighs on me," Hulet senior added, "will weigh on you in your turn and on your children, as it has weighed on others before us. You see, the only way, perhaps, that you have to avert it is a determination exactly opposite the thought you have today."

Pressed to speak more clearly, the despairing old man said,

"You are thinking of getting married and yet for me, the vocation that I would wish for you, would be to espouse a monastery. In order to escape this circle of iron that binds us from father to son. Everything well considered, there is only the religious life for you."

"But father," the frightened young man exclaimed, "You're not the hangman, are you?"

"Perhaps," Hulet senior answered, and fearing he had said too much, he quickly broke off the interview. The humble employment that he held in the Department of Foreign Affairs disguised more formidable functions. A clever cryptographer, he secretly directed the Office of Codes and in addition had the mission, without appearing to do so, of opening all diplomatic correspondence which might have fallen into disloyal hands. He was, in addition, the head of an obscure group of employees working under the name of *Le Cabinet Noir*, or *The Secret Bureau*, and more politely, *The King's Bureau*. They clandestinely opened letters from the interior which had been identified for them by the Director General of the Postal System. For more than a century, as it will be explained later, the central control of that State Inquisition was hereditary in the Hulet family, where it was passed from male to male by the order of primogeniture as is the crown in a dynasty.

By opposing a marriage, honorable and advantageous for his son, which would have carried the original stain on their honor into another family, Hulet was being laudable and honorable. And in fact he was a very honest man. The secrets with which he was entrusted were always inviolable and sacred. Sometimes, without violating the discretion and secrecy imposed on him by his functions, he even saw the way, by certain revelations which came to him, to prevent or repair some wrong. He brought the most eager zeal to that unofficial kindness. He had rendered a service of that kind, without explaining it to him, to the Marquis de Boisbrunet, which later resulted in that liaison which the two families had been on the point of crowning.

A widow for a long time and having lavished on his only son every affection, Hulet senior hadn't expected the complication which had just appeared to create a great worry in the life of that child. His strongest desire would have been to shield him from a profession he held to be despicable. Besides, he liked to persuade himself that the young man had no regard for the vocation. But considering the internal charter of the Secret Bureau, it would seem that the freedom dreamed of by the unhappy father was almost impossible to realize.

In the Secret Bureau, the custom was that all the jobs, as much as was possible, remained hereditary. When the age of twenty was reached, (discretion couldn't be very much hoped for before that age), after a preliminary study and examination of their aptitudes, the subjects who were destined to the delicate functions of the State Police, were taken into the sacred mystery. They were immediately installed as student interpreters with a salary of 6000 livres. If, an infinitely rare happening, some scruple or some resistance were manifest after the fact, by a neophyte, to preserve the secret of the institution put thus in peril, the recalcitrant, by means of a letter de cachet was shut up in a government prison. For him there was no longer any chance, future, or liberty.

As for the children of the employees who, lacking ability, or by the turn of their ideas and their character were considered improper or dangerous to the affiliation, they did not, because of that, escape the fatality of their birth. The watchful and careful politics of the State in charge of overseeing the duration and the security of the work, while leaving them ignorant of their origin, did not, because of that, renounce their oversight and their direction. Being careful to keep them constantly dependent, that cruel mother kept them from advancing in any career. In addition, through the marriages which they manipulated, it was careful to conserve many indirect ties with the shadowy agency, which would have forced them to keep the secret if they had found out about it. As a result a terrible skill made these unfortunate people in some ways passive participants, always under the thumb and index finger of the police. And even abroad, carefully watched, their liberty and sometimes their life, never ceased being at risk, because the least indiscretion must be feared.

Hulet senior then was right. There was, in fact, in a life so strictly mapped out, no other choice but the monastery. He could hope to escape the constraints of the guardianship that must follow him in his daily life by a rupture with all his family to take up the religious life, by the sacred nature of the vows he would have to take, as well as by the protection of the Order of which he must become a member. But even in the sad expedient of the hair shirt and the cowl, the conscientious Director of the Secret Bureau had become aware of another danger.

If his son appeared to show little inclination to become an opener of letters, he didn't seem a great deal more inclined to become a saint. Now, by pushing him toward an ecclesiastic life, wasn't it to be feared that it would make him one of those scandalous monks who, in every epoch, had been a plague and a shame for religion?

However, when the opportunity of marriage with Mademoiselle Boisbrunet came up, seeing the passion with which the imprudent young man embraced the hope of this splendid establishment, it was reasonable to suppose that at no price would he accept the inheritance of the paternal profession. At that point, Hulet the elder no longer hesitated. And foreseeing the frightful future reserved for his well-beloved son if he resisted the King's Bureau, he decided to bring up the necessity for taking up the monastic life, however insufficient his vocation might seem to him. It was obviously not without struggle and resistance that the martyr accepted his chalice. Hearing that a blighting destiny would bar his life, he asked at least to know the nature of that obstacle. Now we know that, in his own interest, that secret couldn't be confided to him.

On his part, he tried in vain to guess. He saw his father enjoying an honest, comfortable livelihood, surrounded by general esteem, and living the most upright life. How could he reconcile dishonor with that pleasant exterior? And he could find out nothing even about the existence of the Secret Bureau. Under the reign of Louis XV, the fact of the surveillance of letters was rather scandalously bruited about, but, nevertheless, during that time, the incognito of the agents was never betrayed. Besides, it was generally thought that since the end of the preceding reign the violation of secret correspondence had ceased. And we have just seen that a king, an honest man, the candid and virtuous Louis XVI, was one of the first to believe it had been abolished.

But it was precisely by the obscure side of his disgrace and his family stain that the pariah was most strongly impressed. He didn't know what phantom to fight. He knew only that with prodigious amounts of talent and perseverance he wouldn't be able to overcome the obstacle in front of which the brilliant dream of marriage had vanished. Faced with that unknown, incalculable destiny, he was seized with a kind of angry despair capable of suggesting the most extreme solutions to him. In that state of mind, a way by which he could see some freedom and space for his existence was opened to him. At last he no longer resisted the paternal suggestions toward the direction of God. However, either because he was frightened of the solitude and the austerities of the cloister, or rather because his ambitious instincts made him see very few chances to climb in Church hierarchies, he refused to enter monastic life. And despite his father's doubt that the secular clergy would be a rather safe haven, he never wanted the necessity for his sacrifice to go beyond the simple vow of priesthood.

Now, having faith in public gossip, endowing Father Hulet's face with an aureole of infinite tenderness, they gave love all the honor for his sad decision.

II. A Woman's Vocation

About three weeks after his father's first overtures to him, the young Hulet started toward the Saint-Magloire Seminary, where he was to stay for several years. It was there that he had decided to do his ecclesiastic studies. An Ortoran, a very learned man and an old friend of his father, taught humanities there.

The day before, like a kind of dying man, the sad young man had put all his affairs in order. After a melancholy lunch with several friends he was leaving, he shared with them the worldly books in his library as well as what he had that was valuable. Some days earlier, in a letter that already was marked by something of that mystical style steeped in piety toward God which is usual in religious life, he sent Mademoiselle Boisbrunet a solemn goodbye.

He went on foot, rather pensive, down the Rue du Faubourg Saint-Jacques. He had already reached the top of Saint-Jacques-du-Haut-Pas, when, under the porch of that church he saw a very young woman showing a very elegant figure under a cloak of black taffeta who seemed to be watching for someone. As soon as she saw Hulet, that beautiful unknown young woman left the place where she had stopped and came straight toward the astonished seminarian.

"Is it really Monsieur Henri Hulet that I have the honor of speaking to?" she asked him.

And receiving an affirmative response, the young woman continued: "There is someone whom you know near here who wants to speak to you. Will you please follow me? I think you will not regret the inconvenience that I have caused you."

119

Hulet wasn't so far advanced in clerical ways that he had to be very frightened of the encounter. Besides, in her voice as well as in all the rest of her person, the unknown woman had an appearance of perfect distinction which would make it difficult to suppose her an adventurer.

"I am at your service, Madame," the nascent Bossuet answered.

Then, going some steps ahead of him, the young woman entered the church, went through it rapidly and left through a door that opened onto a little used street. A carriage drawn by two horses and with a postilion in the saddle was stationed in that location.

"There! In that carriage," Henri Hulet's guide said to him. The astonishment of the young man can be imagined when, approaching the door, where a young woman quickly showed her face, he recognized Victoire de Boisbrunet.

"You!, here, Mademoiselle?" the seminarian exclaimed in a voice that showed more surprise than joy.

"Ah! Don't scold me," the young girl answered with tears in her voice. "Without the deep love I have for you, permitted by my parents…"

"Your parents!" Hulet interrupted her. "After having welcomed me, they let me know I should never again appear at their house. And as for my father, he has never varied in his refusal. So everything is definitely over."

"Could you do that? Your family must soon think of another arrangement for you. And the obsession of their concern for you would be greater if you were thought to be still in love with me. Besides, my father is still young. He is barely sixty-years-old. You can see how far away our projects of marriage are!"

"Nothing is truer," Victoire's friend then interrupted. "And exactly because of that, a decision has to be made."

"A decision!" Hulet repeated, confused.

"So far as I can understand," the confident answered. "The situation explains itself: there are post horses, a carriage. You see very well, sir, that you are taking both of us away."

120

"Victoire!" exclaimed the seminarian in a tone of reproach. "Have you thought about such a step?"

"But Henri, if I don't agree to do that, it would then mean that I would never see you again."

"What's more, sir," the go-between of the two lovers said, "if your logic, which seems to me to be well below your age, lets you find some irregularity in our actions, please, I ask you, reprimand only me. Since receiving your farewell letter, Victoire has done nothing but moan and lament. You can't imagine the trouble I had to make her take some resolution and courage."

"But, Mademoiselle, to thus take over so casually the will of a young woman I have always known to be reserved and prudent, who, then are you?"

"You don't know me, that's true, but I, on the contrary, I know you marvelously well. Victoire never stopped talking about you in her letters. She described you in such a striking way that a while ago, without ever having seen you, I said to myself: That must be him."

"Then I have the honor of speaking to Mademoiselle Adélaïde de la Salle?"

"At your service, and I'm very capable," the young girl answered, bowing very low to Hulet. "I dare say that in bringing me back to Paris several days ago, your star helped you unfortunate lovers in a strange fashion."

"Certainly," the seminarian answered formally, "I appreciate, Mademoiselle, your devotion and your zeal, so much more so, since in the hazardous enterprise in which you have taken control, you are not yourself without running some risk of seriously compromising yourself."

"As for myself, sir, I can rest easy. I don't have to answer for my actions. I have only a very gouty tutor, very occupied with his rheumatisms. I have persuaded him that he should find anything I do good. But I don't believe, in what concerns Victoire, that I am engaging her in what you call such great danger. The difficulty is to get her out of the paternal household and to bring her here. That done, we will go to the

121

house of one of my aunts in Brussels, where we are sure to find asylum. There you will get married, and, after all, I don't see what the most severe judgment could find to say about a three -party elopement.

Without discussing the value of this plan, Hulet said seriously:

"Victoire, you don't know everything. Our parents' opposition to our marriage is not the only obstacle. A family secret raised an impassable barrier, and I must tell you that at no price would I take advantage of your devotion. "

"Well! Sir," exclaimed Mademoiselle de Salle, with disappointment, "you should have spoken sooner. If you had, I wouldn't have pawned the diamonds I inherited from my poor mother with a Lombard yesterday. I turned them into cash to pay for our trip."

"But that secret," Victoire asked, "will you at least tell me what it is?"

"I don't know its nature myself," Hulet replied, "but it's enough that, according to my father, it places me, as far as you're concerned, in an unworthy situation."

"Well! If that's all it is, what does that matter to me?" Mademoiselle de Boisbrunet answered excitedly. "You are worthy of me if I love you, and even if I had to resign myself to the most obscure and the most combative existence with you, do you think I would hesitate a moment?"

But it was just a most obscure and combative existence that didn't appeal to Hulet. He had dreamed of the joys of a splendid and golden existence in possessing his pretty fiancée. To throw himself into all the possible hazards of the adventure offered to him, he didn't feel in his heart that invincible, ardent love that women, on the other hand, can experience better than we can. His decision now was thoughtfully and reasonably taken. To turn him from this path, would have taken something more attractive than a poor, persecuted marriage, running the risk of all sorts of problems which the elopement with a rich heiress rarely spares the abductor. He then again refused categorically to be part of what he called a folly. And he paid with a sermon the poor child wringing her hands in despair and sobbing to break one's heart. He talked to her about an eternity where, sooner or later, they were sure to be together again. For a sixteen year-old girl, you'll have to admit, it couldn't have seemed a very close or consoling length of time.

With the resolute character Mademoiselle de Salle had first shown, her disdain of this boy who was busy preaching and acting prudent instead of jumping with both feet and with his eyes closed into the desperate situation open to him can be imagined. Proudly pushing the preacher away from the carriage door, she got in and with a passionate gesture she clutched Victoire in her arms, telling her not to be so sad, and that at least she still had a friend. At the same time she turned toward Hulet, who remained there at a loss for anything to say and spoke to him in the most disdainful way possible:

"Good-by, Monsieur l'Abbé," she said to him. "Enjoy the seminary!"

That would have seemed a pleasant, witty comment in a less sad situation.

Seeing that the other young girl whom he had brought had again taken her place in the carriage, the postilion thought they were going to leave, and as he didn't feel any great respect for two young girls who seemed disposed to travel without a gentleman to accompany them, he asked:

"Now, my pretty young ladies, where do you want to go?"

Mademoiselle de la Salle hesitated and didn't know what to respond, but in a strong voice and a resolute tone, Victoire de Boisbrunet answered: "Rue de la Ville-l'Évéque, to the Benedictine Convent.

III. Father Hulet's Luck

Mademoiselle de la Salle and the Boisbrunet family tried in vain to make Victoire change her decision. The position taken was invincible and three years later, the same day Henri

Hulet entered irrevocably into Holy Orders, the courageous young girl became a Benedictine nun at Ville-l'Évéque.

As for the seminarian, he was as successful as possible in his studies, and although the ardor of a rather carnal nature, made him a prey to terrible struggles, he was a perfectly well-behaved priest. His strong desire to get ahead in his career gave him the strength to endure all the sacrifices and inspired him with at least the negative virtues of the sacrifice.

Right up to the day when he had the good luck to be noticed by the high protector, that careful administrator of his life hadn't profited by his sacrifice very much. The clandestine activity of the Secret Bureau on the destiny of young men who tried to extricate themselves from its embrace, had, according to his father's foresight, followed him even into Holy Orders and had taken care to keep him in the ranks of the lower clergy. Even after the good luck of preaching before the Court, the cruel influence continued to follow him. He decided to take the result of that diversion from his destiny out of the country. Monsieur de Maurepas, who had tried unsuccessfully to reverse Madame de Lamballe's protection, quickly tried to furnish a specious and at the same time honorable pretext for the reality of that exit.

The Versailles Bureau was then actively preoccupied by the choice of Clément XIV's [58] successor for St. Peter's bishopric, and during the Conclave which ended in the exaltation of Pope Pius VI,[59] frequent communications were

---

[58] Pope Clement XIV (1705-1774), born Giovanni Vincenzo Antonio Ganganelli, was Pope from 19 May 1769 to his death in 1774. He is best known for his suppression of the Society of Jesus.

[59] Pope Pius VI (1717-1799), born Count Giovanni Angelo Braschi, reigned as Pope from 15 February 1775 to his death in 1799. Pius VI condemned the French Revolution and the suppression of the Gallican Church; he was later expelled from the Papal States by French troops from 1798 until his death one year later in Valence.

exchanged between the French Embassy in Rome and the Minister of Foreign Affairs. As if it had been a mission of great importance which could only be given to a subject of transcendent merit, Hulet was in great secrecy sent to carry a letter. And that letter, the contents of which he didn't know, concerned only him. It was suggested to the secretary in charge of the legation's affairs during the absence of the Ambassador, Cardinal de Bernis,[60] shut up in the Conclave, that the bearer of the letter be kept in Rome as long as possible and that he try to involve him in some scandalous affair to be made public.

As a consequence of these instructions, the young Abbé was cleverly introduced to several feminine temptations of the most venous kind and the eye of the police, supported by the ambassador, followed these attempts at seduction with particular care in order to expose them as soon as they occurred. But by his prudence and the strict rigidity of his morals, the young Abbé side-stepped all the traps. They were never able to surprise him into forgetting himself in the slightest.

One opportunity came about, however, where, unless there was some miracle, his good name, if not his virtue, appeared menaced with going under.

In Rome, in those days, there was talk of only one prostitute, one named Bambolina, made to be loved as soon as she was seen. She was really the most capricious young woman that had perhaps ever been seen. She was at that time protected by a cardinal who was madly in love with her attractions. She reigned in his household like a queen.

"My sweet Lord," his mistress said to him, "at least don't keep me waiting a long time for this Pope. Understand that, for me, it must be done at the latest in a week. I won't wait for you past that time. I'll name your successor without a vote or a conclave."

---

[60] François-Joachim de Pierre de Bernis (1715-1794), French cardinal and statesman.

The Cardinal only laughed at the threat, since it did not depend on him alone to hurry the election, which Bambolina meant by that to the seat of Saint Peter. How could he believe that, not getting what she wanted, she would break off with a protector as generous as he?

During the time it took for the Cardinals to elect the Sovereign Pontiff, each day they burned the ballots which had been used for the votes to let it be known if a Pope had been elected or not. At the hour that the auto-da-fé was usually made, crowds of people ran to watch the stovepipe through which the smoke poured. There was nothing if the pipe gave out smoke. On the contrary, Rome and the universe had a Pope the day the pipe remained quiet. As the desire for the election of the Holy Father grew, the first ones were always on time for that rendezvous of the entire city.

"My Eminence," Bambolina was counting, "seven days more, six days more, five days more…" Then she ran to shut herself up in her apartment, where she stayed in absolute seclusion, without allowing any suitor, whatever his rank, to cross the threshold of her house.

The eighth day passed and the Pope was still to come.

"All right," she said, "I'm free. And now let's look around a little!"

It had long been night when, suddenly below his window, as Father Hulet retired to his study to get ready to go to bed, a great light and loud noise broke out.

Curious to see what that might be, he saw a carriage, all lit up in gold, in front of the door. There were twelve to fifteen escorts carrying torches and seeming about to start a fire. At the same moment, the door opened and into the priest's poor bedroom appeared Bambolina, radiant with beauty and finery.

Now, it must be told that the followers of the French ambassador had surreptitiously told the proud young woman that a young priest, recently come from France, found nothing more beautiful than she. And this lying report also said that Hulet, who didn't even know Bambolina existed, had even bragged that if he saw that proud beauty begging at his feet, like a new Joseph, he would know how to control himself wisely and not even leave his loin cloth behind.

God must have given Father Hulet particular grace for the terrible meeting that had been set up for him. Two hours later, touched by the eloquent speeches with which he had represented to that sinner the shame and disorder in which she was living, Bambolina, the effect of her charms having failed, left on foot, confessed and resolved, like another Mary Magdalene, to spend the remainder of her life in penitence.

The next day she gave all her worldly goods to Rome's poor, and her beautiful hair, clipped, shaved and covered with ashes she sent to the cardinal, who received them from her, a cup of despair from which he never recovered.

The same day she entered the convent of the Capucines Reformed Ladies, a strict and terrible house, which the Romans called the *Sepulte vive.*[61] Thus one can see how attempts to seduce our holy young man succeeded.

However, in the long run, governed by a constant obsession, who knows the danger he might run. Fortunately, at that time that love of power which was, to tell the truth, the only passion of his life, made him take a step which might definitively bring about the independence of his future. By chance, he met a Brother of the Order of Saint Dominique. Listening to him discourse on the power of the holy militia of which he was a member, led the ambitious young man to reflect on the wrong direction he had taken in conducting his affairs up until that time.

First of all, it no longer seemed to him that, in France, those high ecclesiastical dignities that he had dreamed of could make him possess the depth and extent of sovereign power equal to his appetite, given certain restrictions and certain limits set by political powers to which it had always had to submit. And considering it more closely, he doubted that, even in Rome, the source of the great Catholic river, the situation of the secular clergy offered a satisfactory realization

---

[61] Buried alive.

127

of theocratic omnipotence such as he understood it. It was only in the center of religious corporations where all the association's strength, delegated to a superior, or to a General, created absolute power, increased and completed by absolute obedience, that he believed that he could find clerical domination organized and functioning according to his ideal.

In this respect, in another time, the Brotherhood of the Jesuits, by the power of their constitution as well as by the strength of its exterior expansion, would have greatly attracted him, but it was then banished, persecuted and on the black list of almost every European country. Looking around him, Hulet could see nowhere except in the order of the frères prêcheurs[62] an association worthy of his zeal.

Once made public, his intention of entering that order did not lack obstacles. But Hulet was one of those exceptional beings that are kept once they come to you. Therefore the General under whom he wished to serve used all his influence to bring about his enrollment and a little more than a year after he came to Rome, the former vicar of Saint Landri, wearing then the white cassock of the Dominicans, mounted the pulpit of the Saint-Louis-des-Français church. There, as at Versailles, he was a very successful preacher but no one dared to hinder his career. The Holy Office was a very different force than the local and laic institution of the Secret Bureau, which did not wish to confront the dangerous Order of Saint Dominique by persecuting one of its members. So, after a little detour, Hulet had come back to the choice that his father had at first advised. And it must be recognized that in the choice of the Order which he had finally entered, he had done well. Wasn't it, in fact, a master stroke to take refuge from the Secret Bureau in the Inquisition?

By his great success as an orator, as well as, perhaps, by the somewhat affected austerity of his life, the young Dominican rose rapidly in his Order, and in 1779 we find him in Malta, exercising in the name of the Holy See, the function

---

[62] Preaching brothers, ie: the Dominicans.

of Inquisitor of the Faith. But, having arrived at that height, he was not fortunate enough to conduct himself with the cleverness that his position would have required. It was only hesitatingly and almost by surprise that the Inquisition had established itself at Malta. There had always existed a silent rivalry with the Magister, or Grand Master of the Order. Therefore it was a power that needed to be exercised with an extremely light touch, and Hulet took just the opposite of that prudent line of conduct. His pretentions, so far as maintaining his privileges and prerogatives, went so far as requiring that the Grand Master's carriage stop in the streets when it encountered his. An argument over the question of precedence broke out and he finally had the worst of it.

In the exercise of his spiritual power there was the same lack of restraint and tact. Violent, argumentative, without forbearance, he wanted to bring reform quickly to the religious houses of the island, to supervise practices with harsh and meticulous rigor. And when he discovered some disorder or laxness of morals, he was very eager to punish, very severe and very subtle in his choice of penitence. For him the punishment seemed very much less a way to correct the guilty one than a kind of sinister voluptuousness that he seemed to find in torturing him.

His zeal, from what one is to believe, finally passed all limits. A terrible and mysterious torture was inflicted on a convent of women. A nobleman of the German language, implicated in that bloody and shady affair, suddenly disappeared from the principal location of the order, without its being possible to find any trace of him. The incident brought together the elements of a strong denunciation of Hulet addressed to the Holy See by the Grand Master Rohan.[63]

---

[63] Fra Emmanuel de Rohan-Polduc (1725-1797), member of the wealthy and influential Rohan family of France, and 70th Prince and Grand Master of the Order of St. John from 1775 to 1797. His last years were troubled due to the decline of the Order because of the French Revolution.

Following an investigation on the spot by a legate sent *ad hoc*, Inquisitor Hulet was ordered to come to Rome to give an account of his administration, and shortly afterward ordered to return to his monastery. There, for several years, his seclusion was so profound and so absolute that his existence was almost in doubt. It seemed that he had gone to rejoin that German nobleman whom no one had heard anything about and who had caused his fall

IV. The Third Nominal Appeal

On the 17th of January in that bloody year of 1793, in a humble apartment on the Rue Jacob in the Faubourg Saint Germain, dressed in that democratic affectation of negligence, which, later, went so far as wearing the short jacket of the ordinary workman and the red bonnet, a man seated in front of a table holding a frugal meal, had just finished eating..

Near him was a woman, although no longer in her first youth, nonetheless remarkable by what remained of her beauty. She was nursing a child, but was not entirely engrossed in that maternal duty. From time to time she glanced toward her husband with a furtive look full of solicitude. It was evident that having to discuss a serious and grave subject she was looking for the right moment to broach that conversation.

That man was one of Louis XVI's judges. In a short time he must go to the Convention where the vote on the third of five charges in the regicide trial would be taken. The votes that evening would concern this: What punishment would be inflicted on Louis Capet?

Seeing his anxious and severe expression, his studied attitude of the *sans-culottisme*,[64] the response of the judge

---

[64] The rich and the poor were identified by the type of trousers they wore; the rich wore short breeches with long stockings, but the poor wore long trousers. During the French Revolution

we're looking at could be foreseen. It was this sanguinary vote that frightened the wife of the Convention member. She wanted to bring him back to ideas of clemency, and was afraid of pushing him in the other direction by an ill-timed contradiction.

In the middle of this silent tête-à-tête between the two spouses, which had already gone on for some time, the doorbell rang. Either through austere Republican ostentation or a very real and effective poverty, they were living without a servant.

Although her infant was still nursing at her breast at that moment, it was the wife who rose to open the door, a detail which showed the somewhat egotistical supremacy of her husband, who showed no intention of sparing her that trouble.

The door hardly opened, the wife exclaimed with joy:

"Ah! My love! Your father!"

And at that same moment, a white-haired old man with a venerable face entered the room which held his son, who rose with an air of deference and respect, but without showing any affectionate eagerness.

"Hulet! I must talk to you," the old man said gravely.

Hulet! Well, are we then in the presence of the Dominican and the Inquisitor whose disappearance we noted in the last chapter? A few words here to explain his presence in Paris and his strange transformation.

Kept a long time in a harsh and narrow prison that the violence of his spiritual administration on the island of Malta had earned him from the pontifical government, Father Hulet had finally escaped and he had managed to regain the soil of France precisely at the time of the first rumblings of the revolutionary storm.

From the retreat where he had remained hidden for some time, very soon seeing that everything around him was crumbling, the throne, the altar, the institutions of the past, he

---

of 1789, the poor were "*sans culottes*," or without short breeches.

fell into deep contempt of everything. He stopped believing that strength was there where he had at first placed it, and, instead of seeing Catholicism, as he formerly had, the first instrument of power, he had more faith in the future of democracy than in a religion persecuted and beaten into ruins, and which seemed three-quarters blotted out and disappeared from the surface of the very Christian Kingdom.

Therefore, through the instinct of ambition, that we had always known he had, the ex-Dominican hurried to associate himself with the side which he foresaw as the powerful and indelible manifestation of sovereignty. Throwing the monk's cowl far from him, he came to make on the altar of the homeland a complete and glaring abjuration of his past. Finally, through the door of apostasy, entering the century, he took the doctrines, the language, and even the costume of the Revolution. He intended by that ardent devotion to substitute a political fortune for the religious fortune that had escaped him.

Soon afterward he found the opportunity to offer to the regime under which he aspired to play a role, some more decisive and more express proof. In the bosom of one of those pious asylums, which Revolutionary decrees had ordered destroyed, lived a woman he knew, to whom he had early been attracted and for whom he had been a powerful fascination. Therefore, one day, at the head of one of those bands of demolitionists who were going about with hammer and pick in hand to invade and devastate the holy sites, even to the sepulchers, he entered the convent of the Ville-l'Évéque Bénédictines. Kneeling and trembling in her cell he found the one he had not dared, at another time, turn away from her family according to men, and didn't then hesitate to turn away from her family according to God.

He didn't need any violence to make Victoire de Boisbrunet follow him, because, in the midst of the sack of the holy convent, he appeared more like a savior than a sacrilegious rapist. Once out of the convent, the nun found herself cruelly abandoned. Her parents, her friends, all those to whom she might have been able to go to seek asylum, had either emigrated or gone into hiding and were fleeing from the Revolutionary proscription. Thus Hulet, who, in the life of the heart, had been everything for that unfortunate girl, again found himself her only resource and her only hope in the life into which she had been so suddenly thrown.

Even after the age of thirty, Mademoiselle de Boisbrunet had remained marvelously beautiful. And the love which the Dominican had experienced for her, as lukewarm as that attachment had seemed, was revived with marked increase in ardor and vivacity. In fact Hulet himself was still in the full strength of manhood and had had to undergo harsh combats to uphold his vows of chastity. In the place of a warm heart, which he had always lacked, he had kept that fervor of the senses which maintains and makes temptation eternal, always reborn and always the conqueror.

Besides, it shouldn't be believed that in the glacial atmosphere of the cloister the fires die out and are extinguished. They slumber in the convent and are deadened, but at the first breath of air they can come alive. Seeing again the man she had passionately loved and who had been the only thought of her life, the Benedictine nun felt her heart again come alive. And while continuing to hold the vows she had taken as indissoluble, she soon knew that they would not be a safeguard against the continuous presence and the plans of the loved being

The situation of the pious creature was strange. Usually a port against the impulses of the senses is found in marriage, which is a form, although less perfect, of chastity. But in this case, marriage only made the sin of the sinner worse and she would have found herself more possible to be forgiven in celibacy.

But this would not at all have been the reckoning of the apostate monk.

Not limiting their attacks to the sovereigns of this world, the Revolutionary Titans aspired to dethrone and suppress the Supreme Intelligence and re-establish it by a decree. In their eyes, therefore, nothing was more precious and more commendable than a priest taking off the cassock and denying its sacred nature by a civil marriage. Wasn't that, in fact, loudly and publicly to untie on the earth what had been tied in Heaven? To put into the civil contract the disputed indissolubility of the religious contract, wasn't that in some way to replace God by the municipal administrator?

Nevertheless, another possible refinement was found to this high degree of Revolutionary perfection. The union of a monk with a nun constituted a new and more striking variety of apostasy that might be called in some way a double flower, and going back to Martin Luther was very much in fashion during that time.

Now, when the ex-Dominican had at hand the opportunity to graft himself to a Benedictine nun, how could he refuse the temptation of a scandal that was a splendid certificate for himself of civic responsibility? And shouldn't he do everything in order to triumph over those importunate scruples which would have fought against this precious result?

Mademoiselle Boisbrunet, however, fought, but having always loved her lover more than God, gave her hand to a union that she regarded as nothing less than sacrilege. It could even be said that this prodigious sacrifice was courage for her, since by doing so she did not doubt that she would thereby lose her soul. And she traded, for several years on the earth with the one who had her heart, an eternity of expiation with which she believed she was menaced in another life.

Nevertheless, on the road to this marriage about to be concluded, an obstacle presented itself. When he returned to France, Hulet had not attempted reconciliation with his father. He knew very well that there existed no point of contact between their political feelings. Not that Hulet senior had been hostile to the Revolution from the first moment. Far from that, like a great many honest and lofty beings, he had greeted the first days of 1789 with enthusiasm. And for himself in particular he had hoped for emancipation and liberty.

His conscience deeply tormented by what he called the ignominy of his hidden functions, he was pleased to believe that in the middle of an immense reaction against the past the shady police institution to which he felt riveted would be destroyed. His heart had been comforted on hearing the beautiful speeches of Mirabeau[65] declaring that the first duty of a free people is to respect family secrets and the sanctity of private correspondence.

But he wasn't long in learning, the good and naïve old man, that, in order to lead the great social troop, young and old shepherds always believe they need the dog and the shepherd's hook. Rarely do all these shepherds of men give up the instruments, however strange they may be, that they find in the arsenal of those who came before them. The National Assembly had platonically decided that "the basis for politics must always be healthy morality." That didn't prevent the old head of the "hackers" after he had read the correspondence of M. de Choiseul and of Mademoiselle de Pompadour[66] from doing the same for the Commune of Paris and of the Jacobins.[67] Only there was a difference that could be seen with the new masters. In the past the secrets revealed by the Secret Bureau risked a turn in the Bastille for the imprudent chatter. But with the terrible levelers of 1793, in such cases he must expect to pay with his head. Now, having become the all-seeing eye of the executioner, made the old man's heart revolt.

---

[65] Honoré-Gabriel de Riqueti, Comte de Mirabeau (1749-1791), leader in the early stages of the French Revolution, President of the National Assembly, a moderate.

[66] Étienne-François de Choiseul (1719-1785), through marriage into the Antoine Crozat family, was important in the administration of the reign of Louis XV. He was, through his alliance with the King's mistress, Madame de Pompadour, the unofficial Minister of the King of France from 1758 until 1770. Together, he and Madame de Pompadour controlled the policies of the King.

[67] The Jacobins were originally devoted to securing a Constitution for France. They were radicalized under Robespierre, author of the Reign of Terror.

His political education done under scandalous, but in essence rather gentle morals, during the regime of the Favorites, he could not now become accustomed to the violent and bloody regime under which he could see very well that he would be condemned to operate. Terrified by the atrocious repercussions that his extracts from conversations might have, he had thought about resigning his functions. But he had encountered two areas of resistance to this projected retirement. First of all, that of the power that, in whatever hands, he did not wish to let disorganize an institution from which he expected excellent service and, next, that of his colleagues who unsealed correspondence who would have feared the indiscretions of a colleague having ceased to work as one of them. He was therefore forced to remain, as he had said, in the mire that now threatened to become formed of blood. And the only way he could find to achieve a little rest for his conscience was risking from time to time a virtuous lie and hiding the danger of their indiscretions from some imprudent people by not making either an exact or complete notation.

On the other hand, Hulet senior had become still more hostile to the ideas of the time. Not having found any consolation for the existence of which he was ashamed more efficacious than that of religion, he was a sincerely pious man. He therefore saw with horror and terror the impious saturnalia of the new regime. So, when learning, almost at the same time, the return of his son to France, his apostasy, and his projected marriage, he saw him about to shut off any way to repentance by the engagement he was going to make. Rushing to the imprudent man, he urged him to stop on the edge of the abyss, begged him on his knees and with tears. And as he found him determined, nevertheless, to go ahead, he was on the point of launching the fire of paternal excommunication. However, he did nothing, because he had long thought that there was curse enough in his family. He went away saddened and stopped seeing this son, who was the culmination of his humiliation and his sorrows. He let him follow the course of his revolutionary fortune far from him,

That course was in fact rapid. By the numerous and striking sacrifices he had made to the dominant ideas, married and soon to be a father of a family, Hulet, the son, gave a high idea of his civic sentiments. And with the help of some of the leaders of the time, he managed to get himself elected to the Convention.

However, the attempt of the former Advent preacher to make himself stand out in that terrible Assembly did not succeed. His speech, which in the past had enthralled the ladies of the Court, didn't carry far enough or transmit enough hysteria to reach the pitch of the great popular pandemonium. He therefore didn't give his father any new worries by obtaining for his political existence the resounding and illustrious showing of which he had at first dreamed.

But the day that Louis XVI was going to be arrested, the most obscure of the votes had the importance and the weight of the most powerful speech. It was clear that at this moment the Revolution was going to take direction. Saving the illustrious accused man, whose life was at risk, would give great encouragement to the manifestation of moderate ideas. On the contrary, his head rolling on the scaffold, must give the tigers a taste of blood. And from that point one must expect to see liberal fanaticism carried to the last excess. In that alternative between two futures, a simple majority could tip the balance. And it can be understood without any trouble that Hulet, the father, had come to make his son decide in the direction of his own opinions and sympathies. But he had a still more personal and more immediate reason to want to influence his vote. He therefore said to the Member of the Convention:

"Hulet, I must talk with you."

"Father, I will listen to you," Henri Hulet answered, "but before anything else, let me say that I rejoice to see you again seated at my humble hearth."

"Don't misunderstand me," the old man replied. "What I condemned, I condemn, and you are not at all seeing me here seeking reconciliation."

"Sir," Madame Hulet then said, "if we are guilty, God has undoubtedly thought that in the exceptional misfortunes of our lives, there could perhaps be an excuse for us. He didn't damn our marriage... Look at the beautiful offspring that he sent to your name!"

And saying this, she presented Hulet senior his grandson that she was nursing just as he entered.

"Time will tell, if we should rejoice at the birth of that child," the old man answered gravely. "In any case, I'm also thinking about his future when I come to warn Louis XVI's judge to consider well the sentence that he is going to pronounce."

"Oh! Father, if you will allow me to call you that," Victoire hastened to answer, "I believe I understand what you're thinking, which is also my thought. Since the beginning of this terrible trial, Hulet has forbidden me to trouble his conscience by what he calls the words of women. But if your venerable mouth also comes to preach clemency, may your word be blessed!"

"Father," Hulet the younger said, to cut short any explanation, "for a long time there has been a profound disagreement between us relative to the conduct of things of the present time. At the moment you come to me, I have made my decision. I have examined my conscience, and nothing can change my resolution."

"So, unfortunate man! Peacefully, and with your conscience believing it a duty and a right, you are prepared to dip your hands in the blood of your King?"

"He hasn't said that, Father!" Madame Hulet quickly exclaimed.

"Be quiet, Victoire!" said the member of the Convention. "I will not deny my vote either before or after. The Convention has unanimously declared Louis Capet guilty of conspiracy against the public liberty and of an attack against general security. As a legislator and as a judge, my opinion is that he has merited the sentence of traitors."

"And you! Traitor to your God and to all of your vows,"

the old man interrupted violently, who, however, had promised himself to be more moderate.

"Sir, spare me the injustice and bitterness of your reproaches. Our point of view is not the same. You can be wounding, injurious, but doing so you will not have more chance of modifying my resolution."

"You are right, son," replied Hulet the elder. "I let myself be carried further than I wished. It was neither with the legislator nor the judge that I wished to discuss. I wanted only to speak to the man. Tell me, do you love your wife and your child?"

"Oh! Yes, Father, he loves us!" Madame Hulet hurried to answer. "And right until now, no matter what your caution has foreseen, our union has been happy. Only your blessing has been lacking."

"Well, if this happiness continues," the old man replied, seeming doubtful, "surely the method to procure its duration is not to change opinions about the curse that has hung over our name for more than a century."

"Father," Hulet the younger quickly answered, "for almost fifteen years you've held a terrible secret menace suspended over my head. That menace has dominated the conduct of my existence in the most terrible way. Either don't mention it to me again, or tell me the secret of that enigma, if you claim that it has something to do with my conscience or my will."

"No more today than yesterday, do I have the right to make you touch our wound with your finger. Know only that it was with a stream of royal blood, having like that of Christ gushed out on the murderer and his descendants, that the curse entered into our house."

"Speak more clearly, I beg you," said the member of the Convention that the partial revelation had seemed to move. "I can then stifle the voice of my conscience under such a horrible secret."

"What else I can reveal to you," continued Hulet, the elder, "is that after having, like the one who spilled that blood, led a sad and blighted existence, each of the first-born of our race has ended miserably and by a violent death. Now that you see the luck of that destiny, do you want to accrue it for yourself and your son?"

"But you, Father, you were the eldest of the family and that curse you speak of hasn't hung over you. Your life has probably been obscure and with few privileges, but I have seen you surrounded by everyone's respect, enjoying an honorable standard of living and defending yourself rather against the caresses of fortune than against its severities.

"And my personal torture!" old Hulet quickly answered. "You've seen it. And haven't I been a fortunate father when I was constrained to impose a situation on you for which you were not born, and which one day might lead you to deny your God. And he has told you the end this God has reserved for us?"

"No, I don't know what the future holds for me, but I know my duty, and should superstition try to turn aside my vote, cause me, in fact, some serious peril, I am a judge and a legislator…"

"Ah! My love, don't go on!" exclaimed Madame Hulet, throwing herself into her husband's arms. "Your father cannot wish to deceive you. Besides, I too feel instinctively that it must be a terrible thing to gamble with the life of kings."

"Kings," replied Hulet, the son, "have but one privilege more than other men. That is to be able to do more evil and to be wickeder than other men."

"Woman! Then I pity you and your son," the old man said with frightening solemnity. "This one, I can see by his blasphemies, is the most damned of all our race. God, that he has foresworn, has marked him in particular with a fatal stamp."

And having thus spoken, he stood up and took several steps toward the door.

As Madame Hulet was trying to restrain him and beg him to retract his horrible horoscope, Hulet, the son, said in a tone of cold impatience:

"That's enough, Victoire. That's all right."

Then with an air of pretended respect, but without adding a word, he conducted his father to the door of the apartment. Once alone with his wife, he would not allow her to try to change his determination by another word.

Fifteen minutes later he entered the Hall of the Convention. The third vote had already begun. By the dim light which scarcely illuminated that doleful scene, the members of the feared Tribunal looked like so many phantoms as they followed each other to the Tribune. And in the middle of a solemn silence their votes could be heard. Timid consciences or implacable enemies of royalty were mixed throughout, some judges believing they should give a reason for their sentence. Hulet was not one of those. When his name was called, he, the thirty-second among the ecclesiastics seated in the Assembly, walked across the Hall with a firm step, mounted the steps of the Tribunal, and with a strong, firm voice said:

"Death." Then, as if to defy his father's menace, he answered in advance of another appeal which had to follow:

"Death," he said again, "and without reprieve."

V. Solitary Inhabitants of the Forest

Some leagues from Chartres, toward Vendôme, there extends a vast area of trees called the Orgères Forest. In 1796, on the edge of that forest, there was an elegant hunting lodge, part of a château situated some distance from the hunting lodge. It, as well as the manor house, had been put up for national sale and bought in a separate lot.

That small dwelling, to which the new owners had added the land needed to plant a small garden, was occupied in the autumn of 1794 by a family that lived there in great isolation. In the countryside that family was known as Vandel. But we can now tell our readers the Hulets were hidden under that name.

In the interval that followed the death of Louis XVI,

right up to the period when we find these new guests established at Orgères, a terrible event had again come to darken their horizon. The sad prophesies of the former head of the Secret Bureau were beginning to become terrible realities.

In spite of the sensation of his regicide vote, Hulet, the son, had never managed to break through the obscurity in which his political life was engraved. He was not made a part of any committee, was never given any exterior assignment. In short, that power of which he had such great aspirations had not come to him at all.

Nevertheless, he had not enjoyed the benefits of that anonymity very long.

Obliged to be the "correspondence opener" for the Terror, Hulet, the elder, was more than ever horrified by his inquisitorial functions. Because he increased the number of deletions he made from the correspondence of honest disloyal citizens, which gave him a little rest for his conscience, he had incurred the wrath of Robespierre.[68] That meant incarceration and soon after, undoubtedly, the scaffold.

Seeing his father's life threatened, Hulet had not acted like Brutus[69] to deny family sentiments. After many strong attempts, without obtaining the release of the prisoner, he had at least managed to delay the moment of his appearance before the Revolutionary Tribunal. But this filial devotion had done

---

[68] Maximilien-François-Marie-Isidore de Robespierre (1758-1794), Member of the Estates General, the Committee of Public Safety, President of the National Convention, and Member of the Jacobin Club. Accused of Danton's death, his group was outlawed. Taking refuge at the Hôtel de Ville, he tried to commit suicide, but his was unsuccessful. He was executed on July 28, 1794.

[69] Marcus Junius Brutus (85 BC-42 BC) Roman politician and Senator, one of the assassins of Julius Caesar. Plutarch in his *Life of Brutus* reports that Brutus was born about the time of Caesar's affair with Servilla Caepionis, and thus was rumored to have been his son.

much damage to his reputation for civic duty. He could easily have been suspected of what could be called filiantisme and négociantisme, and modernisme, the only crimes of that period, that of being a merchant or moderate.[70]

The individual interest that it had in stopping the effusion of blood had little by little thrown the Convention toward the mounting side of those who wanted to stop the daily hecatombs of the guillotine. It had at last found itself near the position of Danton, or as the painters say, in the second style of Danton, proposing to abolish the Regime of Terror and to institute a "Clemency Committee." Hulet didn't at all have the honor of being part of the events of 16 Germinal[71]) in outlawing of the spirited Tribunal, which in the great spectacle of his death would at least have found expiation for his life. But shortly afterward, reserved for an isolated and less brilliant end, he was taken to the Luxembourg prison, where he joined his father, whose execution he had managed until them to stay.

The old man was not ungrateful for this filial devotion.

One evening, exactly two days before the 9th Thermidor,[72] Hulet, the member of the Convention, was called to appear before the Revolutionary Tribunal, and it is almost unnecessary to say, he left it condemned.

His father did not know of this fatal denouement. Taken out from the prison that morning, he had been turned over to the Committee of Public Welfare and was employed all day deciphering decoded correspondence. Taken back rather late to

---

[70] Refers to the Federalists' revolt against the Convention in Provincial France, June to December 1793.

[71] As per the Revolutionary Calendar as revised during the French Revolution to correct the inaccuracies of the Gregorian Calendar: March 21-22 until April 19-20, the seventh month.

[72] July 27, 1794, which ended the bloodiest excesses of the early period of the Revolution. A revolt against the Reign of Terror, began with a vote to execute Robespierre and his followers.

prison, he went to bed without being told anything about the death sentence given Henri Hulet. The next day, in order to spare the feelings of the old man, to leave him ignorant of the Revolutionary Tribunal judgment, it was only at the time of the *fournée* [73] and a little before the executioner came to collect his daily pittance that the condemned man told his father about their imminent separation. And after some touching farewells, he left him for a moment to pick up a letter and some souvenirs he wanted to give him for his family.

In that short interval, death, in the form of a registrar, appeared to harvest from the courtyard where the prisoners were then gathered, and a turnkey began to call the names of those to be carried out that day. Henri Hulet not being there, his old father had a heroic inspiration. He thought that he was almost at the end of his career, that on the contrary, in the strength of age, his son left after him a wife and child, that his son needed time to be reconciled to God and to expiate his sins. And, after all, he was his son. He took advantage then of the great carelessness that had for a long time characterized the calling out of the victims' names. Those who drew up the names for the guillotine were so blasé about their daily duty that they had come to use no other identity than that of the number when assembling their human cattle. And what did it matter if it was a father or a son, if the total was correct?

Completing his substitution successfully, the former director of the Secret Bureau went, therefore, as he had predicted, to terminate his career in a violent way.

An instant later, when the real prisoner named for death that day protested against the misunderstanding, the jailer, refusing to open the door, told him to shut up, that he was an imbecile, that the death cart was leaving, that he therefore had nothing to gain for his father, while he did have, if he insisted, his own head to lose.

Not having been able to make himself heard that day, the next day Hulet, the son, certainly hoped to make restitution for

---

[73] A list of those who were to be executed that day.

the death that had been snatched from him. But the next day, the Revolution of the 9th Thermidor was over, and Providence, which probably reserved him for another destiny, wanted him to gather all of the benefits of the paternal devotion.

Returned to freedom and to his family, he didn't want to take his seat at the Convention again, nothing was more antipathetic to his powerful instincts of control than the anarchistic disorder that characterized that bloody usurpation of all sovereignty. Doing as his wife wished, he left Paris. By means of his inheritance from his father that he had managed to have restored to him, he had a small income. He bought the little piece of property where we find him established. There he waited for the end of the public troubles and, following the principles of the wise man, to be twice as careful in times of revolution, he disappeared from sight; he hid his life.

In that tranquil retreat anyone other than Hulet would have been able to find happiness. But he did not. In the former Convention member's present existence, calm was on the surface. How could it be the same for the interior man who had an account in the past so burdened and so bitter? God, King, father were for him so many poignant memories, and at the price of that battle against all the powers, what had he gained! He had not managed to make himself a place any more in the moral State than in the society of a State in infancy and crisis. In this regard, that family curse, the secret of which the old Hulet had carried with him, wasn't it becoming a very sad reality? If it was true that it had pressed down on him from his birth, to Malta, in his religious functions, to Paris, in his apostasy, to the Convention in his regicide vote, had he not contributed even more to exasperate that occult and threatening force? And, following the paternal predictions wasn't it a very frightening catastrophe that he must believe was reserved for him?

Such, however, are the relief and the consolations that even the most outcast existences can find in taking refuge in nature that after a few years under the tranquil shadows of the trees of the Orgères forest, the unhappy man had obtained, if not absolute peace for his conscience, at least slumber from its terrors and, little by little, dullness of its remorse. It must be said also that in his life's companion he had found a great deal of strength and help. Having as he, her worm eating away at her heart, never, in his presence, had Madame Hulet let it be known that she had regrets for the violation of her monastic vows. However, that pious creature had never let a single day pass without asking Heaven's forgiveness for her having preferred earth with its fleeting and contentious joys. But in motherhood, which is also a religion, she had created a sanctuary where she took refuge against the terrors of the future and the remorse of the past. Gentle, devoted, with a calm personality, even knowing how, if need be, to give the semblance of gaiety, even managing at the same time to communicate it, she was for her husband like the angel of repentance which God permits to console the crime without prejudging the terrible day of the last judgment and the expiation.

For such a sad predestination, was an increase in the family fortunate or unfortunate? Still the fact was that, since their stay at Orgères, Madame Hulet had become a mother for a second time. Three years later, she had given a brother to the son born in 1792. As she did her first son, she nursed him herself. Sixteen at the time she entered the Benedictines in 1771, Madame Hulet was almost forty-years-old in 1795, the date of the birth of her second son. It's impossible to tell the happiness of a mother with these late births, which are like flowers in autumn, opening to the sun during the last beautiful days. Therefore, that tender mother devoted herself to the duties of her last fruitfulness with a kind of passion. At the same time, and probably under the influence of that happy family event, she had the joy of seeing her husband get the better of his dark mood and break away from his somber memories.

Having begun to distract himself by reading books he had always been curious about, the ex-Convention member developed a distinct taste for country occupations. Then, in practicing good works in the countryside, he found another powerful remedy for the poignant anxieties that had until then devoured him. In a short while, having become clever in that small amount of common medicine which can be gained by good sense and a little study, he began to visit the sick in his neighborhood. As he had retained, from his life as a priest, the use of consoling words, which are the soul of medicine, he was true providence for many of the sick.

His renown for medical ability and good deeds only increased day by day. It wasn't long before they came from ten leagues away to ask for his care. And no country doctor had a wider clientele than the good M. Vandel, the name he had taken to break with the past and which he had made famous throughout the region. This success could be explained in a rather simple way: he never took payment for his visits and, on the contrary, it was he who often left some money for his sick, without counting the fact that he invariably furnished all the medications free.

However, a cloud darkened the serenity of that existence regenerated by charity. Sinister rumors began to spread through the countryside. There was talk of travelers stopped and robbed in the Orgères forest. Because of that, it lost its reputation as an honest and peaceful forest which it had enjoyed up until then. Soon, in the absence of an immediate and strong repression, that could hardly be expected of a weak government, such as that of the Directorate, which could prevent nothing, the evil spread and grew. Armed robbery was followed by murder; then the criminals made forays outside the forest, where the danger of encountering them had at first been centered. Dwellings situated outside the population center saw themselves invaded and pillaged. And it was then a matter of atrocious treatments practiced on the victims of these depredations when the victims refused to tell where it was supposed that they had hidden their money and valuable possessions.

Finally, the same horrors they had heard talked about,

around that time in France, spread throughout the Chartres countryside. The brigands walked about in bands even in the middle of communities and villages. They came nightly to lay siege to the houses they had marked in advance for pillage. And it was proved that the Chartres area and a part of Vendôme were the prey of a terrible group of Chauffeurs which must have the Orgères forest as their center of operation. But, despite the late activity deployed by the law, set in motion by the clamor of the population, searches in every direction were useless and no trace of the suspected hideout was found.

At first, when the existence of an armed band was beginning to be proven, the Hulet family's worry must have been extreme. By its completely isolated situation just at the entry to the forest, its dwelling more than any other seemed exposed to an approaching visit of the robbers. And what resistance could the ex-member of the Constitution Committee attempt, aided only by his wife and a single servant? To that must be added that in his constant comings and goings, returning sometimes very late in the evening, the visitor of the poor and the sick seemed inevitably destined to some unfortunate encounter, and thus it might be said that in some way he gambled with his life every day.

Nevertheless, either weary of existence and with a secret desire to be delivered from this manner of expiation, or regret to leave the only asylum where, up until then, he had found a little happiness, or, lastly, by natural courage and a belief in a fate which he found useless to try to turn in another direction, Hulet, despite his wife's insistence, refused to leave their residence. It was of no importance that he saw each day the contagion of fear grow around him, to the point that their servant girl did not want to stay under their roof and it was impossible to find someone to replace her. The courageous country doctor, just as in the time of the greatest security of the roads, walked the fields no less when someone came to claim his services. The only modification in his routine was to pay some attention not to be out too late. And that precaution was taken less for his own safely than for his wife's peace of mind, since at sunset, each evening, Madame Hulet, if her husband had not returned, became so upset and worried that her sanity was threatened.

VI. Chauffeurs and Hospitality

However, things were going better than might be expected. Hulet had suffered no incident for having ignored the perils which seemed to surround him. Nothing to worry him had happened on his rounds and soon something would arrive to complete his security. One morning, it was the 18th of July, the day before the day of his patron saint, Henri, as he was getting up, was more than a little surprised to find, implanted in his bedroom door, which was also that of his wife, a dagger, to which a bouquet was attached. A letter accompanied the bouquet itself which Hulet, with the curiosity that can be imagined, opened. Here are its contents:

My Dear Neighbor,

I have learned that Madame Vandal is horribly afraid of me and of my people. She is mistaken, because if we wanted to harm her, the weapon that you will find this morning stuck in the wood of your door without your being aware of how we got into your house, will certainly convince her that we hold your life, as well as that of many others, in our hands. But we do not wish to take it. On the contrary, having learned that you are a useful and charitable man who does much good in the countryside, although not bragging about doing the same, I am writing you this letter to use as a safe-conduct, should you need one. At the same time, for Saint Henri, your patron saint, I ask you to accept these flowers of friendship, cut and arranged with the hands of a very loving woman, I dare say, for you. In faith of what has been said, I have signed:

Rempailleux
Leader of the Chauffeurs and the Invisibles.

149

From my underground palace, the 14th of July 1799 (old style), seeing that I recognize neither the Republican calendar nor the Republic, nor the Directorate, nor the other garbage of these days

Hulet had to reason with his wife a great deal to persuade her that they must see a kind of good luck in that strange adventure. Not wanting to realize that it meant for them almost complete safety in the future, Madame Hulet was only impressed by the frightening idea that her house had been entered by one of the criminals she feared without knowing how they got in.

"But," she answered all the arguments her husband made, "we are no less at the mercy of these criminals, who, even by their letter, show themselves as daring as to be feared. In any case," she continued, "I have a feeling some misfortune will happen to us."

Perhaps, deep down, his ego flattered by the unusual homage his philanthropic actions had merited, Hulet saw things differently. He continued to believe that he should place absolute confidence in the gentlemen criminals, his friends. And, in fact, nothing happened to justify his wife's fears. She herself finally took patiently the situation she had at first so feared.

One evening, at the end of a hot September day, a storm gathered above the Orgères forest. Rain had not yet begun to fall, but long lightning flashes illuminated the tops of the trees and faraway rumbles of thunder seemed menacing voices. Taking advantage of what remained of the pale light, which was about to fade under the heavy battalions of clouds massing in the distance, Hulet was hurrying to reach his dwelling when, a short distance away, on the road that ran through the forest, he saw a carriage with two travelers, a man and his wife. They were in a strange situation. Frightened by the lightning, the horses were refusing to go forward. Instead of trying to force them to do so, the driver too did not want to go any further. He answered the sharp commands from the travelers by saying that the animals had instincts and were wiser than the Christians. Seeing the foreboding weather, they were right to refuse to go at night into a dangerous place that everybody in the countryside knew was infested with robbers.

In the middle of the deep silence over nature at the approach of the battle of the elements, Hulet didn't lose a word of this argument. He agreed with the coachman. Concerned for the travelers in their insistence to continue on their path, he approached the carriage. After having apologized for having interfered in their affairs without being asked, he warned them that the Orgères forest was far from safe. The state of the weather, dangerous for the peaceful traveler, was, on the contrary, for criminals a convenience and marvelous encouragement.

The stranger then answered in a pronounced English accent that he was well aware of the bad reputation of the Orgères forest but he was armed, and in addition had nothing valuable with him. All of his baggage had been put on the stage coach which ran from Chartres to Vendôme and was well guarded.

Hulet had an answer to that, especially the matter of weapons if he intended to use them against dangerous robbers. They were instead a danger, since these men always attacked as a band, and in trying to resist them he almost certainly ran the risk of being killed uselessly. As for the precaution of having with him only objects of little value, that was another serious inconvenience. These terrible robbers always thought there were things hidden, and to find out where, there were no horrible treatments they wouldn't use. Witness to this was the terrible name of Chauffeurs, which they were the first to give themselves.

It was difficult to believe that such solid arguments wouldn't somewhat shake the traveler's confidence. But he objected that he had only a league through the forest to travel before reaching the shelter where he was supposed to stay. If he turned back, there were at least four leagues to travel to the nearest inn, and that over a road that the approaching storm would soon have made impassable.

Acting then in the manner of ancient hospitality:

"Monsieur," Hulet answered, "my house is no more than fifty feet from here. You will find neither opulence nor luxury there, but you will be given a cordial welcome. Will you please accept a shelter there for tonight?"

The husband seemed disposed to answer with a refusal, but his wife was quick to accept, saying to Hulet that if, in taking advantage of his hospitality, she was guilty of an indiscretion, he had only to take it on himself. The frightening picture he painted of the dangers that he believed they were menaced by, had completely upset her and put her beside herself.

As a man who had made his offer with a sincere desire to see it accepted, Hulet hurried to take the horses' bridle and lead them toward his dwelling. Several instants later the door was opened by Madame Hulet.

The carriage driver, who seemed to show so much prudence, was actually a very great coward. While Hulet was going through the interior of the house to open the carriage door to let the vehicle enter, that man began to let out several lamentable cries. When he had entered and was asked what the shouts were about, he claimed he had seen a huge black ghost who had hit him on the shoulder several times. Beatings were not usually the way of the Chauffeurs. Ordinarily they had something more conclusive to offer those they took an interest in. Therefore they could only laugh at the stupid imagination of this coward, and prove to him that he had brushed against a branch which, since he was mounted on a horse, was exactly at the height of his shoulders. However that might be, he wanted to take advantage of the same shelter as the two strangers. But Hulet had no stable for the horses and, in addition, the team could not remain outside all night without the driver getting in trouble with the head of the rental agency.

Hulet was, however, considerate enough to light a lantern and accompany the poor devil to a place in the road far enough away from the forest for a bad encounter to be a great deal less. But what he couldn't save himself from was the disagreement of getting soaked, since, just as they separated, the storm burst out in all its force. The officious and charitable guide came in shortly thereafter, his garments dripping with water.

Hulet was struck with the pleasant family scene presented by the room which had received the visitors, a gracious contrast to the terrible weather reigning outside. While Madame Hulet was laying the table for the supper, with the help of the husband, who absolutely wanted to make himself useful, the female visitor, still young and attractive, had taken care of the second of the children. She was cradling him in her arms, singing a melancholy English ballad, while, already at home with her, the elder one, hiding behind a curtain, was laughing happily. The pleasant stranger pretended not to know where he was. Seeing his guest thus employed in these household activities, Hulet wasn't short of exclamations and he apologized most of all to the attractive lady traveler, who, just arrived, was transformed into a children's governess.

But the lady replied that nothing pleased her more than these maternal cares. Her greatest regret was not to have them for her own and to have seen Heaven until then refuse her that pleasant responsibility.

The supper was soon ready and they sat down, cheered to the sound of the wood crackling in the fireplace, to a table with appetizing, though simple dishes. During the meal, the foreign woman began again to speak about the regrettable sterility of her marriage, avowing that she had a kind of monomania for maternity. To the Hulets she added that she would give ten years of her life to be the mother of a child half as beautiful as the two angels she was looking at.

Madame Hulet was quick to answer that she was far from being beyond the age of child-bearing. She tried to persuade her that someday, like that other Sarah,[74] her ardent

---

[74] Reference to Abraham's beautiful wife (and half-sister), who remained barren (childless) for a long time.

wish would be granted. But the husband answered that all hope was almost lost for them.

The storm had almost ended at the same time as the supper, however. Madame Hulet, after a moment's absence, came to tell her guests that their room was ready and at their disposal whenever they were ready to retire.

But the foreign woman insisted absolutely on helping to put the children to bed.

During the absence of the two women, the two men talked politics a little. Until that moment Hulet had taken his guests for English, given their accent, and he was astonished to see them freely traveling in France at a time when their government was waging a fierce war against the French Republic. But, by the way the stranger spoke about Washington and the United States Constitution, Hulet came to understand that he was dealing with an American. And then Hulet said to him with a sigh:

"Ah! You have had a revolution also and it was beautiful and pure right up to the end. You didn't stain it with blood, but you had a man to personify it and to lead it. We here had too many drivers for the chariot. We got it stuck and many people perished in that catastrophe."

The women coming back into the room had heard only the end of the conversation and exclaimed: "What catastrophe?"

"We were talking about the French Revolution," the stranger replied.

"Ah!" Madame Hulet then said to Hulet, "Leave that sad subject which always makes you sad. Let's talk instead about the goodness of God who, after the tempest that has just past, has given us this beautiful evening. And going to open a window, she presented the radiant countryside view that their house looked out on. The perspective extended far into the distance, peacefully lit by the moon, while a few rare flashes of lightening were still present on the horizon.

Soon afterward, it was time for all to retire. The strangers were taken to a neat bedroom, where, as much as was possible, all comforts available in the country were present. However, as Madame Hulet was making excuses for not having anything better to offer:

"Do you think so?" the traveler asked. "For people accustomed for a long time to those vile inn bedrooms, this is a palace! And with beautiful white sheets which smell of iris!"

"Yes," Hulet answered, "that's a flower that I always have a lot of in my garden and I suggested to my wife that she put a number of them in the washing water."

Following this housekeeping detail, which we cite here to show to what bucolic preoccupations the ferocious regicide had come, Hulet and his wife retired, saying goodnight to their guests, and some moments later, peace and sleep floated over the household.

VII. The Beginning of the Finger of God

Rather early the next morning Hulet, occupied in his garden, was joined by the American. After a cordially exchanged morning greeting, the American said:

"My dear host, I dare ask you to listen to me for a moment. I would like to talk to you about a certain project. You saw," the citizen of the New World continued, "my wife's great regret at not being a mother. And after, as I told you yesterday, trying all the human and celestial methods, we must consider this misfortune without a remedy and search for some consolation."

"Eh! Does one always know what one desires? And is there not, sometimes, great bitterness in things most ardently wished for?"

"What!" the American quickly answered. "Could that paternity that we envy you be the reason for some worry for you?"

"I don't say so. But who knows the future of these poor little beings that one throws out into the world."

"Perhaps the weight of that care could be lifted from you. I am rich, immensely rich. I enjoy an excellent reputation in business in Boston. As you see, still young, I have retired. For a long time I have considered taking a seat in the American Congress. The husband of an excellent wife, nothing would be lacking to our happiness if God had not afflicted us with the misfortune of not having anyone after us to carry our name."

"So many others," Hulet answered, sadly considering himself, "have regretted being their father's son!"

"I don't think it would ever be that way with the child we adopt. He would be surrounded with care, with tenderness, and we would make him the heir of our great fortune. Now, would you agree to see our choice be that of one of your sons?"

"I can only thank you for your kind thoughts, but I must admit they find me unprepared."

"That's an idea that came to my wife and me almost at the same time, and probably, after such a short acquaintance, it seems strange that I bring up such a personal subject. But according to what I judge to be your economic situation, you have a modest income. And, considering this, supposing that one of your children should become ours, with chances for the most fortunate future, he would have trouble ending up where he would begin with you."

"Would it be the elder that you would like to make your heir?" asked Hulet, seeming to see beyond where that question might lead.

"The elder would be a sadder separation for you," the American answered. "But on the other hand, the younger, still nursing, has more need of maternal care that no affection, you must admit, would ever replace."

"Then it would be the elder that would leave his family to pass into yours," Hulet answered, "if such a sacrifice could be decided on."

"Obviously, for the parents that's a painful separation, but that separation would take place sooner or later! Your son would probably leave you when it was time for his education, and if not for college, assuredly for a career. Well! Consider this! We are offering it to you ready made. In a few years, when our child is firmly attached to us so blood ties need not be feared, what would keep us from being reunited, either if we come to live in France or you come to join us and establish yourself in the United States?"

"Oh, no," Hulet said quickly. "If we agreed to let our child leave, it would be, as you say, in the interest of his happiness and future, and then our sacrifice would be complete. It would be good that he lose even the memory of his other family. This sharing, this being torn between two sets of parents, could only be the source of sad emotions for him."

"You are perhaps pushing things a little to the extreme," the American, who couldn't understand in what sense Hulet had spoken, replied. "Your wife, like mine, would not agree to, I'm sure, that necessity that appears to you, of an absolute separation."

The distinction of the United States citizen was prodigiously naïve, as if, for a mother, there was a relative manner to be separated from her child, as if she could endure that another woman take the place beside her, and with the same title, a part of the place that she occupied in the heart of the one to whom she had given life.

"My dear," she said to her husband, as if she expected to see him carried away by indignation, "don't forget that the gentleman is our guest! The proposition made to us is mad, no doubt, and almost insulting, but however strange it may be, take it, as I have done, calmly and with control."

"Monsieur," Hulet said to the American, who seemed to be trying to explain to the weeping mother, "will you please allow me to talk to my wife alone for a moment?"

As soon as the two spouses could have a private conversation:

"Dear Victoire," the ex-Convention member said, "you know how I love our children, but, exactly because of that pure affection, I wonder if the proposal of these strangers is not providential and if it should be rejected straight off."

"What! Separate me from Alexis! Turn him over to strangers!" Madame Hulet cried out.

"Calm yourself," the husband continued. "Think of my father's terrible prediction that, in his case, was only too realized. In our family, he told us, the first born would be unfortunate."

"He told you that, and you didn't want to believe him. And you were right. What misfortune could happen to my Alexis while I am there to watch over him?"

"I too love him and watch over him, but the atmosphere around our family, alas! it's only too true, is evil. And if God, however, wants to take that child away from a cruel existence, is it for us to stand in the way of his kindly plans by turning down an overture that is perhaps made to us to save him?"

"No, if God wished to strike him down, he would do it in the arms of his mother."

"No, for to be his mother is perhaps already a crime before the justice on high."

"Oh! Mon Dieu! Mon Dieu," Madame Hulet wept in utter despair. "You want to give away our child!"

It was a terrible argument that had just been thrown at her.

"No, you are wrong, I don't want to give our child away, but if that curse that, it's said, hovers over our race, must reach that unfortunate child, wouldn't it be better that that happen far from us? To wish him, all of our life, happy in some corner of the world, wouldn't that be better than to witness the lamentable end with which he is perhaps menaced?"

"But that end, who indeed has foreseen it for him? Aren't we happy and at peace here? And in what way does Heaven seem to be irritated with us?"

"Yesterday morning the Sun rose radiant and in the evening the storm broke out."

"Yes, but an hour later the sky was clear again and now see the state of the flowers and the grass. Doesn't it seem that all of nature is joyous? My Love, don't doubt Providence. The evil foreseen is far away and unknown. What is offered to us now as a blessing is a terrible heartbreak. The very idea is dreadful to me! If our Alexis is destined to undergo cruel experiences, that's all the more reason that he can at least have time to know happiness with us!"

Hulet walked up and down for some time without answering, like a man undergoing a violent interior combat. Finally, going to his wife and taking her hands,

"Listen, Victoire," he said to her, "in order to carry through certain sacrifices, even when reason tells him they are necessary, a father's heart needs support and encouragement. Think about it well before answering. Sending our child away may be his salvation."

"A mother, asked to give up her son, doesn't know anything about calculating and thinking. Take my life if it's necessary, but don't tell me to be separated from my dear Alexis. I don't have that courage, I never will have."

"Let it be as you say, then. I will tell these strangers that we don't accept their proposition. Let God's will be done."

"Thank you, Thank you," the mother said overcome with joy, and throwing herself in her husband's arms. "You'll see. Our love will shelter him so well that misfortune will never reach him."

Just then they heard the sound of horses at the door of the house. It was the carriage the American had ordered through the driver the day before, intending to set out again the next morning. While the vehicle was being loaded, the stranger and his wife rejoined the Hulet couple, in a great hurry to learn their decision. When they heard the negative reply, the travelers did not want to take that answer as definitive. Asking the parents of the little Alexis to reconsider, they talked of coming back in some days to see the outcome of their reflections.

But this time, Madame Hulet, in an impatient voice, answered that a longer delay would be futile and a waste of their time. As for the two strangers, they were people who thought they were making a most attractive proposition. They saw themselves thus turned down out of hand, obstacles thus placed in the way of their fantasies, a situation to which, in general, with their opulence, they were little accustomed, at least in situations that depended on men. Nevertheless, they tried as well as they could not to let certain bitterness in their disappointment show. But they refused to dine before getting in the carriage, and hastening the preparations for their departure, they were on the road sooner than they had planned. So they separated rather coldly and with little cordiality.

As soon as the tempters were out of earshot, Madame Hulet, who had accompanied them to the door, ran to her children and hugged them with unaccustomed effusions of maternal tenderness, the older one most of all. She seemed to be taking possession of him and giving him birth a second time.

Still under the effects of the emotion she had undergone, she begged Hulet to stay with her the whole day. She seemed to need to reassure herself, to see all the objects of her affection surround her.

Two hours later, her maternal feelings and her resistance were justified. The man who had left carrying the two travelers returned, knocking at the hospitable house with news of them. But what news! Mon Dieu! Attacked in an ambush in full daylight by the brigands, the vehicle had been dragged into the deepest part of the woods, where, apparently, the unfortunate strangers had been slaughtered. As for the man who recounted those terrible details, he escaped as by a miracle and was still shaking with terror, so much so that it was impossible for him to add any other details regarding what had happened.

"Well, was I wrong?" Madame Hulet asked her husband. "And just think, our Alexis could have been with those unfortunate people!"

Hulet couldn't deny that it seemed a clear act of destiny. He wondered if the good deeds in his life had not finally turned aside the chalice that his father had said so many times was near his lips.

Begun in sadness, that day was for those poor people one of the happiest they had known in a long time. In addition, Madame Hulet was given a great consolation. From the time he had begun to be associated with the Revolutionary orgy, either because of disbelief, or because of the shame and logic of his apostasy, the secularized Dominican no longer prayed. And it was only in hiding it from him that his wife, morning and night, raised her soul to God. That day, shortly before retiring for the night:

"My love," she said to her husband, "when Sovereign Goodness has been revealed to us in so striking a manner, do we not owe some expression of thanks?"

"I was thinking that," Hulet replied. "Yes! When Robespierre himself was led to recognize a Supreme Being, His existence has been proven a million times."

Then, not making his return half way, he went to get a book of the Gospels. And read with devotion the parable of the return of the prodigal son. And then, kneeling with his wife, he asked God for his protection, for their first night of hope and reconciliation.

God didn't grant that prayer, because just at daybreak Hulet awoke with a great cry. His wife, searching in the dim light of the apartment for the cause of the terrible cry, saw that the entire body of the unfortunate man was bathed in cold sweat and that he was trembling.

"My God! My love, what's wrong with you?" asked Madame Hulet, frightened.

"It's nothing," Hulet answered. "It was only a dream, but what a horrible vision! I saw pass before me a hideous, terrible procession, all those that the Revolutionary scaffold had devoured. They all were headless and carried a human head in their hands, but none of those in the procession carried his own. Young women carried the head of a white-haired old man, and old men the beautiful heads of young women with long blond tresses that were dripping with blood. Among these ghosts I saw my father and another, the most illustrious among all these victims. They had made a horrible exchange with each other. And when my father passed in front of me, presenting me with the head of Louis Capet, 'Alexis should have been allowed to leave,' he told me. 'That was his

161

salvation.'"

"But, my love," Madame Hulet said quickly, "you know this dream was only terrible nonsense. Letting our son leave would have been his loss, because he would right now be in the hands of the Orgères outlaws, unless they had assassinated him without pity."

"Eh! Hulet answered in a somber voice. "To die young, when one is destined to a cruel and bitter life, is a blessing."

"Henri, I beg of you, don't say these hopeless words, that bring misfortune with them. Look, go instead and hug our little Victor who left his nurse very happy last night and ask yourself if, even knowing about the most cruel future, you could be separated from him with indifference."

Saying this, Madame Hulet reached out her arm to the cradle in which the child was sleeping, placed within her reach. But suddenly in a tone of extreme worry:

"Oh, my God!" she cried out. And she jumped out of bed.

"Now what's wrong with you?" Hulet asked.

"Oh! My God! My God!" the poor woman repeated in a more and more hysterical voice.

"But what's wrong?" her husband asked, getting to his feet. And while Madame Hulet was trying to find some light, he tapped inside the cradle and no longer found his son. But less distraught nevertheless than his wife he managed to pull out tinder from the fire and turning back to the little bed, which was definitely empty, in the place of his second son, who had disappeared, he found a large letter sealed with black wax which read:

My Dear Neighbor,

We can live on friendly terms. And I have taken the first steps in order to spare you any uneasiness and even to wish you a happy birthday. Why did you not follow my instructions better? What brought about that madness of stopping travelers on the highway to deprive me of the pleasure of meeting them? Why take away from my business in that way and use thoughtless words about us, calling us "criminals?" And don't deny it! Because I know everything. For the first thing, we'll let that pass. You'll pay for it with one of your children, and you won't see him again very soon, you can count on it. For the next indiscretion the penalty will be greater and that will be the turn of the elder son. If you like, it will then be your wife's turn and finally yours, and you will all be sent to join the nice strangers, your protégés, that we caught so easily the next day. This will prove to you, my dear neighbor, that you would do well to hold your tongue and not run up against

Rempailleux
Leader of the Chauffeurs and the Invisibles.

Not able to accept the idea that her child was in the hands of the brigands, Madame Hulet tried to persuade herself that her guests of the evening before were the authors of the kidnapping ascribed to the people of the forest. But her husband had to contest that consoling thought. The letter was very much in the same handwritings as the one they had previously received. The lack of caution with which he was reproached, he really had committed. The leader of the outlaws, probably hidden behind some bush, had secretly witnessed all that had transpired when he accompanied the visitors to the main road. This supposition was confirmed by the mysterious apparition which had frightened the driver.

"Then there is no God," Madame Hulet cried out, blaspheming. It did not seem possible to her to reconcile the Supreme Goodness and such torture inflicted on the heart of a mother.

"If there is no God," Hulet replied, "there is at least a terrible curse. And here's the beginning; what will be the end?"

VIII. General Finfin

Three years had passed since the sad events narrated in the last chapter. Following that misfortune, the Hulet couple had greatly modified their economic life. Despite the threats, Hulet had nonetheless taken the kidnapping of his child to the Chartres Tribunal. He had even submitted to them the two letters signed by Rempailleux. But that action had produced no result and he thought he could no longer live safely in Orgères. It had seemed to him preferable to live in Paris where one could remain hidden more easily, without counting on the fact that the law was enforced more efficiently there than elsewhere. Needless to say, from the depth of that new retreat he had actively continued his search without any new light shed on the subject. Braving all investigations and all pursuits, the Chauffeurs continued audacious depredations. Their actions were much extended. After having ravaged the Department of Eure-et-Loir, they had infiltrated the Departments of Oise and of Seine-et-Oise, and adventured into the Department of Seine, right up to the doors of the capital, where they began to cause unease and fright.

One evening, as he returned home at nightfall, in the street where he lived, Hulet heard the shouts of three or four of those street hawkers of printed material, which, at the time this story takes place, were, as they are today, one of the major sources of news. Considering the extraordinary energy with which these people were hawking their merchandise, Hulet judged that it must be a question of some interesting news. Listening more closely, he found it was a matter of a great discovery of a band of criminals by means of a young child's presence of mind.

The story was for sale. How much? A sou. And stated that it included the portrait of the author, the portrait of the discoverer, of course, and not that of the writer. Each word of that news story went straight to Hulet's paternal heart. He hurried to buy a copy and rushed to his wife to go over the contents with her. As for the portrait of the author, a father would have been hard put to recognize his son from the horrible bungle of the printer. As for the text of the rag (a technical term), it ran like this:

For a long time, the authorities of the Eure-et-Loir Department have kept an eye on a band of criminals whose hideout was suspected to be in the Orgères Forest, situated not far from the main site of the department. However, despite the vigilance of the magistrates and the work of the National Gendarmerie, only some insignificant arrests have taken place.

The innocence of a young child is the means by which the Supreme Being has wished to reveal that dangerous Association.

Some time ago, two gendarmes were traveling through the Orgères Forest, when one of them thought he saw, in the depth of a thicket, a suspicious object. Dismounting from his horse, he entered the brush. There he saw a very young child, barely covered with rags, who, instead of running away, told him that he was hungry and asked him for bread. Struck by something extraordinary in that child, the gendarme answered that he had no bread to give him, but if he would come with him, he would give him a good dinner.

The child accepted without hesitation. The gendarme put him in the croup of the saddle and they soon came to an inn where the unfortunate little one was amply fed. During the ride, as well as at the meal, the two public law enforcement officers observed him closely, while being amused by his insatiable appetite. They asked him only a few questions, waiting until a good meal had made him more ready to talk. But if he didn't talk while eating, the hungry young one didn't stop moving about. He didn't hide the fact that appropriating everything conveniently near him was the most natural thing in the world. He had taken from the table, and put into his pocket, a place-setting of service utensils, a bottle opener, and he was getting ready to appropriate in the same way a handkerchief and the gloves of one of the gendarmes. Asked then why he was taking all those objects, the child naively replied that it was because he liked them. Summing up the answers to the questions posed to him, it seemed that the unfortunate young child had no concept of "yours" and *"mine." And while practicing it with great ability, he didn't seem to know what the word "rob" meant. Nor did he know the related word "property."*

"And your papa," one of the agents cleverly asked him, "does he also take whatever pleases him?"

"Have no papa," the child answered, "and no mama; there are some that do, but I was found under an oak tree in the forest."

Here, Madame Hulet interrupted her husband's reading, grasping his hand hard:

"Dear love," she said, "there's no doubt. That's our little Victor that those scoundrels have already formed to their way of life. But he has caused them to be discovered, the poor child. There is a God! There is a God!"

Hulet also had conceived some vague hope, but less prompt than his wife to adopt a thought that might be only an illusion, he tried to calm her, and took up again reading the conversation of the gendarmes:

"Are there more little ones there with you?"

"Yes, some little and some big, who are bad as everything; they were beating me to get what I have; so I got away."

"Poor dear," Madame Hulet couldn't help saying, folding her hands.

"But your home," the gendarme asked, "and that of the other children, is it far from here?"

"My home," the child repeated, seeming to attach no meaning to the word.

"Yes, the place where you eat, where you sleep."

"That's not called a home; it's a cave."

"That's what I meant; is it far from here?"

"Yes, it's very far, because it's over there, under the big trees."

166

"And can you take us there?"

"No, I can't. I ran away during the night and I didn't look behind me; they would have really beaten me if they knew I got away."

"And who would have beaten you?"

"Eh! The papas of the others who have big swords and who beat the mammas of the others when they have a reason."

"And those papas and those mammas, you could recognize them?"

"Well, that's something! Would I recognize them?"

"Then listen. You'll have a lot to eat, like today, and what else would you like?"

"Me, I like money."

"Oh, the monsters!" exclaimed Madame Hulet. "Such lessons to that poor child."

"That's good, then" the gendarme said. "It's money then. You'll have some. See, a coin like this one, (he showed the child a two-franc coin) every time you walk with us to show us one of those who lived with you in the cave."

"All right, but I know where you have to go to show you everything at one time."

"And where's that, my little rogue?"

"In the markets and at the fairs where they say they're going to sell a lot of things they carry there. They're the ones who will have money when they come back. Me, I'd like to go to the fairs myself."

Following that conversation, the child was turned over to the authorities. Using the methods already begun, pampered, well nourished, well clothed, within a few days, he was unrecognizable. It was then, accompanied by his two gendarme friends, that he began to frequent the markets and fairs in the area. For every former acquaintance that he encountered, he made an agreed on sign to his two friends and that person was arrested. Very far from growing cold in these investigations, the young informer, having been the object, if he could be believed, of many bad treatments, seemed, on the contrary, to take very great pleasure in the incarceration of the band members. In every hideout where he was taken, he was responsible for many important captures.

The intelligence and the behavior with which he has constantly played his role are admirable and have earned him the title of "General Finfin."

As a result of that precious cooperation, at the end of a few days the authorities had made great strides toward discovering the truth; from a revelation coming from one of the prisoners, they had managed to come right up to the hideout where most of the band had been surprised and put in the hands of justice. The number of those arrested amounted to no less than twelve hundred. The place where they came together was a former quarry in the center of the Orgères Forest. A great part of the stones used to build the ex-Chartres Cathedral came from there. A sort of subterranean colony had formed there where individuals of both sexes lived pell-mell, having their way of life, their police, even their government. That colony, independent of the recruits that it constantly made, forced those it enlisted to undergo terrible tests.

The colony was able to perpetuate itself by taking concubines, and by kidnapping infants who were usually spared in their bloody expeditions, provided they were of an age not to remember their real parents and could be trained in the brigands' way of life. Theft made up the industry of that terrible association. They practiced it with arms over a wide area by means of many pieces of information gathered over great distances from different parts of the territory of the Republic. The noms de guerre of several of those criminals shows the cynicism with which they carried out the perpetration of their crimes. Among those arrested came be noted: François Petit, called Nexel, or the little butcher of the Christians; François Grou, called the Firebrand Warrior of Love, called Oven Baker; Hyancinte Sénéchal, called Toco; Félix-Édouard Dion, called the Priest; Charles Garnier, called little Fatty; Thomas Loutrele, called Cadet Cutty; Jean-

Pierre Aubert, called Thirty-Thousand Devils.

Several individuals of the female sex are also in the hands of the police. The affair is going forward with great activity and will soon be in a state to be submitted to a jury. It is only regrettable that the criminal who hides himself under the name of Rempailleux, and whom the public outcry calls the chief of the band, has been able to avoid all the arrests right up to the present. However, they are on his trail and everything indicates that he will be taken by the justice system with the rest of his accomplices.

IX. Correspondence

Several hours after reading this document, Hulet was on his way to Chartres. Several days later Madame Hulet received this letter:

Dearly beloved,

The hopes I had promised myself not to take too lightly have, in fact, not been realized. As I was telling you, it was hardly probable that our little Victor, who is now only four-years-old, as developed as his intelligence might be supposed, could play the role assumed by the famous General Finfin. And, what's more, let's congratulate ourselves that that child and ours have nothing in common. Through the intermediary of M. the Criminal Prosecutor, who showed us so much interest during the time of our misfortune, I was able to question the little denouncer that they have tried to pass off as another Daniel. With his hideous effrontery face and his red hair, he is at least seven or eight years old. Despite the facts he furnished, which for a moment gained him public sympathy, everything in him denotes a strange development, the most perverse inclinations which have become irresistible upbringing he has received. His instincts toward pillage have not been stifled by the kind treatments showered on him. And if he is so passionate about procuring the arrest of his former family, it is more the result of his feeling of importance and by the natural pleasure he finds in evil than in some good reaction. The future of that unfortunate young boy is henceforth set. He will be either a highway robber, like those with whom he has lived, or a very clever police agent.

I learned nothing from him relative to the one named Rempailleux, about whom I had really tried to get him to talk. He said he had never heard of anyone by that name. Everything leads me to believe that the leader of that band, whose existence, however, cannot be in doubt, exercised an unusual authority over all those people, young and old. No one, in fact, any more than General Finfin, would admit that he is a real person. This is a good tactic to guarantee his safety. And whatever steps the law takes to discover him are thrown off the track. Still true is the fact that right up to the present moment it has been impossible to obtain any information.

As for the miserable little creature, who, by this fact, obeying his command, makes himself an accomplice, I would be inclined to believe that Rempailleux is his father.

However, I am not without some hope of good results from my trip. All the members of the Special Criminal Tribunal show very much sympathy for our misfortune and I am assured in advance that during the gathering of evidence as in the pre-trial, everything about our particular concern will be carefully handled.

Goodbye, Dearly Beloved. I will write again and keep you informed of all my actions. Until then, I send you all the love that you know is yours.

Henri Hulet

Some days later, there was a second letter from Hulet to his wife:

What's to be believed of some discoveries that we have just made? They would be very sad, if they were admitted to be true, but fortunately there is still great obscurity over that abyss of infamy.

A girl named Leturc, arrested with what remains of the band after the police invaded the Orgères cavern, yesterday asked to make some confessions. She started by admitting, as was already suspected, that she was Rempailleux' mistress, proving in this way his existence. She added that, learning, while she was imprisoned. that "her man" escaped to "be nice to another woman, she wanted to make him suffer. She was ready to lead the police to his hideout, if the Criminal Prosecutor would recruit her. As the criminals are very active in relaying false information, bringing about a change of location, thus providing an opportunity to escape, the Criminal Prosecutor, having decided to agree to the Leturc girl's proposition, pressed her for details. He specifically asked her for information regarding the kidnapping of our child, as well as the fate of the strangers who lodged with us, from whom there has been no information after that date. The Leturc girl began to laugh. She finally admitted that she and Rempailleux were the Americans. They were, she said, talented in adopting all sorts of disguises. As for our little Victor, it was at the instigation of that miserable woman, who had always wanted to be a mother that Rempailleux had him kidnapped by a very clever man from Piedmont, who gained entrance via the chimney to commit robberies. In addition, despite all the maternal cares with which she surrounded our child, whom she had chosen in preference to Alexis, as being less of an age to remember and to help in the searches that had to be made for him, she was desolated to see him die in her arms six months ago. His fate would be thereby sadly fixed.

Before becoming a part of the Leturc girl's proposition, the Criminal Prosecutor, in communicating these sad details to me (in which he had very little confidence), wanted me to confront that miserable woman, so as to see if I recognized in her our American woman. If she was telling the truth on this point, he would be more willing to believe her on all the rest.

Once in the presence of the Leturc girl, I couldn't help being struck by a certain resemblance to our stranger. So much more so as she had told the Commissioner that she had visited us wearing a black wig (she herself is blonde). The difference in hair color made me hesitate a great deal in verifying her identity. But in the interval between her first revelations to the Criminal Prosecutor and being interviewed by me, her story had completely changed. She denied having kidnapped our child. She claimed that neither she nor Rempailleux had ever been our guests and swore that she knew nothing about the strangers who had been attacked in the forest. With all this, that shameless liar avoided meeting me. The situation was even less clear than it had ever been.

Finally, two hours ago, the Leturc girl asked to reappear before the Criminal Prosecutor. Entering very excited, she said: "All this bores me; if I don't have the pleasure of arresting him myself, you take him. Rempailleux has to be done away with."

"Here," she added, "take this, since you don't want me to go where he is."

She threw a postmarked letter down on the Magistrate's desk. In it a Piedmont man named Vitluini addressed a love letter to the young woman in custody. To ingratiate himself with her, he told her that Rempailleux was hiding out in Orleans, with a woman he had made his mistress and with whom he was living. He was lodged with her at an inn with the sign reading "Plat-d'Étain" in the Bannier neighborhood. This information seeming valid, the Criminal Prosecutor dispatched a team of agents to arrest the criminal. Me, for my part, with impatience you can imagine, I'm going to get on the road immediately in order to interrogate that man as soon as possible. He is the only one in a position to tell us the fate of our unfortunate child. Good-bye, dearly beloved. I send you tender kisses, and I will write at the least news.

Your very affectionate Tami,

Henri Hulet

It wasn't two days later that a terrible incident excited the city of Chartres. Seized with stomach pains and vomiting after a meal, General Finfin, after a few hours, succumbed to the effects of the most violent poison. At the same time, this letter came to the Criminal Commissioner:

Good Magistrate

You're still a nice fellow. You looked for me in Orleans when I was in Chartres and almost in your pocket, giving to your interesting protégé an interesting bouillon just to teach him discretion. Tell my dear Virginie (the Leturc girl) that I am very happy with the way she played her role and fooled all of you.

And tell her that in a few days I will have managed to get her out. As for you old boy, you can stop searching. I avenged my comrades on their denouncer.

And now, not being able to do anything for them, with or without your permission, I'm immigrating to England to await the end of your government's little shop and happier times. Goodbye, sensitive Magistrate. There are at least fifteen heads that you plan to have the pleasure of getting chopped off, without counting the prisons, the galleys, and other pleasant things, I congratulate you because you probably count on this fat catch to speed up your advancement. But watch out, my little dear, that on my return to France, I don't find you in my path.

A postscript concerning the Hulets was as follows:

You can tell that poor good man who is searching for his child, that it was really me, the American and his wife, and it is also very possible that it was someone else.

Tell him also that the kid who was stolen seemed to me to be dead, just as my Virginie suggested to him in the thirty thousand and one lies which put all of you asleep. I, however, didn't forbid her to suggest that the kid in question was alive.

If you have to write to me, by chance, sensitive Magistrate, address the letter to Monsieur Rempailleux. That will reach me. But in addition, my little lamb, don't fret. Let's take care of our delicate health, as is necessary.

X. A Former Colleague

On his return from Orleans, where we already know that he made a useless trip, Hulet attended the trial of the twelve hundred Chauffeurs, and was even called as a witness. But no additional information came from the testimony. The evening before their court appearance, as Rempailleux had sworn, the Leturc girl disappeared from the prison. Thus, the only person among the accused that could be believed, as to the fate of the unfortunate child, was unavailable to answer the questions posed by the father and the magistrates. What's more, nothing could be learned relative to the American and his wife. The accused impudently denied all the crimes with which they were charged, even those that were more clearly proven than that by which the two strangers had died.

On his return to Paris, Hulet found his wife given over to diverse feelings. If, on the one hand, she was deeply saddened by the loss of all their hopes, on the other hand, an event that her forty-one years made difficult to foresee, seem to have come to compensate for a loss that must henceforth be held irreparable. During her husband's absence, Madame Hulet was certain that for the third time their union was fruitful. Then with that unexpected joy, mingled with sad memories, there was another worry, to know the contents of a letter which had arrived at the Hulet house before his return.

That letter with a bad look (letters have personalities just as individuals) was addressed to Citizen Hulet, aka Vandel, and bore the stamp of the Minister of Police. The former member of the Convention was, then, the object of particular surveillance by the authorities, since they had penetrated his change of name and gotten wind of his incognito.

As a calm wife, accustomed to the most absolute respect of conjugal authority, Madame Hulet, despite her great curiosity to know the contents of that worrisome missive, had not taken it on herself to open it. Opened by Hulet, it carried only this simple invitation: Citizen Hulet is requested to come by the office of the Citizen Minister of Police without delay for a matter which concerns him.

The tenor of the letter known, the ex-Convention Member, was not less intrigued than before the seal was broken. What could the Minister of Police want with him? More than ever, in the middle of his family worries, he had remained a stranger to politics. He was very sure he had not mixed in any business which could merit the suspicious attention of that vigilant power. Besides, since the Revolution of 18 Brumaire,[75] which had just ended, he would have been more inclined to uphold than to hinder the actions of the government.

Loving power a great deal more than liberty, he had been, as has been seen. a revolutionary by ambition and by circumstance. And now he felt a lively sympathy for the personality of the First Counsel, in whom he found all the sympathy of an energetic and powerful director of the public weal. However, some denunciation, as was too common at that time could have been brought up against him, or, a more consoling thought, they could have something to communicate to him relating to his paternal worry. The way to find out was to go where he had been ordered.

He had to believe, as soon as he had spoken to the head of the office, that there was nothing disturbing in his case, because he was greeted with perfect politeness and a few seconds later they had told the Minister of his presence.

Seeing him enter:

"Eh! Good morning, my dear and former colleague," Fouché[76] said to him in the friendliest tone.

The Minister even pushed his affability so far as to draw up a chair for him and ask him to be seated.

---

[75] 18 Brumaire, Year 8, Republican calendar. Successful Coup d'État by Napoleon against the Directoire, thus ending the French Revolution, following three earlier coups.

[76] Joseph Fouché, Duke d'Orante (1758-1820). He organized the National Police and supported Napoléon's Coup d'État; he was called by his enemies an exceptional political animal, a "pure reptile" and a born traitor.

"I'm glad, Citizen Minister," Hulet answered as soon as he was seated, "that you recall our common presence on the Convention benches. That memory will perhaps be for me a promise of indulgence in case, without my knowledge, I have caused some prejudice against my political conduct."

"Who? You, my dear fellow, on the black list? Don't even think about it. I don't know, on all of the Republic's territory, a cleaner and less trouble-making citizen than you. My Word! If everybody resembled you, my Ministry would be the most useless of the sinecures. I pass on finding people in hiding rather slowly. But you, you have played the mole so well that for the last week you have been the despair of my people."

"Since you admit, Citizen Minister, that the taste for obscurity is totally inoffensive, please allow me to see, with some astonishment, the great interest you have wished to take in me."

"And don't I need you! I don't want to discuss with you that life of retirement, where, besides, you have not found happiness, because I now know the cruel family affair that kept you in Chartres. I promise you I will give all my care to the search in which you have failed."

"Considering such kind efforts on my behalf that must give my fatherly heart a great deal of hope, I can only be eager to know, Citizen Minister, in what way my devotion can be useful to you."

"My dear and former colleague," the Minister continued, "in seeing you so deliberately withdraw yourself from the public arena, I must believe that you are not among those who find that our Revolution has been conducted in a way which the far-seeing and judicious would have wished.

"The day Danton climbed up the scaffold I was astonished to find my head still on my shoulders, because, a long time before him I had thought and spoke aloud, saying that the future of liberty was lost by dipping it in blood.

"As for me, I must admit to you that for a long time I was the dupe of certain illusions. Right up to the day I saw a hypocrite without talent, without courage, a Robespierre in fact, aspire to a dictatorship, I thought that we could establish in France a government founded entirely on liberty and equality. To achieve this goal had seemed so beautiful that I did not consider the means."

"Hum! You were terrible phlebotomists!"

"Eh! My friend, the first blood drawn that made that medical practice fashionable was that of the 21st of January, and your opinion was the same as ours. Besides, just as me, you knew in depth one of the two privileged classes that stood in our way. And you knew that the fanatical ancient regime opposed us with frankincense and arms. What did you expect? Every battle energizes the resistance. And at the depth of all my politics there has always been the need and the idea of strong power. Only, I took violence for strength, and today that's an error that you see me come back to."

"As you, Citizen Minister, I believe a strong power, that is to say, only a government, capable before everything of holding back anarchy, can see to the well-being of a State. And because of that if Robespierre had not been a man of blood and I had seen him surrounded with a less hideous luster, I would have been less hostile to his dictatorship. To be successful, Revolutions have always needed to be identified with a man: Cromwell, Washington..."

"Yes," the Minister replied. "That's also my opinion. Someone is needed to take the part of everyone, otherwise the cadaver of the past would be argued about endlessly. It's not even bad that the someone, like Washington or Cromwell, had a saber at his side. That gave weight and authority to his mission. In addition, that's what we have had the good fortune to find in the First Counsel Bonaparte. I believe him, in fact, capable of fulfilling the mandate public confidence has invested in him."

"But my father, or so I was led to believe, was in the Foreign Affairs Department, with modest clerical functions, which don't' seem to me to bring about that particular attention of the Head of Government."

"So much so that you would have no repugnance in accepting some functions under this new government?"

"Frankly, I don't know about that; that's a question to which I have no ready answer."

"So be it! But, nevertheless, I have no doubt of the answer. When a government has just been established, following the terrible crises we have gone through, we must count on the help of all good citizens."

"But, in any case, Citizen Minister, in what sort of public function would you be able to employ me?"

"Oh! On my word! On very delicate matters and with the highest security, I tell you in advance."

"And what would be the output to your department!" asked Hulet, with an intention easy to see through.

"In my department to a certain point," the future Duke d'Otrante answered, "but with this nuance, that you would be the man of the government more than that of a Minister. These aren't functions absolutely administrative, nor purely political. They need a title and I would call them rather... State functions."

"But their title would perhaps define their character?"

"What's more, your father," the Minister continued without responding to the question directly, "fulfilled them with honor, and, you see, although in principle heredity is before anything else, monarchist, my opinion is that, applied to certain duties where it's a guarantee of respect for tradition, it can go very far. It was even that tradition, I must tell you, that decided the First Consul to look in your direction.

"I beg your pardon," the Minister continued, "if I tell you the details which seem to touch very closely the mysteries of private life. Your father, did he confide in you completely? Didn't he keep some secrets from you?"

"Secrets?" Hulet answered with some emotion. "He had one."

"And he never made up his mind to tell it to you?"

"No, despite my eager insistence. But you, Citizen Minister, whose position carries with it knowledge of many hidden things. This secret, would you have known it?"

The Minister then stood up, went to a locked file. Taking out a thick packet bearing the seal of The Republic, one and indivisible. "Here," he said, "are the papers the government found in your father's office at the time of his arrest. You'll find in it great clarity about many circumstances that might interest you. But I can let you look at it only here. If you want to go into the next room, and go over them at your leisure, we'll pick up our conversation after that."

Impatient, as can be well imagined, to see the contents of these mysterious papers, Hulet was already beginning to break the seals.

"No," stopping him, the Minister said, "in a minute, when you are alone."

At the same time he rang for a clerk. The Consul's ministers had already begun to acquire something of imperial etiquette.

"Conduct this gentleman into the blue room," he said, "and be sure he is not interrupted."

The clerk opened the door. Taking leave of him, his former colleague gave him a friendly wave, where there might have been a nuance of protection. A moment later, Hulet entered a room somewhat mediocrely furnished, with light from a single window. It was difficult, at least from that direction, that anything could interrupt him. The window mentioned was covered with a shade that in prison language is called a sack, and in addition was fitted with bars.

Before leaving, the clerk said, "If the Citizen needs anything, there's a call cord in the fireplace corner." Giving that information, he left. A little later, astonished, if not a little disturbed by all these mysterious procedures, Hulet walked on tip-toe across the anti-chamber that preceded the room where he had been taken and went to look through the key hole of the door.

"Ah! Ah!" he exclaimed, noticing that that door, like the doors on public baths, opened only from the outside, "It appears that one doesn't leave here whenever he likes."

When the seal of the envelope was broken, with an eagerness of curiosity that the surrounding precautions were certainly of a nature to elicit, Hulet found a voluminous notebook written in a strong readable hand which he recognized immediately as that of his father. Yellowed on the edges, as happens to papers that have spent some time in clerks' files and in archives, these manuscripts seemed to date back several years. On the first page was written in capital letters: OUR HISTORY AND GENEALOGY.

Later the reader will see the family history unfold before his eyes. The author, by a particular bent of his nature, gave it a more literary than historic form. Right now, while Hulet, the member of the Convention is busy learning about it, we are going to follow the man named Matiphous to London. There we will find that man thrown in the middle of events and characters at least as extraordinary as those that have been seen taking part in the Prologue and the first part of this story.

PART II: GREGORIO MATIPHOUS

I. Where Matiphous Was

In London, where we are now conducting the continuation of our story, in 1799, in two little furnished rooms in a little hotel near the City, separated only by a thin partition, two existences, up until then unknown to each other, seemed to be rushing to their end at the same moment.

On one side it was a man whose health and youth flourished. Despite his European clothes, with his slightly olive complexion, his jade black hair, his wide protruding eyes, and most of all, with the somewhat stern contraction of his mouth, which showed a long range of white teeth, everything in that individual seemed to indicate the Arab.

But considering his myopic expression and his somewhat spindly, not particularly muscular legs, and taking into account other physical characteristics, his nationality could be stated more precisely, because these are two distinctive traits frequently found in travelers from the Island of Malta.

That man, if fact, was from Malta; his name was Gregorio Matiphous.

At the moment of our first encounter with him, he was holding a glass in his hand, in the process of stirring in some unknown horrible mixture with a nauseating and menacing look. In addition, a passionate monologue with which he accompanied these sinister preparations would have finally revealed the meaning. In the clutches of some poignant sorrow, the unhappy man was preparing to ask a refuge in death with what in a moment he was going to drink.

Just as he was going to carry the poison to his lips, a piercing cry rang out from the adjoining roommate. At the same time, from the threshold of the door, a childish voice began to call for help, shouting these pitiable words in French: "Mama! Mama! Ma pauvre Mama!"

The man from Malta, apparently hardened only toward himself, suspended his deadly resolution. He rushed into the room from which the cry of distress had come and hurried to bring assistance to the other sorrow revealed.

His view was at first drawn to a woman, dressed in mourning, leaning backward in an armchair, where she had completely lost consciousness. That woman was still young, and should have been beautiful, but her face showed great ravages of a malady which the fainting spell just suffered seemed to indicate the most dangerous outcome.

As will later be known, Matiphous just happened to possess some medical knowledge. After having reassured a charming ten year-old girl, fallen into terrible despair at the idea that her mother would never wake up again, and with the help of the registrar, who had come running in at the child's cries, and by administering some cordials he managed to revive the sick woman. He did not leave her until he was sure the crisis had passed.

Rousseau was right when stigmatizing suicide, he wrote: *Each time that you are tempted to leave life, say to yourself, "May I still do some good action before dying!" Then go find some indigent to help, some unfortunate person to console, some oppressed person to defend. If that consideration restrains you today, it will restrain you tomorrow, after tomorrow, and your whole life long. If it doesn't restrain you, then die! You are nothing but a wicked man.*

The fact is that, when he returned to his room, the man from Malta was no longer in so very much hurry to end it all. It seemed to him that a feeling of curiosity halted him a moment at the edge of life. He wanted to know who that woman, so abandoned and so unhappy, was. As a result, he locked his poisoned beverage in his armoire and went down to see the receptionist in hopes of obtaining information.

The story of the unfortunate woman, on whom death had already placed its hand, was simple but touching. A girl not of high birth, but remarkably beautiful, somewhat before '89, she married the Marquis de Limeuil and brought on herself the antagonism of a powerful family revolted by that *mésalliance*.

During the time of the Emigration, as much to be a part of the movement drawing the young nobility to the crusade against Revolutionary ideas, as to escape the daily persecution as a result of his marriage, the Marquis had crossed the frontier and gone to serve in Condé's army.[77]

In order not to be separated from her husband, resigned to dangers and privations of all kinds, a mother the first year of her marriage, Madame Limeuil had, nevertheless, followed the Marquis and continued to be a faithful companion to him during all the time that he lived under the flag of the Emigrés. It was only at the time when he found himself condemned to inaction by a dangerous wound that, passing with him over to England, she saw an end to the life of adventure whose fatigues and perils she had wanted to share. A life of sadness and trouble was, for her, the substitute for the excitement of the camps. Struck by an incurable sickness, the Marquis still survived for some time. But reduced, by the sequestration of his property, to the weak assistance the English government allotted to the Emigrants, he soon succumbed in the middle of the torture and poverty which had helped to hasten his end.

Already changed by fatigues and worries, Madame de Limeuil's health was unexpectedly undermined by a last and terrible stomach malady. At the same time, she saw herself struck by the most odious of persecutions. Some of her husband's relatives, emigrants also, were then in London. Continuing to have for the widow the same strong hatred they had for the wife, they were able to portray their unfortunate relative as an adventuress whose marriage had only a doubtful authenticity. The already insufficient subsidies, on which she

---

[77] Louis de Bourbon, Prince of Condé (1621-1686), French general and the most famous representative of the Condé branch of the House of Bourbon. For his military prowess he was renowned as le Grand Condé.

had lived until then, were gradually withdrawn. From that time, the sickness following its course, the worries of poverty, the concern for her daughter's future, the almost total absence of medical help, and, finally, the deprivations of every sort conspired against the unfortunate woman, who, for some time had lived by the charity of her hostess.

Strongly moved by the picture of so much sadness, the man from Malta immediately resolved to continue his charitable help, thinking to put aside for the moment the deadly resolution against himself that he was planning. He went back to his room, put in a purse all the money he had with him, which amounted to about a hundred guineas. Then he presented himself to Madame Limeuil, and without any other preparation he said this to her:

"Since you hardly know me, Madame, I may seem to you a little bizarre. But consider the fact that you are far from being fortunate, and in this foreign country you can't count on any friend. Me, I'm on the point of leaving for a long trip. I have some money at my disposal. With no other condition, will you be my debtor? When we meet again, which will perhaps be a long time from now, you can return that insignificant sum to me. At least I won't leave with the idea that a person of your rank and merit is still in the terrible distress which I just learned about a moment ago."

Following the bad instinct of those of a certain social standing in need, Madame Limeuil first tried to deny her desperate position. But if Matiphous had a good heart, he had a strong hand, and immediately proving to the proud woman that he was perfectly aware of her situation, he put the money he had brought on a piece of furniture. He then wanted to leave, still with his former determination.

"But, sir," the sick woman said to him, calling him back quickly, "that money, I will never return it to you. She added in a low voice so as not to be heard by her daughter. "The person you want to help is a dying woman."

"Probably," the man from Malta answered, "if the situation I find you in continues, your life may be menaced, but with that money you will be in a position to get advice from a knowledgeable doctor. There are still resources open to you, and, believe me, you will live."

"You are mistaken, sir," Madame Limeuil answered. "My life I feel very strongly is coming to an end. In addition, considering what I have suffered, I would bless my approaching end if, in dying, I did not remain racked by a terrible worry."

"In any case, you don't seem to be a great criminal," the man from Malta said gently.

"No, except by marrying my husband against the wishes of his family I don't think I have anything in my life to reproach. And in this I was very excusable. We loved each other desperately and it was neither the will of a father or of a mother that the Marquis disregarded in giving himself to me."

"Well, then, what could disturb your last moments?"

"Eh! Sir," the Marquise said, with some animation. "That unfortunate child that I leave behind me, what will become of her; who will take care of her?"

"Mon Dieu! What you're saying is true," Matiphous answered, without trying to deny the impact of that devastating foresight. And, even going beyond the thought, the mother expressed, he continued: "Still a young girl, and beautiful, and perhaps in a few years exposed all kinds of perils!"

Profoundly worn down, he took a few steps up and down the room. Among the men of the country where he was born, passions, a position taken, good or bad, rapidly explode, which explains the heat of the blood circulating in their veins.

"Listen to me, Madame," the man from Malta said to her: "A while ago I wanted to leave on a long journey, but I can delay it. Better than that, a new interest showing up in my life, might give me the calm and rest I had decided to go look for in a distant place. If it is true, as you think, that Providence is going to take away your life as soon as you think, will you trust your daughter to me? I will act as her father, I promise you."

185

"Sir," the poor mother said, with tears in her eyes, can I believe in the hope you have just offered me?"

"Yes, what I have promised, I will do. And you may perhaps have some confidence in my word when I tell you that the trip I talked about a while ago was that to the next world, where I almost went before you. If I stay behind now, you can know that it is with the feeling that I have taken on duties."

"Oh!, Mon Dieu! You wanted to die, you, with the strength of age and health. You are also to be pitied for having thought about such a fatal resolution."

"I have not had, as do you, Madame, the consolation of being only unfortunate. I have serious faults to reproach myself with. My head doesn't always govern me as well as my heart and I must make you aware of the fact that it is neither a noble protector, nor even a man perfectly worthy of your esteem, who is offering to accept the legacy for which he would be so honored."

"Ah! Monsieur," the Marquise answered with confidence, "charitable hearts can be pardoned many faults! You seem so young! What you call sins may be only the silly behavior of your age."

"No, no, I must not deceive you," the man from Malta replied. "You would not at all be putting your child in to the hands of an honorable gentleman. There are probably many excuses for my follies: the misfortune of my birth, passions as hot as the Sun of the country where I was born, cruel provocations by fate and by men, but that will do as excuses for the heir of a great name. I am a very desirable Governess and you see, Madame, you must accept me as I am, in default of anyone else, and if you don't find another."

"Providence," the Marquise solemnly answered, "would be showing itself very severe toward me, if, deprived of a dear husband and condemned myself to die in the flower of age, I should still have to remain under the terrible motherly anxiety from which you have come to deliver me. I have, in the midst of my bitter trials, never ceased to believe that what God does is right. This isn't deception; it's hope that he sends me in my last hour. Yes, whoever you are, sir, I have faith in you. You will watch over the happiness of the poor orphan with devotion and love. You will be for her everything she has lost."

Here Madame de Limeuil was interrupted by tears and sobs, but a moment later she was able to surmount her emotion and call to her daughter, who was in a corner leafing through a picture book.

"Diane," she said, pointing out Matiphous, "do you see this gentleman?"

"Yes, Mama, and I like him a lot, because he made you wake up when I thought you would never wake up again."

"Well!" the mother continued, "if it should happen that I go to sleep again, for a longer time, you must always love him very much, obey him very much, be very much grateful to him, because he is the one who will take my place."

"That will be like Papa?" the child asked with an unusual mixture of naiveté and logic, so striking in young minds.

"Yes, you have said so, yes, I will be your father," Matiphous said, embracing her effusively. Then, as if carried away by the force of his emotion, he threw himself on his knees before the Marquise, and had Diane do the same.

"Your blessing, Madame, on me and on your child. Bless us now on the earth before blessing us from Heaven."

At that moment Madame Limeuil no longer had a doubt: the man who had just made this pious movement was certainly the protector that she had so often in her prayers asked for her daughter. And God had sent him to her at the last moment.

Full of faith in the future, the Marquise placed her hands, the white skin almost transparent which the approach of death had made cruelly thin. Then, letting her head fall back on her armchair, she murmured very low, mingling the two objects of her confidence and her motherly affection.

Noticing afterward that the excitement of that scene had severely weakened her, Matiphous had her take some drops of calming potion and started to put her in bed.

As soon as he had returned to his room, he went to take

the poison he had prepared and threw it in the fireplace ashes.

"Now," he said aloud to himself, "I have something to do in life!"

A few moments later someone knocked at the door. Little Diane, sent by her mother, came to return his money, that she had been told to say, he had forgotten. This was not the moment to debate the subject; Matiphous took back his money, counting on overcoming the woman's scruples the next day when he had the mother's confidence.

But there was no tomorrow for the Marquise. Toward 3:00 a.m., the man from Malta was awakened by the receptionist, whom Madame Limeuil had called. It seemed the poor woman had reached her last moment. As if she had waited for her daughter's protector to give up her soul, the Marquise tried to smile at him when she saw him enter. Holding a dying hand out to him and murmuring in a barely audible voice, "Remember!" she died.

When everything was finished, Matiphous closed the dead woman's eyes. Then approaching the little bed where the orphan was sleeping, he contemplated his inheritance for some time. With the help of a servant, he gently carried the sleeping child into his room. He thus took possession of his paternity.

II The Other Side of Matiphous

What had he done, this Matiphous, to accuse himself so harshly, and to condemn himself to drink that deadly chalice before unexpected fate alone had made him put that far from him?

His greatest crime, or to speak more accurately, the beginning of almost all his sins, was to have come badly into the world. It couldn't be known at what point, one way or the other, the start of life can influence the moral future of an individual. Later, Matiphous' birth, and all the entourage of romantic circumstances that surrounded it, will be revealed. For today, let's take him to be a poor abandoned child who, one day, was almost miraculously snatched from death by a

Gozzo fisherman.

Kept and brought up by his savior until he was seventeen, he shared his bread, his humble roof, his hard work, To all appearances, in a corner of the hospitable little island and in the bosom of the honest family that had given him asylum, Gregorio Matiphous's days would have passed obscure and happy, if, at first, the lack of education, of intellectual cultivation, and then of love, that terrible domination of human destinies, had not marked his existence for another way.

Among the numerous children of the fisherman who had become his father, the man from Malta, from his earliest youth, had singled out a little girl, born some days before he was introduced into the family, who had been nursed with him.

After having loved her with childish passion, Gregorio had come to love her with a young man's passion, and to make her his wife had become his life's dream. Nothing seemed to oppose this golden dream that the entire adoptive family, to whom Matiphous was dear, seemed to endorse. Unfortunately, his fiancée too had a dream, and she dreamed higher than Matiphous.

With their beautiful vows of chastity, the gentleman of the Order of Malta were nothing less than ordinary men. From 1581, at a time when religious fervor was more intense than it has been since that time, history shows them rebelling against the Grand Master de la Cassière [78] because with a public ban he had expelled from the city of La Valette the women and girls whose conduct set a bad example and forced them to leave the island or retire to villages far from the monastery.

Now, one of the gentlemen of that very chaste order had

---

[78] Fra Jean l'Evesque de la Cassière (1502-581), 51st Grand Master of the Order of Malta, from 1572 to 1581. He commissioned the building of St John's Co-Cathedral in Valletta, and earned acclaim for his bravery in the battle of Zoara in Northern Africa where he had saved the colors of the Order.

fallen in love with the fisherman's daughter, and he had no trouble, with his white hands, his fancy language, and his gallant manners, making her listen to him. Matiphous' fiancée's lack of caution had the worst outcome that could be feared. One day, losing her head, as much as by the fact that her state was about to become apparent as by the abandon of her lover, who, once seduction was accomplished, had begun to neglect her, the unhappy girl decided to admit her sin to Gregorio in hopes that he would kill her on the spot.

Gregorio didn't even address a word of reproach to her. He just asked her the name of her seducer, and he asked that question so calmly and so casually that he seemed to be thinking of acting as an intermediary by trying to bring the flighty lover to better behavior. Thus, in possession of the information he wanted, the man from Malta went to the monastery and had no difficulty finding the gallant monk in his oratory. He asked him bluntly if his intention wasn't, for the honor of the girl about to become a mother, to marry her.

The gentleman answered so as to let it be understood that before he entered the glorious order of Malta he could prove that he had sixteen quarters of nobility, and could never consider marrying a fisherman's daughter. And he added that even if his inclination was toward that *mésalliance*, his vow of celibacy was an obstacle preventing it.

"So," Matiphous then asked, "there is nothing as poisonous as the love of a Knight of Malta, since he gave mortal and incurable wounds to a woman's honor that can never be healed?

The Knight was basically not a bad man, and although his fortune as the younger son was not very considerable, he spoke of taking care of everything, by giving the girl a nice dowry so that she could find herself some honest boy to marry and shoulder the paternity that was put on him.

Matiphous had controlled himself for a long time, because he expected a number of the things he had been told, and had his mind made up when he entered. But that last statement, which was meant for him, seemed to him a moral outrage, and his blood began to boil so violently that his resolution became immediate. Seizing a dagger from his belt which he carried for any circumstance, without hesitating and without saying a word, he plunged it straight into the seducer's chest. He didn't even have time to say "into your hands" before rendering his soul to God.

That done, the terrible avenger, with no more haste than if the conversation had followed its usual course, left the spot where that severe vendetta had taken place. As everything had happened without a sound and with the speed of lightning, that calm behavior and peaceful look, by not sounding the alarm about the act just committed, gave the murderer some hours of safety before they began to look for him.

When Matiphous returned to the fisherman's house, he found the entire family united around a table where it usually dined. Speaking with great calm to his adoptive father:

"Zambola, I was thinking of becoming your son-in-law, but now that can no longer be."

"And why not?" the fisherman answered with astonishment. He was one of those men who, once he gave his word, didn't understand that it could be taken back with good reason.

"Your daughter will tell you," Matiphous answered. "As for me, I have just killed the man who had caused this marriage not to take place."

On hearing Matiphous say that he had killed her lover, the fisherman's daughter became extraordinarily pale. Then, either because she couldn't endure the flash of lightning that her father threw at her, or because the death of the man she continued to love despite his betrayal caused her terrible emotion, she said, rising:

"All right, Gregorio, I thank you," and she left distraught.

When her mother wanted to follow her, old Zambola, restraining his wife, said

"She will do what she will do. Matiphous, tell us everything that happened."

191

Matiphous having told those things as they happened, the fisherman said:

"The law will be here at any moment. Matiphous, you must take refuge in Sicily. I myself will take you there."

The wife and the sisters of the fiancée that had lost her crown (virginity) had at the end left the cabin and gone to look for the poor creature, fearing that she would do something extreme.

On the other hand, the father and the brothers were busy making the boat ready to take to the sea, although the day was windy and cloudy. It seemed scarcely prudent to confront the high waves that had just begun to break violently on the coast.

When everything was ready, the mother and the sisters, who had no result from their search, came to the place of departure, and each in her turn kissed the adoptive brother who was leaving them. Matiphous also embraced each of his brothers who were not to be part of the voyage. As he was going to step into the boat, looking at the places where the sweet years of his infancy and the beautiful years of his youth had unfolded, "Will I ever return?" he asked himself sadly, as if he had a vision of his adventurous future life. But isn't it thus that everyman thinks at the moment of departure, when he thinks of the powerful and capricious wind called destiny that descends from above.

Matiphous' voyage was more fortunate than might have been thought. He soon disembarked in Sicily, where the fisherman and his sons left him with a part of their savings and wished him a tender farewell.

On the return trip, those poor people were already near their island of Gozzo when they saw in the distance an object floating on the surface of the sea. The black and yellow material seemed familiar and as a consequence they maneuvered toward it and soon recognized Matiphous' fiancée that the sea, after having taken her life, sent back to them.

"We have lost two children," the fisherman said to his wife on entering the cabin where they had spent so many happy days. And when the corpse of the dead girl that two of her brothers wrapped in a sail was placed on a bed of algae and seaweed, the family began a great lament. No one thought any longer of the seduced girl but of her deplorable end.

The next day, almost at the same hour, after a sad vigil in which almost all of the fishermen's wives had taken part, the mortal remains of the suicide were taken to a grave dug in the banks of the sand which no priest had blessed. The man killed by Matiphous was taken up, and, then, with all the prayers and ceremonies of the Church, he went with a glorious cortege to take his repose under a beautiful marble mausoleum, where later his coat of arms would be sculpted.

We don't know, but it seems to us that, before appearing before God, it would still be better to be the poor girl buried without prayers than the noble and devout knight over whom the rites of the dead had been so pompously pronounced.

III. Where Matiphous does not make his way

Matiphous did not see any safety for him in Sicily. The Order of Malta, which was searching for him everywhere, had too much influence in that country. He went then as far as Italy where he wanted to enter the service of that glorious French army that had just beaten the Austrians at Arcole and Rivoli.[79] Matiphous should have made a brave and determined soldier, but his star didn't intend him for glory. That bizarre existence, in which the grotesque and the terrible were constantly mingled, came into existence almost through ridicule

The moment he set foot in the French camp, it wasn't soldiers they were looking for. They needed arms for military ambulance and hospital service, for a long time completely disorganized. Whether he would or not, the hot-headed young man saw himself regimented with the nurses. And in a few days he traversed all the space that separated the character of

---

[79] Battle of the Bridge at Arcole: 15-17 November 1796; Battle of Rivoli: 14-15 January 1797.

Pourceaugnac and that of Othello.[80]

That insulting caprice of fortune might, essentially, be considered as one of his advances. It happened that in the job of taking care of wounds and putting on bandages, the ex-Gozzo fisherman revealed a particular ability, showing an aptitude to become a great surgeon. Seeing his fine possibilities, the head doctor of the hospital where Matiphous was serving took pleasure in developing them. And as that instruction took place at the bed of the wounded and on the living, the student profited. About the time of the Treaty of Campo-Formio,[81] in a strange way, he was acting as a secondary major assistant in the 57th demi-brigade.

With a volcanic nature such as that of Gregorio Matiphous, still suffering from a barely extinguished ardent passion, the Paris of the Directorate was a dangerous sojourn. In the middle of the licentious life-style of the tradesmen and prostitutes, he was easily persuaded to seek forgetfulness in pleasure. He rapidly exhausted some savings and soon found himself reduced to the last expediencies.

Unexpectedly, a slippery occurrence for his morality came about. From 1792, a decree of the Convention had suppressed the Order of Malta in France, and also from that period it hadn't ceased being the source of counter-Revolutionary intrigue, active or threatening. On the road, going to the conquest of Egypt, Bonaparte had the mission of trying to shut down that turbulent chief outpost of the Order. In La Valette, the capital of the island, many emissaries sent from Paris, worked to bring about an occupation without using strong measures. They did not want to compromise the expedition by a prolonged siege of a location that had the

---

[80] Monsieur de Pourceaugnac: comedic character from Molière; Othello: tragic character from Shakespeare.

[81] October. 17, 1797. Peace settlement between France and Austria, signed at Campo Formio (now Campoformido, Italy), following the defeat of Austria in Napoleon's first Italian campaign.

reputation of being very well defended.

But independent of this intelligence, working at a distance, the government of the Directorate got together all the information that could contribute to the success of the enterprise. As a refuge from Malta, Matiphous was asked to point out the most assessable places along the coast and the most favorable for a landing.

Like another Coriolanus,[82] and through pure hatred of the people who had wanted to hang him, the ex-Gozzo fisherman had answered those delicate questions. He had then sacrificed to vengeance, which was still his primary passion. That passion can, at any price, lead a man to evil without swallowing and degrading him. But to put a price on his anger, for money as it turned out, to become a turncoat and a traitor, was that not a terrible fall? And when he felt that felony on his conscience, was he wrong to speak in humble terms to Madame Limeuil of his worthiness and of his honesty?

Unfortunately, Matiphous didn't stop himself at that point. First, traitor to his country in the interests of the country that had given him asylum, he behaved like Aesop's fable *Le Cerf et la Vigne*,[83] whose moral teaches that God punishes those who do evil to their benefactors. In other words, in an affair where it was a question of getting France involved either in a failure or ridicule, we see him not hesitating. We see him drawn quickly into becoming officially involved, always for money.

In 1796, Commodore Sydney Smith,[84] he who later, in

---

[82] Coriolanus, tragic character by Shakespeare based on the legendary Roman general Gaius Marcius Coriolanus (5th century BC), who, after successfully defending Rome, was put on trial by the tribunes and fled to lead Rome's enemies against Rome.

[83] The Stag and the Vine.

[84] Sir William Sidney Smith (1764-1840), British naval officer who served in the American and French revolutionary wars and rose to the rank of Admiral.

Syria, competed so disastrously against our arms, in defense of Saint Jean d' Acre, let himself rather stupidly be captured at the blockade of the Seine with his frigate *Le Diamant*. Conducted as a prisoner to the Temple, he remained detained there for more than two years.

The English Admiralty, which considered him, with reason, one of its most experienced sailors, had taken serious steps to secure his exchange, but the Directory, stubbornly refusing to release him, forced the Cabinet in London to secure by intrigue what it couldn't obtain by negotiation.

The Harris and Lloyd Bank, in view of the desired result, was ordered to advance all the sums necessary, and a considerable amount was spent. And by one of those comic contrivances of fate, which at any moment can complicate the conduct of the most serious business, an obscure male dancer at the Opera, named Boisgirard, became the central figure in the long and difficult intrigue which was supposed to free Sir Sydney Smith.

They managed to steal a blank, but signed, form from the Department of the Marine. The Minister, leaving for a diplomatic mission, had left the form in his office in view of some urgent need. On this blank form carrying the Minister's signature with the stamp and cachet of the Minister of the Marine, they wrote an order to transfer the precious detainee of the Temple prison to that of Bicètre. Carrying this false document and disguised, Boisgirard, accompanied by several Emigration agents, also disguised, with courage, a cool head, and an admirable presence of mind, managed to secure the release of the prisoner.[85]

---

[85] Smith specialized in inshore operations, and on 19 April 1796, he and his secretary John Wesley Wright were captured while attempting to cut out a French ship in Le Havre. Smith had taken the ship's boats into the harbor, but the wind died as they attempted to leave it, and the French were able to recapture the ship with Smith and Wright aboard. Instead of being exchanged, as was the custom, Smith and Wright were taken

As soon as he had left his place of detention, the Commodore reached England, carrying with him most of those who had compromised themselves to gain his release. Now it must be said here, contrary to the agreed on version of most biographers, it was not a certain Dalmatian named Wiskowich, but really the man from Malta, Matiphous, who engineered the theft of the famous blank document. As Consultant to the Expedition to Malta, he had access almost every day to the Marine Department. By the intermediary of a girl in the Opera that he was supporting with the handsome money from his first betrayal, he was put in contact with the male dancer Boisgirard. And by a round figure in British money, he took charge of securing the fraudulent document. These were the causes and the opportunity for his going over to England, where, a while back, we met him.

In summary, Commodore Smith, by the imprudent and clumsy maneuver which had delivered him to our gunboat cannons, on his return to England should have expected a

---

to the Temple prison in Paris where Smith was to be charged with arson for his burning of the fleet at Toulon. As Smith had been on half pay at the time, the French considered that he was not an official combatant. He was held in Paris for two years, despite a number of efforts to exchange him and frequent contacts with both French Royalists and British agents. Notably Captain Jacques Bergeret, captured in April 1796 with the frigate *Virginie*, was sent from England to Paris to negotiate his own exchange; when the Directoire refused, he returned to London. The French authorities threatened several times to try Smith for arson, but never followed up the threats. Eventually in 1798 the Royalists, who pretended to be taking him to another prison, helped Smith and Wright to escape. The royalists brought the two Englishmen to Le Havre, where they boarded an open fishing boat and were picked up on 5 May by *HMS Argo* on patrol in the English Channel, arriving in London on 8 May 1798. Bergeret was then released, the British government considering the prisoner exchange as completed.

Court Martial rather than an ovation. But his having been the opportunity for a joke on France recommended him at least as strongly as a victory. His return was, therefore, a sort of triumph. Banquets followed banquets. Matiphous, considered the principal instrument of his deliverance, was invited and sat gloriously by his side. Become the lion of the moment, the adventurous character was immensely popular with the Commodore's following. Soon the same following transfigured him in a strange fashion.

In Paris, he was Major Aide Matiphous, having just the necessary knowledge to fill that humble position, to which, under the casual requirement of the period he had been promoted without a diploma and without an exam.

In London, overnight, and through the authority of the newspapers, he had become the famous Doctor Matiphous, very versed in the knowledge of Arab medicine. And as a doctor in spite of himself, he saw an immense crowd of sick people fill the consultation office which he was in some way forced to open. He cured them as God pleased, but then gravely pocketed the money.

Such an unexpected fate, which could only go to his head, had the most disastrous and most marked influence on his future. Shortly after his return, Sir Sydney Smith was sent to Constantinople on a secret mission. It was a question of adjusting a treaty that England then had with the Sublime Ruler. By the invasion of Egypt, the ownership of one of his richest provinces had been threatened, raising the most serious concerns for his possessions in India. Establishment of French power on the Red Sea would have cut off communication through the Isthmus of Suez.

Sir Sydney Smith had all the French complicit in his escape attached to his mission, and to say in passing, it was a rather able diplomatic act to later persuade the Sultan to put all these people on his staff, including the male dancer Boisgirard. Living in Paris, the dramatic artist had at the same time the military rank he had given himself at eight hundred francs a month from the finances of the Ottoman empire, while he continued, as an employee of the Opera, to still be on the payroll.

It goes without saying that Matiphous was one of the first to be invited on the voyage to Constantinople. Considering that the place of his birth, his instincts, and his temperament gave him in advance great affinity with the Muslim world, it must be thought in losing the opportunity to enter the service of the Great Lord, he unfortunately cut himself off from a chance of fortune and changed the whole economy of his destiny.

But in the first drunkenness of his medical practice, already considering himself as naturalized in England, he did not want, he said, to expatriate, and stubbornly refused to follow the fortune of his companions.

His popularity still persisted for some time. Finally, however, some aggrieved spirits noted that with the prescriptions of Arab medicine, the mortality rate in the City of London seemed to increase rapidly.

Besides, the London doctors did not like, any more than the Paris doctors did, the novelty and the competition that upset old reputations. Justified or not, these celebrities of new ways always cause anger from the former way of doing things. The first instinct is to blow out these meteors which shed important light around them.

In the London Medical College, a kind of coalition formed against the daring stranger. He was denied, decried and dissected for each one of his blunders, even for inevitable deaths, which in current medical practice were excused doctors who were the most able or the most fortunate. Nothing was allowed to the rival they wanted to dethrone and against whom they invoked all the rigorous requirements.

So, driven out of serious medicine, which he was officially forbidden to practice, seeing his clientele diminish day by day, he began to worry about the future. Speaking in mythological terms, he had taken the Styx for the Pactole[86] and had no savings. Taking advantage of the last sighs of his expiring popularity, a charlatan persuaded him to join a medico-industrial association and soon an advertisement appeared in the newspapers: the Malta pills against sea sickness, and that for beauty and the conservation of teeth, the divine water of the famous Doctor Matiphous.

Now, attributing all the pharmaceutical responsibility to him, his loyal associate found a way to keep almost all the profits for himself. And the silly boy managed to strike a mortal blow to his reputation, without even having the consolation of being able to look after his interests. However, this was only a foretaste of the deceptions and disappointments that the soil of the *perfidious Albion*[87] was reserving for him. And, as we shall see, when struck by a more real misfortune, that sinister and deadly inspiration to drink poison came to him, to which some chapters earlier we saw him about to succumb.

IV. Ketty Ketch

That Ketty Ketch was a pretty young girl with the whiteness and the slender figure of a lily and the freshness of a May rose. She was well known in the English Capitol, first of all because of her beauty, but also because of her father's profession. From the reign of Charles I, the Ketches were the public executioners.

It was a family that wasn't less well known than the greatest names in the aristocracy and which had made itself a sort of popular nobility by means of the hangman's noose. Far from diminishing the beautiful Ketty's success, the lugubrious profession of the author of her days had instead surrounded

---

[86] Styx: allusion to the mythical river which, if dipped into, gave invulnerability; crossing it led to death. Pactole: Phrygian river with deposits of gold.

[87] French nickname for Great Britain.

her with admirers and hopeful suitors.

For certain ones she had the special attraction that one finds in women of the theater, that of being very much in the limelight. Or others, as happens with everything that is in contrast, the halo of blood that encircled her ravishing figure appealed in a strange way to the imagination. On the hazy banks of the Thames, where the national character doesn't find repugnance in funereal ideas, she had become so much in fashion that bankers, notorious politicians, and even members of the Royal Family, would have paid fabulous prices to possess her charms, if she would hear of it. But that strange girl seemed to have decided on the path of wisdom, and up until then, none of the temptations had shaken her virtue.

One day, Matiphous was present, with the most fashionable London group, at a boxing match which is still today famous in the annals of pugilism. A certain Broughton, who was the best boxer then in the United Kingdom was supposed to take on another athlete named Humphries. The popularity of the second man was increasing, but it was then only breaking on the horizon. Nevertheless, considerable money had been bet on the chances of the two champions.

For him, Broughton had experience, the confidence that twenty previous victories gave him, and the prejudice in his favor of the great celebrity of his name. But many people were against him and could hardly endure his outrageous airs and the conceit with which he ogled the most titled and elegant women while brandishing his hairy, muscular arms. Besides, almost without a rival for a long time, he had dominated the field. By the same sentiment that had made a citizen of Athens so tired of hearing Aristide called "the Just"[88] they were tired

---

[88] Aristide "the Just" was present at the Battle of Marathon (490 BC). He governed with virtue and was superior in honesty to his contemporaries. His solid character was inclined to justice, allowing no form of lying, flattery, or deception. He died poor, leaving the state to bury him and provide for his daughters.

of constantly seeing victory go to that man. He had rather large bets against him, more by the desire they had to see him lose than by the hope that could logically be formed by that result.

Humphries, on the contrary, had youth, a determined, but modest, attitude, and a reputation for cool-headedness, which augured well for him. He counted Matiphous among his staunchest supporters. The man from Malta had always had the greatest repugnance for Broughton. It was one of those instinctive, inexplicable hatreds.

The fight begun, during the first rounds the advantages were equal and Matiphous' attention was exclusively on the phases of the fight. But, suddenly seeing Ketty, who was noticeable in the opposite camp by her loud and passionate shouts encouraging Broughton, the ex-Gozzo fisherman was struck by a strange resemblance. Almost the same complexion, the young English girl, less tanned and more dazzling, she reminded him of the girl of his own country, that beloved fiancée that he had loved so much and had lost. These kinds of resemblances, in the present and in the past, are known to strike the heart. From the moment he discovered this living memory, the fiery young man could not take his eyes off her. Very probably he would not have noticed the rest of the fight that, despite Ketty's fascination, had there not been a terrible denouement which ended the encounter of the two athletes, drawing his attention away from that distraction.

The fight had already been going on for three quarters of an hour, the two combatants breathing hard, all covered with blood and bruises, to the great satisfaction to the gallery. But having from the outset found Humphries a very difficult adversary, Broughton was weakening and his star seemed to be abandoning him. Dazed, both by the distressing idea of a defeat and by the violence of the multiple blows raining down on him, the Alexander of the boxing ring, was finally disoriented. A terrible blow he received in the middle of his forehead, made him see something like a river of blood passing in front of his eyes. From that moment he was a ferocious beast, no longer trying to do anything but destroy his feared enemy. He forgot the strict rules of the ring, and with the greatest violation of the rules, hitting with his feet as well as with his hands, with a terrible blow to the lower stomach, in the words of the profession's slang, he "finished off" Humphries who lay dead on the floor of the ring.

"Bravo! Well done!" the young girl shouted, nevertheless. But very few of the audience were disposed to find the murderer innocent. In England, boxing is too popular an art to see an attack on its purity without indignation. Considered in general as an assassin, the brutal man who had just made himself guilty of a terrible felony was immediately apprehended by the constables and conducted to Newgate Prison. He remained there accused of a capital offense. He would not fail to be convicted at an approaching court date.

Seeing this treatment of her hero, the young, fanatical admirer of the boxer tried to raise the population to snatch the boxer out of the hands of the police, but that seditious excitement didn't turn out well for Ketty. Recognized, her father's name circulated in the crowd, which couldn't contribute to surrounding her with great trust. Then, as she began to call cowards the assistants who didn't seem willing to take a strong hand, she found herself coming up against public criticism. God knows the treatment that threatened her, the English being the least gallant people in the world. Fortunately for the imprudent young girl, while disapproving her audacious conduct, Matiphous came forward as her hero. Openly protecting the poor girl, that they were already beginning to use roughly, he confronted those set against her. A little later he started on his way to return her to her father's house.

That pretty creature must have made a great impression on Matiphous at first sight, because gossip about her could not have made him ignorant of whose daughter she was. And it seems that, having avoided being hanged in Malta, more than anyone else he should have felt that natural repulsion that the hangman's name usually causes.

On the way, interested in his young protégée, Matiphous was curious to know how to explain the wild devotion with which that boxer, who was neither very young nor very handsome, had come to be honored by that fresh beauty. As a result, with as much subtlety as he was capable, he told Ketty of his astonishment at the great passion she had shown for Broughton's win. He let it be known that a feeling of envy was part of his astonishment.

"Broughton," the young girl excitedly answered, "is the best boxer in the world, the glory of England, and to say that a Humphries could boast that he vanquished him!"

"But nevertheless this Humphries," Matiphous answered, "had valiantly fought a good fight and he was evidently winning."

"Because Broughton was in a bad mood and sick, because he knew very well, the poor man, that there was a plot against him."

"You knew him personally?" Matiphous asked.

"Me? I never spoke to him in my life!"

"Then it was because you felt a certain attraction for him? Because to have such concern for his success…"

"An attraction for Broughton!" Ketty broke in with a burst of mad laughter, "for an ugly man and a woman chaser, a bar fly? Really a nice beau there you think I have…"

"But there are reasons to show that great an interest in a man."

"Then, at the Bear Garden," the pretty girl answered ironically, "when I bet on a courageous bear, at Newmarket when I see Colonel O'Kelley's Eclipse [89] running, I am carried away and breathless; in a cock fight, when I want one of the two champions to win, I am in love with all these animals!"

It would be impossible to say how much good that naïve argument did Matiphous. In fact, she let him know that instead of being a girl with bizarre tastes, Ketty was simply a good Englishwoman loving the strange pastimes of her compatriots.

---

[89] Famous racing horse.

The remainder of the conversation didn't last very long. Walking arm in arm, the young girl and her conductor soon reached the most secluded and somber neighborhood in the City. Not far from Newgate Prison, there was a little Square that the Sun could scarcely enter, since it was at least twelve levels below the ground level of the surrounding streets. On that spot, which was illogically called *The Rose and the Crown,* in the middle of hideous hovels, there was one that looked particularly dilapidated and sinister. Ketty stopped at the door of that sad dwelling. In the English way of letting one of the inhabitants enter, she knocked three times with the door knocker. Then, after having thanked Matiphous, she left him, as one does someone with whom one has spent a quarter of an hour, without thinking or wanting to meet him again.

V. A Visit to the London Hangman

Some months after Humphries' death, Mr. Broughton made an ugly face on hearing that the High Sheriff of London and of Middlesex County had at Session-House addressed him the following kind regards, which, from time immemorial the English law courts had sent to the condemned:

"The law requires that you return to the prison from which you came. From there you will go to the place of execution, where you will be hanged by the neck until you are dead and may the Lord have pity on your soul."

Broughton, however, wanted to put on a brave front, and he audaciously answered the magistrate:

"Judge, don't waste your prayer on me. I've never seen it bring good luck to anyone, and my soul is business between God and myself. I don't think it's at all necessary for you to stick your nose in it."

Two weeks went by after that insolence and that death sentence. One afternoon the great clock of Saint-Sépulcre began to ring a lugubrious toll, which is customary on execution days, to call the condemned to the attention of pious persons. At the same time, an immense crowd of pedestrians, horsemen, and carriages surrounded Old Bailey, where the law carried out its sentences after the old Tyburn was abolished.

The crowd's eagerness was two-fold. First of all, it was a matter of seeing Broughton hanged, a very popular man, as is already known. Then gossip had spread that on the theater where the comedy of his death was to take place, there was to be a debut. Jack Ketch, it seems, was marrying his daughter to one of his aides, a young man, it was said, of the greatest expectations. And that man was supposed to take his father-in-law's place, so as to begin his career in a resounding way.

Nothing in an execution pleases the English public more than the attitude of the condemned man going to the gallows with a composed expression. In this sense it could be said that Broughton satisfied the program in every way. Condemned men were frequently seen to walk toward their execution resolutely and carefree. But carefully considering this courage, you discover either that the condemned man was besotted by gin or whiskey, or feverish excitation caused by the mental state of the criminal. In the case of the boxer, on the contrary, it was impossible to mistake a complete prodigious serenity. Freshly shaved, clothed in his handsomest suit, carrying white gloves and a magnificent bouquet of roses, he seemed to be going to a wedding, and, from atop his cart, he threw friendly smiles and gracious greetings to all around him.

The marvelous courage of the dying man will soon be explained, but as a preamble it is necessary to tell what followed Matiphous' introduction to Ketty.

Jack Ketch's daughter, beautiful as she was, reminding him of the best days of his life, from the first moment he saw her, had made the deepest and most unexpected effect on the man from Malta's ardent and impressionable nature. Having seen that beautiful creature, and just because he had seen himself coldly received, he had passionately wanted to see her again. He began by walking about in the neighborhood where she lived, always looking for an opportunity to meet her. His amorous star hadn't served him very well. The vanity of his efforts increased his desire to satisfy them. One morning, the sad suitor had a great idea. His colleagues who, with reason, reproached him for his lack of medical studies, he therefore had nothing better to do than to complete them. Now, the basis of every science in medicine is, obviously, anatomy. But in England dissection is a difficult practice. The great respect expressed there for human remains leaves very few subjects for the scalpel. Getting in touch, then, with the resurrectionists, a horrible industry dealing in corpses stolen from the cemetery, was at the same time too immoral and two expensive. There then remained Jack Ketch's resources. As he had total control over the corpses of those hanged not claimed by the family, he always possessed a rather nice assortment of those articles of commerce. So there was Matiphous introduced to the father of his beauty, and in the most honest and specialized pretext, he wasn't far himself from paying to learn about anatomy: *Hangmen are not what some people think.*

That is to say, unlike some men having shame, remorse, or pangs of conscious about their terrible mission, Jack Ketch, in particular, was a man who didn't think. From father to son, he didn't hold anything against the hanged men for his services, but he didn't hold anything against himself either for hanging them. He found that by cutting off respiration with the authority of the law, he was practicing a profession like any other. It was even a better profession than many others, because that one provided a good living to its practitioner, which certainly couldn't be said of all the others.

Independent of the fixed salary the state allocated, Jack Ketch had a number of additional resources. Thus the rope, after having done its job, he sold as bringing good luck at the gambling table. Then there was the fat, no less useful than the rope, which entrepreneurs used, effective for rheumatisms and stiff necks. Like all of his colleagues, Jack Ketch knew surgery. He enjoyed something of a reputation for setting fractures as did his wife for bring difficult childbirths to a successful conclusion. But what, more than everything else, made him rich was his knowledgeable studies and reflections about the various differences in knots and nooses with which a man's jugular vein could be severed. Allowed to bargain with him privately, the families, when it was not the condemned man himself, could stipulate a tie of such and such a caliber, bringing slower or more rapid asphyxiation. Just by the ropes he had first introduced into the art of strangulation, Jack Ketch, in a few years had more than doubled the income from his job.

On the outside, in order to instill a certain fear and not to excite envy, he kept the appearance of gloom and poverty about his house that we have seen. Inside it, there reigned comfort that would seldom be encountered at the home of the richest merchant of the City. Having a good fireside, a good bed, a good table, warm rugs, no one on Saint Michel's Day ate a fatter goose, and no one also celebrated with better ale and tastier plum pudding at Christmas, the main celebration of the Anglican calendar.

At that time of the year, groups go about nightly through the streets, giving serenades. When these ambulatory virtuosities presented themselves at Jack Ketch's house, as before that of other middle class people, to ask payment for their nocturne harmony, the happy executioner always paid them generously. He also had pretentions to music, and what's more, it was hereditary in the Ketch family. One of them had been for a long time the organist at Saint-Paul's, and as for the present Ketch, he had a very pleasant talent with the *viole d'amour,* an instrument no longer in fashion. Often, with his wife, his two sons and his daughter, all of whom had good voices and played several different musical instruments, he gave a concert that charmed the whole neighborhood. And it could be seen that there was in action one of those simple family symphonies so often represented in the tableaux of the Holland School. On these occasions, Ketty always took the lead. Born with excellent talent, she one day had the opportunity to be heard by Jean-Christian Bach, called the Englishman, one of the offspring of that famous family of composers which occupies such a high place in the history of the art. Master of the chapel of the Queen, who had imported the German at great expense, and author of several beautiful operas, Jean-Christian had fallen passionately in love with Ketty's voice. He came frequently to give her lessons so as to form her for the theater and he predicted resounding success for her.

Precisely on the day in which Matiphous entered the Ketch home for the first time, in a room adjacent to the one he had entered, the young virtuoso was at her clavecin where she was accompanying herself singing one of the most beautiful airs of Gluck's *Armide*. Busy doing his strange cadaver business with the man from Malta, from time to time Ketch stopped to applaud a cadence or a well-executed refrain or to point out some places which should be repeated.

Naturally, Matiphous was eager to know the source of these celestial melodies striking his ear. It can well be imagined that in discovering in the person already occupying him so greatly, in addition a talent so unexpected and a voice so delightful, he wasn't tempted to put a bridle on his love. On the contrary, to use a metaphor, it galloped even faster.

VI. Where Matiphous must have miscalculated: the The Bottle and the Magpie tavern.

Through his desire to cultivate Master Ketch, Matiphous showed himself such an accommodating buyer and a good-humored fellow, that at the end of a few days, having to his advantage his service to Ketty, he was on the footing of friend of the family. It wasn't difficult for him to come to a point where he could openly show his sentiments.

Accustomed to the highest flown sighs, Ketty wasn't very impressed by the declaration of a kind of adventurer to whom she had decided when they first met to give only a cold reception. In any case, that unapproachable beauty got right down to business. She let him know very clearly that he had no chance of getting very far with her if the love he was declaring had any other purpose but the knot of matrimony.

Hearing that condition, Matiphous couldn't be otherwise than somewhat astonished. However, he wasn't unaware of the brilliant propositions that sought after girl had turned down previously. He couldn't misunderstand her right to speak as she did. "After all," he said, "the obscurity of my own birth scarcely permits me to show myself so touchy on the question of parentage. By means of the theater, to which that child is destined, she could very well know how to cover up her base birth and bizarre point of departure. In some great Italian theater, her beauty and her talent, the passion of an idolatrous audience, they wouldn't be very concerned about knowing what nest this warbler, whose delightful accents they were hearing, came from."

His mind made up by this nice rationale, Matiphous, to the offer of heart, soon joined the offer of his hand. He flattered himself that, by that decision he had flown so well over all obstacles the one he wanted to marry, whom he believed already had his conditional word, he went straight to Master Ketch, from whom he formally asked permission to become his son-in-law.

Ketch declared himself at the same time both happy and honored by the sought after alliance of which his daughter was the object. In her turn, asked for her agreement, Mistress Ketch answered in no less obliging terms. But, as Ketty was the glory and joy of the family, she was a girl who was allowed to have her way in everything. In addition, she had given so many proofs of her virtuous behavior that they could blindly leave the administration of her future to her prudence. The Ketch couple limited themselves to saying that they didn't want to interfere in any way with their daughter's decision. They left their daughter entirely free to choose a husband.

Bolstered by those replies, Matiphous returned joyfully to his pretended. And, not even doubting her consent, he asked her how much delay she anticipated until the happiness of their union.

However, the answer to that question wasn't so simple or categorical as our man in love had figured. With great good sense, the young girl answered him that she knew love was capable of every devotion, even of every folly, when it was a question for him of satisfying a desire and possessing it. Unfortunately, once that was obtained, many things were often lost. And such a woman, desired with such unparalleled ardor, afterward finds herself treated coldly. When the first fervor is abated, the faults and imperfections which the girl might have are given more attention. Now, without speaking of her lack of merit, Ketty knew she had a great flaw, that of being her father's daughter. And at no price could Ketty allow the thought that someday, during one of those cloudy days that too often show up at the horizon of marriage, her husband might reproach her for her birth.

But here Matiphous interrupted and protested against the possibility of such a thing.

But Ketty answered that she had no faith in that. The only way to avoid the danger that she foresaw was to marry someone from a family of performers or a man without prejudices so wanting to please her that he would marry the daughter and the father's profession at the same time.

Matiphous immediately found that was asking too much of him, and after having been assured that was the positive ultimatum of the hard conditions made to him, he resolved to have done with this so very demanding love, the satisfaction of which, from one day to the next, came at a higher price.

Ordinarily these kinds of determinations are formed slowly and with very romantic pride; the misfortune is that they are never executed in the same way.

With unequaled courage, Matiphous stopped, on the spot, haunting Jack Ketch's house. But at the same time he became one of the most regular clients of the famous *Bottle and Magpie* Tavern. Now that tavern, it's good to know, was owned by a sister of Master Ketch. As a consequence, Ketty was seen there from time to time coming to pay her respects to her aunt. During the interval from one visit to the next, the worthy dame had nothing else in her mouth but the name and the praise of Ketty. It would be vain to deny the evidence.

Less easy to be cured of his passion than he had at first figured, the man from Malta, began to frequent, as we have just said, *The Bottle and Magpie* Tavern. He embodied one of those ingenious compromises with which a man in love, while claiming to separate from the beloved object, finds a way to maintain a chance of meeting her and some mysterious contact.

And in fact, aside from that interest, how could the man from Malta's strange taste of frequenting such a place be explained?

Circling London's most famous prison was a belt of dingy and blackish houses commonly called the *Libertis* which formed a special and isolated quarter. That beautiful name of *Libertis* denoted a place of freedom, and had started under the tolerant administration of the Newgate jailer. Unless his administration was prevented by too serious causes, he allowed the prisoners to cross the barrier and go breathe a little outside air, but under the condition, loyally observed, that they not go beyond a certain distance and return to the jail as soon as night fell.

The prisoners who had a little money, to make a profit, quickly took advantage of that freedom each morning when they were let out, filling the *Libertis* with taverns, gambling houses, and other places of pleasure which the floating population of thieves and swindlers were accustomed to.

Among all those dens, the best known and the one with the most business, was kept by Mistress Ketch's sister-in-law. And far from hurting her business, her relationship to the hangman brought her the greatest part of her clients. Criminals, most of them people with imagination, like hearing things talked about that frighten them, as do children and women. Besides, all the instincts and all the habits of their life make the gallows a kind of center for them and the necessary end to which they didn't cease to gravitate.

And it must not be thought that the good hostess tried to maintain the fame of her establishment either by her modest prices or by the superior quality of her drinks. The prices at

The Bottle and Magpie, were the highest of anywhere in the vicinity, and an abominable drink made from the blue violet (gin) was about the only drink they served. And also, in the picturesque language of the inhabitants of the place, considering the pernicious influence and the violet color of atrocious liquor, they always called it the blue death just as the place they came to drink it they never knew except under the deeply significant name of Blue Hell.

Now, it was in this place of pleasure that Matiphous came every day to rein in his amorous dreams. It must even be added that, at the beginning, he more than once ran the chance of being interrupted in the middle of his meditations. In places frequented by the good company where he was mingling, every new or unknown figure was immediately thought to be a policeman. A brutal expulsion, accompanied by some blows, was the least inconvenience that could be expected.

But the Blue Hell's Proserpine,[90] knowing the close relationship that had almost taken place between herself and her habitual client, didn't therefore hesitate to warn the amorous young man. She soon gave him a very different testimony as a sign of her interest which will be explained in the following chapter.

VII Where something surgical is good.

Mistress Aston, the owner of *The Bottle and Magpie*, had picked up the somewhat chivalrous habit of speaking rather familiarly, without distinction, to all those who frequented her establishment.

One evening, and when there was already talk of Broughton's near execution, "Don't leave, boy," the tavern keeper said to Matiphous. "I have some business to talk to you about as soon as my big crowd has left and the gentry of

---

[90] Roman mythology: daughter of Ceres, goddess of the seasons; wife of Hades, or Pluto, ruler of Hell. Based on Greek myth of Demeter and Prosephone.

Newgate is under lock and key. I will tell you something I was sent to say to you."

Matiphous was very intrigued with that opening, because he had some reason to believe that Ketty would be spoken about.

At the signal that announced the closing of the prison, the bar was immediately emptied. Mistress Aston was busy a moment longer adding up some figures on a slate. Afterward, coming to sit in front of Matiphous, she began by deeply inhaling tobacco, leaning her two, fat red arms comfortably on the table. Then, in a mysterious tone, she began to say the following:

"What I was commissioned to ask you, my almost handsome nephew, is if you had ever thought about earning a lot of money?"

"It's not about Ketty," Matiphous said to himself, greatly disappointed.

"That depends," she answered, in a cold, rather than excited tone. "It seems," Mistress Aston continued, "that you know quite a lot about surgery?"

"That's not always what the gentlemen at the College of London said."

"Yes, I know, envious people," the hostess answered in a knowing tone, "I have some of them too, but my establishment doesn't suffer from it. But an opportunity to confound all those vicious tongues is offered you, boy, to bring about a cure that, I assure you, will be talked about."

Matiphous couldn't keep from showing some curiosity.

"You know," the tavern keeper continued, "that poor Broughton will be hanged a week from now? The Minister has rejected his appeal and the best London society wasted its time in his behalf."

"Then," Matiphous continued, "Jack Ketch has only to prepare one of his quickest nooses, because it's said Broughton is well fixed, and, to be promptly sent on his way, money to him would be no object."

"He would be even less concerned about money,"

Mistress Aston answered in a tone of secrecy, "if it was for a rope that could leave him still able to breathe. And would you really believe, beautiful bird, that this great miracle, it's you who must bring it about?"

"Me!" Matiphous answered. "May God damn me if I can imagine any way to keep a sliding noose from closing."

"There is one, however," the hostess answered. "It appears that you haven't kept up with the progress of science. But I can explain how it's done, and afterward you will see to arranging it."

Committed then, it goes without saying, to laying out the procedure:

"You must know," Mistress Aston continued, carrying things a bit further, "that about a dozen years ago a rich London butcher had the idea of operating on gentleman like him almost like he did on animals. That fantasy led him to commit several murders, following which he was condemned to say the great farewell. People comfortably situated like him and Broughton, like being hanged even less than other people. He tried then, with his money, to avoid hanging, but neither magistrates nor jailors would listen to his proposals. And there would have been no hope for him if it had not been for a young surgeon named Chowel, who got it into his head to make him avoid this bad step."

"How the Devil could he go about it?" Matiphous interrupted.

"Ah! this Chowel," Mistress Aston answered, "was a clever man and as knowledgeable as you can be, but, what's more, he was a man who took care of business, who didn't waste his time like you sighing and thinking stupid things! A man, really thinking only about his future, who made revolutions and, voilà, this is what he invented. Getting himself introduced to Gordon, as soon as they were alone, he took out of his pocket a little silver pipe shaped like a whistle. And with this instrument he proposed to save the life of the butcher. Gordon at first thought he was making fun of him, but Chowel answered that he had made very careful experiments on animals, and by means of a very small incision made to the throat, with the pipe lodged in that opening, a man could breathe very comfortably."

"In fact," Matiphous said, "the thing is not impossible, but the rope must be tightened above the air conduit, because if it's tightened below it…"

"Exactly, Mistress Aston interrupted, "you've found the answer and the experiment tried on Gordon should certainly have worked. But first of all, he was powerfully built so that his weight increased the pull of the cord and, then, the devilish cravat wasn't advantageously placed by the executioner that hadn't been let in on the secret. That didn't prevent the fact that, hanging more than an hour from the gallows, when Chowel had him transported into office, and had opened the vein, he still showed some signs of not being dead, sighing deeply and motioning that someone give him something to drink."

"Very well, but to come to terms with your brother-in-law, Jack Ketch, such an incorruptible man, who is rich and doesn't need money!"

"It's certainly a matter of Ketch," the hostess said, shrugging. "The same hand that's supposed to open a window into a man's throat must pass the rope around his neck, that's understood."

"Mistress Aston," Matiphous asked deliberately, "did the idea of using me come from you?"

"And why not?" the tavern keeper answered. "According to Mr. Matiphous, isn't the owner of *The Bottle and Magpie* capable of having an idea?"

"I don't say so, but there exists a certain person in the world who has always shown a great deal of interest in Broughton."

"Oh, well, interest, everybody is interested in him. Me, first of all; like half of London I'd like to save him. But at the same time, I'd like to take care of another affair. On one hand, I see you withering away; on the other, my poor Ketty does nothing but moan and cry."

"About the approaching death of Broughton?" Matiphous asked.

"No, you simple man, because you are harsh toward her and refuse to give her the only proof of love that she's asked you for."

"But, Mistress Aston, I ask you, is Ketty reasonable, and can a man be asked…?"

"Anything can be asked of a man to know if his love is solid," Mistress Aston answered sententiously. "But for everything else, I don't see any more difficulties between you, since I've found the way to solve everything."

"To take care of everything!" Matiphous repeated quickly. "And how, if you please?"

"Come now! Understand a little," the tavern keeper said after having taken another long puff of tobacco. "Isn't it true that Ketty, for her guarantee, asks that you pitch in, and you, don't you want to do her that gentlemanly favor?"

"That's all right," Matiphous answered, "but you're asking a gentlemanly favor where she doesn't have too much to do."

"Finally, to sum things up, since with you it's necessary to weigh words, Ketty would like for you to hang and you, you don't want to hang, is that not the question?"

"Perfectly," said the man from Malta, "impossible to say it better."

"Well! To hang Broughton? That's Ketty's business. And at the same time not to hang him? That's also Ketty's business and also that of all the boxer's friends, and yours also, my dear. So, please, find something more ingenuous."

"But, my poor Mistress Aston, whether Broughton is well or badly hanged, I will nonetheless be forced to be present for the whole ceremony, to appear with him in the cart and on the gallows."

"Yes, but when it's learned the next day that Broughton is still alive, and it is by great skill that he triumphed over death, then people will no longer say that Matiphous is the valet of Jack Ketch. They will say that Matiphous is the greatest benefactor of humanity; Matiphous is the author of a cure that has never before been made in medicine, that of resuscitating a dead man. When this news begins to spread, please come take a walk to *The Bottle and Magpie* tavern and you will see if, among the gentlemen from Newgate, you don't enjoy general esteem."

"And I will also enjoy the general esteem of the sheriffs, who, to congratulate me on the way I have carried out stopping justice, will have me apprehended and perhaps put in Broughton's place."

"So, and with an enormous sum of money that the other one would give you, would you be so simple as to stay there waiting for them? You would have already walked off."

"And if I have to leave London, what will happen after all that escapade, so far as Miss Ketty is concerned?"

"Can you read?" Mistress Aston asked, drawing a piece of paper from her pocket.

"A great surgeon like me! That's probable."

"Well, then, read this letter to me."

The letter was from Ketty.

"Dear Aunt," the young girl wrote, "suffering so much today in soul and body, because of the sorrow I confided to you, instead of coming to see you, I'm writing you about your idea for poor Broughton. I would, like you, undoubtedly, be happy if the life of that famous artist could be saved. But I don't approve that you use the person in question. It isn't the same thing to me if he agrees half-heartedly to what I wish, or that he jumps at what I wish, I admit to you that for my peace of mind, and not to be exposed afterward to insults, I would rather marry someone of the profession. But, as I have complete confidence in you, if you find that commits the recalcitrant person far enough, and if you hold to your idea, I will be satisfied with simple willingness, because I believe M. Matiphous is basically an honest man and I am weak enough to be in love with him a little"

"That says a lot," Mistress Aston observed.

"Go ahead, then and arrange that with him. But there is a

very great obstruction. My father would never forgive him for that deception and the magistrates would be angry. Therefore, as soon as the job is done, the poor young man must leave England. But, then, what about our marriage? It doesn't mean that there is no way to reconcile all that. M Christian Bach says I am ready to debut, and he assures me that I will have an engagement at the Carnival in Venice. I could then leave the very evening of the day the unlucky artist has been condemned. And if M. Matiphous wants to take the same route as I, it would certainly be impossible for me to prevent him. Perhaps even, instead of being alone on the open road, which is not safe for a girl my age, it would be better for me to travel in his company and under his protection. If you find, dear Aunt, that things could be arranged in this way, I won't oppose it, and I leave you free to take care of everything as you mean to."

Matiphous, who didn't yet know his pretended's style, found the manner in which she suggested an elopement completely charming and delicate. What's more, in a postscript, she showed that she had calculated every detail of the business, because she added:

"You must still arrange with M. Broughton about a substantial sum paid in advance, because we will need money for that trip. And although, for a long time, dear Aunt, you have wanted to see me in the theater, in order to raise the reputation of the family somewhat, I won't hear of your paying for our trip to Italy. The man to whom one renders such a great service, should not bargain about money and should pay generously."

"Certainly," Matiphous said, as he finished reading. "That isn't a good deed he should be allowed to be stingy about."

"So, you approve all this arrangement," Mistress Aston asked, "and we can count on you?"

"That is to say, I'll think about it," Matiphous answered, "and you'll have your answer no later than tomorrow morning."

For a tavern keeper, Mistress Aston really didn't understand too much about evil in the human heart of men. The same evening, after that conversation, she had Ketty told that everything was arranged, and that Matiphous had agreed.

VIII. The Decision that Matiphous Made.

The next day, going to Jack Ketch's house, because they were undoubtedly expecting to see him take that step, the man from Malta had agreeably confirmed what was insinuated relative to Ketty's state. He found her very pale and with a very worn look. That thinness and that pallor seemed to testify to the deep sorrow that the rupture of their matrimonial negotiations had caused the poor child. They were, for our man in love, sweeter to see than the rosiest complexion.

If the adventurous boy had not already made his decision, *in petto*, the lovable flattery he saw of the ravages made by his absence would certainly have completed his resolution. Besides, everything was marvelously arranged for the success of the plot in which he had decided to enter.

That same morning Ketty had her father's aide fired. Because of what he had heard about the beautiful child not wanting any husband but a man in the profession, that man had allowed himself to address too ardent a courtship. His still warm job was at Matiphous's disposition; the man from Malta had only to show his ambition to enter the profession, than he was immediately hired.

Taking immediate possession, he moved into the former lodgings of his predecessor, began eating with the family, and finally was part of the household and the declared son-in-law.

That high position, as well as that of Jack Ketch's substitute, beginning the next day, made him worth an aubade that was given to him by oboists at Christmas. At the same time the musicians offered him a symbolic bouquet composed of roses and marigolds, a melancholy gallantry that it was customary to give to the executioners of criminals to welcome them into the harsh profession.

However, there remained a somewhat serious difficulty: the agreement of Master Ketch, who always insisted that the work be done properly, that a subject of Broughton's importance could be put in the inexpert hands of a beginner. Miss Ketty had great influence with her father. She began by pointing out to him that she couldn't marry a beginner, and that it was indispensable that the man who would be her husband show himself, before their union, on some auspicious occasion. Ketch, while admitting the validity of that argument, hesitated, however, to agree. His pretty daughter tried cajoling. Throwing her alabaster arms around his neck, she told him that Broughton could be her dowry and she asked him for it as a wedding present. The worthy Master Ketch was always defenseless against those little ploys. Matiphous was definitely destined to the honor solicited for him. But they didn't hide from him that great confidence in him brought great obligations and that he must try to profit by the hasty education that his father-in-law, from that moment, undertook to give him.

Another equally important business was to get in contact with Broughton.

By means of a disguise, and by the intermediary of Mistress Aston, who, understandably had many kinds of intelligence in Newgate Prison, Matiphous rather easily reached his client, but it wasn't as easy to come to terms with him.

Boxing, as well as taking a part of all the purses from the fights, Broughton had made a rather round sum. He was therefore in a position to pay his savior generously, and that was what he at first had contracted with Mistress Aston. Another reason for him to be generous in his arrangement was that he had a horrible fear of dying. Nothing was more common among gladiators and ruffians than taking care of their life, pushed right to cowardice, outside the occasions in which they usually put it in jeopardy. But among other villainous faults, Broughton had that of avarice, and that passion for penny-pinching made that interview between

Matiphous and him rather comic.

When Matiphous entered the prison, where he was expected, he found his client so deep into reading a book of sermons that it was hard to get his attention. However, when our people were alone, and Matiphous had introduced himself as the person sent by the hostess of *The Bottle and Magpie*:

"Ah! Good! Mistress Aston," the boxer said casually, as if he had not been told of Matiphous' visit. "…then is that unusual idea that she suggested to me really serious?"

"Very serious," Matiphous answered, "and it's an operation that couldn't be simpler, now very well known in science. Pushing caution to the extreme of having me send you off myself, we can be sure of success."

"Sir, I am very obliged to you for your kind intentions, but, frankly, my ideas are not turned toward taking advantage of them."

"What? You mean to let things go forward?"

"I've thought a lot in my solitude, and I've had long and serious conversations with the Prison chaplain. And, everything considered, leaving this valley of misery a little sooner or a little later, does that really make a lot of difference?"

And he continued this way in a moralizing tone until Matiphous, finally losing patience, told him he should have had those pious reflections earlier and not waited for the conclusion of certain serious preparations that his prodigious detachment from earthly things had suddenly interfered with.

Changing tactics then, fearing that he might finally be taken at his word, the crafty boxer seemed to be touched by this reproach. As if he had resigned himself to trying to live, through complaisance and respect for his word, the boxer almost managed to shake the man from Malta when he asked what sum he intended to offer him for allowing himself to be operated on.

"What?" Matiphous shouted. "You expect to be saved from the noose and still be paid?"

"But, of course," Broughton answered with admirable

calmness. To give his claim some foundation, he pointed out that if the anatomists were in the habit of bargaining for corpses, he, a living cadaver, agreeing to lend himself to a dubious operation, should reasonably make himself a golden bridge for science. Science had everything to gain for him to give up this great taste for death which had suddenly visited him.

What was the reason for all that chicanery to show himself difficult, from a man who, far from delving into his purse, claims on the contrary that he is being taken advantage of? The result was that for a consideration of one hundred guineas, haggled over for a long time, Matiphous's crafty client signed the contract insuring him against hanging. The price finally stipulated, it was in addition agreed that the evening before the day set by the sheriffs, the man from Malta would find a way to get into the prison. Then, after the successful operation, the sum agreed on by the parties was to be paid.

Returning to find Ketty, Jack Ketch's substitute was somewhat apprehensive of being badly received, given the meager salary he had finally accepted. But he had the pleasure of hearing his pretty fiancée say that if that sum wasn't enough for their flight, she had some savings in reserve, counting on the fact that, if necessary, Aunt Aston wouldn't fail to provide for everything very generously.

Thus reassured, Matiphous himself was satisfied with his bargain. Although, up until then, he had been only moderately squeamish about the means of getting money, it wasn't because he was greedy. On the contrary, he had this good side to his character. He was a million leagues from loving money for itself. If he desired money, it was in view of his needs and perhaps to spend it a little more liberally than he would have.

IX. What Happened to Broughton

Providence seemed to wish that in Matiphous' hands, after having been for a long time a surgical utopia, pharyngotomy as applied to taking care of hanged men should become a reality. In fact, all the obstacles our philanthropist could find in his path he saw successively level out and disappear.

Thus the operation to be practiced on Broughton, consisting of a small incision in the thyroid cartilage, successfully initiated, the man from Malta wasn't without worry the next day. While giving him the primary role, his father-in-law had announced his decision to serve as his second. And wasn't it to be feared that, with his wide experience, that devil of a man would, at a glance, see how the rope had been placed and ruin everything by his unfortunate intervention.

But, just the morning of the day the boxer was to appear at Old Bailey, Jack Ketch was ordered to go to a distant county where the Master of Works there had just died, postponing an important execution. It was a matter of at least a dozen wicked heads that, at the occasion of an increase in the price of food supplies, caused a riot. When the people begin to feel stomach pains, governments always find the situation serious. And the less they do to prevent anger caused by famine, the more they are disposed to punish it vigorously. That lightning justice, no one had the talent to do it better than Jack Ketch. They had, therefore, requisitioned him with an order to leave without delay and to be at his bloody task as soon as possible.

One can imagine with what unusual care, at the moment of starting on his way, he renewed his clarifying instructions to his son-in-law. If they had only believed the conscientious functionary, they would have put off Broughton's execution until his return. But before introducing his son-in-law to the sheriffs he had answered for his great ability. The orders for the execution given, the condemned man informed, everything ready, and half of London on the way, it was therefore decided to go ahead, notwithstanding the absence of Jack Ketch. This fact wouldn't, in case his double committed some blunder, prevent him from being held responsible, as the chief executive of the business.

Now, there should be nothing astonishing about Broughton's behavior going to his hanging. Possessing his safety valve, and counting on being hanged only as a formality, he enjoyed calm and fearlessness at a bargain price, receiving the flattering murmurs and admiration of the crowd as he passed by.

However, once he was on the gallows platform, at the moment of the last formality when Matiphous' slightest mismanagement could have dire consequences for him, fear began to dog him. Several times, his lips trembling and his forehead pale, he begged his dear doctor to be very careful with what he was doing.

As a man who had profited by his father-in-law's lessons, Matiphous flippantly threw the noose that he was careful to adjust below the incision. Then he very cleverly maneuvered the balance lever that was supposed to take away the platform under the patient's feet, so that he was launched into his provisionary eternity before he was aware of the movement that precipitated him there.

That rapidity caused the audience not to hear a very beautiful discourse the condemned man had prepared for the occasion. But, considering the despondency into which the equipment had thrown him at the last moment, it is doubtful that he would have had calmness and presence of mind enough to have delivered it. In fact, he acted like many members of Parliament who daily hold back magnificent pieces of rhetoric and content themselves with being great orators inside their own heads.

As was the custom, the unfortunate Broughton remained on exhibit for an hour, and during that time, Matiphous thought of standing guard over people in the crowd, because he wanted to prevent the relatives and friends of the hanged man from coming to pull down on the man's feet. He knew that philanthropic attention, the purpose of which was to shorten the suffering of the patient by increasing the pressure on the rope, was tolerated and admitted. However, in this situation, it couldn't be more inconvenient. One might say that charity had never been so badly dispensed.

The hour over, Jack Ketch's substitute was in a hurry to unhook his client and wanted to have him transported to the executioner's domicile, where he was going to doctor him. But here there was another battle to fight. The boxer's union had made superb funeral arrangements for their most important member, and they had even for a moment had the audacious thought of interring him in Westminster, beside the glorious men of the past. Money could obtain that honor. Having been a pugilist wouldn't have been an obstacle to Broughton's apotheosis. It would perhaps have been a little more expensive for him than for some other great man. But as the quality of the hanged man had brought up more serious difficulties, they had given up the idea of a national monument. And it was in view of rendering modest duties to the victim's remains that they had come at that moment to reclaim them.

Fortunately, foreseeing the dangerous homages with which he might be threatened, Broughton had thought of avoiding them by means of a document in good form left in the hands of his surgeon. It read like this:

By these witnesses, I, Tom Philippe Broughton, esq., first pugilist of M. the Prince of Wales, give and transfer to Matiphous, a great scientist and doctor of surgery, who accepts it, the posthumous ownership of my body. I charge him with dissecting it with care, propriety, and decency. Given the unusual beauty of the skeleton, a skeleton the doctor commits himself to use as an ornament in his office, letting it be understood, however, that the skeleton will repose on a pedestal, and not be hung from the ceiling as is usual. Independent of the inconvenience of that position, there is almost always in this climate, the disagreement of finding oneself in the company of lizards and snakes stuffed with hay and crocodiles stuffed with straw.

Showing that document that, with the well-known character of the English, could just as easily come from a condemned man going seriously to his death as from a jovial person who had every expectation of avoiding it, Matiphous put aside all preparations and was finally at leisure to have the sick man transported to a back room of Jack Ketch's house, where he began the resuscitation.

X. What Happened to Matiphous

Resuscitate was really the word. Either because Broughton, in the trouble he was in, didn't know how to use the alternate airway that had been put in, or by the thoughtful attention of his dear ones and his friends stubbornly pulling down on his feet, his situation was greatly aggravated. When Matiphous got him down, his face was swollen and livid, there was a deep bruise around his neck, and foam began to soil his mouth, unmistakable signs of confirmed death.

The first therapeutic sign was vigorous bleeding, but under the lancet not a drop of blood appeared. The subject's circulation had already stopped, another conclusive reason to doubt the possibility of saving him.

In the middle of the man from Malta's emotion at the failure of that first attempt, he heard a knock at the door and recognized the voice of Ketty, who asked to come in. He at first refused to open the door, not wanting his pretty fiancée to see the horror of the scene under his eyes. But the self-willed young girl insisted in such a commanding way, shouting through the door (the family of Jack Ketch certainly knew what a cadaver was), that the man from Malta decided to open the door to her and have her witness the attention he was continuing to give his sad client.

As soon as Ketty entered, she ran to the table where he was stretched out. Seeing his pitiable state, she cried out: "You have stolen the money of this unfortunate man! He is dead and can never be brought back to life!"

Thus questioned, Matiphous fell back on the officious eagerness of the patient's friends to hasten his death. Then, although he himself didn't have very much confidence in what he was saying, he claimed that the case was far from desperate and that, with the numerous resources his art made available to him, he could banish that appearance of death that Ketty had asked him to explain in such unfriendly terms.

"And there you are wasting time and acting intelligent" the impetuous girl answered, "when each minute takes away chances! Get busy then. Do something, if you aren't the most ignorant of all medical men!"

The man from Malta couldn't help thinking to himself that his future wife didn't at all show the sweetness and easy temperament that he had at first supposed. However, since that great excitement could very well be the outpouring of a good and charitable heart, he gave her the benefit of the doubt, and without saying anything, he hurried to the pharmacy which he had prepared for the situation. He poured a strong dose of smelling salts between the patient's lips. The activity of that sharp volatile liquid stopped the coagulation of the blood, but for the same purpose the exterior must be violently rubbed. This posed great embarrassment for Matiphous.

He didn't dare, in Ketty's presence, take off the sick man's clothes. Understanding the extreme chastity of English females' ears, he was even kept from explaining to his fiancée why her presence bothered him. Fortunately, Jack Ketch's daughter was far from being as prudish as her compatriots. She herself saw the difficulty and hastened to leave so as the patient could be put in the delicate position the treatment required.

Shortly afterward, she again knocked at the door, which was partially open, and through which she passed to Matiphous a large wool covering. When everything was decently arranged, she went back into the mortuary room and wanted to help with the proceedings.

While the surgeon exerted pressure and friction under the unfortunate patient's covering, she began to rub his arms, his neck, his chest outside the cover. She did the job as a nurse with such dexterity that it would scarcely be expected of an experienced matron.

Unfortunately, all this care was a waste of time and although Matiphous was preaching perseverance, citing the books he had consulted, saying that almost all cases of asphyxia ended well, provided the care and necessary follow-up. Her arms almost broken with fatigue from the action she had continued for several hours, Ketty finally threw down the wool pad soaked with alcohol that she been courageously using, and turning angrily toward her poor fiancé.

"It's really hard to resist the hangman's job," she said bitterly, "when this situation proves to us that you have so much talent for it."

"But, dear Miss," Matiphous said, catching his breath in his turn, "that's a strange argument to make to me. The gamble that you subjected poor Broughton to was never a sure thing. The differences in temperament have great influence on the circumstances. The preparations for the operation were perfectly successful. The rope was tightened only where it was supposed to. All that was humanly possible to do, I have done."

"Give that up. You have never pardoned that poor man for your Humphries' death, and seeing a chance to pay him back…"

"By Heaven," Matiphous quickly interrupted, "I didn't expect to see the memory of Humphries brought up in this situation!"

"Yes! Yes! We know about you. The people of your country are demons enraged with vengeance, and when a man from Malta finds an opportunity to satisfy that terrible passion, there is nothing he won't sacrifice."

"Come now," the poor surgeon replied, shrugging, "you're unreasonable. Instead of listening to your unjust reproaches, I would be better advised to fall back on a last method."

Saying that, he put some cloves and a few caraway seeds in his mouth, crushing them between his teeth. Then, making a pipe from a feather, he staunchly pushed the aromatic air into the asphyxiated man's stomach. Perfectly disagreeable and almost ridiculous to administer, this remedy produced no more effect than the others.

"On my word," Matiphous said, "I give up." And thereby admitting that death had won. "God probably didn't want this unfortunate man to escape death, Miss Ketty."

He asked a moment afterward, "Passing on to another subject, don't you think it's time to think about us? It's almost night."

"Me! Run away with you!" the girl shouted, in a voice full of disdain, "with the wickedest and most perfidious of men, with a treacherous and underhanded hangman!"

"You really astonish me, Miss Ketty," Matiphous answered with dignity. "Here you are reproaching me for having carried out too well the strange conditions with which you recompensed my love. Executioner, no doubt I am, but to please you, against my will. And when I try to save Broughton's life, you didn't think about adding the unreasonable condition that I must of necessity succeed in the experiment I was undertaking."

"But, also," Ketty answered, her fiancé's harsh tone seeming to cause her to get control of herself, "you start talking to me about your love, standing beside the dead man. Do you think that's proper and well advised?"

"Eh! And you yourself, this prodigious interest for the salvation of a murderer, after all, do you find that proper and justified?"

"Well, yes! I admit it," the girl answered with abandon. "I loved him, that poor man, as the greatest of the pugilists that England has ever had. And I thought he could be saved, and now when I see him stretched out there, without strength and without life, that has a strange effect on me. I would hold it against God himself, if he were here, for not having let such a great artist live. And you can be sure that He can't make such another whenever he wishes."

"All right, give some tears to the dead, but the living, should you be so harsh on the living?"

"But, Master Matiphous," Ketty said very clearly, "do

you think at the depth of my regret, the greatest part of it isn't for you! I saw you, by saving that man, winning glory and European fame. I was going to be the wife of the world's greatest surgeon. And now I'm reduced to being that of a bloody companion."

"As much as, and more, than you, I deplore how this has turned out, but who has wanted and required this humiliation, or the sacrifice; was it from your side or mine?"

"I know, I was wrong," said Ketty, shaking her pretty head sadly. "I have greatly regretted my wicked caprice which came to nothing."

"However that may be," Matiphous replied, "after that attempt, when the secret gets about, living in England is no longer possible for me. You have given your word to leave with me, and I don't believe that you're thinking of taking back your word."

"No, of course, and I will follow you. But it can't be said that there is absolutely no hope. And consider, that after our departure, a fortunate chance, although very improbable, was going to be lost because of a lack of perseverance. Nothing is pressing us. My father is going to be absent for several days. Can't we therefore wait until tomorrow evening before starting out?"

"I would certainly prefer to leave immediately, but I share your human reasoning. It could in fact be possible that all our care will take effect afterward. Nature often does bizarre things. And I admit that it would be better to be here to act as her assistant."

At that moment they heard the piercing voice of Mistress Ketch, shouting as if the Tower of London were on fire.

"Ketty! Ketty! Matiphous! Come on! Supper has been ready and on the table for a quarter of an hour. Where the devil are you?"

"Go, Ketty," the man from Malta then said. "I'll follow you. I'm going to open the windows and place our patient near one of them. If there is now any chance of revival, it will be by introducing a great mass of air into his lungs."

Ketty left first; Matiphous followed several minutes later. And in the room where so much useless medicine had been practiced, poor Broughton remained, and in his case, he had no need for supper.

XI. Of the Newgate Chaplain. Of his Ideas about Nobility. Of an Encounter as Extraordinary as it was Unforeseen

On entering the dining room, Matiphous saw a kind of Hercules with plump, cheerful cheeks that it seemed to him he had met somewhere before, and, what's more, he was supposed to meet again, but a great deal later on a solemn occasion.

That man was the Newgate chaplain. That same morning he had fulfilled his usual role as the gallows pastor, and it was in the company of Broughton that Jack Ketch's substitute had seen him.

Very certainly, foreseeing the lugubrious ministry that he must someday occupy, it had pleased nature to give that florid athletic person a sort of perpetual living contrast to the pale visage of the man he escorted. As soon as he saw Matiphous enter, he went to him and shook his hand.

"Young man," he said, "may I compliment you! Such self-possession and nimbleness in a beginner and how quickly you sent your man on his way. I have accompanied many condemned men to their death, but never, I must say, have I seen any dispatched as skillfully."

Matiphous accepted that strange compliment with marked coldness.

"No," the worthy chaplain continued, taking Matiphous' reserve for modesty, "I claim that Jack Ketch himself couldn't have done better. What's more, when someone as healthy as you…"

"In fact," the man from Malta answered, "I don't feel bad, but I don't see exactly what my good health can have in common…"

"Not bad!" the unusual man interrupted quickly. "You are honest, my dear fellow. Say then that your constitution is one of those that can be called admirable. Your complexion, without being called flourishing, is resplendent with life and strength. The blood can be seen flowing freely under your skin, your nerves, your muscles, all your viscera function with perfection without equal and with a sort of beatitude. I certainly pride myself with being solidly and well built, but in the game of having a good physique, you could give me points and still win. No, I can certainly say that, in my life, I have never met a man as well built as you."

On hearing that tirade, Matiphous' first thought was that he was dealing with a maniac. As that thought couldn't do otherwise than be reflected on his face, the chaplain continued:

"It seems to you that I am very bizarre and very extraordinary. No, my robust friend, I am only deeply aristocratic. As much as I think well of, and willingly feel drawn to the privileges which Providence has bestowed on a solid and powerful organism, I am as much repulsed by weakly and disinherited creatures that have been condemned to a suffering and sickly existence. Health! That's all of man! With it, he can will anything and attempt anything. Without it, he is only a vegetable, and I trample on him!"

"It's certain," Matiphous said, "that health is very desirable, but I wouldn't have thought it that precious."

"Very desirable! Say rather that it's the first of all good things, the only one that is to be wished for. And add that it is the only true nobility, the stamp that the hand of God is pleased to place on his elected vessels. You, my dear fellow, I admire you and I believe you capable of succeeding in everything, because you carry yourself like Westminster Bridge. But, see, the director of the prison, where I have the honor of being the chaplain, he is considered an able man. Well! Do you think that I have the least respect for him? A sick man, prey to gout, who never walks without a cane, and spends two-thirds of his life with his leg stretched out on a

233

footstool. A while back he asked me to dinner, but I refused, while I gladly came at Mistress Ketch's invitation, knowing that everyone here, father, mother, children and son-in-law, all breathed well-being and health."

"However," the man from Malta answered judiciously, "the same hand that sent health also sent sickness. It seems to me that, especially for a man of your character, it would be the duty of Christian charity to be more patient with human infirmities."

"Those are just words," the chaplain answered, getting excited. "God knows why he gives some a good constitution and others existences scarcely roughhewn. What's more, I fulfill, as you say, my duties as a good Christian to these sick people. I sympathize with them, I even help them when I can, but I have no confidence in them, and I don't lower myself to them. In order for the world to be well run, everyone must keep his rank where nature had placed him. And say what you like, you will never make me treat as an equal an asthmatic, a consumptive, a hospital gallows bird, and cemeteries, where they should be left."

Listening to the opinions of that amusing paradox, the supper passed more pleasantly for Matiphous than he would have thought. It wasn't the same for Ketty. Pouting, not talking, and at the risk of offending the Chaplain, she finally complained of a violent migraine. She left the table before the guests and went to shut herself up in her room, after having told her fiancé a rather cool goodnight, which the most casual stranger might expect.

At first, the man from Malta didn't pay much attention. But when supper was over, when he found himself alone, and most of all after having looked in the mortuary room, he had the disagreeable realization that, instead of doing an act of surgery, he had decidedly stopped justice. He began to greatly regret that fatal chore, for which he found himself so poorly compensated.

Because after all, in all of this, his fiancée had almost showed her true character. All day she had spoken bitterly.

When the time came, she had put off their departure, and now she left him with such cold behavior that no one could think there was great tenderness of heart, nor that perfectly calm temperament desirable in the woman with whom he was going to share his life.

The complication of all these cares being far from giving him a pleasant state of mind, the sad young man saw that his night would be troubled and restless. He feared an agitated sleep, painful dreams and fatiguing insomnia. But needing movement, instead of going to bed, he went out and began to walk down streets in an effort to lessen his care.

After having beat the pavement aimlessly for several hours, Matiphous came to edge of the Thames, toward Blackwall, which is the place from which one embarks if he wants to go from England to Scotland by way of the sea. There, on a beautiful autumn night lit by the Moon's pale rays, in the shadow of one of those large hangers that holds merchandise, he sat down to get his breath. Listening to the clapping of that silver wave that broke against the barge, he recalled the soft evenings spent in the past with his fiancée under the wonderful starry sky of Malta, where the far away smell of orange trees wafted on the breeze.

Suddenly, forming a sharp contrast to the happy memory of the past, a frightening scene, or at least an unusual one, snatched the dreamer from his reveries.

Under the sinister light of several torches, he saw a cortege approaching That cortege was composed of a hearse, two coaches of mourners, and a large group of people dressed in black following silently. Once abreast of a small launch moored some distance further out, that nocturnal pomp halted. Lit both by the Moon and the torches, Matiphous distinctly saw a coffin taken from the launch and placed in the longboat. Once on the shore, it was placed in the hearse and started slowly toward the interior of the town. All those accompanying the hearse assisted, with great indications of sorrow and respect.

These funeral arrangements at such an untimely hour,

which, however, had nothing furtive or clandestine about them, were already something bizarre. But to add to Matiphous' astonishment, immediately after the funeral cortege had passed by, here's what he witnessed: Its sad burden placed on the ground, the launch didn't move on; two whistle blasts were exchanged between those getting into the launch and those on shore. At this signal, passing by like two shadows, a man and a woman hurried to get into the longboat, which, its passengers once on board, rowed away. Then, an extraordinary sight! In one of those mysterious passengers, in the full moonlight, by his pale face, his athletic figure, and always a little theatrical, draped in his dark colored cloak, one would have sworn he recognized Broughton!

That was probably one of the bizarre phantasmagoric effects caused by blonde Phoebe (Goddess of the Moon), however, for our nocturnal walker, that hallucination became the reason to return to Jack Ketch's house. Let's say that this time he took the shortest way. It must also be added that his speed and the excitement in his walk, made him seem a man who had begun to doubt and didn't want to neglect anything to be quickly enlightened.

XII. Where Everything Is Explained

First of all, there is one point to explain. Instead of finding himself peacefully in the holding spot where he had been placed, like an honest and well behaved hanged man, Broughton had disappeared. On entering the mortuary room, Jack Ketch's substitute no longer found any vestige of his unusual client.

Now, what to think of that disappearance? Was it really the boxer who, a quarter of an hour before, had been seen boarding a ship ready to lift anchor? But in that case, given the ship's strange cargo, wouldn't one be led to believe in some event outside the laws of nature. Wasn't it rather Broughton's ghost instead of his flesh and blood personality that would have been seen?

At another period in his life, Matiphous wouldn't have doubted the existence of some superhuman fact. Fishermen and people of the sea are rather given by their nature to naïve beliefs and superstition. But since he had had a touch of civilization and medicine, the man from Malta seemed to have become strong minded. And it was only in the realm of terrestrial possibilities that he sought an explication of the bizarre circumstance he had encountered.

Therefore, it wasn't Broughton that he had seen a moment before. Then Broughton was, for him, still very dead. If he was no longer found where he was left, he must have been stolen, either by the resurrectionists for the purpose of dissection in the amphitheater, or perhaps by the boxers' cooperation which didn't want to be cheated of his funereal pomp.

Whichever it was, Matiphous searched to find out how the theft had occurred. But for this, there was no clue, no trace of breaking and entering, so that indicated as the probable author of the larceny, a person familiar with all the people in the household and the routine of the house.

That fact brought forth a very natural idea which didn't lack, it has to be admitted, a certain foundation. That aide to Jack Ketch, that Matiphous had so abruptly replaced, had possibly got it into his head to seek revenge by doing him that bad turn. Who knows if that man, in one way or another hadn't been brought into the actions taken to bring about Broughton's salvation? Given that fact, there was no joke; the case was becoming very compromising. If this miserable thief took it into his head to go to the magistrates, and to show them the corpse, they would find the incision in his throat, the little silver pipe, the trace of the cord there where it shouldn't be. Then, how could so many accumulated proofs be explained?

While going over all these ideas in his head, Matiphous continued his worried search. Day breaking already, Mistress Ketch partly opened her bedroom door and began to shout: "Well, Matiphous, what fever prompted you to run through the entire house the whole night?"

"What! Run about all night? I just came in a while ago, and, my word, I found a lot new."

"What do you mean with your *new*? I repeat, that since midnight there have been footsteps walking about, going up and down the stairs, opening and closing doors. Although you tried to be quiet, I heard very well. I sleep only with one eye closed when Jack Ketch isn't in the house."

"Then you should have gotten up and shouted there were burglars, because instead of me, those were thieves you heard."

"Thieves in Jack Ketch's house! Are you mad? Then what did they steal?"

"Broughton, that I left yesterday on the table in the big room in a condition that you wouldn't believe he could move out all by himself and without help."

Mistress Ketch didn't lend any great credence to Matiphous' words. And instead, she was tempted to think the poor boy had lost his mind. Finishing dressing, she came, however, to check what he had said. When she had verified the boxer's disappearance, since she knew her sons played jokes, she thought they had perhaps played a joke on their future brother-in-law. She ran to wake them to get an admission of that prank. But they defended themselves in such a way as to be found strangers to what had happened. Then, there remained Ketty to ask if she had heard anything.

However, Mistress Ketch didn't want to burst into her bedroom. To wake the poor child suddenly, a girl so delicate and so impressionable, and who, just the night before had gone to bed with a migraine. Who could be that cruel? However, the day wore on and no sound was heard in the young girl's bedroom. Mistress Ketch became impatient and she finally went to pound rather loudly on that door, which had been so sacred to her some time before.

At the first loud knock, there was no answer; second call, with fist and voice, still followed by silence. Then an explosion of shouts and using all the means to overcome sound sleep. But still no answer.

Overcome with astonishment and worry, she asked Matiphous, who was no less worried, to go find a locksmith. When the door was opened, everyone's stupefaction can be imagined! Not only was Ketty not in the bedroom, but her bed had not been slept in. Disorder and confusion were everywhere and in the armoires and the drawers of furniture they noticed that all the absent girl's clothing had been removed.

In the presence of that new complication, Matiphous made no comment. He left Jack Ketch's house rapidly and some minutes later entered *The Bottle and Magpie* tavern. It wasn't the hour that the Newgate prisoners were free to assemble there. Sitting at her counter alone, Mistress Aston was busy organizing the bills from the night before when Matiphous appeared.

"Well! Is that you, boy, so early?" the tavern keeper asked. At the same time he saw an equivocal expression of amusement on her face which, in the best light, Matiphous could suppose that he was being greeted with a smile. Taken in the worst sense, he was being mocked.

"Yes, it's me," Matiphous answered, "who's come to announce some unfortunate news. Your niece Ketty was kidnapped last night."

"Ah! My niece kidnapped! And by whom?" the tavern keeper asked, without her face showing any astonishment.

"That's exactly, my dear Mistress Aston, the question I was going to ask you. You were much in Ketty's confidences. And my instinct tells me that you could tell us many things, if you would talk."

"Eh! Eh!" Mistress Aston said, without contradicting that statement.

"Talk, then. I'm listening."

"I understand you. You're going to get hopping mad."

"Me? Not at all. I'm calm, perfectly calm."

"Well, my dear, it would be pointing out the obvious to tell you that you've been used a little."

"Ah! I've been taken advantage of?" Matiphous asked,

still pretending to be very calm. "Well, true, I'm beginning to suspect that."

"But also, my dear jewel, you came like a foolish youth, and threw yourself right in our laps. You became passionately enamored with Ketty without even knowing if her heart was free. You had talent for surgery, and then that animal Broughton went and got himself in trouble with the law!"

"So then," Matiphous, who, from all that he had heard, had been struck by only one idea:

"Before knowing me, Ketty loved someone else?"

"Eh! My Lord, yes, my poor treasure! For an infinitely long time without telling anyone, not even the devilish object, didn't that little girl get it into her head to be mad about Broughton!"

"But listening to you, Mistress Aston, I was the one she had fallen passionately in love with. How did you arrange that, if you please?"

"She certainly found you an honest and likeable boy," the tavern keeper answered. "But, you know, when the heart has spoken…"

"Yes, yes, as you say, the heart should be respected, and now that Broughton is dead, I'm not going to be jealous of the past."

"Nonsense! Jealousy, that's alright for idiots. And besides when he found he wasn't dead, Broughton…"

"But then, is he alive, is he dead?" Matiphous asked excitedly. "A while ago I thought I saw him in rather passable health, and although that fact seems to me a miracle, if you are swearing to me that he had recovered…"

"Well! My great surgeon, you have to know; you can pride yourself with having made a superb cure and the grand operation had great success."

Hearing that, Matiphous' face lost much of its color; his lips contracted, and he clinched his hand in order to grab a long kitchen knife which the tavern used to slice a large piece of roast beef from Hamburg for its customers. Finding herself alone with Matiphous, and for the first time understanding her danger, Mistress Aston had an inspiration. Without seeming afraid, "Will you please leave the knife where it is, or you won't learn anything."

The impetuosity of the most violent movement can turn from its direction if it encounters the smallest obstacle. Substituting his curiosity for his interest in vengeance, halted Matiphous' bloody intention. He went to sit down on a bench that was to one side, and put his head in his hands.

"Speak," he said to Mistress Aston. "I'm all ears." He kept his eyes fixed on the floor for fear that the sight of the one who had so cruelly played with him would rekindle the furious resentment which he had managed to master.

Wanting, as much as possible, to put herself on the right side, the tavern keeper poured some gin into a glass and, wheedling, presented it to Matiphous, saying:

"Take it, dear. Drink this glass for me. That will put the heart back in you. It's amusing how you immediately took on the look of a dead man!"

"Thanks," Matiphous answered. "I'm not thirsty." Then, when Mistress Alton insisted, "I tell you once more, I don't want a drink," he said, stamping his feet. "Say what you have to say. That would be better."

"All right, then!" the tavern keeper said, moving cautiously toward the door. "I have first to tell you that I would have much preferred a nephew like you to another of Broughton's kind."

"Go on," the man from Malta said dryly, without showing any reaction to the flattery.

"I can assure you," Mistress Aston continued, "I used everything I had of good sense and words to that little hard head to get this unfortunate love out of her mind. But, you know women, once that's gotten into them, the more it's unusual and badly chosen, the more they cling to it, young girls most of all."

"Continue," Matiphous said, seeing that Mistress Aston seemed to be smugly settling into satisfaction with the finesse of her observations.

"Finally," that woman continued, "I saw that little girl losing her mind and perishing, particularly since her Broughton had been condemned. I didn't know what to do to console her, when one day she came to show me the old story of your colleague Chowel, and that a man can be hanged without dying and there are no side effects. 'Very well, then, I told her. 'I have in fact heard about such a thing from the gentlemen at Newgate. But a surgeon to bring it about? It's not just anybody who can do it. It still takes a clever and experienced hand.'"

"Oh, if I had only known!" Matiphous said in a cavernous voice.

"And that would have been the right thing," the tavern keeper answered, entering with good or bad faith into that regret. "But me, do you see? I had given my word. I had promised that little girl that I saw shaking and weeping, to arrange the business with Broughton."

"And also with me?" Matiphous interrupted.

"Yes, with you," Mistress Alton continued. "I won't say anything about our interview, since in fact you know the rest. But, truthfully, I thought I was also doing it in your best interest, because, say what you will, the operation you performed was magnificent. It will be talked about throughout Europe and even in the Indies. To think that a surgeon as young as you…"

"Then," Matiphous said, bringing the tavern keeper back to the subject, "you were charged with negotiating this affair with the boxer?"

"As you say, regretfully. But seeing it was my responsibility, I went to see Broughton and suggested that he marry Ketty. And, would you believe it, he asked me what Ketty would bring him as a dowry! 'Your life, you miserable man,' I told him, 'do you count that for so little?' To sum up, the business was concluded, and although Broughton, while still alive, was going to be considered dead as far as the law was concerned, his heirs could come claim their inheritance, as he willed me all his property. So you see, he is entirely dependent on me. If he doesn't treat Ketty as he should, I'll have a way to make him think better of it, don't you see? I don't have a good feeling about this marriage. I would rather have had you."

"Oh! You miserable go-between," Matiphous shouted angrily. "Why then did you act in Broughton's favor?"

"What did you expect, my boy! Ketty before everything else! She's my joy and I have never known how to refuse her anything."

"But," Matiphous said, still wanting to doubt his failure, "neither you nor your niece knows more about medicine than I do. Broughton, when I left him, had certainly ceased to live, and now you tell me he has been resuscitated!"

"Ah! My friend! The miracle of love! Despairing after seeing him senseless after all the care you gave him, Ketty, about midnight, couldn't help going to visit her monkey, thinking she was going to gaze on him for the last time. But, suddenly, his pretty fiancée was no sooner at his side than that unusual corpse began to cough. Then he sat up, asked for the time. Things went so well that a quarter of an hour later, the couple knocked on the door of this room where I was waiting for them with the Newgate chaplain I had asked to come bless a marriage, without knowing the names of the couple."

"So, they are married?" Matiphous asked, standing up with a threatening look.

"Not at all. On the contrary they are not. That strange chaplain, when he learned that it was a matter of uniting Ketty and Broughton, got terribly angry. He said he would never consent to marry a cadaver. Broughton tried to pass himself off as hale and hearty, explaining the way in which he had been saved. 'Ta, ta, ta, temporary health,' that maniac kept repeating. 'Does anyone ever come back from such an experience? With your incision in the throat? That little girl must be mad to want a husband from the next world,'" and he left without being willing to listen to anything."

"A worthy and holy man!" the man from Malta shouted, and he sat down, half consoled.

243

"Well, yes," Mistress Aston continued, seeming to agree with Matiphous. "But I don't think we have gained very much. They left a while ago for the Isle of Wight, where you know people can get married on short notice."

"In any case, they went there on a yacht, which should bring them good luck if the sample I saw pass by resembles his lovely cargo."

"What!" the tavern keeper exclaimed. "You saw the funeral of that poor Lady Colqhoum? Another amusing imagination!"

"You find amusing a casket, a hearse, and a troop of people in mourning?"

"Enough! Let me explain," the tavern keeper said in a competent tone.

"Mistress Aston, was it probably you that got Ketty passage on that yacht?" the man from Malta asked.

"I was without a doubt, me," the audacious woman answered, taking the precaution, however, of moving toward the door. "Like all *bon vivants*, Colqhoum is one of my friends. I knew that his yacht, after having brought his wife's corpse here, would stop at the Isle of Wight. I then asked him asylum for our lovers. Shouldn't you finish what you start?"

"Keep your fear for later," Matiphous, who had noted the cautious maneuver of Mistress Aston, said solemnly. "It isn't in full daylight and on the sill of your shack that I mean to take your skin. But remember my words, you, Broughton, your charming niece, and your friend Colqhoum, I know how to find you later. Ketty told me yesterday, 'People from Malta are enraged with vengeance!' Well, I'm from Malta! I have one of those personalities that doesn't forget if one lives a thousand years! And vengeance is a dish that can be eaten cold. Good-day, Mistress Aston".

And he left.

XIII. The Prince of Asturies. What Colqhoum was

"Colqhoum," Matiphous said to himself on leaving *The*

Bottle and Magpie tavern, where so many things that cruelly wounded his ego had been told him. "Colqhoum! I think I remember that name."

And his memory began to torture itself, trying to recall where and under what circumstances he had heard about the person Mistress Aston, Ketty's aunt, had pointed out as an accomplice in the secret of which he was a victim. But suddenly his mnemonic work was rather disagreeably interrupted.

After he had left Jack Ketch's house, in the corner of a mirror in Ketty's bedroom, had been found a letter where, telling her family goodbye, she had revealed the name of her strange ravisher, and telling how he was still capable of being a very acceptable husband after having been hanged.

It would have been better for Jack Ketch's wife if she had kept the whole adventure secret. Although he was absent, her husband remained nonetheless responsible for the choice of his aides. On his return, he might be very annoyed by the authorities and later the escape of the boxer. But, undone by despair, the worthy Mistress Ketch couldn't keep from pouring out her maternal despair to some gossips in the neighborhood. Despite the discretion asked and promised, by secret circulation the gossip about that extraordinary event came to the ears of the sheriff with all of the details. He immediately gave the order to apprehend Matiphous wherever he could be found and to take him to Newgate. This rigorous order was executed almost at the instant the poor dupe left Mistress Aston's house.

The popular rumor had in the same way equally made its way into the prison, situated at a very little distance from Jack Ketch's house. When Matiphous was brought into the prison, he found all the prisoners assembled to do him honor. A speaker addressed a beautiful speech to him, in which the service he had done to humanity was praised almost to the skies. The conclusion of the compliment was that instead of having to pay for entering, as was the custom, the surgeon was humbly asked if he please accept a banquet which had been unanimously voted for him.

Matiphous gave a rather cold reception to that brilliant reception, not because he took his imprisonment and the sheriff's anger much to heart, far from it. To see it declared by being arrested that he had failed his job of hangman would rather have seemed rehabilitation to him. But his incarceration was going to put an obstacle in the way of his plans for vengeance. That continued to be his major preoccupation. He counted on obtaining some information about Colqhoum, whom Mistress Aston had said was one of her friends, from the habitual customers of *The Bottle and Magpie*. He responded to the curiosity of those who had come forward to compliment him.

"Pouf!" he was answered, "to know what Colqhoum is! You really aren't squeamish. A lot of others before you have wanted that, but that man is a bottomless well that no one has yet flattered himself that he has sounded its depth."

At the same time, an officious rolling fire of explanations crossed each other in front of Matiphous. They formed the following litany: "Colqhoum? He deals in contraband;" "A nabob;" "A learned naturalist, who knows the philosopher's stone;" "A counterfeiter;" "A retired merchant;" "A charitable and generous man;" "The good angel of artists;" "A bon vivant, but not proud, who comes to drink blue death with us at Mistress Alton's tavern;" "A hermaphrodite, neither man nor woman. Or rather, both a man and a woman, like the Chevalier d'Éon."[91]

With this last comment, Matiphous' memory was put back on the path of memories he was seeking. He remembered that during his sojourn in England, the newspapers had several times entertained the public with a character about whom they published various eccentricities, notably his sex, but also that of the Chevalier or Chevalière d'Éon. He was, exactly at that time, residing in England, and was the object of considerable bookmaking. But Matiphous thought at the same time that he

---

[91] See Note 32.

remembered having seen this living puzzle several times at Mistress Aston's tavern. It was not under the name of Colqhoum, but a Spanish name, and that was the name the newspapers had used for him.

When the man from Malta remarked on this, the numerous prisoners around him answered:

"That's right! In the past he was a Spanish marquis, but today he's come up in rank and he's a child of Old England."

"What's more," one of those giving information continued, "if Your Grace wants to know more, you may talk to the Prince of Asturies walking over there with the look of a dethroned emperor. He's a man who says he's well informed about Colqhoum, with whom he seems to have had differences."

Matiphous glanced toward the person who had been pointed out under the name of Prince of Asturies. The name was obviously a prison nick-name to justify his haughty manners and lack of communication with those who gave him that name.

In this Spanish prince, made in England, Matiphous saw a tall, blond young man with elegant bearing and a gentle and melancholy demeanor. The man from Malta was drawn to talking to him and went to meet him. After having apologized for taking the liberty of disturbing his solitude, he asked him if he would please tell him what he knew about a certain Colqhoum, a man about whom he had reasons to be informed.

"Yes, certainly," the solitary walker answered. His face had become animated at the name he had just heard. "I can speak knowingly of this shadowy person. It's because of him that I am here, under condemnation of capital punishment. But you, sir, who are you?"

"Me! I am Doctor Matiphous."

"Ah! the one who resuscitates the hanged! I may perhaps recommend myself to your talented services."

"I like to think there won't be any need."

"God's will be done," the prisoner said in a resigned voice. Then, coming back to Matiphous' question, "Well, sir, you honor me by asking about the personality of the infamous Colqhoum. But that story might very well seem long to you."

"What does that matter? Here where we are, don't we have time to kill?"

"You're right," the Prince answered, and he began as follows:

"I belong, sir, to an honest family of merchants in the City. My father, of whom I was the only child, left me considerable wealth when he died. I could therefore have had an honorable and happy life without the deplorable passion that I let myself fall into for our great tragic artist, Miss Anna Oldfield.

"Sought after by the greatest names in aristocracy, proud and capricious, for a long time that girl wouldn't pay any attention to a love that, with a thousand sacrifices, I had tried to make her accept its homage. Suddenly one single attention fulfilled my wishes. One of her caprices was to eat woods' strawberry in the middle of February. She had had them looked for in all the London fruit merchants. I learned that at one of the hothouses of the Duke of Northumberland, Sion House, famous for the magnificence of its gardens, I had a chance of procuring that delicacy for Miss Oldfield. I exhausted a horse to cover the twenty-four miles, coming and going, that separated Sion-House from the capitol. Before twenty-four hours had elapsed, I had sent to the beautiful actress a little basket containing forty, three-fourths ripe strawberries, for which I had paid one guinea each. An hour later I received a note that invited me to come to the great tragedienne's dressing room after the drama. The next day I had nothing left to desire."

"Hum!" Matiphous said, "that taste for early fruit, that's a conquest that would slowly exhaust the inheritance."

"What you say is only too true," the young man answered. "With her ruinous fantasies, Miss Oldfield was a bottomless pit. Once our intimacy was established, she began to dip into my purse with an ease and abandon which my love's foolish abandon made me find infinitely charming. I had already begun to notice the state of my affairs when a man began to show up in London who was to have a disastrous influence on my life's economy.

"He arrived from the Indies, but that, however, it was said, wasn't the least of his peregrinations. He brought back a fortune from his long voyages; at least that was what was supposed by the amount he soon began to spend on his living quarters.

"He began by renting the magnificent old Ancaster town house, where by using as bait a fabulous rental rate, he managed to dislodge the proprietor of this marvelous edifice, a master work of our architect Inigo Jones.[92] He established a menagerie that he had brought with him, which for its rarity, if not for its number, even rivaled that of the royal menagerie. A natural history gallery, a library and a collection of ancient pictures that he added to by numerous orders and purchases of modern artists, constituted a princely dwelling for him. Into that sort of museum, the public was biweekly admitted with more freedom and courtesy than in any of our national establishments.

"As for the proprietor of all this magnificence, often taking the trouble to entertain those eager to visit, he was without equal in affability and courtesy. Furnished with letters of introduction, and in addition, better recommended still by his opulence, the newcomer had soon insinuated himself into aristocratic salons. Gambling heavily, winning with indifference, losing with laughter, intrepid fox hunter, betting heavily at New Market, he knew how to fit in rapidly to the customs and elegant habits of the country where he was asking hospitality. In all of England it would have been difficult to find a more accomplished model of the perfect gentleman. His

---

[92] Inigo Jones (1573-1652), English architect of Welsh ancestry, who left his mark on London by single buildings, such as the Queen's House and the Banqueting House, Whitehall, as well as the layout for Covent Garden square which became a model for future developments in the West End.

popularity grew with the revelation of several charitable acts, for which he managed to get necessary publicity, while at the same time, afterward, seeming to be very annoyed at its being noised abroad. Finally, lodging in his house artists, literary people, pensions given to several others, and two or three dinners, where he brought together the most elegant London company, and which the newspapers published its sumptuousness, made him the hero in fashion. Never, in the annals of fashion, had there ever been seen a more complete success.

"After some time, however, a little mist began to form around that shining figure. First of all, there was his strange effeminate exterior, his high, shrill voice.

"Yes, I recognize that voice," Matiphous interrupted. "I once had the opportunity to hear it."

"Well," the storyteller continued, "that so little virile appearance wasn't long in bringing out some ridicule. That was the cause of a duel in which one of the precious offshoots of the great families of the peerage died. That misfortune began to lower his popularity.

"That direction once taken, certain things, which up until then he had been credited as having, emerged as being important. They started looking into his past and his antecedents, about which, it was noticed, he, in fact, had never opened his mouth. They wanted to know the reasons for his presence in England. On this subject, it was never possible to obtain any answer. Without asking him the question directly, they cleverly got information from his servants about the supposed origin of his huge opulence. Instead of clarification, they got impertinence. Infinitely less talkative and communicating little, his house servants seemed to have received orders. They unanimously answered that this Croesus had become rich through dealing in whalebones, which sold in Europe for women's corsets. This explanation was obviously derisory and was designed to throw curiosity off the track by mystification.

"Things were at that point, and without any outward sign

yet appearing, there was the small sound of the demolition of the high pedestal on which the bizarre character had at first been placed. Then a lamentable star threw me into his path.

"It had been noticed for some time that this problematic person was very often at Covent Garden, but only on the days that Miss Oldfield was on stage. He showed the highest admiration for her monologues and her acting when she was center stage.

"I made a mistake, but not by showing jealousy of a rival whose exterior was so little attractive that I saw not the shadow of danger. Several jokes were aimed at me relative to the possibility of a rival. I made the mistake of answering scornfully and I alluded to the unusual gossip about the man they wanted me to be jealous of.

"One afternoon I was with Miss Oldfield. Suddenly in the street under her windows there was an unusual sound. That noise was produced by an assortment of curious people around a splendid carriage which had just stopped at the door of the house. In the noise made by that crowd, I seemed to hear the name of that nabob. In fact, just at that moment both doors opened. Probably fascinated by the notoriety of the person, without coming to ask her mistress if she wanted to be seen, Miss Oldfield's chamber maid announced: Marquis Vicente de Samaniego!

"Walking calmly toward my mistress, the newcomer took her hand cavalierly and brought it to his lips; then in a slightly German accent and in his ridiculous soprano voice,

"'Would the most beautiful talent and the most splendid beauty of England,' he said to Miss Oldfield, who looked at him in amazement, "'please pardon me for being late in offering her the homage of my admiration?'

"'But your Excellency owes me nothing,' the actress answered him. 'He has nothing to be pardoned for, and his visit will find me grateful at whatever time he wants to honor me.'

"'Oh, but he does! He does!' the stranger quickly answered. 'My behavior would be uncivilized and inexplicable if I didn't have an excuse in the attention that I had to give my house to receive in your person, charming Miss, the pearl of three continents.'

"'That's already taken place, sir. I have been your guest, just like all of London. I have visited your royal townhouse, in which I found only one flaw; the master wasn't there that day.'

"'Oh! That's not the way I mean. I don't want you as a visitor. Your apartment is now presentable. I am here to find out when you will be pleased to come live in it.'

"'How's that! I'm to come live in your townhouse?'

"But of course, my very adorable one,' the impertinent visitor replied, glancing around at the room where he had been received and where I had spent a considerable sum for the furnishings. 'You are suffering here in a veritable rat's nest. It isn't an apartment, but a temple that your beauty needs, and, as much as possible, I have provided one for that religion.'

"'Allow me, sir,' I said, intervening, 'it's first necessary to know if Miss Oldfield wants to accept your unusual offer, and if, first of all as a preamble, she wouldn't have to ask the agreement, or, to put it better, the advice of some friends.'

"'Is that you, Master Fauntleroy?' the nabob then said to me, seeming to notice me in the apartment. In a protective tone that it's impossible to describe, I answered:

"'Yes, sir, and I dare say that I have that honor.'

"'The son of a Master Fauntleroy, a merchant in the City?'

"'Yes, sir, a man whose fortune has a known source, and who is only English, without being Spanish in name, German in pronunciation, and whose face, whose bearing and the sound of his voice have no known origin.'

"'Well, Master Fauntleroy,' the bizarre character continued, without seeming to have noticed the insult contained in my words, 'I am charmed to meet you. I intended to come visit you one of these days, and preach a little sense into you. Honor, position, is not tenable for you. While doing things in a mediocre way, your fortune is already compromised. Your revenue is slowly diminishing, and we are dipping into the capital. Miss Oldfield is a crushing expense for you. And on her side, she cannot eternally resign herself to the requirements of your paltry resources, which are blowing away, when someone comes to lay millions at her feet.'

"'Sir! That isn't me, but Miss Oldfield that you're insulting!'

"'Come now, Master Fauntleroy,' Miss Oldfield said, laughing, 'don't get upset. You see his Excellency has a joking and original personality, and, besides, he actually could be somewhat right.'

"'No, by God, I'm not joking,' the audacious person answered. 'I am very seriously claiming the honor of being your host. And to speak like a certain great lady of incorrigible virtue, I will give you this much, this much, and this much if you will graciously consent not to finish ruining this poor young man. As for him, if he still feels himself insulted, in a quarter of an hour not only will I be completely at his orders, but awaiting how interesting his position may be, I formally commit myself not to kill him.'

"'That is too much,' I shouted with a menacing gesture.

"'My dear, you are foolish, and as a result very inconvenient,' Miss Oldfield said to me, throwing herself in front of me. 'You know how I abhor the manners of a boxer, and in my presence, at least, you will restrain your fiery irritation.'

"While in this way my mistress indirectly seemed to take the part of an insolent rival, he approached the fireplace. Finding there a richly incised dish holding some valuable rings that were there on approval, he opened the window and threw them one by one to the crowd that was still outside the house.

"'But, Marquis, what are you doing?' Miss Oldfield exclaimed, seeing where her rings were going.

"'Oh! Miss, I'm throwing those gems which dishonor you to the people. I brought some stones from the Orient that I beg you to be willing to accept. You will recognize that these here are not worth even a glance from your beautiful eyes.'

"That prodigious self-possession seemed to impress the

actress."

"'Well, Miss Anna,' I asked, 'is it this gentleman or I who must cede his place?'

"'Those who find themselves in the way here,' the queen of the theatre proudly answered, 'are perfectly free to leave. I'm not dismissing anyone, but I'm also not holding anyone back.'

"'That's not an answer, and at least have the courage...'

"'Come now, young man,' the infernal stranger said. 'Miss Oldfield knows life too well to give you that tiresome compliment you seem to be soliciting. Understand how things are: we promise to be at your house in a quarter of an hour, and what's more, we will take care of you.'

"'Anna,' I shouted as I left, 'the lowest tavern servant has less of my contempt than you.'

"The actress was content to shrug. While casually stretching out in an armchair, my vanquisher seemed to be taking charge of the property he had come to acquire."

XIV. Continuation of Fauntleroy's story.
The Duel. The Reconciliation.

On leaving that house where I had just witnessed an insolent triumph of gold, I rushed to my house, picked up two dueling swords, and less than a half hour after the scene that had just taken place, I was in my carriage at Miss Oldfield's door, where the Spaniard's carriage was still parked. A little later, seeing him appear, I quickly put my head out the carriage window. As soon as he saw me, he asked me if I still had the same intentions.

"'Sir,' I answered him, showing him the swords, "'here are the weapons. Are they satisfactory to you?'

"'They are both satisfactory to me. But seconds?'

"Hearing my answer that we could do without them: 'As many killed as wounded,' as they commonly say, there will be nobody dead. So be it, my dear enemy. To Hyde Park, isn't that right? Go ahead of me, my carriage will follow.'"

Arriving at a little frequented path, we got out of our carriages and went into the bushes. As soon as we found a favorable spot, I wanted to cross swords.

"'No, jackets off, please,' my adversary said to me. 'I like formality and I want things to take place in the regular way. Besides, I like to know where I strike, and that I have cut my gashes properly.'

"I believe I have some ability in swordsmanship, but if I had been crossing swords with the foremost London master, I wouldn't have found myself more outmatched. My strikes were those of a frenzied man. I paid no attention to being struck provided that my blows carried. But with an imperceptible turn of his wrist, without making a counter stroke, that dangerous adversary turned away all my cuts. And when he had, for several minutes, taken my attacks, with a little curt strike, he sent my sword flying. He hurried to pick it up, and presented it to me courteously.

"I was too beyond myself to recognize the generosity of that act, so that when he asked me if I wanted to continue:

"My life or yours; that's why we're here."

"'Ah! You want blood,' the Marquis said to me, smiling. 'So be it, my dear fellow. There will be some.'

"The combat on my side began again as furious as ever. My adversary, on the contrary, kept his cool head and serenity. But in a moment, as I was recovering from a thrust, after having lunged with all the strength I was capable of, with a thrust as fast as lightning, his sword struck me in the chest. That was all for me. I would have been pierced from side to side, if, with a sureness of hand that can't be imagined, this prodigious swordsman hadn't brought back his sword to only mark a cross on my chest, a long scratch of no depth, only piercing the skin. At the same time, repeating the disarmament strike which he had already used, my sword again flew out of my hand. But, this time, instead of picking it up, he threw his own to one side and said:

"'Since I can't, my dear sir, spend my life running after your sword, we'll leave it there, if you agree. Does your inclination now turn to pistols, with which you are perhaps more familiar? I am ready to oblige you, but as a preamble, I dare ask you to watch one of my recreations.' Saying that, he clapped his hands several times, and an Indian, whom I had already noticed behind his carriage, immediately appeared, wearing the picturesque dress of his country.

From an expensive box, the servant took out a beautiful, living butterfly with the richest colors and presented it to his master. Pierced through with a golden needle, struggling at the end of it, the insect was fixed to the Indian's headdress like some sort of cockade. Picking up a pistol, the Marquis stepped back thirty paces. He readied himself to aim at the living target. Standing out so little from the headdress, the butterfly's constantly rotating wings seemed to make the shot impossible, even for the imagination.

"'Sir! Sir!' I shouted, with a kind of terror. "'That is useless. I don't doubt your competence and your dexterity.

"'Don't worry,' he replied, laughing. 'This is something I have done a hundred times in my life. Look and see if our assistant is worried.'

"My eyes, with a sort of fascination, were drawn toward the Indian. His expression, however, was completely impassive. The weapon was fired; the man hadn't been touched. Just after the detonation, he followed the line of the bullet. In a moment he presented me with the needle, twisted by the force of the shot, and from which there hung some remains of the butterfly.

"'That's how I shoot,' the Spaniard told me coldly, 'and that's not because I want to discourage you, because with the pistol, I don't fight without witnesses. And any case, that would mean setting up another meeting. Besides, it's possible that by tomorrow you will have completely changed your mind. So, goodbye, then, my amiable adversary,' he added in a very gracious voice, and followed by the Indian, who had helped him pick up his jacket, he left me in prey to all the feelings you can imagine.

"An hour had scarcely gone by since my encounter with

the Marquis, when, to my great surprise, he was announced at my apartment. After some hesitation I agreed to see him.

"'Dear, sir,' he said to me, 'I've come to finish with you what we started. Honor has such demands that, even without owing it to you, I thought that it was proper to give you the satisfaction that you desired from me. Now, would you please allow me to give you some explanations?'

"'Your actions, sir, are not such that could be explained,' I replied. 'Taking advantage of the most shameful of superiorities, that of money, you came to destroy my happiness!'

"'That means,' the Marquis said, interrupting me, 'that without hearing what I have to say, you have used a tone with me that immediately causes bitterness between us. But what if you were mistaken, what if I had no claim on Miss Oldfield, and if, in a word, I wasn't in love with her?'

"'It would be impossible to tell you what happiness rushed into my heart at that declaration. However, I thought I owed it to my dignity not to show this movement of joy. And avoiding coming around too soon, I replied.'

"'Your conduct in that case would be even more unpardonable, because only an overwhelming passion could justify your attempt to supplant me.'

"'But it wasn't the least in the world an attempt to take your place. I find your liaison with Miss Oldfield, the most respectable and the most fitting, and my only ambition is to be there as a third party, on the footage of a friend.'

"'I admit, sir, that some proofs to support this completely new point of view, seem to me necessary and difficult to give.'

"'Ah!' the Marquis answered, 'now we've come back to explanations? Well, then, please listen to me. Up until now, if I haven't mentioned it, I have used my fortune in a passably honorable and intelligent way.'

"'Yesterday, I would have been the first to agree.'

"'Without,' the Marquis continued, 'passing myself off as Léon X, or as a male Medici or a female Medici, I have done things for the arts and science, two professions by their nature somewhat disadvantaged, that required some sacrifices, for which I have been given credit. Today, I have as guests in my house, painters, sculptors and poets. I have, in addition, brought together art collections, which, as far as I am able, I have made available to the public. But have you not noticed that in that temple of intelligence there was lacking a soul, a visible divinity under whom my pious institution was placed? That idol, dear sir, I have found in the person of Miss Oldfield, who unites two crowns at once, that of talent and beauty. In coming to ask her to please sanctify my habitation with her presence, my thought, I must persuade you, never went beyond that.'

"'That wasn't the result of your words, and you positively presented yourself as a declared rival.'

"'Because, without letting me explain the object of my visit more clearly, you yourself began acting unreasonable. But, while inflicting the small chastisement it seemed to me your jealousy deserved, I nevertheless respected all your rights. Please question Miss Oldfield. She will tell you, when you were not there, in no way did I go beyond the limits I pose here.'

"'However that may be,' I replied, 'I must point out to you that there are insurmountable difficulties! How can the public take the role destined for me in that party of three? Would I not seem to be obliging to a situation that would seriously compromise my reputation?'

"'Ah! You're concerned with public opinion!' the Marquis said disdainfully.

"'With no doubt; that's a power that must be deferred to.'"

"'Me, I prefer to defy it, and fall back only on my conscience. But, actually, what would that prude have to be concerned about here? Isn't Ancaster House a vast enough building for Miss Oldfield to be lodged there at the same distance from me as if she just lived in the same street or the same neighborhood? Do I ask you to stop visiting her? Wouldn't you always be admitted as in the past at any hour of the day or night? After that, you must consider that Miss Oldfield has the honor of being the most celebrated actress of her time. This profession, it seems to me certainly has some exemptions that can very conveniently be invoked in this situation.'

"'But, if all that were true, where does this fantasy lead?'

"'I've told you. First of all to crown the pediment of my temple by placing a magnificent statue there; and, then, if you forbid me to love Miss with my heart, would you also forbid me to adore her with my brain? Is it a crime in your opinion to want to see up close and informally the one I have twenty times seen and applauded on stage? Does possessing the charms of your mistress give you a monopoly of her whole life?'

"'I am certainly not so ridiculous,' I answered, 'and confronting an offer that I believed for an instant a threat, I was never jealous.'

"'Well! There where you thought you saw a danger, there was never even a threat. I am, certainly the object of much curiosity, and I have never opened my past to anyone. But, since it's absolutely necessary to reassure you, for you I will be indiscrete vis-à-vis myself. Come dine this evening with Miss Oldfield at Ancaster House and to a certain extent I promise you an inviolable secret; I will show you who I am. You can then judge for yourself if you should fear rivalry from me.'

"'But to accept your invitation with Miss Oldfield, I must know if she has forgiven me for my recent behavior in front of her and then if she would accept.'

"'All that has been done,' he replied. 'As a fine actress, Miss Oldfield has studied the human heart too long not to recognize a troublesome and mean jealous outburst. Her vengeance was limited to laughing a little at your solemn curse as you departed. As for my ambition of having her to dine today without the permission of her lord and master, she has agreed.'

"'Agreed for the dinner,' I answered, 'but if you will

remember, a short time ago you told Miss Oldfield and you told me myself that I was exhausted as a provider, while you had millions to put at her feet. Now, you understand, that's one of the situations that's impossible for me. The pleasure of enriching the loved one is happiness that can't be shared.'

"'Come now, let's be reasonable,' the Marquis continued. 'I doubt very much that would be our stumbling block. I have my list of arguments ready. The great fortunes that the queens of the theater often make, where do they come from? First of all, the money comes from the public, which comes to their hands after having passed through the hands of the theater manager, where the greatest part stops; then from gifts from some of their admirers.'

"'That's enough,' I replied.

"'Well, because, instead of pouring out drop by drop, shilling by shilling, penny by penny from the pockets of the middle class or the apprentices in the City, the money to a great artist would come all at once, in a wave, as the tribute from one ardent admirer, that artist would be compromised and everyone wouldn't have the right to give to her according to his ability?'

"'That reasoning has something specious about it.'

"'And what is more than specious,' the Marquis answered, 'is a verifiable and palpable truth that the gifts from a platonic and disinterested admirer, as I pride myself in being, would make possible an endurable future for an illustrious artist are infinitely less insulting to her than those from an egoist like you, who puts them out at interest. My way, sir, raises genius by endowing it, while yours dishonors it. At least dishonor it on a grand scale and pay her honor all the price it's worth.'

"'Mon Dieu!' I answered, a little stung, 'I know I will never be able to compensate at its just value Miss Oldfield's prodigious talent.'

"'And until now,' the Marquis cleverly replied, 'that has been your glory, because that's a proof that you are loved for yourself, and that your sacrifices are only those of a friend.

But a friend can do only so much. The glory days of the theater are used up and pass quickly. And one fine day, a woman will find that she has sacrificed her talent and youth to later come up against poverty because she has gambled everything on a respectable but ruinous attachment.'

"'You seem to have logic on your side,' I replied, 'but nevertheless there is a certain instinct in me that resists your rhetoric.'

"'Let's sum things up. If a King of England or some Prince of the blood had the idea of making Miss Oldfield's fortune at one fell swoop, would that lower her reputation?'

"'Certainly not. That would be homage to her inimitable talent.'

"'Well,' the Marquis said, getting up, 'then you come this evening and I will show you that I am greater than the King of England and all the Princes of his family, because I'm more powerful than they are.'

"That said, that unusual man probably didn't think it was possible to add anything to that magnificent boast. Without waiting for my answer, he took his leave.

"When I was free, I first of all had to hurry to Miss Oldfield, to whom I had, in any case, to apologize for the outrageous and violent way I left her. I found her carried away with the mind and manners of our future friend. In addition, her ego having easily persuaded her that it was a matter of homage, as generous as disinterested, paid to her talent, she was too excited to even think of chastising me. Appearances, she was the first to admit, were against her. Only, I must understand, she said, that she didn't seriously seem to agree to what we both had at first taken as a proposition from the Marquis.

"As for the answer that would be given to his proposition, Miss Oldfield seemed to me to be strongly inclined to the solution that would install her at Ancaster House, and a great part of Don Vincente Samaniego's argument came from the mouth of my beautiful mistress.

"The summary of our rather long consultation was that

before making a decision, we should look into it. As a result, a few hours after our furious encounter, I was pleasantly seated at my adversary's table waiting for the very conclusive secrets that he had made us hope for.

"The meal was exquisitely presented. A mass of exotic products that our Amphitryon had brought back from his voyages, as they were served without affectation, truly gave us a very curious course of gastronomic geography. After dinner, counting on the effect of that seduction, our host insisted that we go visit the apartment he had furnished for Miss Oldfield. And despite my secret repugnance to enter into the proposed arrangement, I was forced to admit that in furnishings nothing could have been designed that was at same time as sumptuous and as stylish. Luxurious items from every country in the world, oriental, Japanese, European, Chinese, those from the two Americas, even primitive items, were mixed and married with consummate taste for the future tenant for life of all that magnificence.

"One thing above all must have seemed priceless to her that was the care with which her monogram had everywhere been mixed with the trappings of tragedy.

"Finally, foreseeing a propriety that was not, for me, an indifferent guarantee, the lodgings destined for Miss Oldfield were in a separate wing, at such a great distance from the apartments occupied by the Marquis that it would scarcely be possible to claim that he and his beautiful tenant lived under the same roof.

"That visit to the locations once achieved, I could not hide from myself that my queen of the theatre's decision was, if not already decided, at least three-quarters taken. There remained only the secrets we had been promised and the Marquis began them in something like the following:

XV. Continuation of Fauntleroy's Story. The Cabalist

"'I'm going to tell you about things,' Don Vicente Samaniego told us, 'so far outside the ordinary realm of life, that I find myself placed between the danger of being held as a visionary by you and that of seeming to want to insult your credulity. However that may be, I dare, nevertheless, solicit a promise of absolute discretion from you. Two and one make three, and confiding to your two loyalties the secret of which I am the depository, I remain in the limit of the *TRIADE*. Dispersed beyond this fatal and privileged number, *science* would turn against us, and then there are no dangers or misfortunes to which we would not be exposed.'

"Although not understanding a great deal of the mystic words with which we had just been greeted, we hurriedly took the engagement asked of us, and then the Marquis continued:

"'You are too young,' he said, 'my excellent friends to have known Count Alexandre de Cagliostro who, following a long sojourn in France, came, in 1786, to live in the English capital, where he resided about ten years.[93] But you surely have heard talked about that extraordinary man who made marvelous medical cures. Called by the envious a charlatan and adventurer, he had access to the greatest Lords, with whom walked as an equal. Finally, without possessing an

---

[93] Not quite. Count Alessandro di Cagliostro (1743-1795) was the alias of the occultist Giuseppe Balsamo. On April 12, 1776 Balsamo was admitted as a Freemason of the Esperance Lodge in London. In December 1777, he and his wife left London. In February 1779, he traveled to Mitau. In September 1780, he made his way to Strasbourg. In October 1784, he traveled to Lyon. In January 1785, he Balsamo went to Paris in response to the entreaties of Cardinal Rohan. There, he became involved in the so-called "Affair of the Queen's necklace," was prosecuted and held in the Bastille for nine months, but finally acquitted. He was asked to leave France, so he returned to England, but soon left to go to Rome, where he was betrayed to the Inquisition. On 27 December 1789, he was arrested and imprisoned in the Castel Sant'Angelo.

ounce of land under the sun, he could draw considerable sums from bankers in all the world's capitals, which he dispensed with generosity and liberality. He did so as a man perfectly free from the worry of seeing that source of infinite riches dry up. Who was this marvelous personage? Many people have asked themselves that.'"

"Has anyone, in fact, ever explained who that man was?" Matiphous asked Fauntleroy, interrupting his story.

"It was thought," Fauntleroy replied, "that he possessed some advanced knowledge in chemistry, and that his great resources of money were explained by his affiliation with the Freemasons; but such was not the opinion, at least the apparent opinion, of the Marquis de Samaniego, because," continuing to address Miss Oldfield and me, "he said to us:

"'...All the explanations given on the subject of this great man remain, whatever is said, surrounded with inextricable difficulties, and only you will have the key to the enigma when I have told you,' the Marquis added, lowering his voice, 'that Cagliostro was a man in business with the elementary spirits, in a word, a *cabalist.*'

"At that statement, Miss Oldfield and I looked at each other, as if to be in agreement as to the way in which we should take that somewhat grotesque confidence of our new friend. But just at that moment, the Marquis stood up, and, from a piece of furniture that he opened with three keys, one of bronze, the next of silver, and the next of gold, he took out a superbly bound little volume. On the fastener, which was of gold, and on the corners which were of gold set with precious stones, as well as on the cover, that one would have thought was of green-veined marble, but that our host told us was of Vesuvius larva, there was a crowd of strange signs bizarrely interlaced. Inside there was a parchment manuscript enriched with precious miniatures representing flowers and fantastic animal figures. The writing, so far as I could believe, were neither Hebrew, nor Arab, and perhaps they were all fantasy and did not belong to any known language.

"When he had let us consider this little volume for a moment, that, in any case, could be taken for a valuable object of curiosity, the Marquis continued:

"'The way in which I came to possess this valuable treasure is most unusual. I was born in Spain, as my name shows you, but the greater part of my youth I spent with my uncle who occupied a high position at the Imperial Court of Austria. At his death, then a possessor of an independent fortune, I gave myself over to an inordinate passion for travel that I had always had, which, as you are going to see shortly, hasn't turned out too badly for me.

"'About ten years ago, I visited Egypt. So, like all tourists, I didn't miss going to visit the Pyramids. At that time, like everyone, I saw only in that fabulous mass of stones the gigantic work of humans. However, on the subject of the Great Pyramid, the erection of which is generally attributed to King Cheops,[94] an Arab serving as my guide, told me a story that has stuck in my memory. According to that legend, King Cheops hadn't managed to procure those immense monoliths which form the basis of the monument, except by giving his own daughter over to the eager attentions of a genie, or spirit of the earth, who took charge of furnishing him those colossal stones, stipulating that shameful condition. The truth is that, aside from the genie, King Cheops' infamy is set down in Herodotus' history, where I recall perfectly, having read it.

"'As for why the odious monarch wanted to raise at any price that mountain of stone, that interest was vanity. He destined that great pyramid to serve as his sepulcher. And it was there, in fact, according to all the historians, that his mortal remains were placed.

---

[94] Khufu, also known under his Hellenized name of Khêops or Cheops, is the name of a Fourth Dynasty ancient Egyptian pharaoh, who ruled in the first half of the Old Kingdom period (26th century BC). He is generally accepted as having commissioned the Great Pyramid of Giza.

"'The desire struck me to visit the royal crypt, where, it seemed to me, no one before me had entered. Some clearing work done, accompanied by two guides carrying torches, I went first into a vast, vaulted room in which I saw nothing remarkable. To go beyond was a matter of going into a passageway that plunged rather rapidly into the depths of the monument where, in that narrow passage there was no access to a ramp, so my two companions became afraid. It was therefore alone that I, after somewhat disagreeable work on my stomach and my knees, came to a second room. It was a great deal more spacious and much more ornamented than the first.

"'In the center of that second enclosure, there rose a black marble sarcophagus, probably the one I was looking for. During my sojourns in Muslim countries, I habitually adopted the dress of the country. I therefore carried a dagger in my belt. That weapon was made of the hardest Damascus steel, and with it I wouldn't have been afraid to cut through steel if I had tried to. Curious to know what my King Cheops, who must have been marvelously embalmed, had become after two thousand years, with the help of my dagger's blade, that I had managed to slide between two pieces of marble, I tried to raise the tomb's lid. Although it must have been terribly heavy, the block budged under my efforts. And I had an almost indistinct sensation of having moved something with my efforts. But, at the same instant, a dull noise told me of the folly of my effort.

"'The steel blade, forged as strongly as it was, had given way to an immense resistance, and I found I had nothing more in my hand but the blade's handle. The blade that I had engaged right up to the hilt, remained caught between the two pieces of marble that I had tried to separate. However, just the width of the space made by the presence of that thin foreign body was an immense result for me. By that opening, hardly visible to the eye, I saw a thick vapor escape. Its smell recalled the particular perfume given off by the earth following a long dry spell after it has just received a rain downpour. That vapor soon condensed, took on bodily shape, and finally there stood in front of me a little man who, in the light of my torch did not produce his shadow. From that, I judged he was a spirit...'"

"Ah, well, so what?" Matiphous said to Fauntleroy. "It seems to me that your Marquis told you some very oriental stories."

"That's also how it seemed," Fauntleroy continued, "to Miss Oldfield and to me. Nevertheless, I must say that he told his story in such a perfectly convincing tone and with an air of such astonishing good faith, we would have taken it for a mental derangement rather than an attempt to mystify us. What's more, the end of his story was not less extraordinary than the beginning. To believe him, that spirit, for whom he found he had provided an exit, was exactly the same one who had made that infamous business deal with King Cheops which consisted of trading a royal heir for some monoliths. At the death of his contraband father-in-law, the spirit, to make amends for his lechery, had been buried with the dead man in the marble sarcophagus, where he had to stay to do penance until the moment that some chance would deliver him. The instrument of that liberation, the Marquis, had everything to expect as gratitude from that elementary spirit, which, in fact, did make him a gift of that little volume that we had just seen. And what a treasure was that volume, which was none other than the real *Clavicules de Salomon*,[95] an immense and precious repository of all the formulas known to evoke spirits."

"And in all of that," Matiphous remarked, "where were those guarantees that you should find against M. de Samaniego's rivalry?"

"Ah!" Fauntleroy answered, "with the advice of his friend the spirit, who had begun by putting at his disposition incalculable treasures, the Marquis had been very careful not to come in contact with the dark spirits of the abyss. Doing

---

[95] *The Keys of Salomon, a.k.a. Clavicula Salomonis*, is a grimoire incorrectly attributed to King Solomon. It probably dates back to the 14th or 15th century Italian Renaissance. It is a typical example of Renaissance magic

business with that infernal breed, that ultimately is always paid very dearly for his services; he preferred those of the elementary spirits, which are always gentle, kindly and natural friends of mankind. And devoting himself with rare passion to a study of the *CABALE*,[96] he came to live with them in such familiarity that he had finally left his heart in the hands of a sylphide[97] of whom he claimed to be the happy lover. But to arrive at that ethereal voluptuousness, the road was hard and difficult. It was only after years of unknown chastity that he managed to obtain the good graces of that celestial lover.

"'Now, my dear Fauntleroy,' the cabalist said to me in finishing, 'you can judge if, engaged in a liaison that has made me completely happy for a long time, I can think of following on the heels of yours, and besides exposing myself to the terrible vengeance my infidelity would incur.'"

"'Hum! Hum!' Miss Oldfield broke in, 'I have at least the merit of being forbidden fruit.'

"'No, my beautiful friend,' the Marquis answered. 'For me, you are not at all to be feared. And should your ego suffer somewhat from that admission, I will go so far as to say that between me and the charming spirit of the air, you would instead be one more tie. Invisible witness to all my actions as to all my thoughts, she was sure that, by putting me on the dangerous slope of a sweet familiarity with the most loveable and the most beautiful of mortals, I don't take away from her even the slightest attraction. So, Miss Oldfield, the thing is understood; it is my admiration, my friendship, that I offer you, but nothing beyond that.'

"'Marquis, that makes me competitive,' said the actress in the same joking tone. 'A woman is still a woman, and you tempt me very much to move into your place.'

"'That is just as I understood it,' replied Samaniego.

---

[96] French for *Kabbalah*, an esoteric method, discipline, and school of thought that originated in Judaism.

[97] Female genie, nymphette, spirit goddess.

"Then, just as we rose to take leave of him, affecting a great air of solemnity, he said:

"'My good and excellent friends, I have used the privilege which the laws of the *Cabale* allow me to place my secret among three people. But I can't point out to you too much how. Beyond that number, indiscretion begins, and the consequences between us could be disastrous. Look, I will cite you the example of a certain French priest named Montfaucon de Villars.[98] Having obtained, I don't know by what means, some rudimentary cabalistic information, he found it amusing to confide his pretended knowledge to the Parisian salons by publishing under the title: *Le Comte de Gabalis ou Entretiens sur les sciences secrètes* [99] some rather impertinent revelations about the world of the spirits. He didn't bear the pain of his profanation and of his blasphemies very long. Three years after the first edition of his book, at scarcely thirty-eight years of age, he perished, murdered on the open highway without anyone being able to put their hands on his murderers!'

"That insinuating remark thrown out with an air of majestic gravity, the Marquis offered his hand to Miss Oldfield to conduct her to her carriage, and during the somewhat long journey, as a man perfectly sure of the result of our interview, he didn't say a word relative to the decision which we still had to make, everything seeming to him already agreed on."

XVI. Continuation of Fauntleroy's Story. The Nights of Ancaster House

"The next day, Miss Oldfield had, in fact, decided. She found the Marquis' actions in appearing to have given us a

---

[98] Nicolas Pierre Henri de Montfaucon, Abbé de Villars (1635-1673) was a French occultist. He is famous for his book *The Count of Gabalis, Discourses on secret sciences* (1670), where he claims to reveal the mysteries of Kabbalah and the Rosicrucians.

[99] Note in the text: Paris 1670. q.v.

grave and serious confidence, pleasant and in very good taste, and actually having told us nothing. Me, I was rather disposed to see in that manner of dealing with us a nuance of impertinence, and I continued to resist a project where I foresaw a thousand inconveniences in the future. The deliberation even menaced turning into a quarrel, for my beautiful mistress had finally reproached me, saying that my defying her showed very little consideration. But, suddenly, by an intervention to which Samaniego was probably not a stranger, the question was definitively settled. Miss Oldfield was, at Covent Garden, in continual beauty and talent rivalry with one of her colleagues, Miss Wolfington, and, in competition, these two women wished each other everything bad it's possible to imagine. Right in the middle of our quarrel, that charming enemy appeared. She held in her hand a copy of the *Morning Herald,* and came, she said, to give Miss Anna explanations relative to an article she had read some minutes before:

"The foyer of Covent Garden was, yesterday evening, very upset by commentaries of every sort which told the news of flagrant hostilities coming between our two queens of tragedy. Transported by an admiration without equal for Miss Oldfield, the opulent stranger who has shown for our artists such an enlightened protector, came to beg the beautiful actress to honor him by accepting in good faith, a splendid apartment intended for her that he has caused to be set up in his townhouse. On learning that dazzling homage to a rival, Miss Wolfington, thrown into despair, sworn to create an obstacle to the stranger's opulence. In this charitable end, she searched out Sir Charles F***, a person who claims some right of surveillance over the activities of Miss Oldfield. She persuaded him so well of the great inconvenience of the proposal made to his protégée that, during the day, an encounter between the Marquis de S*** and Sir Charles F*** took place. God be thanked that no misfortune resulted from this combat, where it appears, however, the generous intention of which Miss Oldfield was the object went no further. That, at

least, is what Miss Wolfington said this evening. She wanted it
understood, congratulating herself on having maintained her
and her rival on an equal footing that an unfortunate distinc-
tion had tried to attack.

"The attitude Miss Wolfington had chosen for that day
was that of a good and excellent comrade, coming to protest
against a tissue of lies and calumnies. But basically the goal of
her visit was to know exactly the state of the Marquis de
Samaniego's munificence claimed by the newspaper.

"Miss Oldfield had nothing to gain by letting her curious
friend ignore the truth that she had come to verify. She therefore hastened to answer her that in fact an apartment had been
offered her at Ancaster House. And she added that the best
answer to make as to the accuracy of the journalist's information was that she intended to go that very morning to occupy the lodgings of honor.

"At that, and after a few words, where, in the middle of
protestations of an unalterable friendship and devotion, the
bitter and the ironic were at any moment on the point of bursting forth, the two enemies separated and from then on, I had
only to bow my head. Miss Oldfield's ego was then involved
in the matter and I wouldn't try to fight against such a force.

"Once my beautiful love was installed in the Marquis'
domicile, I must say that it was perfectly convenient. He celebrated her coming with a banquet, where I was invited with
London's most elegant dandies. And on that occasion he tried
and succeeded with rare goodwill of thought and expression to
publically assign the true character of his relationship with
Miss Oldfield, that is to say, of the enthusiastic admiration he
had for her talent, and of which she had deigned to accept a
shining example. On the question of gifts, he was no less admirably reserved, and if he sometimes risked some of them, it
was always in my presence and usually finding some specious
pretext. On some occasions, he noticed in the tragedienne's
costumes something reproachable in the matter of good taste
or richness, and humbly asked permission to remedy these

271

imperfections. Sometimes coming from an afternoon representation he had found, the evening before, Miss Oldfield's talent so glaring and so incapable of imitation, she was elevated to such a height and had brought such emotion to him that in gratitude he came to deposit his modest offering on the altar of the goddess without ever hoping to properly acquit the debt for the admiration which overwhelmed him.

"On another occasion, taking me aside and testifying by entering into detailed circumstances that he knew the secret of my affairs, which were then becoming seriously in disorder, as well as I did myself, he generously offered to intervene to set them straight, and it was only with great difficulty that I refused his generous insistence. In brief, everything in our relationship was going marvelously and I had to reproach myself for the scruples with which I had at first wanted to keep myself estranged from such a generous man when, however, on our peaceful horizon a cloud appeared.

"One morning, we, the Marquis and I, happened to arrive at the same time at Miss Oldfield's. Suddenly she, without any preamble, asked her host if his great familiarity with the spirits didn't pose some danger to those who lived under the same roof as he.

"The Marquis willingly let himself be scoffed at in the matter of the *Cabale*, but never on that issue entered into a joke. With inexorable seriousness, he maintained the sincerity of his conviction as to the existence of an invisible world and never missed an occasion to exhibit faith in that kind of religion. Not satisfied with witnessing by his words, he proved himself by his actions also an adept zealot. He was known to engage in frequent conferences with the Swedenborgists,[100]

---

[100] Swedenborgianism is the name for several historically related Christian denominations that developed as a new religious movement, informed by the writings of Swedish scientist and theologian Emanuel Swedenborg (1688–1772). Swedenborg claimed to have received a new revelation from Jesus Christ through continuous Heavenly visions which he experi-

disciples of the theosophist Swedenborg, who several years before had obtained the tolerance of their cult in London. He frequented their chapels and was one of the rare subscribers to their journal, *The New Jerusalem Magazine.* Then when Miss Oldfield posed him that question he was asked to respond to, he inquired with serious curiosity how the words of the charming Miss should be understood. She replied that the previous night something hardly reassuring took place in her bedroom.

"'What was that?' the Marquis asked. 'You must explain.'

"'I had just awakened,' Miss Oldfield answered, 'and I counted two o'clock striking on the clock when it seemed to me that I heard, very distinctly, walking in my bedroom. Naturally, I asked, *Who's there?* No answer to my question. However, the noise ceased and I thought I had been dreaming, but a quarter of an hour later, instead of the sound of footsteps, I'm perfectly sure that I heard a sigh. I then pulled the bedside cord. My maid arrived with light, and after the most minute searches we found...'

"Here, since Miss Oldfield had stopped: 'You found?' the Marquis asked.

"'Nothing,' Miss Anna said, smiling, 'but I wouldn't any less swear that last night someone walked about and sighed in my bedroom, and you see me still a bit shaken.'

"'In all of this,' Samaniego replied, 'there is a very likely possibility; you were having what is called a waking dream. That is to say, you were in a state half-way between sleep and waking, where you were in some way conscious of the two states which were for a moment in perfect equilibrium, too perfect to tip the balance to one or the other side. Thus, you

---

enced over a period of at least twenty-five years. In his writings, he predicted that God would replace the traditional Christian Church, establishing a New Church, which would worship God in one person: Jesus Christ. The New Church doctrine is that each person must actively cooperate in repentance, reformation, and regeneration of one's life.

dreamed the steps, then afterward dreamed the sighs. As for the intervention of the supernatural world, I can't answer anything and don't take it on myself to explain anything. But, Miss Anna, you don't believe in the supernatural world.'

"'The thing is nonetheless very extraordinary,' I said, interrupting.

"'What thing?' the Marquis asked drily, 'that Miss Oldfield had a dream?'

"'No, but if, as she is sure she was not dreaming, someone can secretly get into her bedroom...'

"'Ah! but my dear fellow,' Santiago said to me impatiently, 'before you go to the end of a bad thought that I can very well foresee, you must halt at the idea, still possible, of a burglar. Because, no matter how well kept and guarded a house is, a criminal can still get in.'

"'That's true, but he doesn't vanish like a spirit.'

"'Very well, I am suspected' exclaimed the Marquis, standing up energetically. 'So, my dear sir, you're going to come with me to visit that bedroom; we will all go back, and if some passageway exists, you will certainly have to find it.'

"Thereupon, he passed impetuously into Miss Anna's bedroom where, for a moment, we hesitated to follow him. However, hearing him move furniture about, and showing unusual good faith by turning everything upside down, Miss Anna feared that, in fact, she had taken for reality a mistake of her senses.

"At the moment we entered the suspicious room, to join him there, we found him tearing down and shredding the bed's drapery, which was of magnificent Chinese satin.

"Lost, like the woman she was, on seeing the destruction menacing that beautiful material, Miss Oldfield cried out that she was now sure it was her stupid imagination, and that his proof by denuding all the walls of the apartment was completely unnecessary.

"At that, the Marquis calmed down, but, nevertheless, he demanded that I accompany him to minutely examine all the nooks and corners of the apartment. That done, without anything suspicious having appeared, Samaniego said:

"'Miss Anna, I will not say that I require, because I don't have the right to demand, but in the name of my honesty, so strangely suspected, I dare to beg you first of all to change bedrooms, and next not to sleep except with a nightlight and your maid sleeping in the same room.'

"'I won't change bedrooms,' Miss Anna replied. 'That would injure you, my dear host. As for the nightlight and my roommate, I accept, not as a precaution and safeguard, but to avoid in the future some misunderstanding as ridiculous as that today.'

"That said, peace was restored, and truly I was in good faith in the excuses I gave our excellent friend for the somewhat thoughtless words with which I had wounded him.

"Sometimes Miss Oldfield and I thought we perceived that, from that moment, he was not for us exactly the same man. He didn't have for the great tragic actress those bursts of tender admiration to which he had accustomed us. Our affair then was beginning to fly with only one wing when Samaniego announced a short absence to us, a business trip of two or three days to a neighboring county.

"The day after his departure, in the middle of the night, I heard violent knocking at my door. I soon saw Miss Oldfield's maid entering with a frightened air and begging me, in the name of her mistress, who had just been transported, dying, to her former domicile, to come to her without delay.

"My haste to accept an invitation couched in that way can be understood without any trouble. I found Miss Anna in bed, not dying, but very haggard, and bathed with sweat, like a person who had scarcely recovered consciousness. Pressed by the twenty questions I asked her all at the same time, she told me she had gone to bed immediately after returning from the theater, because she was tired and feeling ill. She went almost immediately to sleep, having her maid in a little dressing room in range of her voice and with a lamp that gave off enough clarity into the apartment that all the objects could be distinguished.

"About midnight, as near as she could calculate, she was drawn out of her sleep by the sound of sweet, melodious music. But at the same time, she saw that the bedroom was plunged into deep shadows which made her immediately suspect danger.

"Just as she, her roommate should have been awakened by that serenade which followed. However, neither that sound nor her mistress' repeated calls were enough to produce any result, and Miss Oldfield remained under a silent terror, that just the circumstances of that supernatural sleep created in her. To the melodious cords that continued to be heard, there soon was added something else strange. Little by little the room was filled with a vapor, thin at first, and then thicker and penetrating. And finally Miss Oldfield distinctly heard a dull shuffle on the rug which seemed to be advancing toward her.

"Leaning over then to the bell cord placed within hand's reach, she pulled it violently two or three times, rapidly put on a house robe, and in her ignorance of the nature of the danger menacing her, she threw herself out of the bed where she would have been less in a position to face the peril. She could also then go to her maid, have a chance of awakening her and getting her help and assistance in the terrible situation in which she was placed.

"Walking on the rug without her house shoes, Miss Oldfield had hardly gone a few steps when her foot touched an object cold as death which reacted with soft plasticity under pressure. At the same moment, she felt something like a ribbon of viscous glass encircle her leg, and under that sensation of understandable horror, she fainted.

"The rest of the adventure Miss Anna knew only through her servants, who came running at the sound of her bell. Having forced open the door, they saw that a frightening silence had followed the distress call that had drawn them. Searching in all the recesses of the apartment, nothing. The maid, despite all the noise that had been made, continued her sleep which had something of lethargy to it and from which she couldn't be awakened without stimulants and infinite attention. Finally, what had to be supposed in the preparation of all these inexplicable facts was criminal premeditation. Destined to burn all night, the lamp, sometime after midnight, had consumed all its oil.

"Conscious after her fainting spell and persuaded that the horrible object she had felt must have been a snake, Miss Oldfield didn't want to live a moment more in that cursed house. And she had me called so as to repose on the heart of a friend after the terrible fright from which she had just been liberated. Our discussions were innumerable, and if Miss Oldfield's and my mind had turned toward superstition, we would have fallen into believing in some supernatural event and some *conte brun*.[101] But in the individuality of the Marquis, for which I had always felt an instinctive repulsion, in the mystery in which he took pleasure in surrounding his life, in his looks, in his unexplained and inexplicable wealth, finally in that unusual cleverness with which he had surrounded us in order to draw Miss Anna to him, were united all the elements which could constitute a monster of wickedness, asking only human means and an evil genie for the success of his frightful projects.

"If my advice had been followed, the law would have immediately received a complaint, and perhaps the investigation, immediately begun and pursued vigorously, would have traced many other dark mysteries. But Miss Oldfield wasn't of a very forceful nature; she was afraid of scandal, and for the moment it remained agreed that I would stay quiet, except to take more vigorous action when we were less under the influence of emotions hardly grown cold. The next evening I stayed with Miss Oldfield; her day had been quiet and she was beginning to recover from the brutal invasion of the night before.

---

[101] Horror tale.

"Judge, sir, of our indignation and our surprise when we were told that Marquis Vincente de Samaniego was there and demanding to be received. My first movement was to go confront the impertinent visitor and to rudely show him out. But women are curious, and Miss Oldfield was persuaded that, coming himself to meet us, that man actually had some excuses or some explanations to give us. She therefore insisted that we let him come in. At the same time, she was careful to suggest moderation and prudence to me. A second later, the Marquis was introduced.

"We noticed on his entry that he was in full mourning, and Miss Oldfield had her mouth open to ask what was the misfortune in his family, but he himself prevented her by saying:

"'Tell me, then, charming Miss, what happened during my absence for you to have so hurriedly left my house.'

"'Sir,' entering the conversation, I answered him, 'more than anyone you should know, because who doubts that you were the organizer of that infamy.'

"'Dear M. Fauntleroy,' this prodigy of impudence, said to me calmly, 'I have the honor to point out to you that I am at this moment at Miss Anna's home, and that my aim in coming here was to search for the explanation of a fact about which I have until now the most incomplete information. Violence, so far as I know, has never brought light to any business. Please, for the moment, let us not have yours. I'm not speaking of later, when it's in its place.'

"'Me? That I once more risk my life against a professional duelist? No, sir, it's face to face with the law that people like me are met.'

"'As you please,' replied the Marquis without emotion. 'But, to come back to the purpose of my visit, please, Miss Anna, I ask you, tell me a little about that adventure of which I know nothing but the broad details and the very nebulous tale of my servants.'

"Miss Oldfield then told him in detail what had happened. He listened with very well acted attention. He demanded some explanation about several points which he seemed not to have completely understood at first. Then, when the expose was finished:

"'That's what I was afraid of,' he said, 'and it was a great fault of mine to be absent.'

"Naturally, Miss Anna pressed him to explain. 'Tell me, then, dear Miss,' he then asked, 'the first time I had the honor of having you visit my menagerie, don't you remember that a serpent with a big round head stripped white, brown and yellow, attracted your precious attention for a moment?'

"'Yes, I remember,' Miss Oldfield said.

"'Don't you also remember that you told me, that despite your very pronounced horror of reptiles, you didn't experience for that one I showed you any strong repugnance. You said he seemed gentle, debonair, and that his eyes, which were bigger and more slit than those like him, had a charming expression?'

"'Yes, I said all that about a serpent, from the coast of Guinea, if I recall your knowledgeable explanations correctly.'

"'Well! That's exactly where all the trouble comes from. You turned the head of this unfortunate reptile who thought that you loved him.'

"'Sir,' I interrupted quickly, 'that joke in the present situation is most intolerably misplaced.'

"'But, sir, I wasn't joking and you will understand when I have confided to you that under that form, which found favor with Miss Anna, is hidden my friend the genie. You probably recall the adventure with the daughter of King Cheops. I don't want to say for a fact that the obliging words of your beautiful friend were taken as a declaration of love. And certainly when I was present he would not have allowed himself the caprice which now falls back on me. But all the trouble comes from the flattering compliments that my audacious friend had gathered from the mouth of Miss Anna. In the past the serpent caused the woman's downfall; now you can say that it's the woman who has condemned the serpent.'

"My mistress and I were so stupefied with the impudent self-assurance that presented that stupidity to us that we let him continue to the end of his tirade.

"When he had finished, I stood up, and underlining with gestures all the indignation I felt, I told him, showing him the door:

"'Not a word, and not a moment more here, or I will call Miss Anna's servants.'

"'On the contrary, one more word,' said the Marquis, whom I had seen change expressions under that insult. 'You do not believe,' he added, 'either in the spirits or in the *cabale*. That's your business. But nevertheless you have promised me, both of you, to keep as an inviolable secret everything I have revealed to you on that subject. Be careful, my friend, the genie is closely mixed up in that nocturnal adventure which has already gone too far. The form under which he is pleased to hide can foretell, it seems to me, the nature and the extent of his vengeance. If there is a lack of indulgence for one of his weaknesses and if his existence is divulged, remember the fate of that indiscreet Abbé Montfaucon de Villars. That is what I came to tell you.'

"With that, he gave a low and ceremonious bow to Miss Oldfield; then he left."

XVII. Continuation of Fauntleroy's Story.
The Genie in Love. The Sleepers' Club

"'Immediately after the Marquis had delivered us of his odious presence, I at first wanted to laugh at his amorous serpent,' Miss Oldfield told me, 'but his last words frightened me. His expression, when he was speaking to us, showed terrible cold irony. He's a man who shouldn't be pushed too far.'

"'Oh! He doesn't frighten me,' I answered. 'On the contrary, he's an outstanding cheat who has to be unmasked.'

"Miss Anna then strongly insisted that I not bring the law into that affair and that I not have another duel with this dangerous adversary. I promised everything she wished. I had my own project. I must tell you, my dear listener, that I sometimes dabble in writing. Even at the period that the ruinous possession of Miss Oldfield had begun to put some disorder in my fortune, I could see, without too much trouble, the moment when I would be drawn into complete ruin. I thought that I would live by my pen and poverty would be my muse.

"While waiting, I had, it appeared to me, in the business that had just passed with Samaniego, an excellent opportunity to exercise my talent and to stand up to his threats, as well as to revenge myself brilliantly on him. Under the title, *The Genie in Love,* I published in one of the magazines the most in vogue, a short story under a pseudonym, but with a transparency that I took care to make perfect. Our Marquis played the principal role. Miss Oldfield's adventure naturally was the basis of that little novel. But I took care to join a certain number of embellishments taken from my own imaginations. Embroidering on what I knew of the man, and even on what I did not, I made of him a figure of the total and complete adventurer. At the dénouement, to which the unusual exterior that you know lent itself, he was transformed into a former eunuch guard of Timur Shah,[102] King of Kaboul's harem. In that way I explained the fabulous fortune he was seen to possess.

"When she knew about that audacious publication, that I had not consulted her about, Miss Oldfield was seized with fear. She was expecting terrible reprisals from Samaniego, but when he didn't budge, and what's more, *The Genie in Love* becoming an immediate scandalous success, she finally was reassured and didn't hesitate to give the details of her sojourn at Ancaster House which people everywhere pressed her for.

"However, from the day the Marquis had appeared before us dressed in mourning attire, a revolution as sudden as unusual had taken place in his life. By a transformation that could pass for flattery addressed to the somber tendencies of our national temperament, suddenly he passed from worldly

---

[102] Timur Shah Durrani (1748-1793), the second ruler of the Durrani Empire, from 1772 until his death.

behavior and all the splendors of fashionable life to the most somber and desolate eccentricities. Under the most profound sorrow possible, in all his person and in the complete change of his life's habits, he manifest symptoms of the most terrible access of spleen that England, that classic country of dark melancholy, had ever been called on to observe. Struck by a kind of funereal monomania, he began by hiring an architect and a sculpture of renown and instructing them to create in Westminster a rich sepulcher, for which he himself furnished most of the plans.

"Following the logic of that dark disposition, he dismissed from his townhouse all the artists it had pleased him to give asylum to, and for the royal magnificence that he had in the past assembled, he substituted a funereal luxury deployment only seen in the funeral rites of the highest personages. Outside of his home, and without doubt to accumulate all the forms of manifestations adopted by human sorrow among the different peoples of the world, he began to wear mourning in white, as is the custom in China. Dressed all in white, like the statue of the Commander,[103] without caring about the strange effect that his appearance in the streets produced, he rode about in a carriage draped in white, drawn by two white horses, with a coachman and lackeys wearing white. Many people began to assume there was something wrong with his reason.

"Following the customs of the English aristocracy, that has its yacht on the Thames, as they in Venice have their gondola, he acquired a little vessel that he baptized the *Sarcophagus,* taking care that the dark color given to dead things and by the dark and severe aspect of the vehicle's rigging, its lamentable name was fully justified. He was seen to make frequent voyages on that gloomy craft, the goal and direction of which were vainly investigated. It is not necessary to add that, modifying completely the milieu in which he had lived until that time, the relations in the fashionable world that he had at first cultivated, he replaced with the strangest haunts.

---

[103] From Molière's *Don Juan.*

"He was frequently seen to go into a tavern, habitual rendezvous of criminals and recognized swindlers, and it was claimed that he had recruited the crew of his little boat in that wicked place. From that point, a thousand untoward rumors circulated about him and credited that fortune he had come to use so miserably to sources that could be the least admitted and the least justified. While for several he was accepted as adept at occult sciences, for others he dealt in contraband, a counterfeiter. They went so far as to suggest that exercising, in fact, for some Muslim prince, the bizarre functions I had ascribed to him, he had come to Europe with the goal of recruiting for his master's harem and that those secret and frequent voyages had no other purpose.

"The last and the most inexplicable oddity, in his townhouse and under his Chairmanship there began to assemble a club, a mysterious and austere association, the object and purpose of which were searched in vain. But what appeared the height of the bizarre, in fewer than six weeks, three members of that shadowy band perished by voluntary death, and all three, by wills in proper form, stated as their heir, excluding relatives they might have, Don Vincente de Samaniego. That circumstance couldn't fail to draw the attention of the authorities. The man who benefited in a way so notable in the murderous fantasies of his co-associates, should he be considered a stranger to them? As a consequence of that presumption, truly founded on reason, he was summonsed to appear before the Lord-Lieutenant of Middlesex County. On that occasion, between the High Magistrate and the accused man, something close to the following dialogue took place:

"'Sir, under your patronage and in your house, there took place meetings of a club whose functions I am authorized to ask you the name and status.'

"'My Lord,' the Spaniard replied, 'I really believe I'm not mistaken. As the authors of comedies say: *the scene takes place in England.*'

"'That's how it appears to me,' the Magistrate ironically replied.

"'England, as I am led to believe, is a free country?'

"'That I can positively affirm, the most free on Earth.'

"'Where, as a consequence, freedom of association must rule?'

"'Without doubt, but what are you getting at?'

"'To not answer any of your questions, My Lord. If I have freedom of association, I am not obligated to give an account to anyone about the composition and the title of my society. You desire some *information*. It's up to you to procure it and not to me to furnish it.'

"'But, sir, with every liberty there must exist limits and control. When an association hides in the shadows, and these shadows which surround them, as well as its strange...'

"'Pardon me, My Lord, for interrupting you, but as for being bizarre, the club that I have the honor to preside over, is it more so than the Fatmen's Club, or the Skinny Men's Club, or the Slices of Beef Club and what of the October Beer Club? I hold as just as unusual the famous Silence Club, where, for having let himself announce aloud a great English victory against France which had just been reported, a member was expelled without pity. And what about the Eternals' Club, where the meeting place must always be occupied by one of its members who act as soldiers on guard? And the Dafi Club where they can drink only juniper berry brandy? And the Four-in-hand Club where they must be able to drive four horses without a postilion? And the Lame and the Ugly Men's Club? And the terrible Calf's Head Club, where every year, on January 31st, they eat, in fact, a calf's head, in commemoration of the other head that Cromwell had cut off from King Charles? And finally, sir, you talk of eccentricity, but haven't the ultimate limits of the strange been reached by the bloody club of the Duelists, whose members, at least once in their life, must have fought in single combat?'

"'At least, sir, the diverse associations that you have, with remarkable erudition, just enumerated, remain public and open to everyone, while the object of your meetings...'

"'...Is not a secret for anyone, Magistrate.'

"'Witness your hurry to show it, when you have been solemnly invited to do so by the authorities.'

"'It is exactly that solemnity and that intervention by power that closes my mouth. My silence is only a reserve of right. Solicited by you, My Lord, in an official manner, you would have found me in a hurry to give you explanations.'

"'Eh! Sir! Officially, officially, what does it matter to me provided that you answer truthfully and openly?'

"'As for that, I have the honor to tell you that our Club is called the *The Sleepers' Club*. And for this purpose we meet to enjoy together the sweetness of sleep, as stated on the inscription placed on the door of the meeting room: *Here is the sojourn of eternal peace.*'

"'But that inscription would go just as well over the door of a cemetery, and the fact is that, in your shadowy association, they kill themselves a lot...'

"'That is to say that, in a short time, we have had the misfortune to lose three of our colleagues.'

"'From whom you have also had the misfortune to inherit.'

"'Just as they would have inherited from us if we had been similarly carried away, because our statutes provide that each of our members who die leave all his possessions to the Associations, in the person of its President.'

"'All that, sir, seems to me very nebulous and very foolish. To come together to sleep, as if one could sleep at will.'

"'Yes, you can when, as I do, you have carried from the Island of Borneo the secret of a precious narcotic instantly procuring sleep and peopling it with delicious dreams.'

"'After all, it isn't just your Club; it's your whole life that is an enigma. Where do you come from? How do you provide for your enormous expenditures? That's what can't be explained.'

"'But we have said that *the scene takes place in England,* the country *par excellence* of liberty. I would have believed that at least I wouldn't have been asked to tell my cook's memoirs.'

"'In every country, sir, one likes to know who one rubs elbows with in the street.'

"'Well, My Lord, still officially, and in order not to irritate you as a private man, I can tell you that I come from almost every part of the world, where I have traveled successfully and become rich through commerce.'

"'What, the trade in whale bones?' the Magistrate said in ironic belief.

"'A little in whale bones, a little in spices; then I was in the trade of Blacks, if it doesn't displease the honorable M. Wilberforce[104]; then some objects of natural history. One has to earn one's poor living. As for the small amount of money I threw on the London pavement, I am astonished to hear myself reproached for it, as La Fontaine, the great writer of fables, noted: *La République a bien à faire / De gens qui ne dépensent rien.*'[105]

"'You discourse marvelously, sir, but to come to the facts, you are suspected, since I must tell you, of being affiliated with a band of counterfeiters.'

"'Look, My Lord!' the Marquis said gaily, and he deposited a handful of guineas on the Judge's desk.

"'And what is certainly,' the Magistrate continued, 'of a nature to lend credence to the strangest interpretations, is your regular attendance at one of the most infamous places in London. What does a man like you, I ask you, do in a tavern like *The Bottle and Magpie,* the rendezvous of all the prisoners from Newgate, and whose hostess is a sister-in-law of the hangman?'

"'I go there, first of all, precisely because of that hostess, a woman with a very gay and very original personality, and

---

[104] Note in the text: "The first promoter of the abolition of the slave trade." William Wilberforce (1759-1833), English politician, philanthropist, and a leader of the movement to abolish the slave trade.

[105] The Republic has no business / With those who lay no money out. *L'Avantage de la Science*, Livre VIII, fable 19.

whose casual way pleases me more than the stiff little purse mentality of all your ladies. As for thieves, that's perhaps an unusual taste, but I like their company. These adventurous men who have declared war on society, and put each day their head in play against it, I have a sort of respect for them, sympathy. And then in these lower class and energetic characters, I find in them an effect missing in your socially acceptable people, the uniform compression of the great social mill. Finally, one reason worth all of them, in the country *the most free on Earth:* I have believed in the freedom to move downward and the inalienable right to get drunk on gin and to frequent people of doubtful or odious character.'

"'You have answered everything,' the Magistrate, who was made ill at ease by that cold irony, announced on finishing. 'But be careful. Your path is tortuous, and other rumors, not less strange, are circulating about you. I see very well it would be useless to enter into explanations with you. Take care not to go outside the law, that up to this point you have brushed against without breaking. At the least infraction, I warn you, the authorities are decided to apply to you the most severe punishments of the Alien Act and make you settle everything at the same time.'

"The Lord-Lieutenant's clerk, from whom I got all these details, added that the Marquis was told to take back, before he left, all the gold he had left on the Magistrate's desk. The Marquis answered that that would go toward the tax of the poor, a destination where there would be no way to argue with him."

Fauntleroy had come to that point in his story, when he was interrupted by a prison door employee who had come to ask Matiphous to go to the prison office. A few moments later, the man from Malta, came back with a radiant expression. By a highly placed and powerful individual, his detention had just been lifted and he was now legally free to leave Newgate.

"I congratulate you on this happy dénouement," Fauntleroy said sadly, "and since the cage is open, you aren't waiting a moment to go breathe the pure and living air of liberty."

"No, not really, Matiphous answered. "I've come to hear the end of your story. Now that I am free, I need more than ever to know exactly what Colqhoum is. I too have a score to settle with him."

"Oh! Be careful," the son of the London merchant said to him quickly. "That man, I'm here to tell you, is a dangerous adversary."

"We'll see," the man from Malta said in a positive tone. "But first, the continuation and end of your story."

"Mon Dieu!" said Fauntleroy, "There you are asking me to bring up very bitter memories, and I would really prefer to stop at a point where a fortuitous circumstance suspended my narrative."

"Come now," Matiphous said. "Have a little courage. Who knows but what I am your vengeance?"

Fauntleroy shook his head in a gesture of profound disbelief. "All right," he said, "you wished it," and he again took up his sad story in the way you will see in the following chapter.

XVIII. Continuation of Fauntleroy's Story.
An Actress' Dressing room. Self-love and love

Resuming his story, Fauntleroy said:

"A considerable amount of time had gone by after the rupture with Don Vincente de Samaniego. He had given us no further sign of his existence, and everything led us to believe that he had ceased to honor us with his attention and his memory. One evening when Miss Oldfield had had one of the greatest successes of a tragic actress in the memory of the annals of the English theatre, I was in the dressing room of my beautiful mistress, enjoying the enthusiastic congratulations given to her from all directions, when Sir Henry Grosvenor arrived. He was a baronet, an old pillar of the theatre wings, constantly on the trail of all the news of the world of the theatre, which he prided himself on being informed about before anyone and always first hand. Making himself a pathway through the crowd of Miss Oldfield's admirers, the Baron said:

"'Well, adorable Miss, do you know the news?'

"'What news,' Miss Anna asked.

"'What! You have yet to learn what must at this moment be the subject of all conversations in the London salons, the marriage of Miss Wolfington?'

"'Miss Wolfington is getting married?' asked her rival with an air of disdain.

"'Yes, with a man that you know, your former platonic suitor, the Marquis de Samaniego.'

"A general laugh of disbelief having greeted the name of the spouse: 'Laugh, gentlemen, as much as you please,' continued Sir Henri Grosvenor with the greatest seriousness, 'but the thing is no less done. I had the honor of being the intermediary to make the proposal to Miss Wolfington, and am supposed to be one of the witnesses.'

"'But that's impossible,' was the response from all sides. 'Miss Wolfington must be mad.'

"'Not so mad,' the Baronet replied. 'I have the contract, and when you make a woman a kind of queen! However, in a certain way, I admit that Miss Wolfington is sacrificing herself, because she won't become a Marquise.'

"'And why?' I asked.

"'Because Samaniego himself is not a Marquis'

"'Some news!' Miss Oldfield said. 'Whoever doubted that man was an imposter?'

"'No,' the Baronet continued. 'He has only the title he gave himself, and he's not even named Samaniego, and is not at all Spanish. He's English. His real name is Colqhoum and he comes from an honest Devonshire farm family, so he very candidly admitted to me.'

"'Oh, well, Miss Wolfington will make a very nice farm wife,' Miss Oldfield then said. This alteration of her colleague's happiness seemed to amuse her a great deal.

"'But,' the Baronet continued, 'that frankness is only honorable in our fellow countryman, for he was right to reveal his plebeian name. It isn't only by his wealth that he is important. Since his position as Prime Minister and perhaps the successor of a great Indian princess, isn't to be absolutely disregarded.'

"'Then why did he come to London instead of being governor of his principality?' one of the questioners asked.

"'He said he came to England to see his family again, that he left very young, and having had, according to what he said, the misfortune to find them all dead, that's how he explained all the funereal eccentricities you saw in him. But I believe he's here on a diplomatic interest that all this bizarre behavior is meant to hide.'

"'That great princess whose Grand Vizier he will be,' I asked, 'can we know her name?'

"'Of course,' Sir Henri Grosvenor answered. 'It's Princess Sirdhana, the old Begum Sumru.'[106]

"'I've never heard of that respectable lady,' said a young Peer not yet seated in the House of Lords, not having yet reached the required age.

"'Ah!, my dear Duke,' the old Baronet answered, 'for a future political man, you aren't too up to date on foreign af-

---

[106] Begum Joanna Nobilis Sombre (c.1753-1836), popularly known as Begum Samru or Sumru, *née* Farzana Zeb un-Nissa, started her career as a dancing girl in 18th Century India, and eventually became the ruler of Sardhana, a small principality near Meerut. She was the head of a professionally trained mercenary army, inherited from her European mercenary husband, Walter Reinhardt Sombre. This mercenary army consisted of Europeans and Indians. She was also regarded as the only Catholic Ruler in India, as she ruled the Principality of Sardhana in 18th and 19th century India. She died immensely rich. Her inheritance was assessed as approximately 55.5 million gold marks in 1923 and 18 billion deutsch marks in 1953. Her inheritance continues to be disputed to this day. An organisation named *Reinhards Erbengemeinschaft* still strives to resolve the inheritance issue.

fairs. *Begum,* in Farsi means Princess, and *Sumru,* which must be just translated as *Sombre,* is the correct name of that Elizabeth of the Indies which she took from a Frenchman to whom she was married. Far from being a person to laugh at, the Begum is, on the contrary, a very serious and almost frightening figure. She has been able to defend the independence of her principality against all our enterprises. She has always administered it in a very virile fashion. Her ministers must not make a misstep. When she thought she had some peccadilloes to reproach two of her functionaries, they were, by her orders, tied to the mouth of a canon and sent to the devil in the guise of cannonballs.'

"'An amiable and gracious sovereign,' one of those present said.

"'Among other things, the chapter of the heart is a very delicate matter with her,' Sir Henri Grosvenor continued. 'Suspecting that one of her slaves had for Lord Sombre some weaknesses a little too tender, she just had that rival buried alive. Next she ordered that they set up a tent for her over the grave of the victim. For three days she drank and ate there, and finally inflicted a banquet there on her unfaithful spouse.'

"'Well! There's a beautiful subject for a tragedy,' said a little dramatic poet lost in the crowd of shining courtesans of the great actress.

"'And this beautiful marriage, when does it take place?' Miss Anna asked casually.

"'Oh! As soon as possible, because it doesn't appear that our diplomat's stay here can last very much longer.'

"'Miss Wolfington must have a terrible desire for a husband!' Miss Oldfield said to the Baronet. 'Without talking about how strange he is, to go live in a court whose manners you have just described to us, and with a man who has against him, as a recommendation, how he acted toward me, that's really rare courage.'

"'Ah! The story of the serpent,' Sir Henri Grosvenor said. 'I spoke to him about that. He laughed a great deal. He said that you are a coward and he told you a rather pleasant story about that.'

"'On that subject, as on all the others,' Miss Anna replied drily, 'he's a man who can't say a truthful word.'

"'So truthful that in the great admiration that he continues to feel for you, I believe him to be truly sincere. He speaks of your person and of your talent with an enthusiasm which certainly has nothing feigned about it,' the Baronet replied.

"'That's why,' I replied, 'he wanted to arrange a horrible death for her.'

"'Oh, no, my dear sir,' replied Sir Henri Grosvenor, 'it seems everything happened by chance. A cage left open, the prisoner went to seek asylum in Miss Anna's bedroom; that's how that great crime can be explained. In any case, the dark intent, if there was a dark intent, didn't go beyond the bounds of a little misplaced joke, because I've seen up close and touched that Lerne monster.[107] It's a fetish serpent, still young, of the race that Negroes on the coast of Guinea honor with a religious cult. There is no species more inoffensive and charming. '

"'Ah! Well, my dear sir,' I said to the Baronet, 'you are very intimate with Sir Colqhoum, for him to have honored you with confidences of such extenuating circumstances?'

"'That is to say that he came to visit me to ask me to intervene in regard to his proposal to Miss Wolfington. And afterward I kept him informed of my actions. Naturally, in view of learning about the morality of a man for whom I was vouching, I had to talk to him about an adventure which had caused some scandal. It was then that he spoke to me of Miss Oldfield in terms of regret and admiration and to make me believe that you were somewhat hasty in judging him severely.'

"'One question, my good Sir Henri,' Miss Oldfield then said. 'Are you acting as a double diplomat?'

"'Why?' Sir Henri Grosvenor asked.

---

[107] The Lernean Hydra, second of Hercules' Twelve Tasks.

"'That's because with a few more of the kind things that you are saying about M. Colqhoum, I would believe you were also charged with a proposal for me.'

"'On my word, I won't say I wasn't, if you were free and if you hadn't rejected him more quickly.'

"'See here, Sir Henri,' I then strongly interrupted. 'I demand closure on talking about Colqhoum. I find he's a great deal too much talked about. Don't you have any other news to tell us?'

"'And I, Gentlemen,' said Miss Anna, on seeing the woman who dressed her awaiting her good pleasure with a dress over her arm, 'I ask that I be allowed to take off my Cleopatra dress and put on a town dress.'

"With this dismissal, everyone began to leave, I just as the others, and I asked my beautiful mistress if a quarter of an hour would be time enough for me to come pick her up to take her home. She answered that that wouldn't be necessary; that she was dying of fatigue; that to hold a conversation was beyond her strength; that she would see me the next day in the morning.

"The next day, I found Miss Anna terribly sullen; she was suffering with a terrible migraine, she said, and instead of being well received, some jokes I chanced to make about Miss Wolfington's happiness, were received with icy coolness.

"Knowing that migraines like solitude, I didn't prolong my visit and took my leave, announcing my intention to come back later to find out about her indisposition.

"So, a little before the dinner hour, I was on my way to go see Miss Anna, when, just as I turned into the street where she lived, my carriage was almost turned over by a cabriolet pulled by four horses running at a gallop. At an unusually well chosen moment, at the same instant, a head showed itself in one of the vehicle's windows and gave me a gracious nod. That man who greeted me in the quarter of an hour that his cabriolet put my life in peril was Colqhoum, assuredly called the Marquis of Samaniego!

"Sudden seized with a vague worry, I rapidly reached Miss Oldfield's lodgings. Received at the door by an old housekeeper, I learned that my mistress had just started on a rather long voyage. She said that I must even have met her carriage, which a few minutes before had been stationed at the door."

"Ah! Wretched woman!" Matiphous exclaimed. "She left with Colqhoum."

"You said it, sir," Fauntleroy replied. "When I learned that news, you can imagine my sentiments."

"More than you could know," the man from Malta replied. "Not any later than the night just passed, I even had the same adventure."

"May yours," Fauntleroy said, "not turn out like mine, because that was the first link in a chain of misfortunes that were going to surround me."

XIX. Continuation of Fauntleroy's Story.
An Actress' Dressing room. Self-love and love[108]

"Wanting to know as quickly as possible the details of my terrible disappointment, and, in addition, feeling the need to vent my anger on someone, I even went to see Sir Henri Grosvenor, whom I was not far from regarding as an accomplice in Miss Anna's kidnapping. I didn't find him at home; he had just received a letter, his domestic told me, that had caused him to leave in all haste. I supposed that important missive could be from Miss Wolfington, and, taking a chance, I ran to that other Ariadne[109] where I had, more than anywhere else, a chance of being informed. I wasn't wrong. Summoned suddenly by his beautiful client, the negotiator had been informed about a very cold, although very respectful, note in

---

[108] When starting the fifth volume of *Le Cabinet Noir*, the publisher appears to have reused the same subtitle for Chapter XIX as Chapter XVIII.

[109] See Note 38.

which Colqhoum had made known to his future bride that the marriage project couldn't take place because *a former engagements with Miss Anna Oldfield created for him another duty and other arrangements.*

"The real indignation of the Baronet persuaded me that, in all that affair, he had played a perfectly upright role. However, he and Miss Wolfington, already employed in the same sense, had been, in the clever and infernal hands of Colqhoum, made obedient and naïve marionettes. Everything right up to the choice of Sir Henri Grosvenor going everywhere to carry his news, must have been calculated in the choice that had been made of him to serve as the pivot of all that intrigue. It was impossible for me to see Miss Wolfington, who from the moment she received that note of rupture, had not ceased having a succession of nervous attacks, of which nothing foresaw the end. As for the Baronet, if I had myself been less sadly affected, I would have found him rather delighted with his claim to have been right about Colqhoum's action, and once assure that I had no clarification to expect from him, I left him shouting his head off that he wasn't mystified, and that things didn't happen that way.

"Several days went by. I went to stay at a little piece of property that I possessed several leagues from the city, in order to let the greatest part of the scandal pass. There I received a circulation letter which at the same time was spreading across London. It was a letter postmarked from Gretna Green, in which Colqhoum announced his marriage to Miss Oldfield, which had just celebrated before the blacksmith.[110] A month

---

[110] Note in the text: "Everybody knows the unusual privilege of a blacksmith who, at Gretna Green, on the frontier of Scotland, has the right to marry without restraint or formality the couples who come before him." Gretna Green is a village in the south of Scotland famous for runaway weddings. It is in Dumfries and Galloway, near the mouth of the River Esk and was historically the first village in Scotland, following the old coaching route from London to Edinburgh. It is one of the

later, I had more explicit news from my faithful one. In the hurry of her departure, she had left in London a great number of objects that she used which she now needed. Her maid, taking care of a thousand things of that type, had at the same time been charged secretly with a letter for me. That letter, which I'm going to read to you is a masterpiece of feminine perfidy and cleverness..."

Fauntleroy then took a piece of paper from his wallet and, after unfolding it, he read what follows:

"Dear M. Fauntleroy,

"Following our long acquaintance and familiarity, I would believe I was lacking in all proper behavior if, after having let the voice of the public inform you of a resolution that must have surprised you, I didn't let you know the completely personal motives which decided me:

"That M. Colqhoum, having obtained my consent, gave me the most frank and most loyal explanations, especially about his conduct which must have seemed nebulous, is what, I think, you do not know. For a long time, he had been in love with me. He had hoped, by managing frequent opportunities to see me, to make me share his passion. Discouraged by the fervor of our passion and dominated by an invincible timidity which made him take more care to hide his true sentiments than others would have taken to show them, he confessed that one night, in an excess of despair, he had gotten into my bedroom through a hidden entry, of which only he had the secret. But that insolence was only a more outstanding proof of his respect, since, in the delicate situation in which I saw myself,

---

world's most popular wedding destinations, hosting over 5,000 weddings each year. The local blacksmith and his anvil have become the lasting symbols of Gretna Green weddings. Scottish law allowed for "irregular marriages," meaning that if a declaration was made before two witnesses, almost anybody had the authority to conduct the marriage ceremony. The blacksmiths in Gretna became known as "anvil priests."

he didn't even have the courage to let me know of his presence and he still tried to deceive me about his actions. As the adventure which put an end to all our relationship with him, he continued to persist that it was a simple product of chance and, in any case, it was proven that it never put my life in peril.

"These explanations given, M. Colqhoum didn't leave me in doubt that in offering his hand and his fortune to Miss Wolfington, he gave way to furious spite, that he didn't have any love for her, and his only aim was to put a person that he knew had been in rivalry with me for a long time in a position to distress me about her luxury, which would be his vengeance for all the torments that I had caused him. I admit that this reasoning unusually impressed me, not that I took very much interest in the attitude of superiority that Miss Wolfington might take vis-à-vis me. God be thanked, I know how to estimate her value and mine; I never thought that her rivalry bothered me very much. But you, dear M. Fauntleroy, great, generous, you would never have allowed that a person honored with your feelings could be humiliated in something by a hope....

"Nevertheless, to fight with oriental opulence, he was going to spend everything in caring for his ego, I had already contributed to weakening your fortune; the competition into which you must inevitably have rushed, would have completed your ruin. I had to decide. In the name of the solid friendship which had little by little taken the place of the first ardors of our liaison, I have thrown myself across this fatal marriage which was supposed to be your loss, and with my person I have paid your ransom. Will you be grateful for that? I don't at all dare hope so. Do you understand all the grandeur of my sacrifice? Later, perhaps. While waiting, I keep my conscience as a witness and the feeling of a great duty accomplished.

"Therefore, please believe, whatever happens, in the sincere attachment and the unceasing devotion of your very affectionate,

Anna Oldfield.

"As for me," Fauntleroy continued, "I admit that that apology for Miss Oldfield's conduct was on the point of convincing me. What made her, in fact, write to me? Some of the things you do cannot be excused. Had I created a mirage of the ardor of an unbelievable devotion? Was she, in fact, persuaded that the option which she talked to me about was necessary, and, did she really believe she was doing a laudable act by ruining me in matters of the heart to save me in matters of money? That illusion, if it hadn't vanished of itself with the least reflection, wouldn't have been kept alive by the messenger, a chambermaid, that Miss Oldfield had sent.. She was an intelligent girl above her condition who had gone to work for her mistress only in the hope of learning from her and entering the theater. She said she had talked with her and made all the necessary objections possible to turn her from a union where everywhere there could be seen only doubts and shadows.

"However, the Machiavellian calculations of Colqhoum had won the day. Wanting to taste the celestial pleasure of crushing a rival, Miss Anna, without hiding from herself the dangerous game she was playing, dashed headlong into that marriage, which had as an intermediary a furious attack of envy."

"But then," Matiphous asked naïvely, "why write to you?"

"Ah!" Fauntleroy answered, "That's how women are made. The occasions in which they are the most evidently wrong, are most precisely the ones where they show the most passion to give themselves at least an appearance of reason.

"Now," he added, "here's what happened to that beautiful marriage, according to the chambermaid. Instead of bringing his wife back to London, as she was expecting, the new spouse had taken her to Hanover, not far from Hamburg, where he had, he said, some business matters. Their residence was an old chateau, for a long time uninhabited, which Colqhoum had recently acquired. Received by her vassals, as in feudal times, Miss Anna was at first very amused by her

298

position as chatelaine. But she wasn't long in noticing remarks and making discoveries that gave her something to think about. On first setting foot in his chateau, Colqhoum was very moved and one of his first acts was to go to the chapel where the tombs of the former owners were conserved. Kneeling near the funereal stones, he prayed devoutly, but most of all in the presence of the rather recent tomb of a certain Carlotta de Kormer, according to her epitaph dead at the age of thirty-seven, without having been married. The visage of the living puzzle, ordinarily so impassive had appeared to be animated by the impression of the saddest sentiment.

"Several days hadn't passed when another curious incident surfaced. An old majordomo, who remained the only guardian of the chateau since the death of its former inhabitants, had taken advantage of the time when Colqhoum was deeply occupied looking over the archives and titles to the property of his domain, to mysteriously approach the chatelaine, and excusing himself in advance for the audacity of his curiosity, he finally asked her if she had known her husband for a long time, and if she was very sure that he had always worn the same name.

"Miss Anna, who had seen him change once already, was not at all offended by his doubt and, on the contrary, she encouraged the questioner to explain himself freely. When the man had recounted that about twenty years before the period of 1799, the period they were in then, the chateau that had just been sold was the theater of a mysterious domestic event, which for him, an old servant who was confided in, still remained unexplained.

"One day, the only son of his master, Baron Kormer, had left the antique manor with such haste and despair that it gave his abrupt departure all the character of an exile. What had been the cause of the misunderstanding suddenly arisen between the father and his son? Only conjectures could be formed on that point. But soon after the departure of the young man, his first cousin, Mlle Carlotta de Kormer, a young orphan, as fortunately endowed on one side with the advantages

299

of the mind and the figure as she was unfortunate on the side of property and fortune, was suddenly struck by dark sorrow. It had even been a question at that time, that she leave the chateau where, since the death of her parents, she had resided under the tutelage of the Baron, her uncle.

"From all that, couldn't some secret intrigue of the heart between the two cousins have been discovered which opposed some other projects of the Baron? The character of the son, passionate and impetuous, and that of the father, completely domineering, and jealous of his family's illustrious name, could only make that supposition seem very likely. However that may be, the departure of the young Kormer, whom his mother loved almost to idolatry, had spread deep melancholy over the existence of all those in the chateau. Some letters, further and further apart, from the absent son, was the only diversion that seemed to bring a little relief from the troubles of the Baroness and those of her niece. The effect of one among all of those letters was remarkable. It appeared to increase the young girl's troubles without producing on the Baron and Baroness a similar impression.

"But several years still rolled by and a package sealed in black brought the last wishes and the news of the death of the young Kormer, which devastated the entire family. What's more, from some words of reproach addressed to the Baron by the poignant sadness of the two women, it was easy to understand that they found him responsible for the premature death of his son, who, in addition, had died in circumstances of a nature to deepen even more the inconsolable regret of his loss. From that moment, not a ray of joy shone in the house that had seen disappear the one and only hope of its rejuvenation. Mme Kormer, eaten away by a mother's sadness, was the first to leave to join her cherished enfant. Ten years later she was followed by the Baron, whose conscience had become his executioner. Heiress to all their fortune, Mlle. Kormer would not hear of any marriage. Some years later she died with consumption, a result of her sad fixation and persevering in the reclusion of her solitary life. With her, the Kormer family was

300

extinct. Without her having left any will, state taxes had inherited, and the new owner had bought it to settle them.

"Now, according to the old majordomo, between the stranger who had come to take a seat in the foyer of his former masters and the young man whose death had not until that moment been put in doubt, there was noticed, despite the passage of years, striking features of resemblance. Now, to this first and rather conclusive clue, if there is added Colqhoum's emotion on seeing the places where he was supposed to have passed his childhood, then if there was considered the little likelihood that a man arriving from a distant country where he would have spend his life, would just by chance put his hand on this so little attractive domain, lost in the depth of Hanover, wouldn't it seem less strange than it appeared that he was hiding his true name under a borrowed personality?

"Greatly intrigued by that multiplicity of personalities and nationalities revealed in her glorious spouse, Miss Anna had taken it on herself to cleverly insinuate to him the doubts inspired relative to his supposed identity. On his side, Colqhoum answered that on his return to England, he took some trouble to demonstrate in an unequivocal manner that he was descended from the Colqhoums of Devonshire. As for the acquisition of the Kormer chateau, what was more natural than that a man having important business matters in Hamburg, would have wanted to set up a *pied-à-terre* in the neighborhood of that city? Finally, should it be considered so strange that, in taking possession of the domain where he followed a noble family, he had gone to render a pious homage to their grave and that the striking testimony of the nothingness of human grandeur has seemed to move him a little?

"As to whether the two spouses lived together, the chambermaid could only claim to know the surface, and that surface, it had to be admitted, was satisfactory. Colqhoum was full of courtesy and attention to his wife. Almost every day, in the area around the chateau, which was magnificent, he went on horseback rides with her. More talkative than the mystery of his funereal outfits with which he surround his life would

301

have made it appear, his conversation, nourished by souvenirs of his long voyages, was always interesting and full of details, and had at moments unusual gaiety. This did not prevent his showing Miss Anna the most extraordinary gallantry that could be imagined.

"From time to time, he went to Hamburg, where he had, he said, commercial interests. One day he returned with an assortment of boxes whose contents remained a secret for almost a week. Suddenly, he said to Miss Anna, 'I must show you the great curiosity that I brought back from Hamburg.'

"She was then taken into a room entirely draped in black material where two iron lamps suspended from the ceiling cast their wan light down on all the objects. There, on a table covered with a tapestry of the same color, she saw bones of bizarre shapes whose use at first glance didn't seem easy to guess. The middle of the tapestry was filled pell-mell with letters, their seals still intact, but which the reddish color of the paper attested to a very respectable amount of age. These letters also served to point to the pantomime the bones lent to each of the actors of that infernal scene. Some of them extended their arms as if to fish from that mass of correspondence. Others spread them out opened, and seemed to read them closely, or, pen in hand, were busy making excerpts. Others pretended to close them after having read them. One of those horrible parodies of nameless workers was above all remarkable for his attitude. Delicately holding one of those letters used in that scene between his fleshless fingers, he opened it, halfway, right up to the height of the now dried orbit where in the past his eyes had been, trying to read it, without opening the seal, absolutely as if it made his mistress' love letters a fresh and exciting, pert young woman.

"Terrified by that frightful scene, Miss Anna took some steps to leave.

"'Stay,' Colqhoum said to her. 'You and I will be like that one day. That's an idea it's necessary to get used to.' Then he added: 'I'm going to explain that happy band to you, which you very surely don't understand. Recently, in Hamburg, some repairs had to be made to an old building called the House of the Senate. All the objects under your eyes gathered here were in the foundations of a subterranean room. As there didn't appear to be any entry to that room, it was soon apparent that it had been sealed. There is almost no doubt that the unfortunate people whose lamentable remains you see were enclosed there to starve to death. That's what brought about the desperate positions in which they were found.

"'Now, as nearly as I can guess, those people were employed in violating the secret of the letters found with them in their tomb. It is not known what unknown circumstance made their death necessary, nor what preceded that terrible execution in the manner that was discovered here. Known in Hamburg as well as in London with liking to acquaint myself with ideas about funerals, I was invited by the architect conducting the work to come visit his findings, and I didn't have much trouble, by means of a good price I gave him, to become the owner of all that historic anatomy. His design in telling me about his discovery, which he had kept as secret as possible, was to make me a part of that speculation.'

"At the same time, Colqhoum announced that he intended soon to exhibit those sad relics in London:

"'That's a good lesson in morality,' he added. 'From that it can be learned that it's not always good to interfere in other people's secrets. Besides, there is more respect for the dead in what I'm doing than might be believed. Right now the funereal monument at Westminster that I'm having built is for the Colqhoum family, of which I am the last son. My purpose is that this tomb be that also of these poor letter openers. They would at least have the consolation of an honorable burial after their sad end.'

"In fact, a short time after these unbelievable details were given by Miss Anna's chambermaid, Colqhoum arrived alone in London, and in his townhouse, as he had announced, the lugubrious act took place. It was too much in the Shakespearean taste of my fellow countrymen not to be the greatest success. But the government, which wasn't without some small amount of remorse relative to certain epistolary curiosities which it had also permitted, apparently considered the person behind the spectacle that took place at the Ancaster House, and under the pretext that it was an attack on public morality and religion, ordered it closed.

"Contrary to what would have been expected of Colqhoum, who in another encounter had shown himself less deferential to the authorities, he submitted to that injunction without any resistance. A few days later, it could hardly be doubted that he was really from the family whose name he had taken, when he was seen having all the necessary authorizations which couldn't have been given to him without conclusive justifications of family relationship. He conducted the burial in the pompous ceremony which transferred the Colqhoum ashes to the royal tomb that had been prepared for them. After that, as if that pious duty over, all his lugubrious aims ceased to preoccupy him. He re-established all the apartments of his townhouse on their former luxurious worldly footing, announcing that he soon expected his wife to preside over the festivities he intended to give there.

"His wife! He then didn't have any other word in his mouth and never had a husband seemed more in love. Every day he sent her some present from London. Notably, the opportunity to buy an admirable Arab horse, for which an insane price was demanded, and which a prince of the royal family had backed away from, was bought by Colqhoum, and he immediately sent it by his faithful Indian to his well beloved Anna, not withstanding her approaching return to London, and to give her that beautiful present some days in advance of her return.

"At the same time, walking one day in Hyde Park, I met this detested rival and you may certainly believe, M. Matiphous, that I was in no hurry to confront him. But he came up to me with a air full of grace and ease and although I gave him a more than cold greeting:

"'Now that my period of mourning is over,' he told me, 'as soon as Milady Colqhoum is in London, we will have, I dare to believe, a pleasant house and will receive good company. Can we, my dear M. Fauntleroy, sometimes hope to have the honor of your visit? Anna, I can certainly assure you, has kept a place for you in her affections, and this feeling must be contagious, since she has come to make me share it. Until then!'

"'I am leaving in a few days for Scotland,' I replied, 'but in two weeks at the most, you will hear from me, and there is not the least cloud between my wife and you.'

"From the date of that conversation, where I hadn't been able to get in a word, being so astounded at the behavior and words of that scoundrel, a series of truly astounding misfortunes began for me and the conclusion of which could only be in this place where we are united."

XXI. The End of Fauntleroy's Story. Matiphous' Vengeance

"A large part of my fortune," Fauntleroy continued, "was placed in an industrial enterprise, based on stock shares. Until then, those stocks had done very well and had each year brought me beautiful returns. Suddenly, in one of those stock market reactions, which the most experienced brokers haven't yet explained, the enterprise was shaken right down to its foundations, and for me there was an enormous loss. I had hardly finished liquidating from this sinister loss when my silver, my jewels, the cash that I had on hand, and even valuable titles or papers were stolen in a night theft, committed with unparalleled audacity and cleverness.

"To that other misfortune, there followed almost immediately fires at several farms that I owned in various distant counties. Under the blow of so many disasters, I saw myself pursued for some debts that, in other times, I would have considered insignificant. Out of the hands of the original carriers, the titles had passed to entirely unknown creditors who would hear of no delay. Those people, evidently collection agents, would not give me any break until I had been locked up as an insolvent debtor in the King's -Bench prison.

"One day, I was alone in the modest lodging the keeper of that sad shelter had assigned to me, trying to understand that very marked and continuing persecution of my star, when I saw enter a personage whose large green eyeglasses, a beard that hadn't been shaved in several days, and a large hat over a black silk head scarf pulled down over his eyes, giving at the same time a sick and grotesque appearance. To that man's request for a moment's interview, I answered that I was ready to listen to him; but in reality I wasn't expecting anything else but some proposition of a usurer.

"'Sir,' that bizarre unknown man then said to me, 'I know about all the misfortunes that have befallen you for several days. I am interested in your situation, and, although having the honor to speak to you for the first time, I don't despair of having you accept my official assistance in the difficult circumstances in which you find yourself.'

"'I appreciate your good intentions,' I answered, 'but in what manner do you think you may be able to help me?'

"'I can't hide from you, sir, that I'm usually considered an odd man; but people have to be taken as they are, so much more so in that my greatest peculiarities, I dare say, are based on a great depth of love for my fellow man and a sincere desire to be useful to them.'

"All that preamble seemed to me to smell more and more like a professional money lender, so much so that I put a little harshness in asking him what he was getting at and what he meant.

"'To get to the point,' he answered me, 'I have the honor to lay out to you that I am what you may call a master of the game of piquet.[111]'

---

[111] French card game for two players requiring skill and cunning. It is one of the oldest card games still being played and was first mentioned on a written reference dating to 1535, in *Gargantua* and *Pantagruel* by Rabelais. Although legend at-

"'I'm delighted to know you have this talent, but in what way, if you please, can that help me in my present position?'

"'Please let me tell you. I have even developed an ability so superior that I can no longer right now find a single adversary capable of competing with me. I would have then been, just by the excess of my ability, in the hard necessity of giving up a pastime whose privation would have caused me infinite sadness, if I hadn't finally been aware that the only person who could compete with me, and for whom, I dare say, you, like me, have the greatest veneration.'

"'Who is that person?' I asked.

"'God!' my visitor answered me with the greatest coolness.

"'God! You play piquet with God?'

"'I have the honor to play a game with him every day, and to let you know how the choice of this high and mighty adversary can interest you, here's the way in which we go about figuring our losses and gains, that, let it be said in passing, come to me rather often. I have noticed that in one form or another, lately, my conscientious debtor sends me the total of my winnings. If, on the contrary, I happen to lose, I have no trouble taking to his address the sum which I lost. God, sir, has on the earth an infinite number of bankers and the poor who are in need. It's in their hands that I pour the money that I owe. Their benedictions and their gratitudes are a receipt with which I am well assured of having satisfied my creditor.'

---

tributes its creation to Stephen de Vignolles, also known as La Hire, a knight in the service of Charles VII during the Hundred Years' War, it may possibly have come into France from Spain. Piquet is played with a 32-card deck normally referred to as a piquet deck. The deck is composed of all of the 7s through to 10s, the face cards, and the aces in each suit. Until the early 20th century, piquet was perhaps the most popular card game in France, occupying a similar position to cribbage in England.

"Seeing that I looked at him with a kind of astonishment, this unusual philanthropist continued:

"'Now, my dear sir, is what I can do for you. You will need two or three hundred guineas to satisfy your creditors. Would it please you that in your presence I play them *with the person in question?* If I lose and you are lucky, because I don't feel in good form today, I will give you the sum total of my debt and you will be free.'

"'I understand, I answered, "'and certainly your manner of opening your purse to me is as ingenious as it is delicate, but I can't take advantage of your obliging offer. It is clear that you are going to arrange it so you lose and you don't want to make here anything but a charitable detour.'

"'No, by the Devil! And don't you pride yourself in that. I always play a very close game with my august adversary. Maybe a little while ago, it seemed to you that I was a rather bad player. I admit rather naively that I don't at all like to lose, and, when that happens, I get angry and show a little more temper than I should.'

"'Well, then,' I ended by saying, 'there may be a way to reconcile everything. Promise me, when I have put a little more order in my affairs, that at the first game where you've been lucky, you will come to me to pay off God. Only on that condition will I become indebted to you and make myself the holder of the sum that you anticipate you might lose today.'

"'How's that? I like that arrangement a great deal! You understand that with a player who could so easily bankrupt me, I shouldn't be too annoyed to have a deposit.'

"Everything agreed on in that way, and my ingenious benefactor having first given me his address and name, which was in fact that of a man rather well-known for his inexhaustible good works and bizarre behavior, he took two new packs of cards out of his pocket and a little green tapestry. Then he began to deal, announcing the points of each play for himself and his invisible adversary. Then he simulated a very serious game and pushed even to comedy, showing himself in a very bad humor, and letting escape some very irreverent oaths, when he didn't win.

"Needless to say, God didn't win, and, before leaving me, my helpful visitor paid me in bank notes more than what was necessary to secure my liberation. I immediately asked to be taken to the clerk's office in order to obtain my release from debt. While the clerk was busy making out the necessary papers, I returned to my cell to get ready for my departure and, in thinking about the unexpected way in which I had been gotten out of my trouble, I could do no less than admire the ways of Providence, which had brought forth this unusual person to whom I was going to owe my freedom. But I was suddenly told to go down to the office of the Prison Director, who interrogated me as to the origin of the bills with which I had *pretended* to pay my debt. The manner in which the question was asked and the severe tone of the official addressing me, was a terrifying and sudden illumination.

"'My God!' I exclaimed, "aren't these bills real money?'

"'They are counterfeit,' the Director answered me, 'and although counterfeited with a rare talent of imitation, the band which puts them in circulation, and which has long been on the wanted list, will no longer be able to pass even one. That's what you can tell him, sir, that man of goodwill, while waiting, was going to pay for everything.'

"Seeing myself thus placed under the most terrible of accusations, because the bank on which that counterfeit money was drawn had already had considerable losses and would pursue vigorously the creators or accomplices of that damaging industry, I thought I was doing a miracle in recounting how those detestable bills got into my hands, but how could you make anyone believe in the reality of such an occurrence? In the place of the liberty that I thought I already had, everything ended for me by my being transferred from the King's Bench Debtor's Prison to the criminal Newgate Prison. Before the Justice of the Peace and then before the Jury of the Accused, I could give the fullest explanations, give details about the infamy that had made me a dupe, and finally change my unlikely story for all the chances it would have to be believed and accepted.

"But what interest could that false individual have had to make me his victim? And the appearance of acts of goodwill that the criminal used, the results of a lucky fabrication, where would the thread lead for them? Moreover, faced with the famous philanthropist whose name my dangerous benefactor had taken, I was obliged to recognize that there was no kind of likeness to the man with whom I thought I was doing business. What most likely remained then to be thought was that in collusion with the audacious counterfeiters, who had for a long time disturbed public credit, I had taken charge of distributing their product and now was trying to circumvent justice by a rather poorly imagined fable.

"That, at least, was the point of view the jury came to, and, as a consequence, I was condemned to capital punishment, which for several months now should have ended my misfortunes. But, in hopes of obtaining some revelations from me and with the help of the Lord Mayor, an old friend of my family, a delay had been granted. As for the rest, if I had for a moment been able to have a doubt about who had made that cruel fate press down on me, I would have been edified the day my arrest was pronounced. As I left the court room, a man wearing a wide hat like those worn by the Quakers [112] and wrapped in a cloak, found a way to approach me. In a rapid movement, he uncovered his face which I recognized as that of the traitor who caused my condemnation. At the same moment he said to me:

"'The Marquis de Samaniego and Colqhoum send you their compliments.'

"And he threw himself into the crowd where I lost him from view.

---

[112] Perhaps coincidentally, Paul Féval used the same disguise to cloak his villainous mastermind Henri de Belcamp in his classic *John Devil* (1861).

"So, everything that happened to me was only revenge by the detestable man whose ego I had offended by some indiscrete suppositions and by the publication of the *Gnome in Love*!

"As for the unfortunate Miss Anna, here's what was her fate: Several days after my condemnation, Colqhoum reappeared in London in view of the return of his wife, who was expected at any moment. The miserable man had told the truth when he said that the most elegant society wouldn't refuse to appear in his drawing rooms. He had managed to excite such extreme curiosity that, passing over the inconvenience of having to encounter the Master and Mistress of the house, a part of the gentry had accepted the invitations for a gala, to see the infinitely magnificent things he had recounted.

"But one day, all the newspapers published sinister news. One morning, as Miss Anna was mounting, the magnificent horse Colqhoum sent to Hanover had run reared. Thrown violently to the ground, the poor woman, despite the courageous devotion of the trusted Hindu domestic who was accompanying her, and who had done everything to stop the fiery animal, she had been dragged more than five hundred feet, and she had survived that terrible accident only a few hours."

"Ah! The miserable man!" Matiphous exclaimed.

"It was vengeance for the scandal always associated with him and, better than anyone, Miss Anna would have made herself the echo.

"As for me, who from experience knew the man in depth, I didn't for one moment doubt that scoundrel. But public opinion, on the contrary, remained completely duped and saw only an accident where there had been a crime and the bursts of hypocrite sadness of the executioner found belief and sympathy everywhere. The infamous man even dared to ask the government's permission to bring the unfortunate spouse back to England in order to bury her in the sumptuous family tomb. A few days from now another sacrilegious parody can be expected."

"It's already been acted out," Matiphous said quickly. "Last night, I saw the remains of poor Miss Anna disembarked. A word escaped from Mistress Aston, that hag who seems to be in the confidence of the horrible Colqhoum, strikes me now and, in fact, must make some new information suspected. But I'm free now; I too have an account to settle with that person, and right now I'm going to make my suspicions known to the authorities."

"Be careful," Fauntleroy again warned. "You can't imagine the prodigious danger that anyone can run by entering into battle with that man.'

"For what I now have to do in life," Matiphous replied with melancholy, "it little matters what I expose myself to. Besides," he added, "it's not only my vengeance, it's your salvation that I'm pursuing, because once your persecutor is unmasked, the drama with which he has victimized you will appear in the open and perhaps there will be a review of your case."

Fauntleroy didn't seem to put much faith in that hope and once more asked the man from Malta to proceed with extreme caution in the combat which he appeared to have decided to engage in. Shortly afterward they took cordial leave of one another and taking advantage of his freedom, Matiphous hurried to cross through the Newgate office.

XXII. *"A good deed is never wasted."*
Where Matiphous begins to take vengeance

The reader will not perhaps be unhappy to learn the name of the highly placed and powerful personage through whose protection the fortunate Matiphous was so quickly let out of prison .He hasn't at all forgotten Commodore Sidney Smith, the man that Matiphous in the past helped escape from Temple Prison, and, who, afterward, went to the Orient to oppose the French invasion of Egypt. The conqueror at Saint Jean d'Acre where the French army, after prodigies of valor, had been forced to lift the siege, the man formerly obligated to

Matiphous had arrived in London precisely on the day that the imprudent young man had decided, for love of Kitty, to be the substitute of Jack Ketch. Learning almost immediately through the public outcry what had been the deplorable denouement of the philanthropic action of his former liberator, the Commodore saw the opportunity to pay his debt of gratitude. And one can easily understand that the man to whom the city of London had just given a magnificent sword of honor and the rights to the city, the one the King had wanted to honor with a new coat of arms bearing the device, *Lion Heart,* finally, the man the people in the somewhat hyperbolic drunkenness of its enthusiasm, didn't hesitate to greet with the name *Sea God* ,when he decided to obtain Matiphous' pardon, he had only to state his wish to see his desire immediately crowned with success.

On learning the name of his illustrious protector, the man from Malta, couldn't keep from a sad comparison of their very different destinies: he fallen so low, while the man he had refused to accompany to Constantinople had, in the interval, pushed his fortune so high. Thus, he never had the courage to go offer his thanks to this favorite of destiny, who was to him as a living reminder of the stupid direction that he himself had given to his life. He was content with sending his written gratitude to his savior. Besides, he was preoccupied with other cares. He had first of all to definitely break with the Ketch family, then to put irons in the fire for the bad plans he nourished against Colqhoum. Fauntleroy's story had made him seem sufficiently despicable even when that man's interference in Kitty's abduction didn't particularly recommend him to his ardent dislike. After having rented a furnished room in one of the least frequented London areas, Matiphous went to Jack Ketch's lodgings in order to pick up the clothes he had taken there when he had gone to establish himself under the double title of son-in-law and substitute.

At Jack Ketch's house, the escapee from Newgate encountered a great simplification to his projects for revenge. Come to visit her sister-in-law, the executioner's wife, Mistress Aston, was in the process of explaining to that disconsolate mother, the way in which she had been led to meddle with her protection in the love life of her daughter with Broughton, when Matiphous appeared. He had to get from Mistress Ketch's hands the key to the room where his clothes had been put. On seeing him enter, Mistress Aston was not agreeably surprised. She had thought, until she heard any different, that he was solidly behind bars. However, putting on a pleasant expression, and if absolutely nothing had happened in the past between them:

"Well, my boy, it's you," she said to him. "They said the sheriffs had put you behind bars."

"They told the truth," Matiphous answered, "but here I am outside, and in fact I don't at all regret the few hours I spent in Newgate."

"Not true, they're wrong when they make that prison a monster? That's what all my customers say."

"Oh, there's not much rejoicing there," Matiphous answered, "but they talked to me a lot about your friend Colqhoum, a curious and interesting person, on my word."

"If that was all it was, my little rabbit, you didn't need to go take a turn in jail. Colqhoum is one of those men that people in London talk about the most. And just at my place, in the past, you could have heard a lot of things about him. But at that time, it's true, you were so love-struck that you wouldn't understand if it was clear daylight and you didn't even read newspapers."

"Do you know," Matiphous cleverly continued, "the burial of his wife about which you were so mysterious this morning was a funny thing of the imagination!"

"What!" the tavern keeper asked, rather quickly, intrigued. "You were told all about the thing?"

"Oh! They told me everything. Several of those gentlemen that Colqhoum met at your place, are well up on his affairs. And do they have secrets at Newgate from the great surgeon that they no longer call anything but *Death Deceiver*?"

"At least," falling completely into the trap Matiphous had laid, Mistress Aston said, "I don't advise you to talk about the business, because if the customs people learn about it, there could very well be a fight and with Colqhoum, look out; in case he gets angry, you're done for."

"Possible," Matiphous answered, "that I could run some danger, but you, little mother, some stain could very well splash onto you, since Colqhoum would surely know that it was through you that I found out."

"What! On me?" the tavern keeper shouted with great emotion.

"But there's no doubt; if this morning you hadn't let the word escape that Mistress Colqhoum's burial was a *funny imagined thing,* would I have had the idea to go find out?"

The tavern keeper was apparently very impressed by the strength of that reasoning, since without even waiting for the end of that sentence and without taking leave of her sister, she threw her shawl on her shoulders and started to leave the company. That rapid exit said enough about Mistress Alton's intention to go warn her mysterious friend about the danger menacing him. So, Matiphous ran after her and gently forcing her to sit down:

"But are you crazy, my poor Mistress Aston," he said with an expression of goodwill, "do you think I'm going to sell the secrets of the worthy M. Colqhoum? At first I held it against him for having contributed to Kitty's abduction. But then, I recognized my responsibility for the conduct of that little stubborn girl. Since she was in love with someone else, I am, truly, charmed that she has done it openly. And I swear that I have enough esteem for myself not to be jealous of Broughton. After that, I told myself: 'When I am three-quarters consoled, why then would I hold it against a man that I don't know? Looked at in the right way, he only did a service for a friend and perhaps didn't know what he was doing against me.'"

"He undoubtedly didn't know," Mistress Aston answered. "But no later than this morning, you were talking about wrecking everything, and now that you know one of his secrets..."

"Yes, but there is something else I also know. The character of the person, it seems, is not easy. They told me all the history of that poor Fauntleroy, and I don't want to expose myself to wind up like him for not having held my tongue."

Was Mistress Aston convinced or was she still defiant?

She appeared to believe in the cautious disposition of the man from Malta, since, after having complimented him, she took off her shawl and very calmly began to chat with her sister- in- law. Shortly thereafter, Matiphous left the two gossips, leaving them with a friendlier appearance than he had at first promised.

In an instant, he had gathered his clothes, given a delivery man the address of his new domicile, then at the same time he went on his way to the Customs Board, where he introduced himself as the bearer of very important revelations. He was very easily admitted to an official trained to receive denunciations. All the official information that the customs agent could receive was somewhat nebulous at that moment, but Colqhoum was a man who had for a long time been suspected of delivering contraband, and the agent told Matiphous that great attention would be given to his incomplete revelation.

Matiphous didn't hold back when asked his name.

"Ah! Ah! The famous M. Matiphous!" exclaimed the clerk who had already heard all the story of the man from Malta, including the interest that Sir Sidney Smith had taken in him. "It's good that you are devoting yourself in this way to the public order," the scribe added. "Perhaps with your help, we're going to put our hand on the most dangerous adventurers and hardest to charge with facts. You could not in a more worthy fashion recognize the clemency the government had given in your case."

With that said, they separated very satisfied with one another. Matiphous must naturally believe that his revenge against Colqhoum was on the right track.

XXIII. The Isle of Wight's Hangman

In relation to his misadventure of the heart, Matiphous had acted the stout-hearted man with Mistress Aston. But in fact we know what to think of it. And the evening of that day so filled with so many diverse fortunes for him, in the furnished room where he had just transferred his belongings, alone with his thoughts, he asked himself how he would manage to fill the emptiness Kitty's departure had created in his life, when, a visit, as unusual as it was unexpected, seemed to open a horizon for him in the direction of that dangerous girl, with whom, he felt too well, he had not gotten over. The man who had just entered was a white-haired old man whose honest demeanor spread through all his person, acting in his favor as soon as he appeared.

"Sir," he said to Matiphous, "let me before anything else congratulate myself on the circumstance that brings me the acquaintance of a young colleague distinguished by the elevation of his character."

"You're a surgeon?" Matiphous asked, bowing his head deeply in acknowledgement of the compliment.

"No," the stranger answered, "I don't exercise the healing art, or, at least, I only undertake to heal social wounds. I am, at your service, the executioner of the Isle of Wight, the colleague, as a consequence, of Jack Ketch and his intimate friend."

"Then," Matiphous rather rudely interrupted, "you will please erase from your documents that relationship for which you congratulated me. For one morning, and in the interest of a surgical experiment, that I could execute only at that price, I consented to become Jack Ketch's substitute."

"But now that you no longer hope to become his son-in-law," the old man nicely interrupted, "you don't want to be one of us. I know all that."

"Then, the purpose of your visit?" Matiphous asked abruptly. A man so well up on his affairs began to please him only slightly.

"Sir," the stranger began again, "this morning on the Isle of Wight I was walking on the beach when a small boat that looked very unusual had just dropped its anchor. I saw the daughter of my friend Jack Ketch, the charming Kitty, disembark in the company of a man with a very bad appearance."

This beginning couldn't keep from seeming interesting to Matiphous. It was therefore on his invitation that the old man continued.

"Rather astonished to see that young person disembark on our island, I went to her and I saw that the man accompanying her was clearly in a very drunken state. At that moment, recognizing me, the poor child threw herself in my arms, crying:

" 'Oh, dear sir, it's Heaven who sends you. You are the old friend of my father. I beg you, save me!' "

"But what danger was threatening her?" Matiphous asked. "Didn't she willingly leave with that miserable man who is with her at the moment?"

"The story of that folly is known to me," continued the colleague of Jack Ketch. "The very devoted passion that you had for that child, the shameful manner in which she abused you, she didn't withhold anything from me. But I will add, repentance followed very soon after the fault. She was scarcely in the hands of her kidnapper than she recognized him as a coarse man with no finer feelings, and who, in the short sail from London to the Isle of Wight had found time to put himself in the shameful state that you see. In short, she didn't want to hear of becoming his wife mentioned and she begged me to take her under my protection."

"You undoubtedly tried to deliver that man escaped from the gallows to the law very quickly?" Matiphous asked.

"No, with Kitty's insistence, I consented to let him go. But immediately considering the interests of the poor child, with her I boarded another ship which was leaving and, with a brief delay, we reached here, where our first care was to look for you."

"It seems to me the first care of a gallant man, as you seem to be, should be to restore the fugitive to her family."

"Such was, in fact, my intention; but Kitty answered that, with the agreement of the respectable authors of her days, you were her fiancé; that she had failed you in the most essential way, and it was proper that before everything she place herself at your disposition. Finally agreeing with that feeling, I consented to go with her to Newgate Prison, where public gossip said you had been imprisoned."

"But not finding me there," Matiphous asked, "how did you go about finding me? I have resided here only a few hours and nobody knows my address."

"Not even the man who transported your belongings?" the old man asked.

"That's right. You could have found out through that man."

"From Newgate," the old man continued, finishing his story, "after having placed Kitty in a respectable family, I went to Jack Ketch's house, where I thought I would find you. You had just left, and if, in the middle of the information I had gathered in the neighborhood, chance hadn't thrown you on my steps the Commissioner you had just used and who lead me here, it is very likely that we would not have met."

"But, my star having otherwise decided, you are here for what purpose?"

"To know if you will agree to be taken to Kitty. You will find her, I assure you, willing to give you every type of satisfaction."

"But," the man from Malta answered, "without welcoming that overture with the eagerness it would have been supposed, you really wanted to speak to me about Miss Ketch's desire to take the first step toward me, and right now it's a question of my going to her."

"It seemed regrettable to you, a little while ago, that I had not before everything taken the fugitive to her family. Now, undoubtedly, you aren't maintaining that it is proper to

319

take her to you even before truly knowing what might be your intentions."

"Well, you have just offered to take me to a place where I'm supposed to meet Kitty?"

"Precisely."

"Well, being absolutely frank vis-à-vis your kind offer, I will tell you that in all this business I have already encountered a great many miscalculations and duplicity. In addition, my position vis-à-vis other persons who have played a more or less secondary role in these subterranean maneuvers, isn't as perfectly simple as I would like. Considering all of this, at this hour in the evening and not having the honor of knowing you, I don't find going to Miss Kitty very pressing, and it's also what I could do tomorrow in the morning, after the night has brought me council and matured my determinations a little more."

"Please allow me, sir, to tell you," the old man answered, "that you don't seem to me to be a very ardent lover. But I concede that a little ulceration still remains in your heart, and that explains to me the coldness of your answer. But as for your reason of caution, I feel myself perfectly authorized to tell you that they can't be taken seriously."

"And why, if you please?"

"Because you seem to me to be a man of resolution and courage, and I can't imagine the peril to which, in leaving with a man of my age, you could believe yourself exposed."

"But," remembering very well Fauntleroy's warnings that hadn't been lost of him, "a man of your age, despite his look of honesty, could very well lead me into a trap."

"Let's leave it there," said the old man, rising with a look of injured dignity. "I'm going to tell Miss Ketch that she is dealing with a matter of resentment more irreconcilable than we supposed. And now, if she chooses to come up, because that's how women are, the more they're treated harshly, the more they come to the hand pushing them away, I will be the first to oppose that act I would find as humiliating as misplaced."

"What," said Matiphous, struck by one word among all the others, "if Miss Kitty decided to come up! Then she is below?"

"No, sir," the old man continued, "if you now decide to go to her, your courage would be put to a most dangerous test. Your incomparable bravery would have to go beyond the threshold of your outside door and dare to look inside a rented vehicle where the poor weeping girl is waiting."

"What are you telling me?" Matiphous, getting up ready to leave, quickly asked. Then, however, stopping and taking the time to justify this first involuntary move. "If you knew, sir," he continued, "what perilous difficulties and what deceptions my life has been strewn with to this point, you would even pardon me an excess of caution. But let's not leave Miss Kitty any longer at the door. A woman, whatever her faults, always has the right to courtesy, and I would be truly desperate..."

"No, sir," the stranger said, getting ready to restrain him. "I'm going to tell Miss Kitty your refusal to see her, and after that I'm going with her to her mother, where you may see her tomorrow."

"But, dear sir," Matiphous said, smiling, "you won't keep me from going down with you."

"So be it, but you also won't keep me from jumping into the carriage and ordering the driver to leave. I don't hide from you that your suspicions have profoundly offended me."

"Oh! sir, consider what a poor wounded heart is in all these emotions!"

And speaking thus, Matiphous rushed out of the bedroom and rapidly descended the stairs, followed by his visitor, shouting at him to at least wait until he had time to announce him to Kitty.

There was, in fact, a rented carriage stationed at the door, the door partially open and the floor board lowered. As preoccupied as he could be to meet his deceptive mistress, Matiphous threw a rapid glance around the outside of the house. Nothing seemed suspicious to him: the street lights were lit; there were a few passers-by; the coachman was on his seat, smoking his pipe; and the very calm horses must have put him a hundred leagues from the fear of a planned attack.

Approaching then the carriage door, that he opened completely, he saw no one in the carriage but a woman whose face was covered by a veil and who, seeing him, began to sob.

"Come now, Kitty," he said, trying to take the hand of the beautiful weeper, because the usual effect of the loved one's tears is well known. "Calm down. Your faults no doubt are great, but you see me ready to hear all your explanations."

Kitty replied only with a new outburst of sorrow, and instead of her sweet voice, Matiphous heard that of the Isle of Wight hangman saying in his ear:

"You must let me explain to her. Now we're going to have a scene; at least get in the carriage so that we don't gather passers-by."

The man in love found the advice good to follow, and clearing the floorboard, he sat down beside the fugitive who, while continuing to weep, gave him one of her hands, while the old man took a third seat in front, intervening then in the reconciliation:

"Come now, my child," her protector said to Kitty," you must not be upset like that. M. Matiphous let himself be led here with some difficulty it's true, but he's not a tiger. And when you've explained to him the way in which your Aunt Aston pushed you to commit that flighty act, I'm sure he will forgive you."

With that promise of pardon, as if carried away by a new movement of repentance, the young girl, crying more than ever, threw herself into her lover's arms. While pressing her to his heart, Matiphous tried to pull away the veil that hid the adored features. But as soon as that obstacle was put aside, he exclaimed in surprise: "That's not her!"

He found the vehicle had rapidly started off full speed, and at the same time he felt his throat gripped by a snare that must have been thrown around his shoulder by means of the false Kitty's movements of tenderness.

"Not a sound, not a word!" the false Isle of Wight hangman said to him in a commanding voice, "or it means your life."

And in fact, at the effort the prisoner had made to release himself, the pressure of the snare increased even more, so that his respiration was almost cut off. Forced to resign himself, Matiphous wasn't kept very long in that painful situation. Fewer than fifteen minutes after it had started, the carriage stopped in a spacious courtyard of a townhouse, where it was as bright as midday. There he was asked to please stand on the ground and the abductor took off the snare. He understood that he was in a place where his enemies reigned as masters and where all resistance would be superfluous.

There was nothing more frightening added to the rest of his adventure at that point. After having climbed a splendid staircase, still accompanied by the man who had led him into that trap, he went across a long series of sumptuous apartments and came to a back room with a gloomy and severe aspect.

He was left alone with the understanding that he was to stay there a moment. While waiting, an inscription above a door met his eye. He approached it and read in white letters on a black background:

Here is the sojourn of eternal peace.

That explained everything. He was a victim of a new plot by Colqhoum and brought to the Ancaster mansion, according to all appearances he was going to penetrate the mysterious location of that strange club called *The Sleepers' Club*.

PART III: THE SLEEPERS' CLUB

XXIV. Inside The Sleepers' Club.
The Secret of the Letters in England. Rempailleux.

The English are a strange people in every way. They have found the way to tax even death and to put it at the service of that commercial instinct and manufacturing which is the foundation of their national wealth. The linen sack, through immemorial use, the President of the Chamber of Lords sits on, states the importance attached to one of the most importance branches of British commerce. But another encouragement of a very unusual kind has been given by the law to the production of linen cloth. All the objects used in the burial of the dead must be made of linen cloth, or suffer a tax of fifty pounds sterling. Even the thread used to sew the shroud together must be of the same material and the civil officials are charged with verifying not only that the deceased is really dead and doesn't run the risk of being buried alive, but that only linen has been used in all his apparel for the other world. It therefore follows that the Englishman who, during his lifetime, had managed to withhold something from every tax, always ends by paying tax on his wardrobe for the next world. It follows also that in England the dead wear a uniform that consists of a linen bonnet attached under the chin, plus a pillow covered with linen, on which it is customary to place the head of the dead.

Now, on entering the alcove where, after several minutes' wait, the unfortunate Matiphous was introduced, what first struck his eyes was the spectacle of a dozen caskets lined up side by side on a low inclined platform. In the caskets, dressed in the ceremonial costumes just described, reposed twelve human figures. From their closed eyes, as well as from their complete and frightening immobility it could be supposed that, conforming to the inscription that Matiphous had read above the door, they were sleeping the sleep of eternal peace. There was another object not less frightening: at the bottom of the platform there appeared a thirteenth coffin. That one hadn't yet engulfed its prey that it seemed promised in the person of an unfortunate man seated very near it already wearing his dress for the tomb. His hands and feet tied, that man had a gag in his mouth. The only sound that could be heard in that gloomy alcove was his labored breathing and panting under that instrument of torture. A pale and wan light like that of the moon, combined with the solemnity of the silence, made it one of the most striking sojourns that could ever be imagined. The phantasmagoria that today no longer frightens anyone but children and their nurses wasn't then invented, or at least it wasn't as cleverly used to frighten.

It was undoubtedly by means of that optical illusion that soon after the shadows were created, Matiphous saw himself surrounded by lugubrious and frightening apparitions to which the sound of thunder, violent winds, torrents of hail, formed an accompaniment full of horror. Then from the depth of a faraway perspective he saw appear, enlarge, and advance, a figure that in every point resembled the portrait of Colqhoum that Fauntleroy had sketched to him and that he retained. That apparition came within several steps of him, Waves if light flooded the room. All the illusions ceased, and the man from Malta found himself face to face with the mysterious personage, who said to him, affecting a tone of perfect urbanity:

"Sir, I have been advised from several directions that you would like to take a very particular interest in my affairs, and it's in part with the intention of satisfying your curiosity that by a little ruse of war I've had you brought here. A few hours ago, my excellent friend Mistress Aston took the trouble to let me know that you claim to be completely up to date on all the mysterious circumstances that can accompany the funeral arrangements of my adored wife; and from another direction, even the terms of a denunciation that was immediately transmitted to me by an employee of the Customs Board to whom you took the trouble to report, without even knowing that he was my man. The result for me was proof that you were very imperfectly informed. In two words, and to bring your curiosity more up to date, this is what happened: Mistress Colqhoum, my well-beloved wife is resting tranquilly at Hanover where I conscientiously removed her and in her place in the coffin that ostentatiously contained her mortal remains, I had Flemish lace and other small objects transported for about six hundred thousand francs of merchandise. That was, you will agree, a charming joke played on the customs officials, because you can be sure that I will dispense with paying duties on that cargo. This merchandise, you can be sure, is very safely disposed of, because the coffin that you see there, open and empty, is the method of transport, but I'm not a man to cheat the grave. Even tonight, filled with its more probable contents, it will be placed in the sepulcher that I long ago had made for my poor dead family and for my cherished spouse. Only when it is opened, because I have to tell you, sir, that your denunciation won't be wasted, and that a certain moment, which will only be that of my arrangement and my convenience, the customs agents will be notified, and instead of finding Mistress Colqhoum, who has always been absent, they will find the gentleman you see present here..."

While speaking, Colqhoum pointed to the unfortunate bound man. And if the use of speech, as that of all his other members, had been taken from him, it was clear that the freedom of hearing still remained to him, since at that explanation of the destiny awaiting him, the entire body of the victim pointed to became agitated, trembling with fear. He made some violent efforts to get free which were totally useless, since he was so soundly bound that even the strength of Samson wouldn't have been sufficient to deliver him.

"Now," Colqhoum continued, "since I have generously brought you up to date on my affairs, here's the part of intervention in all of this that I've reserved for you. That man is very guilty and has merited ten times the death reserved for him. However, I want things to take place legally. He will therefore be judged, condemned, and executed. Now, sir, this last article concerns you. You are Jack Ketch's substitute, and they say you acquitted yourself of your delicate functions with perfect dexterity. Everything is ready for the ceremony; a noose has been affixed to the wall; there is a packet of ropes over there, and you have only to hear the verdict."

"There is in all your arrangements, sir," Matiphous then replied, "just one difficulty. That is that I am not Jack Ketch's substitute, and even if I had the misfortune to be, I would still refuse to participate in an execution carried outside all legality."

"Oh!" Colqhoum said, "there you're making a ridiculous difficulty. What! Because I'm not wearing clothes made in a particular fashion, and wearing a big wig, I can't rid society of a monster that I find in my path? One thing must be remembered: the favor asked you as a service could be imposed on you as a punishment. In fact, all your actions toward me amount to nothing less than putting me at odds with British justice. And that is without pity in such a case. To defraud taxation is, in their eyes, the greatest and the most unpardonable of crimes, and nevertheless that is what you are accusing me of."

"You do with me whatever you please," Matiphous said, "but very certainly I will not be an accomplice to the *new* murder you want to commit against this unfortunate man."

"Come now, let's not get passionate," Colqhoum replied with ironic moderation. "First hear the accusation I have to make against this man. He is right now before his peers. Wait for the verdict of the jury, and then afterwards you will decide."

Having said this, he pushed forward a chair and Matiphous was told to sit down. Then, turning toward the caskets as if speaking to an assembled tribunal:

"My Lords and dear colleagues," Colqhoum said, "the man you have there before your justice is a Frenchman named Dulac, who, at the age of twenty left the city of Marseille, his homeland, to go search for adventures. I saw him for the first time in 1786 in Peru, in Lima. He had deserted from the ship he arrived on. There was at that time a young Spanish girl named Insilla Lopez, very remarkable for her beauty, and with whom he fell very much in love. That girl, who didn't share his feelings very much, finally told him one day that she wouldn't consent to marry him until he could put a great fortune at her feet.

"As I'm not an enemy of the bizarre and the extraordinary, and, besides, touched by the fervor of the passion of the unhappy lover, who was talking about cutting his throat, I told him to go to the Virgin Islands. There on a completely uninhabited point, of which I gave him a minute description, he would find buried a treasure of ten thousand Spanish quadruples[113]

"In my many voyages, my habit has always been to create for myself little subterranean hiding places on various points of the globe, so as to find myself constantly near capital in case my current resources had just dried up. Once master of the sum that I settled on him as a dowry, it seemed that Dulac's grand passion was transferred entirely to the quadruples, since neither I nor Insilla Lopez heard anything more from him. I learned later that he had gone back to France, where he lived an expensive life-style. In 1789, just at the moment his country's Revolution began, he had dissipated all the fortune I had made him master of, and was totally out of funds. Becoming associated then with his Provençal compatriots who had come to Paris to help bloody the cause of liberty, he became part of all the excesses of that time. When the guillotine's reign stopped, he took on the mask of the Royalists and served for a while in the ranks of the Chouans.[114] Passing then to non-political theft, he became head of a band of criminals who rampaged throughout several provinces. In that last

---

[113] Note in the text: About 40,000 francs.
[114] Peasants of Western France who rose against the French Revolutionary government in 1793.

transformation of his adventurous existence, he gave incontestable proof of unusual cleverness and fearlessness. At the same time, under the *nom de guerre* of Rempailleux, presiding over an infernal association of murderers who put their victims to abominable tortures, he gained one of the most terrible names for ferocity that the annals of crimes has ever recorded.

"It was at that time that the caprices of fate placed this miserable man in my pathway. The vast commerce of contraband by which, since my arrival in London, I found relaxation from the roughest work, extends from England, to Germany, and to France. In this last country, to bring in my prohibited articles, between Dieppe and Tréport, not far from the little town of Biville, I had noticed a steep cliff that rose more than two hundred and fifty feet above sea level. The foot of that cliff is a bank with scattered reefs which cannot be approached except by small boats, and then only on condition that they are very cleverly maneuvered. Afraid of the difficulties of approach, the French customs agents completely neglect surveillance of that part of the coast. I then had the idea of fixing a long knotted rope at the top of the cliff down to the reef just above the water level. In that way, my people and their merchandise could be easily lifted up. To keep this aerial path secret, I had set up a widow of a fisherman, an intelligent and courageous woman, some distance from the reef, and provided her livelihood. Helped by a young man, her nephew, with whom she took turns, her mission was every night to wait for a signal to throw us the rope once the customs' convoy had passed. She then was responsible for pulling it back up and hiding it in a fissure of the rock.

XXIV. Inside The Sleepers' Club (cont'd).
Force is still a Law

"Everything went well for a while, but love, that eternal obstacle in human affairs, came to disrupt the regularity of that service, and complicate my customary arrangement by a tragic event. The nephew of the keeper of the rope, that my men called the *'mother of the smugglers,'* was an odiously deformed boy with a repugnant face: solemn, deceptive, taciturn and with a not very open character. There could not have been a less appealing personality. That didn't keep him from claiming to be loved by one of the prettiest girls in the town of Biville, where he sometimes had occasion to go. Without knowing it, he had as a rival one of the most enterprising men that I employed in my business: alert, attractive in personality and in expression, a song always in his mouth, this rival had a million times more a chance to be preferred; and in fact, he was.

"Finally aware of his misunderstanding, the disdained lover formed a plot for a terrible vengeance. Here's how he made it a reality: One night, during a terrible gust of wind and rain, being on guard at the cliff, he heard the signal to throw down the rope. He knew his rival was one of the first to scale the wall, but to be certain he was once again, he shouted down to the convoy:

"'Eh! Williams, how do you like the weather tonight?'

"The voice he hoped was at the bottom answered him:

"'Superb for smugglers.'

"At the same moment, the oscillation of the rope, becoming stationary under the weight, testified that the ascent had already begun. The miserable man waited until Williams had covered two-thirds of the cliff. Then quickly detaching the cable, he shouted down:

"'I know that one day or another, the girls of Biville would finally turn your head. There! As you lose your balance, go see if I'm down below!'

"Thrown from a height of one hundred and twenty feet onto the rocks which spread throughout the abyss, the unfortunate young man died a frightful death, and to add to the horror, two of his comrades closely following him and to whom the traitor had nothing against, were sacrificed at the same time.

"For a short while, we lost hope of getting our hands on the murderer, who, once the crime was committed, left the country. But some days later, one evening when I was at the home of the *mother of the smuggler,* trying to get some information from her mouth, two men with sinister faces brought us the criminal. They carried a letter from Rempailleux for the Commander of the Station of the Swindlers, that is to say, for me. That letter informed me that the fugitive had come from very far away to enter the troop of the *Chauffeurs and Invisibles,* as Rempailleux's band was called, and believing the prowess of that act would gain him entrance, he told all the details of his felony.

"My opinion," my honorable correspondent added, "is that, among people who live at war with society, betrayal is more punishable than anywhere else. As a consequence, he sent me Williams' assassin so that I could deal with him according to my justice and will.

"The aunt of this criminal, who was a woman of strong caliber, didn't oppose in the least that he be given the punishment he merited. She began praying for the salvation of his soul, and as soon as she heard the detonation of the rifles which did away with him, she came piously to bury him and helped us transport him to the tomb she had dug at the same place where he had committed the homicide for which he had just atoned. As for Rempailleux, whom I didn't yet know was my former protégé from Lima, I sent him word that, if the course of his adventurous life, he found himself in need of an asylum, he was always sure of finding one aboard my yacht, the *Sarcophage*, and I gave him a signal by means of which every time we were close to the coast, he could call us to him.

"Not much time went by until the occurrence I had foreseen came about. The Chauffeurs band was dispersed and given over to the law, and, one fine day, I saw come aboard the former lover of Insilla Lopez, who didn't find himself face to face with me without certain apprehension. But, everything considered, I was indebted to him, and, in addition, he was my guest. I then didn't allow that, between us, there be even a question of the past.

"Later, I pushed my goodwill and forgetfulness even to his admission into the club we had founded. Now, that faith, according to that man, which must be particularly kept among non-believers and atheists of the social order, would you like to know how he understood it and practiced it?

"After having taken his generous share of the benefits of our association, the day came to sign the contract, not only did he decline the most fundamental legal prescription, but to get out of the duty his cowardice recoiled from, he plotted to denounce to the police our mysterious gathering place. If through my vigilance he wasn't able to succeed in that betrayal, the government, today, would possess all our secrets. In those circumstances, My Lords and dear Associates listening to me, what punishment does this felon appear to you to merit?"

"DEATH!" with one voice cried out a dozen phantoms, who, to Matiphous' great surprise, sat up in their coffins.

"You see," the President of that unbelievable club then said to the man from Malta, "there's not one voice to invalidate the sentence. To work then, and let's finish it."

"I have told you," Matiphous answered, "a hangman I am not. But if I did this work, I would still refuse to lend my position to carry out the orders of secret and mysterious justice. In addition, the theatrical forms and procedures don't intimidate me."

"However," Colqhoum said impatiently, "it probably doesn't enter into your plans to take the place of the one you want to spare, to fill the unused funeral coffin over there?"

"Is it my life you're threatening to take?" Matiphous asked in a profoundly indifferent tone. "You can do so; I won't resist, and it would perhaps be more a service to me than you think."

"Are you telling the truth, young man?" asked Colqhoum, who seemed deeply impressed by the words of the man from Malta, and seemed to pay renewed attention to him.

"Go ahead; you can do it without any peril; I am one man against all of you."

"Yes, I find you, in fact, unusually disinterested in life," continued the bizarre personage in a strikingly softened voice. "If that's how it is, we could come to an understanding. Besides, something in your youth, in your melancholy and resigned voice, provokes my interest. We will talk again about that; but first, let's be done with this miscreant!"

He clapped his hands several times. The Hindu, already seen several times in Fauntleroy's story, immediately appeared. After a few words exchanged between that man and his master, he went to a corner to pick up a rope and got busy making a slip-knot, perhaps one like the *thugs* or *stranglers* in India habitually use with their victims. But at that moment there was a loud noise at the door of the room, suddenly invaded by a swarm of constables with a police magistrate at their head.

"What is this?" Colqhoum cried out, rushing to meet the brigade. "In a country that claims to be free, the domicile of a citizen violated, invaded!"

"In the name of the law, I arrest you," said the magistrate, "and summons you to follow me to Newgate."

"You will at least produce your arrest warrant," the one addressed cried out, in a more menacing than intimidated tone.

The magistrate then gave him a paper, that Colqhoum pretended to read slowly and calmly.

"That's all right," he finally said, seeing that the warrant concerned only himself. "Over there are a dozen honorable gentlemen who offer to post a bond for my liberty."

Speaking thus, he pointed to the twelve members of his club who, at the arrival of the magistrate, had arisen in disorder from their funereal couches.

"You are a foreigner," the magistrate answered. "The law doesn't allow you to post a bond."

"A foreigner! My name is Samuel Colqhoum, a farmer from Devonshire, my birthplace, which I can prove cannot be questioned."

"It is, on the contrary, contradicted by one of your strongest allies in a letter he addressed to you two hours ago. He called you *Monsieur le Marquis.*"

"And who, then," the accused proudly asked, "can claim to know the content of my letters?"

"The government," the magistrate answered without hesitation, "when it is dealing with a certain class of accused persons has never questioned its right to intercept their correspondence. This afternoon, an employee in the Customs Bureau that you bribed, and who didn't dare to come to you in person, used the mail as the safest intermediary to let you know about a denunciation that had just been posted against you on the occasion of the transfer of your wife's remains. That missive came directly to you, but you have for a long time been under suspicion and the eye of power read your letter before you."

"So!" Colqhoum exclaimed, the powerful British lion is only a ferret! But, after all," he continued, "that denunciation doesn't state any details, and under the glorious administration of William Pitt, is being denounced sufficient then to be found guilty?"

"The customs office has verified its contents, sir; it made certain that the casket of Mistress Colqhoum has never been placed in your tomb."

"Oh! The beautiful free country! Where letters, tombs, and domestic foyers, all are violated for fear of a little deficit in the customs revenue!"

"This is too much talk," the magistrate finally said. "You have seen my warrant. Please come with me."

"But I don't see that this warrant has anything to do with the dozen honorable gentlemen present here."

"As you note very well, this warrant doesn't concern anyone but you. English law doesn't forbid anyone dressing up inside the home, and the honorable gentlemen present here, just allowing me not to find their masquerade in very good taste, are *provisionally* free to leave."

While the gentlemen members of the Sleepers' Club, hurried to take advantage of the permission given them.

"And that one over there," the magistrate asked, approaching Rempailleux, "what's he doing here?"

"That man," Matiphous said, taking charge of giving the explanation, "was going to be put to death. You will learn a great number of things from him, and you arrived in time to save his life."

"Matiphous!" shouted Colqhoum, on seeing him work with the constables to untie the prisoner, "We have a big account to settle because it's through your indiscretion that all this has happened!"

"Add to the account," the man from Malta replied, "that six hundred pounds of contraband merchandise has been put into what was supposed to be the casket of your wife, whom you murdered, and I state these two facts against the honorable person present here for the law and the King."

"All right, sir," Colqhoum answered, "you add to the measure; we would have done better to kill you."

The magistrate took down all that was said, and Colqhoum, as calm as if nothing that had taken place concerned him, with a taunting ironic expression, watched him do it. When the magistrate had finished writing:

"Have you finished, sir," the prisoner asked, in the tone of a prince dictating to his secretary. "When you please, let's go!"

XXVI. Colqhoum's Farewell

Immediately after the arrest of Samaniego, a.k.a. Colqhoum, the doors of his townhouse were sealed, the government took possession of his yacht, and finally everything of value or objects belonging to him that could be discovered, the customs officials quickly impounded as a guarantee for the enormous sums which it appeared he would be fined. That didn't keep the prisoner, during two days at Newgate, from dispensing princely sums of money.

The second day, under torrents of gin, whisky and port, that he made flow all day long, there was unrest in the prison, where there was soon a riot and a fire. In the middle of the disorder born of those two events, the Marquis disappeared and the following day, in a brochure that flooded the streets of London, this unusual man expressed himself thus:

THE FAREWELL OF THE MARQUIS DON VINCENTE
DE SAMANIEGO TO THE HEROIC BRITTANIC NATION

Englishmen,
   Soon to leave each other, let's settle our debts; good bookkeeping makes good friends. Who am I? You still don't know. As for me, I know everything about you. I have seen up close your terrible tyranny in India, and all the evil I could do to you, I swore that I would do it. For ten years, friend and lieutenant of the famous Paul Jones,[115] I have been a part of all the defeats you have suffered and you also owe me a part of the warm execration with which you have surrounded his name.
   Later, enemy and conqueror in my own right, for some ten years, aboard a fast schooner, flying a black flag, I competed with your claim to the mastery of the seas. Scourge of the Indies, at your expense I amassed those immense riches that with wide eyes you have seen me throw to the wind of my every fantasy. One among all the others, I took to heart; without ever being able to see my face and know my name, you have put a price on my head twenty times. Willing to be known, it pleased me to come in the center of your power to mystify proud merchants. Satiated with your human remains,

---

[115] John Paul Jones (1747-1792), Scottish American sailor and the United States' first well-known naval fighter in the American Revolutionary War, after fleeing England to avoid a civil trial. He is credited with answering a British captain who asked during a sea battle if he would surrender: "I have not yet begun to fight."

337

the vulture one day descended to your island. There he made his nest at one of your palaces and let his talon grasp there happily. The most beautiful of actresses made me the owner of some few fists of gold and I rejected them as flavorless fruit. At this, for your cockneys[116] *I am no longer a man, and someone toward whom I had acted most outrageously was glad however to accept me as a husband. To other curious people I must give an account of my birth.*

To cut short all the questions, I acquired a family. Money can buy anything in England, even a family relationship. Have I wept enough for that illustrious farm family who, at Westminster, now has its tomb beside your kings and your great men! Near my august parents in that glorious tomb for which I have the receipt in my pocket, the remains of my beloved wife, Anna, was supposed to repose. But I found that to put in her place some hundreds of thousands of francs worth of prohibited merchandise would also be as sweet to my heart as the presence of her remains. That speculation didn't at all succeed, and the pious customs officials, learning what they called my sacrilege, had me arrested and carried to Newgate, where I am writing you. It is not that I have very much to complain about. On the whole, and since I have been in London, it's at least three hundred pounds sterling that I flattered myself I have not paid the customs, without counting the bank notes I have actively counterfeited in precisely the time I was believed to be occupied sleeping in my famous Sleepers' Club.

This club, oh, Englishmen, is not a joking matter because it is founded on a strong, deep and profound psychological thought. At the present time, according to all appearance, unmasked by an indiscreet person I'm going to punish, the secret of that holy association is known to your government, but they are too cautious to give the key to that enigma. In a country like yours, they are too afraid of that idea.

Englishmen, in sending you my farewell, there is one justice I am glad to attribute to you. In no country in the world

---

[116] Note in the text: "What in Paris we call idle onlookers."

could you encounter a more varied choice of criminals, more audacious, more intelligent, and better company than your population of thieves and swindlers. In them I found the most useful and the most active cooperation. And as I am at the point of leaving London, to unite me with these honest men has been a real favor from your government, since I can give them in person my strongest gratitude. However, this duty accomplished, you cannot hope that I will remain indefinitely at Newgate, because after all, everyone has his own business, and despite the infinite kindness that you display here, I cannot remain here mystifying you until the end of time. Perhaps on several other points of my adventurous existence you will be willing to see me give still more explanations. But I have the habit, in my most intimate confidences, to keep a certain reserve. And I think I would have made a great diplomat, because I like the secret for itself. Some few curious people, during my sojourn among you, have tried to oppose me on this chapter, not finding it good merchandise. I leave behind me something to be liquidated in this matter, which I strongly regret has been imposed on me.

However, I want to end by an act of clemency. Suspected of distributing my false bills, the man named Fauntleroy is shaking at this moment under the keys of Newgate. Now, the punishment of death to which you have condemned him, I want you to know, is a very wicked act. Having talked a little too much about my affairs that is the only crime of this man, thought to be a counterfeiter, that my vengeance had cleverly led into a trap sprung by the law.

Now, everything between us, I think, is well discharged. Good-bye, then, Englishmen, my good dupes, Later, we will have the advantage to meet again, because you have sequestered my yacht and I am returning on my schooner. But then, I warn you, I won't be so completely in a good mood. And God save you from Samaniego the Pirate in the middle of the solitude of the ocean.

XXVII. Why Matiphous Wanted To Commit Suicide

Passionate above everything else for eccentricity, the London population read with avidity more than anger the insolent farewell of a man who had occupied that role a long time and kept it right to the end. In his particular case, Matiphous, although the facts contained an evident menace to himself, couldn't keep from recognizing a certain greatness of character in that powerful and audacious individual. Aspiring to the great as well as to the bad he was able, nevertheless, to bring about what he wished and knew so well how, by energetic irony of action, to carry out the bitter irony of his word. As for the indulgence which, at the last moment, Samaniego had shown toward Fauntleroy, it probably wasn't very merited, since the desire to compromise English law in revealing the gross error it was about to commit toward an innocent man, could have as well have been inspired him by a true spirit of clemency. Nevertheless, Matiphous was glad about the denouement of the terrible Marquis, and in remembering the kind of long dislike that this unusual man had at first shown him, he almost regretted letting himself be drawn into hostility in their relationship which was ended as soon as begun. That kind of revelation that the Marquis appeared disposed to make to him, spoke strongly to his imagination. Who knows but what if associating his destiny, already passably adventurous, with that other destiny that unfolded with so much mystery, would not have been good business for him.

Whether in hopes of again putting himself on the path of that inexplicable personage, whether the desire to obtain a little more information about him, whether still feeling the need to talk again about Kitty, and have news about her, a few days later Matiphous decided to visit Mistress Aston's tavern. But since he had been to that location, many changes had taken place in the outward appearance of the *Libertis*.

Audaciously taunted by Samaniego, and not being able to take out their bad humor on that guilty man who had escaped them, the police took revenge on the neighborhood frequented by those he claimed as his accomplices, with what could be called a coup d'état. Under the pretext that that *The Bottle and Magpie* had been the location of all the intrigues so insolently admitted in Samaniego's farewell, this respectable establishment had been closed and the Newgate concierge forbidden to let his charges leave as in the past. It was to that double measure taken soon after the Marquis' arrest that must be attributed the riot that made his evasion possible. And it could be well imagined that, if in that moment Matiphous had gone inside the prison, it would have been something very different than a banquet that Matiphous would have attended, since they hadn't pardoned him for informing on the Marquis, the cause of all that had happened. Nevertheless, since thieves don't voluntarily lose the habit of going to the places they are accustomed to frequent, and since the population of Newgate was henceforth under lock and key, their friends and acquaintances no longer encountered anyone in the half-deserted taverns but constables and police detectives, so a great number of these men still went to the *Libertis*. But that no longer had the lively and animated aspect that was formerly seen in the neighborhood. People drank and got drunk in silence, and each face seemed to be in mourning for that excellent Colqhoum, who at his departure had given such a beautiful testimony to the gentlemen of the thieves corporation and had so greatly honored them by his brilliant comment.

Finding the door at Mistress Aston's closed, and struck by the gloomy aspect of the adjacent streets, Matiphous wanted to know the explanation for all that change, and an old beggar woman, to whom he had given some pennies, was in the process of telling him when he saw approaching one of those bands too often encountered in the streets of London. It was a naval officer followed by some companions in charge of recruiting, voluntarily or by force, for the Royal Marines. As a foreigner, Matiphous believed himself less exposed than others to an outrage like that, so he let the troop of canvassers approach him without suspicion. He was more than a little astonished when he heard the sergeant recruiter say to his men: *Grab this stout fellow!*

That was quickly done. Without having time to get his bearings, Matiphous was pushed into a tavern of an infinitely more hideous aspect than that of the defunct *Bottle and the Magpie*. There, some men with vile expressions were busy drinking and gambling. But, although the unfortunate man protested and fought with all his might, no one in those gathered there seemed even to pay attention to the scuffle, which ended with Matiphous' being violently thrown into a sort of cave or cellar which suddenly opened in front of him.

At the end of some twenty steps down, rolling rather than walking, in the middle of the obscurity the unfortunate young man found himself in a vast vaulted room where a smoky lamp suspended from the ceiling illuminated some sinister faces. In the middle of them there appeared the false Isle of Wight hangman, the one who had so suddenly led the man from Malta into Samaniego's net.

"The devil! Young man, we've had a lot of trouble catching you," said Samaniego's bodyguard in a tone of friendly reproach. "Well! How have you been since we've seen you?"

Matiphous glanced at him n disdain without answering.

"Don't be angry, friend," continued the agent of the Marquis' revenge. "It's not a matter, as you might think, of going to serve on his Majesty's vessels, but simply a question of giving you a little lesson."

"Lessons from a miserable man of your sort?" answered Matiphous, who, resolved in advance for anything, brought about at least, by these provocative words, to speed up the catastrophe.

"Yes, sir," answered the venerable person, "a lesson of discretion whose memory will remain always with you so that it won't be lost on you."

"Have done with your menaces," said Matiphous, still with the same tone of contempt, "and since I am in your power, get to the fact."

"Not at all. I must first make you aware of our procedure vis-à-vis you, because we like to have right on our side. You will learn, then, for the first point, that here and elsewhere, we hold your informing very much against you because it deprives us of the useful and pleasant society of the Marquis de Samaniego. What's more, with your loose tongue, which has so much compromised that worthy man's interests, you are the cause of the loss of the only privilege that could make a stay at Newgate endurable, and also the cause of the death of several honorable gentlemen who died defending it."

"Add," replied disdainfully Matiphous, "that you are in the pay of the Marquis for his revenge, and finally finish it."

"Now, ordinarily, with informers," continued the false hangman, without showing any reaction, "here's what we do. You see there a trowel, a trough, two sacks of cement, and the gentleman over there, a mason."

At those words, the man pointed out gave the prisoner a deep bow. "Now," the orator continued, pointing out an excavation in the wall a great deal higher than broader, "a man in that little room could be comfortable. We take our man, strangle him, place him like a saint in his niche, then, sir, with some pieces of rubble and some handfuls of cement, you're like a building in front of him. This in technical terms means *walling up a man,* and that, I repeat, is the punishment given in the code of the *gentlemen of the night* [117]for the crime of informing."

A shiver ran throughout Matiphous's members at the thought of that horrible end.

"Ah! Ah!" said the Marquis' agent, "that masonry, it seems to me, doesn't please you very much. Be reassured; we

---

[117] The term appears to be borrowed from Paul Féval's *Les Mystères de Londres* (aka *The Gentlemen of the Night*) (1843-44), the first novel in the loosely connected saga of *The Black Coats* (available from Black Coat Press). The grim fate of "walling up a man," is, in fact, used by the leader of that criminal society, the Colonel, in Féval's novel *'Salem's Street*.

are just and merciful. We won't forget that if you are guilty of serious imprudence, the beautiful and philanthropic operation practiced on Broughton gives you some right to our indulgence. Your punishment has then been commuted, but in letting you live, we maintain that a certain memory of your carelessness of language is still with you. The operation is neither long nor painful and, with your permission, we will begin it without any more delay."

"But what do you intend to do?" asked Matiphous, struggling in the hands of several of the assistants who, having grabbed hold of him, were beginning to undress him.

"No, only the right shoulder," said the one carrying out the torture, and taking a white hot iron from the hands of one of his assistants that had gone to get it from a stove, he approached the shoulder of Matiphous, who in the meantime had been stripped naked so the unfortunate young man could no longer be in doubt of what type of torture was meant for him.

"Kill me instead!" he cried out and in a desperate effort he tried to deliver himself from the restraint holding him.

"Be still, sir," the agent of the Marquis said cold-bloodedly, "or otherwise it will wound you."

That said, with a rapid movement he pressed the iron on the shoulder of Matiphous, who cried out in rage, while a small cloud of smoke spread throughout the atmosphere of the subterranean room, carrying with it a strong odor of roasting flesh.

"You see, if I'm not the hangman of the Isle of Wight, I could be without too much study," ironically said the executor of that terrible justice. "Now," he added, "I can lessen the disagreement you've just undergone by a small consolation. What for eternity has just been written on your shoulder are the sacramental letters *TP* usually placed on prisoners condemned to forced labor for life.[118] In your particular case the

---

[118] Travaux forcés à Perpétuité.

letters simply mean *Trop Parler*.[119] And if you would like, I am ready to give you a certificate saying so."

Matiphous understood almost nothing of that terrible facetiousness. In a paroxysm of pain and rage, he had almost lost the use of his senses.

When he came to himself, he had his clothes back on and was sitting on the edge of a sidewalk in the middle of some passers-by who had stopped to help him. At first, he didn't have a very lucid memory of what had happened to him, but when his memory had managed to push aside the veil under which it was still obscured, he let out a cry of despair, rose up like a madman, and pushing violently aside everything holding him back, he ran until he had reached the edge of the Seine.

Then the sight of the water stopped him. He seemed to think for some time, then, calmer, he began to walk through the streets until he came to a pharmacy. There be bought the first dose of poison. A little later, in the same frame of mind, he went along the same way, adding to his provision of poison, because not only the idea, but the form of his suicide had been decided on. Back at his hotel, we saw him about to put the poison in his veins when the cry from the bedroom of Madame de Limeuil halted his resolution. That resolution was completely extinguished by his generous adoption of the little orphan, to whom henceforth he devoted his life.

What he did with that paternity, what became of the Marquis de Samaniego and how his existence and that of Matiphous came to be attached to that of the Hulets, whose story will soon be taken up again, is what the reader will learn in reading the 3rd, 4th, 5th, and 6th parts of our story.

XXVIII. The Encounter

Since 1799, the period in which the major part of the facts recounted in the second part of this story took place, eleven years had passed. It was then 1810. Come into by

---

[119] Too talkative.

means of his power, and introduced by an Archduchess of Austria, what has been since called, rather ridiculously, *The European Concert,* Napoleon had established rigorous etiquette for his court and for his palace. Badly explained by a ridiculous element of vanity, it must soon be taken for repatriated politics attached to and surrounding his monarchy with the greatest brilliance. Whatever it was, a comparison of the *Almanach Royal* of 1789 with the *Almanach Imperial* of 1810 shows that Louis XVI, in the hands that were to break the scepter of the old French Monarchy was reduced to a Grand Chamberlain and to six Gentlemen of the Chamber, while the service of the Emperor's chamber was comprised of a Grand Chamberlain and fifty-nine ordinary Chamberlains.

Without satire here, it could be said that the prodigious number of personnel needed to show in visitors, must be attributed to the cruel antechamber where, for more than three-quarters of an hour, where, in one of the Tuileries' waiting rooms, the unhappy solicitor of an imperial audience had been waiting. A letter of introduction indicating the day and hour when he would be received by his Majesty the Emperor and King, had nevertheless made him hope for a less laborious admission.

Since we have time to consider in some detail the characteristics of the man whose patience has been put to such an extreme test, we will say that his thick blond hair was turning gray and that some very deep wrinkles pointed to the approach of fifty years. He was short, had a pale face, was beardless, effeminate, and had one of those thin flute-like voices to which one is always tempted to give a foolish interpretation. But going past the first look, considering his sharp and commanding voice and the impatience of all his actions which emphasized the torture of the wait, it was impossible not to see one of those rough and energetic natures standing on his own two feet, rebelling and revolting against the least attempt at his independence or dignity.

"Well," said the person who had scarcely sat down after an agitate walk around the room, leaving his seat again, "isn't the Chamberlain on duty available?"

"Impossible," the office usher, who had just been called, responded drily. "When his Majesty wants to see you, the Chamberlain will ring for me to bring in those to be given audiences."

"Well, then," the man who had been asked to take a new lease on patience, said abruptly, "since the masters and the valets are both invisible, here are the telegrams from the Governor of the Isle de France which I have been charged with putting only in the Emperor's hands. You can say that, tired of waiting, I have left them." And he deposited on the usher's desk a voluminous envelope with an ample red seal.

"But, sir," the usher said with a kind of terror, "an audience with his Majesty!"

The man that exclamation tried to hold back, shrugged disdainfully, and he was already getting ready to leave and when at the door he had just opened, he found himself face to face with someone whose unexpected encounter produced a strong impression on him. Holding under his arm a green Moroccan leather briefcase, and walking with that administrative self-assurance, which is characteristic of heads of departments and services, when they go to work in *high places*, the man entering paid no attention to the face that had just presented itself in his pathway. But it wasn't the same for the man who had deserted the imperial audience. He retraced his steps and speaking to the usher, while the object of his curiosity went into the Emperor's office without being announced by the Secretary.

"Can you tell me the name of the person I have just seen enter?" he asked.

"But you were in such a hurry to leave!" the man wearing the chain of office said maliciously, without giving the information solicited.

"My dear fellow," the questioner then said, seeming to return to his interrupted words, "how is it that among so many powerful people you see file through here under your eyes without ceasing, not one of them has thought of giving you a present!"

"What's that!" said the usher, aghast at the unexpected question.

"But you're dipping into a wooden snuffbox there that shouldn't be allowed in the Emperor's palace," said the man with the telegrams. "Here, look at this one!" and at the same time he drew from his pocket a delightful gem in malachite.

Although he was somewhat startled with being spoken to in such a way, the usher couldn't help but agree that he did in fact have under his eyes an object of exquisite workmanship.

"Well! Here's what must be done with this other horror," the incomprehensible person said, and almost snatching the humble snuffbox from the hands of the usher, he threw it into the big fire burning in the fireplace.

"But are you crazy, sir?" exclaimed the unhappy proprietor, who had just been thus dispossessed.

"Not at all, my friend; you like my snuffbox. You keep it. Yours hurts my eyes, and I have done with it what it deserves. You see everything is for the best."

"Eh! Sir! I don't need your presents!"

"You don't understand me, my dear fellow; it's not a matter here of a present. It's just that I abhor things of bad taste, and I make pitiless war on them wherever I find them. Such as you see me, I have gems of all kinds in one of the richest collections that exist in all of Europe, and the object that I have begged you to accept is a simple bit of nothing found at hand. But at least don't go believing that I want to make you the object of some roundabout seduction, because, you see, I'm no longer talking about the information that I at first hoped to get from your mouth."

"Oh, well, there's no great mystery there, and I certainly would have committed no indiscretion when I told you that the person you're inquiring about is named M. Vandel."

"Vandel! And you're sure it's not Hulet?"

"At least I know him only under the name of Vandel."

"And in function does he come here, with that air of being part of the household?"

"That I ignore completely; I only know there is an order to let him see the Cabinet Secretary at any hour without announcing him."

"He's more fortunate than I am," said the questioner, changing the conversation, "because it seems that I definitely will not be seen today, so," he continued, "I again put you in charge of my telegrams," and saying this, he went toward the door.

"But, sir," the usher shouted, "let me give you back your snuffbox!"

"Keep it; it's less than nothing," replied the man who carried the telegrams, and without hearing of any restitution, he definitely left that time.

About a quarter of an hour after his departure, the man with the briefcase was seen crossing the courtyard of the Tuileries, and reaching the nearest public carriages, he got into a cabriolet with a high number.

After having been parked a long time in the courtyard of the Palace, an expensive carriage left almost behind the man with the briefcase. At the moment the rented carriage started off, the brilliant equipage followed at some distance, taking care not to pass it. That convoy wound up at a townhouse of a rather gloomy appearance situated in the Rue Barbette, in the Marais. While the man with the briefcase knocked at the door of the house, which soon opened to him, the man of the snuffbox had gotten out of the rich carriage, stopped for a moment to consider the façade of the townhouse where, in his turn, he knocked. Having then gone to the concierge's lodgings, he asked:

"Is this the correct address for M. Vandel?"

On the affirmative address he had received, he hurried back to the vehicle, which had immediately driven away, burning up the pavement. So, the questioner wasn't wrong. Vandel and Hulet, as the reader already knew, were one and the same person, and it really was Hulet, the ex-Dominican and ex-member of the Convention, the one who, at the end of the first part of this story we left with the Minister of Police, busy reading a manuscript given to him by Fouché, that despite the change of name caused that unusual curiosity shown by the unknown man, who had only met him at the Tuileries. What's more, Hulet hadn't noticed in any way that someone was following him. If he had, perhaps he would have been able to make sense of a large letter addressed to him received the evening before under his pseudonym of Vandel which contained absolutely nothing but these words:

> *Raro antecedentum sclestum*
> *Deserut pede claudo.*[120]
>
> > *Horace, livre III, ode II.*

But since he was ignorant of the action taken against him, which was probably not well meant, he attached little or no attention to that first message. To seriously arouse his attention it took a second letter some days later, infinitively more significant and more menacing to impress on him the classic idea of vengeance so unusually placed under his eyes. Written in the same hand as the first, this new missive told him:

> *Les chats ne poursuivent pas les animaux qu'il ne voient pas; ils ne les chassent pas; ils les attendent, les attaquent par surprise, et après, s'en être joué longtemps, ils les TUENT.*[121]
>
> > Buffon, *Histoire naturelle.*

---

[120] Translated in a footnote in the text: Rarely does lame-footed punishment miss reaching the crime that it is following.
[121] Cats do not hunt animals they cannot see; they do not chase them; they lie in wait for them, attack them by surprise, and afterward, having played with them for a long time, they KILL them!

It would be difficult to show a man more clearly than with nothing but the way some of the words of the citation had been underlined that someone had something against him, first of all affecting his repose and next his life. However, some days passed without anything happening to give a body to these vague menaces, but one morning there was deposited with the concierge for him at his address at the townhouse where Hulet lived, a package carefully wrapped and tied. When the packet was opened, he found it served to hold a delightful small rosewood box enhanced with incrustations and carvings.

However curious the ex-Convention member might be to know the contents of that packet, he only opened it with extreme caution using the key he found suspended by a rose favor to one of the ornaments in relief. He remembered a family misfortune which also should have warned him against some infernal machine that could lurk in the flanks of the valuable little box. But Hulet wasn't at first aware of that hidden malicious intent which at first didn't reveal everything in depth, and most of all the procedures of the shadowy persecutions which, the more novel and unexpected, were intriguing.

As soon as the cover to the little box had been lifted, like that other box of Pandora, a whole world of hideous and harmful insects escaped. It seem to have been a deputation of each of the most repugnant species that the entomologist had ever classified: fleas, bugs, wood lice, ants, kites, *perce-oreilles*, earwigs, Spanish flies, locusts, slugs, English moths, pill bugs, scorpions, spiders, centipedes, wasps, had been carefully brought together to form a venomous assembly that immediately flew away or started away to infest the house. At the bottom of the box, seeming to be the king of that aggregation, there was enthroned an enormous frog, wrapped in hemlock leaves and asafetida.

With this blow, Hulet could no longer misunderstand a prelude to that anonymous vendetta, previously demonstrated to him. What's more, it was in vain that he thought and tried to recall; he could not remember where he had incurred that secret hostility which manifest itself in such strange and odious refinements. Apparently the invisible persecutor was not in haste for a denouement, since, for several weeks he let his victim breathe and it was only, when, with a hellish shrewdness, he found a sensitive and vulnerable spot in him that he began to strike again.

Hulet had always loved books; age, leisure brought about by the ease his functions, and to which a considerable salary was attached, which we will talk about later, had finally given his tastes as a bibliophile the development and the characteristics of a true passion. Soon the possessor of a valuable library, he almost never spent a day without enriching it with some curious acquisition. His notoriety as a knowledgeable amateur had finally become European, and as soon as some important library collection was put up for sale, either in Paris, or abroad, the flower of the collection was offered to him, because he was known as a good judge and in a position to pay what things were worth.

One of the great pastimes of Hulet's existence, very withdrawn since the period when we saw him ordered to the Commissioner of Police, was to go each evening to the Bullion Hotel or the Silvestre shop. There, whether it was a book, a manuscript, an autograph, he rarely let escape an article that he had once fixed his choice on. But, suddenly, on his path there appeared implacable competition, and soon it was no longer possible to bid at an auction than there was immediately a counter bidder, trying at any price to out bid him. Only those who possess the mania of a collector could understand the strange hold that kind of *idée fixe* can have over the reason and the will. Everyone will tell you that in that incessant battle, where he also was incessantly the looser, the unfortunate bibliophile must be overcome by a sort of despair, and, nevertheless, beyond this first torture, still more, encounter that of never knowing the hand striking him. At each encounter there was a new proxy, often someone unknown, often just a bookstore owner having instructions to bid excessively high in order to take possession of the object on which he had bid.

The object that he had only thought about was disputed in advance. You would have said it was a supernatural instinct that somehow had guessed, to kill in their germ, even his least expressed desires.

To that fierce battle only one end was possible. Discouraged and always vanquished, Hulet had to retire from the lists, and thus his life remained without the innocent and only distraction that he had. Unfortunately, in the devilish progression the sad collector's invisible enemy seemed to want to give to his vengeance, that cruel influence was still just harassment and, in some ways, just pin pricks. As we shall see in a little while, it still had a great amount of bitterness to distill to him.

XXIX. Continuation of the Hostilities

In speaking about the extraordinary amount of meditation Hulet, once he was a public official, had introduced into his life, we haven't said to what point that life was serious, austere, and profoundly withdrawn. The house, whose entrance we led him to only a moment ago, was one of those townhouses formerly inhabited by the parliamentary magistrature where the architecture married brick to stone, and above all where their long and narrow windows had an aspect so characteristic and so melancholy. In that antique dwelling, the second floor was inhabited by a family with a dignified and patriarchal lifestyle.

Everyone would have considered living near them and those who visited them as good fortune. Living on the first floor and always having an opportunity to meet some members of that honorable family, not only had Hulet not shown any need to form ties with them, but keeping himself carefully at a distance, it was with a coldness pushed almost to rudeness that he had discouraged their frequent advances to him. Early in the morning, winter and summer, without waking the concierge, he habitually left through a door opening into the garden from his apartment onto a side street. And as for the curiosity that this habit of leaving so early might arouse, it is explained by a pious custom that the ex-Dominican had of going daily to hear the first mass in his parish. His official duties over, retired into his library as into an impenetrable sanctuary, he practiced his favorite pastime, Hulet received only rare visits, and except for the evenings when he went to auction rooms, when ten o'clock, at the latest, struck, every light was extinguished and every sound of housekeeping was hushed.

Madame Hulet had always had a great taste for solitude that remained from the religious life where she had spent her most beautiful years. Being then about fifty-years-old, more than ever she liked a retired life, and far from feeling any opposition to the somewhat confining regime, she was happy to find in her husband such a sympathetic position, and she would have applied herself to bring it about rather than oppose it.

Already in the world the year Hulet gave his regicide vote, and therefore near to finishing his nineteenth year, Alexis, their elder son, would perhaps have preferred, because of the energy characteristic of his age, to have some diversion from the gloomy economy of that existence. But, having been for a long time a scholarship student at the *Arméniens du lycée impérial,*[122] was at the moment with *Les Arméniens* in Constantinople,[123] where he was considered one of the most distinguished students.

During the absence of their well-beloved son, whose return they soon expected, Madame Hulet concentrated all the ardor of her love and her maternal care on an eleven-year-old girl, the last fruit of her marriage. She was a child, if the read-

---

[122] Note in the text: *Les Armeniens* was a secondary school for young men whom the State trained to become *drogmans*, or interpreters of Oriental languages. After beginning their studies in Paris at the *Lycée impérial*, to which they were attached, they were sent to complete their education in Constantinople in an establishment funded and kept by the French government since Louis XIV.

[123] Istanbul.

er remembers, that she reminded her husband was a consolation at the time when the most exhausting searches had made them understand that the loss of their second son, kidnapped at Orgères, under mysterious circumstances that we have reported, was irremediable. Her sweet name of Hélène[124] did not lie, but promised that child would be as beautiful as her mother had been and everything foresaw that, as far as the heart was concerned, she would have the most loving and tender character, not excluding all the gifts of the mind.

In a few days, a ray of joy was going to descend in the middle of the serious and so sad life of the paternal household. She was preparing herself for one of the sweetest events in the life of a young woman and, prepared by Christianity for this great act of the Catholic faith, she had reached the moment desired for her first Communion. If there is not a mother, however frivolous she may be, who does not look into herself and feel her heart tremble at the approach of that celebration of childhood, the religious emotion with which Madame Hulet awaited this day can be imagined. In her, beside the mother of a family and a companion of the man, there still survived the servant of the Lord and the wife of the Mystic, and by all the practices and the most ardent devotion, the former Benedictine sought for a conciliation of her present with the past whose oaths she had violated. But to that woman, still secretly obsessed with pious scruples, it seemed that the young communicant must be a powerful mediator to achieve her reconciliation with Heaven, and she looked forward to that holy ceremony as a final station in the sad path to her repentance. Kept back by the duties of his occupation, Hulet could not be part of the happiness of that day. After going to the church, clothed in the white dress and the veil, symbol of virginity covering her face, Hélène came, brought by her mother to kneel before her father. By serious and heart-felt words, he reminded her of the grandeur and beauty of the act she was going to fulfill. Next,

---

[124] Allusion to Helen of Troy, whose abduction started the Trojan War.

he solemnly took her hands, and embracing her with great emotion, he told her goodbye until the hour she would return *nourished with the bread of the angels and having accepted her God.*

Seated in the row of the young communicants, her heart filled with holy joy, Hélène mingled her voice to the canticles that accompanied the majestic harmony of the organ, when suddenly, with an abrupt and commanding gesture, the priest who had prepared her for the supreme Christian initiation, signaled to her to leave the bench where she was sitting and to come to him.

That day, Madame Hulet had only half her soul in prayer and with a distracted look at every moment drawn toward her daughter, she had seen that call. At the same moment a conversation seemed to have started between the priest and the child; then the child pointed to the direction in the church where she knew her mother was seated. Then, followed by Hélène, whom that incident had filled with confusion, the priest approached Madame Hulet, and in a commanding and severe voice said:

"Will you, please, Madame come with me to the sacristy?"

Arrived there without having been able to receive any explanation, the mother heard the girl ordered to kneel in a corner, after which addressing her:

"Madame, I have just now received this letter. Read it and answer."

Trembling, and instinctively guessing its contents, Madame Hulet took the paper from the hand presenting it to her, and here's what was written there:

Vicar,

You will perhaps be edified to learn that the young Hélène Vandel, who just now was going to approach the holy table, is the daughter of a defrocked Dominican and a Benedictine who violated her vows. You see that with an origin as "sacred" that child has a particular right to the benedictions of the Church. However, there are some minds, badly formed, that could claim that certain stains on the lives of the parents could rub off on the life of the child. They add that civil law, vis-à-vis the natural child, admits certain reservations, incapacities. So religious law can and should also recognize them in regard to the spiritual bastard when the scandal of two apostates and two perjurers have thrown it into life.

That letter was written in the same hand that had twice written to Hulet in a threatening way; it was neither dated nor signed, and had no stamp.

"Well, Madame!" said the vicar, while with her face washed with tears, and without daring to raise her eyes, the accused held out the denunciation for him to take back.

"My father," said Madame Hulet, for any response letting herself fall at the feet of the one questioning her, "What expiation do you need? You see me ready for any."

"You are asking?" evidently carried away by an excess of zeal, the priest asked. "How can a scandal be repaired except by making it go away."

"But at least," the poor woman continued, " never let my child know the stain on her birth, and most of all may she not be rejected from the sacrament."

"There's no question of that today," the vicar answered. "The cure is too busy right now for me to take up the question with him. Tomorrow when you have made your necessary submissions, we will see what can be done."

"But, sir, this is a terrible affront that you are preparing for an innocent. It means transforming into a day of mourning what should be one of the happiest days of her life. You see me right now willing to do anything."

"I repeat that I can't take the decision on myself. Take the child away with you, and we will let you know in a few days."

First a suppliant, and then irritated by what she finally called an abuse of power, Madame Hulet, as much as she could, declined the cruel injunction. Even though the letter was addressed correctly; it had arrived in the hands of a man in whom a holy and extreme ardor of regularity was not accompanied by all the desirable enlightenment. He remained then inflexible in his refusal. Finally, under the threat of seeing the reason for the continuing debate revealed to her daughter, the unhappy mother was constrained to give way. As for Hélène, not understanding anything about the humiliation that had just struck her, she saw disgrace and sadness beginning for her the same day and hour that her soul should be filled with that celestial joy that, even by the admission of those to whom the ways of salvation are the most foreign, is not experienced twice in life.

At the moment the two victims returned, Hulet was not at home. At his return, Madame Hulet was still so influenced by the blow *to her daughter's heart* that, forgetting her position as a wife, and remembering only her position as a mother, her first word was for a separation, which the happiness and the future of her children seemed to demand.

Hulet didn't try to fight either with logic or the heart against the resolution of a despairing woman. He tried only to calm her, and without losing a moment, he went to the archbishop. There he laid out to the Directing Prelate the excessive pretention of the priest who wanted to make the child responsible for the sin of the parents. At the same time, just in case that intolerant jurisprudence had found favor in the place he had come, he didn't hesitate to add value and favor to his request by making known the functions and great confidence the government had invested in him.

The request didn't undergo the shadow of a difficulty, and an hour later he brought the parish priest express and imperative commands from the Archbishop that Hélène be allowed to commune. But the evil that had been done could not be repaired. The poor child was admitted to the holy table only the next day and then alone and at a furtive hour without the radiant pomp with her companions of the day before. From that ceremony accomplished, there remained for her the vague and unexplained feeling of an open family wound that poisoned all the joy for her. The same event had injected leaven into what had been, until then, the very happy family life of her parents.

Madame Hulet's scruples, long asleep, awoke and in the man with whom she had associated her life, from then on he appeared to her as an accomplice rather than a husband. Following these deplorable events, the question was whether Hulet had the ardor to discover that invisible enemy who, accurately and piece by piece, demolished his life's happiness.

Absent from the paternal house at the time of that sad outrage, the young Hulet had yet escaped that wind of unhappiness blowing over his family. But shortly thereafter he arrived from Constantinople, and soon had his share of that relentless persecution that seemed to hover over the former Convention member in all that was dear to him, before striking him.

Hardly had he returned to Paris than, by the ardor and inexperience of his age, Alexis Hulet was drawn into a liaison with a woman who, in every way, presented herself as an adventuress of the worst sort. Duped by cunning and shameless advances, the young man was nothing but some sort of wildlife that she had been told to catch. From the first drunkenness of his dangerous happiness, surprised by a rival who was later known to be traitorously planted, the imprudent young man saw himself challenged to a duel, where, just as into his sad liaison, he went head first. An encounter followed. Completely unfamiliar with handling weapons, Alexis Hulet crossed swords with a dangerous swordsman who, apparently, had been told to take his life. The crime, however, was not consummated and in that terrible tribute of hatred and vengeance raised against his family, Alexis Hulet, in paying with his blood, had at least the good fortune not to be mortally wounded.

There is something better. About the time, healed from his wound, he could seem exposed to some new ambush, suddenly the secret of that hidden hatred, of which he had almost fallen victim, was revealed, and it was finally given to his father to tear away the cloud from which the lightning incessantly came. But even the production of that revelation was surrounded by truly extraordinary circumstances and their exposure has its place here, prior to every explanation.

TO BE CONTINUED IN
THE BROTHERS OF DEATH

MYSTERIES & THRILLERS

M. Allain & P. Souvestre. *The Daughter of Fantômas*
A. Anicet-Bourgeois & Lucien Dabril. *Rocambole*
Guy d'Armen. *Doc Ardan: The City of Gold and Lepers; The Troglodytes of Mount Everest/The Giants of Black Lake*
Cyprien Bérard. *The Vampire Lord Ruthwen*
A. Bernède. *Belphegor; Judex* (w/Louis Feuillade); *The Return of Judex* (w/Louis Feuillade); *The Shadow of Judex* (anthology)
A. Bisson & G. Livet. *Nick Carter vs. Fantômas*
André Caroff. *The Terror of Madame Atomos; Miss Atomos; The Return of Madame Atomos; The Mistake of Madame Atomos; The Monsters of Madame Atomos; The Revenge of Madame Atomos; The Resurrection of Madame Atomos; The Mark of Madame Atomos; The Spheres of Madame Atomos; The Wrath of Madame Atomos* (w/M. & Sylvie Stéphan)
Félicien Champsaur. *Homo-Deus; Nora, The Ape-Woman; Ouha, King of the Apes*
Jules Clarétie. *Obsession*
V. Darlay & H. de Gorsse. *Arsène Lupin vs. Sherlock Holmes: The Stage Play*
Harry Dickson. *The Heir of Dracula; Harry Dickson vs. The Spider*
Séamas Duffy. *Sherlock Holmes in Paris*
Alexandre Dumas. *The Return of Lord Ruthven*
Paul Féval. *The Black Coats (The Parisian Jungle; Heart of Steel; The Sword-Swallower; 'Salem Street; The Invisible Weapon; The Companions of the Treasure; The Cadet Gang); Gentlemen of the Night; John Devil*
Paul Féval, *fils. Felifax, the Tiger-Man*
Louis Forest. *Someone is Stealing Children in Paris*
Émile Gaboriau. *Monsieur Lecoq ; The Casebook of Monsieur Lecoq*
Goron & Émile Gautier. *Spawn of the Penitentiary*
G.L. Gick. *Harry Dickson and the Werewolf of Rutherford Grange*
Léon Gozlan. *The Vampire of the Val-de-Grâce*
Georges Grison. *The Heads that fell in Paris*
Paul d'Ivoi. *Around the World on Five Sous* (w/Henri Chabrillat)
Paul Lacroix. *Danse Macabre*

Jean de La Hire. *Enter the Nyctalope; The Nyctalope on Mars; The Nyctalope vs. Lucifer; The Nyctalope Steps In; Night of the Nyctalope; Return of the Nyctalope*

Rick Lai. *Shadows of the Opera: Retribution in Blood; Sisters of the Shadows: The Curse of Cagliostro*

Etienne-Léon de Lamothe-Langon. *The Virgin Vampire*

Steve Leadley. *Sherlock Holmes: The Circle of Blood*

Maurice Leblanc. *Arsène Lupin vs. Countess Cagliostro; Arsène Lupin vs. Sherlock Holmes (1. The Blonde Phantom; 2. The Hollow Needle); The Island of the Thirty Coffin; 813; The Many Faces of Arsène Lupin* (anthology)

Gaston Leroux. *Chéri-Bibi; The Phantom of the Opera; Rouletabille & the Mystery of the Yellow Room; Rouletabille at Krupp's*

Maurice Limat. *Mephista*

Jean-Marc & Randy Lofficier. *The Katrina Protocol;* (anthologists) *Tales of the Shadowmen 1-12; The Vampire Almanac* (2 vols.)

Richard Marsh. *The Complete Adventures of Judith Lee*

William Patrick Maynard. *The Terror of Fu Manchu; The Destiny of Fu Manchu*

Frank J. Morlok. *Sherlock Holmes: The Grand Horizontals; Sherlock Holmes vs Jack the Ripper*

Jean Petithuguenin. *The Adventures of Ethel King*

P.-A. Ponson du Terrail. *The Immortal Woman; The Vampire and the Devil's Son*

Georges Price. *The Missing Men of the* Sirius

Antonin Reschal. *The Adventures of Miss Boston*

Norbert Sevestre. *Sâr Dubnotal vs. Jack the Ripper; The Astral Trail*

Eugène Thébault. *Radio-Terror*

P. de Wattyne & Y. Walter. *Sherlock Holmes vs. Fantômas*

David White. *Fantômas in America*

Pierre Yrondy. *The Adventures of Thérèse Arnaud*